THE TWO LOVES OF

Sam Taylor is a novelist and literary translator. His previous novels have reached an international audience, and his award-winning translations include works by Laurent Binet, Leïla Slimani and Marcel Proust. Born in England, Sam was a writer and editor at the *Observer* before moving to France. He now lives in the United States with his family.

by the same author

THE REPUBLIC OF TREES
THE AMNESIAC
THE ISLAND AT THE END OF THE WORLD

as Samuel Black

THE GROUND IS BURNING

THE
TWO LOVES OF
SOPHIE STROM

Sam Taylor

faber

First published in 2024
by Faber & Faber Ltd
The Bindery, 51 Hatton Garden
London EC1N 8HN

This export edition first published in 2024

Typeset by Faber & Faber Ltd
Printed in the UK by CPI Group (UK) Ltd, Croydon, CR0 4YY

Extract from *Notre-Dame de Paris* by Victor Hugo, translation © Alban Krailshaimer 1993, published by Oxford World's Classics. Reproduced with permission of the Licensor through PLSclear

Extract from 'The Meaning of Psychology for Modern Man' by C. G. Jung, published in *Civilization in Transition* by C. G. Jung, 1964, used with permission of Taylor & Francis Informa UK Ltd, permission conveyed through Copyright Clearance Center, Inc.

Extract from *The Interpretation of Dreams* by Sigmund Freud, translated and edited by A. A. Brill, published by The Modern Library, 1938

This is a work of fiction. All of the characters, organisations and events portrayed in this novel are either products of the author's imagination or are used fictitiously

A CIP record for this book
is available from the British Library

ISBN 978–0–571–38011–4

Printed and bound in the UK on FSC® certified paper in line with our continuing commitment to ethical business practices, sustainability and the environment.
For further information see faber.co.uk/environmental-policy

2 4 6 8 10 9 7 5 3 1

for Kathy, at last

and in memory of my dad,
Keith Taylor (1945–2021)

The dreamer . . . is like two separate people closely linked together by some important thing in common.

FREUD

In each of us there is another whom we do not know.

JUNG

PART ONE
VIENNA

1933

MARCH

Afterwards, when he thought back to that evening, the last he would ever spend in the apartment on Prinzenstrasse, Max Spiegelman couldn't be sure if what he remembered was real or a dream. Half of him felt certain it had truly happened; the other half suspected it was something his imagination had woven from the tangled threads of sadness, loss and desire.

It was late afternoon: sun disappearing behind rooftops, the first hint of chill in the air. Max and his best friend Josef Müller were walking home after a game of football in the Augarten. Max had to yell to make himself heard over the drone of traffic and the thump of the scuffed leather ball that Josef was bouncing against the concrete; he was reminiscing about the goal he'd scored to win the game that afternoon. Josef said nothing in reply, just stared glassy-eyed at the ball. He'd been strangely quiet all afternoon.

The sweat on the back of Max's neck was starting to cool. On the other side of the street his father's musical instruments shop glimmered red and gold. Max's parents lived in the apartment above the shop, and Josef's in the flat above theirs, so the two boys always walked home together. They waited for a tram to pass then ran across the road. A car horn honked, a man shouted. When they reached the opposite pavement, Max noticed a girl sitting at the Bösendorfer Imperial grand piano that dominated the shopfront. He couldn't hear the music she was playing but by watching her hands he could tell it was a simple piece. He found himself staring at the tendons in her neck as they fluttered beneath her skin.

Max was thirteen years old. He'd always liked girls but in the past year he'd begun to be troubled, even haunted by them. The girl in the window had long dark hair tied in a ponytail, and a few stray hairs curled over her exposed nape. Her ears were pretty, Max thought. He felt as if he were breathing underwater. He stepped closer and saw his own reflection, half-obliterated by the colours of dusk, and that was when he noticed that Josef was no longer beside him. Max looked around but his friend had vanished. He wondered vaguely if Josef was angry with him. Then he looked back at the girl and realised he could hear the jaunty, repetitive, half-familiar melody coming faintly through the glass. What *was* that song?

He was close to remembering when his concentration was broken by the sound of raised voices. He turned and saw three boys, older than him, in matching beige shirts, running in his direction. He couldn't tell if they were laughing or hostile, if they were shouting to one another or at him, but some instinct propelled him towards the arched passageway between SPIEGELMAN MUSIK-INSTRUMENTE and SCHNEIDER APOTHEKE. He walked quickly through the cobbled shade and the sound of the boys' yelling died away, along with the other city noises.

From the inner courtyard Max climbed the exterior iron staircase that led to his parents' apartment. He walked inside, dropped his school bag on the floor, kicked off his shoes. The yellow walls of the living room glowed a flickering orange in the sunset. The air smelled sweet, almost edible. His mother must be baking a dessert. As he walked through the living room, he ran his hand along the smooth lid of her piano. The comforts of home.

Frau Spiegelman was in the kitchen, wearing an apron, muttering to herself as she looked at a recipe book. Flour on her hands, red circles on her cheeks. This was not Max's favourite version of his mother; he preferred her when she was playing music or getting ready to go out because there was a serene precision to her gestures then. Cooking brought out her nervous side.

'Mmm, apple strudel,' Max said. 'Is it a special occasion?'

She looked up at him distractedly. 'Oh Max, there you are. Yes, we have guests tonight. I told you yesterday, remember? The Schattens will be coming, with—'

'Ugh, not the Schattens!'

'Don't be rude,' said his mother mechanically. 'And they may be bringing Karl, so you'll have to entertain him.'

In his mind's eye Max saw Karl Schatten's massive body and square head, his small cold eyes and sneering lips, those fists the size of cannonballs. He felt a lurch of dread.

'Karl doesn't like me.'

'Have some compassion, Max! He was there when it happened. After everything he's been through, of course he's going to act out a little bit . . .'

It was true that Karl's younger brother Oskar had been killed the year before, and that Karl had witnessed the accident, but Max had once heard Karl making a sick joke about his brother's death, so he did not believe for a second that the school bully was grief-stricken. But there was no point trying to tell his mother that.

She was washing her hands now and her words came in little bursts from between tensed lips. 'Anyway . . . he might not come . . . Apparently he has a Scout meeting on Wednesdays . . .' She dried her hands on a tea towel and looked up at the clock on the wall. 'Goodness, is that the time? Max, go downstairs and tell your father he needs to get changed! He should have closed the shop twenty minutes ago . . .'

There was a trapdoor in the floor of the kitchen. Max opened it and descended the wooden stairs to his father's office. It was the usual mess – desk littered with piles of paperwork, instrument cases strewn across the floor – but Max liked it here. In many ways he preferred it to the shop. To Max, each room was like a version of Franz Spiegelman: the shop, with its thick carpet and elegantly displayed instruments, its smell of polish and money, was the respectable face that his father presented to the world; the office was the Papa of home, the unshaven man who played the trumpet in his pyjamas and winked reassuringly when Mama was angry.

There were two doors out of the office: the one to the left led to the courtyard outside, the other to the shop. Max opened the door to the right and saw Franz Spiegelman at the far end of the show-room, trying to look interested as he listened to a woman with very short hair speak rapidly in a foreign accent. Max tiptoed towards them, afraid to interrupt, and noticed the woman's daughter lean-ing against the wall by the entrance, watching him with a half-smile. There was a book in her hand, but she wasn't even pretending to read it. He stopped and stared at the carpet, blushing hotly. It was the same girl he'd seen earlier. The one with the pretty ears.

'Maman,' said the girl, interrupting the cascade of words.

'Oui?'

'I think it's time to go. This gentleman has to close his shop.' The girl spoke in faultless German. She was facing her mother now, so Max was able to observe her in profile: swanlike neck, bony nose, rosebud lips. 'And his son is waiting to speak to him.'

Everyone turned to stare at Max: the girl looked amused, the woman surprised, his father embarrassed. 'Max? What are you doing here?'

Max had to cough and clear his throat before he could speak. 'Mama says you have to come and get ready. For tonight.'

His father stared at him blankly. He must have forgotten about the dinner party. To underline the urgency of the situation Max surreptitiously made a shape with his right hand: thumb and index finger a few inches apart, the gap steadily closing. It meant: *Mama's getting upset.* In the periphery of his vision he was aware of the girl watching him. His father understood and quickly made his excuses as he ushered them towards the door: 'Ah! Sorry, ladies, duty calls.

But it was delightful to speak with you both . . .' The woman asked Max's father if he knew of a good music school in the city, and while he answered her the girl turned to face Max. They were almost exactly the same height. 'What do you play?' she asked in a friendly voice.

Max thought of football and frowned. 'What do you mean?'

The girl smiled and he noticed that her front teeth were slightly crooked. She gestured at the shop behind him and said: 'You don't play an instrument?'

'Oh,' said Max, feeling stupid. 'Yes. The violin. And you?'

'She plays the piano, Max,' his father said gently, and it was only then that Max realised the adults had stopped talking and the two of them were watching Max and the girl, waiting for them to finish their conversation. 'That's why they were looking at the Bösendorfer.'

Max blushed. 'Oh yes. Of course.'

'Perhaps we could play a duet together sometime?' the girl said to Max, gripping her book tight to her chest. She looked straight in his eyes as she said this and he had to remind himself to keep breathing. Her eyes were grey and yet simultaneously somehow multicoloured, like a rainbow seen through mist.

'Yes,' said Max, struggling to think of a way to convey the full extent of his enthusiasm for this idea. 'Yes . . . okay.'

'Come tomorrow if you like,' his father said graciously to the girl's mother. 'These two can practise while we try to find something to suit your budget.'

Max felt dizzy from looking in the girl's eyes, so he glanced down at the cover of the book she was holding. Goethe's *Faust*. Max felt a little intimidated. The woman must have said something that Max didn't hear, because his father was now telling her the shop's opening hours. 'Drop by whenever you like.' Herr Spiegelman looked distractedly at his watch. 'But I'm afraid I really do need to—'

'Yes, of course,' the woman said, hurrying outside and pulling her daughter by the arm. As his father locked the glass door, the girl turned around and waved at Max. He waved back.

'Sorry about that, Max,' his father said, winding the handle that lowered the metal shutters. 'She just wouldn't stop talking . . . Ugh, what is wrong with this thing?'

The shutter mechanism had jammed. Mama's voice called, shrill and panicky, from above. Father and son exchanged a glance. 'Never mind, I'll deal with this later.' They walked to the office and began climbing the stairs to the kitchen. 'So . . . guests?'

'The Schattens,' said Max. 'Arriving at seven.'

'Ah, the Schattens. They're not bringing that brute of a son with them, are they?'

'They might be. Frau Schatten's supposed to call.'

'Oh dear. Well, my fingers are crossed for you, Max.'

'Who were they, Papa?' Max asked as he followed his father through the open trapdoor.

His father turned, puzzled. 'Who were who?'

'That woman with the foreign accent. And the girl.'

'Oh, she's some artist, apparently. French. Just moved to Vienna. She was looking for a piano for her daughter, so I let her play the Bösendorfer. But as soon as I mentioned the price . . .' Franz Spiegelman closed the trapdoor and smiled knowingly at Max. 'You seemed very taken with—'

Just then, Max's mother appeared in the kitchen. The circles on her cheeks were larger and redder than before, and she started to chide her husband for his tardiness. Franz stroked her arms and looked into her eyes. 'Don't worry, Liebchen, everything will be fine. I'm going to get changed now.' He kissed her on the lips and went upstairs, and just for a moment Ana Spiegelman looked calm.

Then she noticed her son standing beside her. 'Max, what are you doing? Get washed and changed! Karl isn't coming, but it's already so late. At this rate you'll still be eating your supper when they arrive, and I can't have you looking like that in front of our guests.'

An hour later the rabbit stew was simmering and Max was tuning his violin by the living-room window, gazing out at the street below. He had eaten his supper alone as the sky darkened to violet. Now the streetlights were shining on Prinzenstrasse and inside the apartment the lamps had been lit, casting parts of the living room into evening gloom. Often this time of day would make Max feel melancholy, but today he was still bathed in the afterglow of euphoria: that girl had practically asked him out! Well, not *out*, but she had wanted to see him again. And she was pretty. Intelligent too, he could tell. Only then did it occur to him that he'd forgotten to ask her name. Oh well, he could ask the next time he saw her . . .

Franz Spiegelman came downstairs in a crisp white shirt. Before adjusting his tie in the mirror at the foot of the stairs, he winked at Max and made a movement with his right hand as if stroking an invisible cat. All is well, thought Max. He began playing 'Ode to Joy'.

Ana Spiegelman appeared on the stairs a few minutes later. Max stopped playing and turned to look. 'Will I do?' she asked her husband shyly.

She was wearing a white dress with large pink flowers on it, high heels, earrings . . . What else had changed? One by one, Max noted the subtle differences. Her hair was down, falling in waves over her shoulders, softening her face. Then there was lipstick, eyeliner, a hint of powder, thickened lashes. She was wearing perfume too, a scent Max associated with nocturnal adult pleasures: forbidden, mysterious. Franz went over and whispered something in her ear. He kissed her neck and she smiled. Max looked away. He used to be happy when his parents hugged and kissed because the air was so much lighter than when they argued, but now his chest tensed.

An image of the girl leaning against the wall in the shop flashed into his mind and it was a relief when the doorbell rang.

Herr and Frau Schatten came inside, along with a gust of cold air. Max was glad that Karl wasn't with them, but he still felt awkward. Their younger son Oskar had died the previous summer. He'd been run over by a car on Prinzenstrasse and Max's mother had been the first to console Frau Schatten. The Schattens lived just around the corner on Trauergasse, so Ana and Katharina had become friends despite having nothing in common.

The four adults exchanged greetings and a silence descended. Herr Schatten was a watchmaker but he looked more like a funeral director: a tall, sombre man whose face appeared to have been carved from wood. He stood close to the door with his hat on and nodded at Max as if they were passengers on the same tram. But Frau Schatten, who was short and round and alarmingly loud, spotted Max and ran over to him like a goose after bread. 'Max! Little Max!' she exclaimed, pressing him to her ample bosom. 'Oh, but I shouldn't call you that anymore because you've grown.' She held him at arm's length. 'You must be . . . fourteen now, is that right? Thirteen? Ah yes, you were in the year below poor Oskar, weren't you? You look like him, actually. You have the same eyes. Such kind eyes . . .' Max froze with panic as Frau Schatten's own eyes suddenly filled with tears. For a moment she looked like an opera singer about to launch into a tragic aria, then she dabbed at her face with a handkerchief while the others crowded around sympathetically. 'Yes, yes, I'm fine, sorry, I know it's embarrassing when this happens.' Max made a hand signal to his father: *What should I do?* Franz made a flicking gesture with his little finger and Max escaped up the staircase.

Around nine his parents came to his room to say goodnight. Papa smelled of wine and told Max he had no idea how lucky he was not to have to listen to Katharina Schatten for hours on end.

He gave his son a brisk hug, then went back downstairs to entertain the guests. Mama knelt beside Max's bed and stroked his hair. Her eyes were mistier than before. She gave a wobbly smile, then hugged him. Max got a mouthful of hair and had to turn his face to the side so he could breathe. She was gripping him much more tightly than she normally did and he could feel strange spasms in the muscles of her back. 'Mama?' Max whispered after a minute or so. 'Are you all right?'

She released him and sat back, smiling, eyes glistening. 'I'm fine,' she said, in a too-bright voice. She turned away for a few seconds and Max saw her take a handkerchief from her sleeve. What was it with all these weeping women tonight? After a few seconds she turned back to him and said: 'I think it was just—' Her voice caught. 'It was seeing Katharina get so upset . . . about Oskar.' She swallowed and there was a long silence. 'I know I get annoyed with you sometimes, Max, but—'

'I know,' he said, trying to pacify the storm of emotion he could sense brewing behind her eyes.

'Ich-liebe-dich.' She said it very quickly, the words bursting from her mouth with the involuntary force of a sneeze, then screwed up her face as if she was in pain. 'Very much. You won't ever forget that, will you?'

'No, Mama.'

It was strange: she sounded as if she knew, as if she were saying goodbye to him. Or was that only how he remembered it afterwards?

There was a brief silence, punctuated by the sound of Frau Schatten's staccato laughter from downstairs. His mother sighed. 'Don't worry, I'll ask them to keep the noise down. Although it shouldn't be so bad with the door closed.'

She stood up and smoothed down her dress, looking calm and composed again. Max felt a mingling of relief and disappointment.

'Could you leave the door open?'

'Why?'

'I want to hear you play.'

She leaned down to touch his cheek. 'That's sweet of you, Max, but I don't want you staying up on a school night.'

He looked at her imploringly.

'Perhaps you'll hear me play in your dreams, though. Would you like that?'

Max shrugged. His dreams usually evaporated as soon as he woke, like breath from glass. 'Yes, Mama.'

'All right, go to sleep now.' She turned off his lamp, kissed his cheek, whispered into his ear: 'Süsse Träume.'

When the door had closed and the sound of her footsteps had faded to silence, Max reached down under his bed and picked up his book and his torch. Inside the yellow-glowing cave of bed-clothes, he opened *Peter Pan*. This was the fourth or fifth time he'd read it, and he felt a little embarrassed at that thought, having seen the girl holding her copy of *Faust*. Was it time for Max to grow up? But as soon as he began to read, he forgot this idea and became lost in the story. He breathed in his own breaths, his skin scented with his mother's intoxicating perfume, and after a while he had to lift his head above the sheets and swallow the cold dark air of the bedroom. He listened hard, but there was still no piano music. He wanted to keep reading but found himself wrestling drowsiness: as his head sank into the pillow, the faint light around the bedroom door started to pulse in time with his breathing, to loom close and grow yearningly distant, as if he were slipping, against his will, into darkness, and then catching himself. *Stay awake.*

In the end he got up, put on his dressing gown and padded onto the landing, where he sat on the top step of the staircase and lis-tened to the hum of voices below, the clink of glass and china. His eyes followed the burgundy carpet runner as it descended the wooden steps through dimness and shadows to the pool of warm light on the bottom landing. Muffled by walls and distance, the adults' voices were like musical instruments: Herr Schatten a tuba, low and steady; his wife a cat jumping onto a piano keyboard, unpredictable and occasionally jarring. Max's father was a trumpet, of course, blaring a joke now and then, but he couldn't hear his mother, perhaps because she was busy in the kitchen.

At last their voices fell silent and Max heard the first notes of *Rêverie*. He lay down with his head on his arm and closed his eyes to listen. His whole body relaxed. As Debussy's weightless melody floated through him, he found himself thinking back over the evening. He remembered the goal he'd scored at the park and Josef's odd behaviour. He remembered the girl in the shop and the constriction he'd felt in his chest when she smiled at him. He saw again the orange walls, the violet sky. He smelled his mother's apple strudel. The whole evening, it seemed to Max, had been haunted by the nagging sense that something magical or important had just happened, or was about to, as if his parents' faces, the contents of their apartment, the words in the book he was reading were all haloed by some unearthly light. He tried again to remember what song the girl had been playing when he'd heard her through the window, but it was swept away by the music from downstairs. The song and the girl . . . Max felt as if he were retracing a series of steps that had taken him to the threshold of a strange new world. Those notes and chords played on the piano. The lineaments of the girl's smile, the sound of her voice. The swelling of his heart. Was that all it would take to lead him out of his old life? No, there had to be something else. Something that had not yet happened.

But did Max really think that then, as he lay at the top of the staircase? Or was it just how he would remember it later? Already, as he heard voices below, the front door clicking shut, already as his mother began to play a more jaunty, familiar tune and Max felt his eyelids grow heavy, already the scene was blurring, dividing in his mind. In those final moments suspended between waking and sleep, between the old life and the new, his memory was transforming, warped by an inkling of the tragedy to come, by the untraceable distortions of hindsight, by the knowledge that nothing would ever be – that nothing ever was – the same again, after.

That *he* was no longer the same.

Max woke with a start and almost fell downstairs. He was lying on the top step and when he opened his eyes he saw the staircase unfurling vertiginously below him. His heart was racing and he assumed it was because he'd almost fallen. But it wasn't.

His fingers and toes were numb with cold. He must have nodded off while listening to his mother play the piano. He looked up at the grandfather clock: eleven minutes past one. Rubbing his eyes, Max wondered what had woken him. A noise, he thought vaguely, something violent and discordant. A dropped plate? The piano lid slamming shut? A sound in his dream?

And then he heard something else: voices outside, the distant smash of glass. From downstairs, he heard his mother ask: 'What was that?' and his father reassure her: 'Only some drunkards in the street.' His parents' voices grew louder, clearer. They were coming towards the stairs. Max clambered to his feet. Feeling dizzy, he put one hand on the banister to steady himself, then crept across the dark landing. As he reached his bedroom, his mother's voice grew anxious: 'But what about . . . radio today . . . Katharina was . . .' The landing light came on. His parents started climbing the stairs and his father said something soothing in reply. Afraid of being caught, Max shut his bedroom door. His mother laughed softly and the landing light went out.

He hugged himself between the icy sheets and soon he could hear the regular squeak of bedsprings, the thud of the headboard against the wall. Knowing he would not be able to sleep while they were doing that, Max picked up *Peter Pan* and the torch again and covered himself with the sheet and blanket. The layers of fabric muffled the noises they were making, but still he found it difficult to concentrate. His mind kept drifting to the memory of the girl who had played the piano in his father's shop. When he reached the part of the book where a nameless fear clutches at Mrs Darling's heart and Michael asks: 'Can anything harm us, mother, after the night-lights are lit?', Max found himself seized by nameless fears of his own.

He pulled the bedclothes down and listened. Silence. His parents must have finished what they were doing and fallen asleep. He should go to sleep too: the alarm clock would wake him early the next morning. Max plumped his pillow and tried to get comfortable. Then he noticed that the air in the room was no longer cold; in fact, his temples were damp with sweat. Perhaps his father had lit the stove in the kitchen. He turned onto his side and closed his eyes.

The longer he listened to the silence, however, the more he seemed to detect a sort of soft purr beneath it, like wind on a stormy night. Curious, he tiptoed to the window and opened it. He unfastened the shutter. The rusty hinges made a birdlike screech. He felt no wind on his skin but he could still hear that quiet booming sound. What could it be? As he closed the window again, he remembered the jammed mechanism of the shop's metal shutters and wondered if his father had ever gone back down to close them.

Wide awake by now, Max went downstairs to investigate. As soon as he reached the kitchen, his stomach twisted with apprehension: it was so hot in here that beads of sweat pricked from the pores of his hands. He opened the stove door: only a single log, smouldering on a bed of embers. The air was hazy and he started to cough. He closed the stove door, then noticed that the floorboards were warm beneath his bare feet. He opened the trapdoor and a wave of smoke engulfed him.

In a panic Max let the trapdoor fall shut. 'Mama! Papa!' he shouted. Silence: they were probably fast asleep. Should he go upstairs and wake them? But what if they were having sex again? He had walked in on them once before and his father had been so angry. His mother had covered herself with the sheets as if concealing some shameful horror. And she was always telling him to show more initiative . . . Max felt paralysed by indecision. Do something, he told himself. His eyes darted from the dirty saucepans in the sink to the tray of wine glasses on the countertop. All too small. Frantically opening cupboards, he found a tin bucket. He held it under the tap. The noise of the running water drowned out the roar below, drowned out all thought. The bucket swayed under its handle, almost too heavy to carry. Max put the bucket on the floor and opened the trapdoor again. Less smoke this time, he noted hopefully. Holding tight to the wooden handrail, he carried the bucket downstairs.

The room smelled strongly of smoke, but Max was relieved to see only a single patch of flames – on the lower part of the door that led to the shop. He tossed the contents of the bucket. The flames sizzled and he thought he'd doused them. But a few seconds later the orange tongues started to flicker again through the gap around the door, higher and angrier than before, as though he'd only prodded the monster. He heard it growl.

Run upstairs now, he thought. Warn them before it's too late.

But it already was.

The door was opening. Not the way a door was supposed to open. It was falling, very slowly, on top of him. He had time to think but not to act, as if the seconds were expanding and only his mind was racing, uselessly, through this slowed-down moment. He had time to curse himself for all the bad choices he had made and to notice the appearance of the door's other side: the blackened paint, the writhing flames. Only when a shadow fell suddenly past his eyes and something unbearably hot grazed his face did Max let out a yell that brought him back to the reality of heat, smoke, fear, pain, noise. Only then did time speed up again.

The stairs to the kitchen were on fire. He tried to shout loud enough to rouse his parents, but his voice was lost amid the roar of the blaze. Half-blinded by smoke and tears, he staggered across the baking floorboards to the back door.

Out in the black night air, the cobbles smooth and cool under his hands, Max crawled across the courtyard. He had to reach the street, to tell someone what was happening. Perhaps it wasn't too late to save his parents, to save Josef and his family too. He tried to climb to his feet, but his body was racked by a coughing fit and he spat dark sputum onto the ground. He took a moment to catch his breath, then forced himself to keep crawling until he felt a sharp pain in his right palm and looked down to see a shard of glass stuck in his flesh. He carefully removed it and watched the blood stream over his wrist, staining the sleeve of his pyjamas.

Through his tear-blurred vision he saw a dazzle of light to his right: the house on fire. Figures on the street ahead, silhouetted by lamplight. He tried to yell, to get their attention, but his throat was scorched, his lungs shrunken. Avoiding the glitter of broken glass on the cobbles ahead of him, Max kept crawling slowly forward.

The right half of his face was hot. He patted his cheek to make sure it wasn't on fire and felt something too soft and jelly-like to be skin. The horror anaesthetised him. For several seconds – or several minutes, he couldn't tell – he lay there wheezing, struggling to fill his lungs with air, the night-time scene around him fading in and out just as the light around his bedroom door had done earlier that evening.

He opened his eyes and saw a woman, shoulders shaking, hand covering her mouth, being ushered away from the crowd by a tall man. Mama and Papa? 'Help,' he called, his voice a hoarse whisper. Summoning all his strength, he tried one last time: 'Help!' The woman froze. She turned in his direction. It was Frau Schatten.

At last a hush descended. The bright blaze grew darker. Just before losing consciousness, Max heard a distant scream. The sound of glass shattering.

Max woke with a start and almost fell downstairs. He was lying on the top step and when he opened his eyes he saw the staircase unfurling vertiginously below him. His heart was racing. What had woken him? A noise, he thought vaguely. A sound in his dream? He caught the fragments just in time, before they vanished: the fire in the shop, the scream, the sound of a window breaking. Max shuddered. His nightmare had seemed so real.

And then he heard something else: voices outside, glass smashing. He heard the piano lid slam shut and his mother ask: 'What was that?' His father reassured her: 'Only some drunkards in the street.' Sitting up, Max stared at the grandfather clock behind him. Eleven minutes past one. Was he still dreaming? He touched his right cheek: the skin smooth, unhurt. He examined his palm and saw no dried blood, no cut. 'But what about those reports on the radio today?' his mother asked anxiously. 'You heard what Katharina was saying, didn't you? About the new laws in Germany . . .'

Max sat paralysed as his parents appeared at the bottom of the stairs. His father switched on the landing light, put his arm around his mother's shoulder and said: 'Oh, you know Katharina – she does tend to make elephants out of mosquitoes. Anyway, this isn't Germany.'

The clunk of their shoes on the wooden steps, their tipsy smiles: Max had not witnessed any of this before, yet he felt certain that it had all happened – every moment, every impossible detail – in his dream. Catching sight of him on the stairs, his mother stopped. 'Max!'

His father sighed. 'Time for bed,' he said, making a movement with his fingers that Max knew meant: *Vanish.*

But his mother knelt and touched Max's forehead. 'Max, what's the matter? You're all pale and clammy. Are you sick?'

In a faltering voice Max told them about his dream. He watched the series of expressions on his mother's face as he spoke – puzzlement, concern, tenderness – but somehow he knew he hadn't been able to convince her of what the dream meant. That it was a warning, a premonition.

'Max, you're not a Kleinkind anymore,' his father said, slurring his words slightly. 'It was only a dream. Just go back to bed and everything will be fine.'

'Franz, I'm not sending him to bed like this. He might have another nightmare.'

'Oh, come on, Ana . . .' Franz slid his arm around her shoulder, nuzzled his mouth against her neck.

Shaking her husband off, Max's mother took him by the hand and led him downstairs. 'I'll make you some cocoa.'

In the kitchen Max heard the purring sound that he'd heard in his dream. He looked up at his parents: they'd heard it too. His mother nervously stirred the milk in the saucepan. 'I think you should go down and take a look, Franz.'

'Seriously?' Franz kneaded his forehead. 'All right, all right, I'll go.' He lifted the trapdoor. No wave of smoke. 'See?' He climbed down the steps, walked around the office, shouted up that everything was fine, then stopped. He'd heard something. They watched as he opened the door to the shop and smoke blurred the air. He slammed the door shut and his feet hammered up the stairs.

'We need to leave.' Franz's face was pale. He looked suddenly very sober. '*Now*.'

Max felt his elbow grabbed. He was pulled out of the kitchen and through the living room. At the foot of the staircase, his father crouched beside him, eyes fierce. 'Max, go to your room and find some warm clothes, then come straight down. Be as fast as you can.'

Max ran upstairs and collected an armful of sweaters, trousers, socks and underwear from his chest of drawers. He was on his way out of the bedroom when he spotted his violin case amid a battalion of toy soldiers on the floor. He squatted down to pick it up, sliding his thumb under the handle, and saw *Peter Pan* under the bed. His mother shouted his name, an edge of fear in her voice. 'Coming!' he called, abandoning the book and hurtling downstairs, clothes spilling from his arms.

'I'll get them,' his father said. 'Max, put your shoes on and go outside with Mama.'

Max looked at his father, who was holding his trumpet case and the old cake tin that contained their cash savings. Suddenly he felt optimistic: everything was under control. There was even something quite exciting about it. Just wait until he told Josef about this . . . And then he remembered that his friend was in the apartment above theirs, that he and his parents were probably asleep. 'The Müllers!' he said. 'We have to warn them.'

'I'll do it,' his father replied. 'I'll meet you in the courtyard. Go.'

A minute later, as Max and his mother were making their way from the courtyard to the street, eyes fixed with horror at the flames pouring from the windows of the shop, his father caught them up and said he'd rung the bell and banged on the door of the Müllers' apartment but there had been no answer. 'And the door was locked. I'm sorry, Max, there was nothing else I—'

Franz stopped talking as they emerged onto Prinzenstrasse. He was staring straight ahead. Max followed his gaze. A line of people standing on the far pavement. Neighbours, friends, strangers. And there was the Müller family, watching expressionlessly as their home was consumed by flames. Max wanted to run to Josef, to ask how he was, how they'd escaped, but that felt like the wrong thing to do. They crossed the road and took their place among the silent audience.

Max could hear sirens in the distance but he knew it was too late: the blaze had already reached the first-floor windows. Sweat glued his pyjamas to his skin, and when he touched his face his fingers came away black with soot. His mother held his hand; her grip tightened as she watched the Bösendorfer burn. The embers started to crumble, like incandescent dominoes. Max remembered the girl who'd sat at that piano only hours ago. What would she think when she came here to play a duet with him and there was nothing left? Would he ever see her again?

'Ana! Franz! Max! You're safe!' Frau Schatten was running towards them, her husband trailing behind. 'Oh, I'm so relieved. My neighbour called to tell me there was a fire on Prinzenstrasse and I said to her, surely it can't be the Spiegelmans, we just left there! I can't believe it. Your beautiful home . . .'

They all turned to look at it, and Max thought about *Peter Pan*. His mother had given him that book for his tenth birthday. There were so many memories in their apartment, being devoured one by one. The whole of his childhood.

'Where will you stay tonight?' Frau Schatten asked.

'I don't know. We'll find a hotel, I suppose,' said Max's father.

'A hotel? No, you must stay with us. For as long as you like.'

'Katharina, that's very kind of you,' Max's mother said, 'but we—'

'Oh, nonsense! It will be our pleasure. Won't it, Helmut?'

They all turned to look at Herr Schatten, who was watching the blaze and did not appear to have heard.

Later that night, Max was lying in a dead boy's bed. He could hear Karl Schatten breathing, close by. Max's parents were in the spare bedroom down the hall and he wished he were with them instead, but Frau Schatten had been adamant that he should take Oskar's bed. Karl would be thrilled to have a roommate again, she'd said.

Max remembered the cold look on Karl's face when he had come in late from his Scout meeting, still wearing his beige uniform, and found these people in his home. He recalled the strange atmosphere in the living room soon after that when Frau Schatten had gone to the kitchen to make tea and he and his parents had been left alone with Karl and his father, who stared at them, silent and unsmiling. Still, it was only temporary, until they found a new apartment. And at least the bed was comfortable, the sheets smooth and fresh.

Suddenly exhausted, Max closed his eyes and the memory of his dream returned to him in flashes. The burning door. The hot floorboards. The horror when he realised it was too late to save his parents . . . He sighed and turned over. They were all safe now. His muscles relaxed and he started to drift round and down into the black whirlpool of sleep and then he coughed, so hard it half-woke him, and when he opened his eyes the room was in daylight and Frau Schatten was sitting in a chair next to the bed, reading a magazine. Max realised that he must be dreaming again. He felt as if he were floating a few inches above the mattress: a strange but pleasant sensation. There were plastic tubes attached to his arms and something was partly obstructing his right eye. He reached up with his hand and his forearm stung in several places as the tubes pulled taut. He touched his face. What he felt wasn't skin. He gasped. But a heavy weight had settled on his chest and he couldn't suck enough air into his lungs. Wake up, he told himself. He closed his eyes. *Open your eyes. Wake up!*

He woke in Oskar's bed, heart pounding. The shutters were open and his pillow was soaked with cold sweat. He looked around. His mother was sitting in a chair next to the bed. 'Max, how are you feeling?' She leaned forward and touched his forehead. 'You were moaning in your sleep just now. I was worried you were having another nightmare. Although I suppose we shouldn't complain . . . It was your dream that saved us, after all.'

Max stared at her, suddenly afraid.

'What is it?' she asked. 'Did you have another dream?'

Max shook his head. Breath from glass, he told himself. 'I don't remember. I don't remember what I dreamed.'

APRIL

Hans

The nurse sat on the edge of the bed, the curve of her hip against his thigh. She leaned close to him – so close he could feel the warmth of her breath on his nose and lips – and carefully changed the bandages.

He had been at the hospital for the past three weeks. The first week he barely remembered: he'd been on morphine, asleep most of the time. Since then, the hours had dragged. He had not had many visitors: a few distant relatives he'd never met before and who didn't stay long, perhaps afraid they would be asked to take care of him; various police officers and social workers, asking about the fire, his next of kin; a psychiatrist who questioned him about his feelings and his dreams (he said he couldn't remember them). Josef had not come to see him at all. His only regular visitor was Frau Schatten.

She was there now, sitting in her usual spot beside the bed. Ever since the night of the fire, Frau Schatten's eyes had been wells of compassion, but now she looked as if she was bursting to tell him something. Wonderful news! He could imagine her using those exact words.

The nurse prodded his scar with a piece of cotton wool. 'Does that hurt?'

'No.'

It never hurt now. It never felt like anything. As if part of his face had disappeared. He still hadn't looked in a mirror with the bandages off. When he pictured his face, he imagined a hole in it, like a missing jigsaw piece.

Most of the time he managed not to think about the fact that his parents were dead, that he would never see them again. But in odd moments reality would flutter down from the ceiling like a giant black dragonfly and land on his chest, making it hard to breathe. In such moments he felt as if he'd been buried alive, six feet of solid earth pressing down on his face, and his heart would thud sickeningly inside his chest as he thought about all the love they'd shared, all that happiness and security, stolen from him in a few awful minutes.

The only way he had found to lighten that weight was to think back to happier times. He remembered playing a Mozart sonata with his mother on the Bösendorfer one night when the shop was closed, helping his parents paint the living-room walls sunshine-yellow two or three summers ago, throwing snowballs with his father in the Volksgarten one Christmas morning . . . Each memory was a coin discovered at the bottom of a pocket, to be polished and treasured. Each one released the pressure on his chest, making it easier to breathe. Yet the more he thought about these memories, the thinner they became, as if by polishing them he might end up rubbing them away completely. Had he really thrown snowballs with his father in the Volksgarten? Perhaps, but when he tried to pinpoint an image in his mind – crisp snow, leafless trees, pale winter sky – it started to dissolve. And there was no one he could ask about the truth. He felt so guilty when he thought about this: nothing remained of his parents' lives except what was inside his head and he couldn't even look after that properly.

He kept trying to remember what tune his mother had been playing just before he fell asleep at the top of the stairs. It wasn't Debussy, he felt sure of that. She had finished her rendition, the Schattens had gone home, and she was just messing about on the piano, the way she did sometimes when she was happy. A descending melody, an elusive chord . . . It was such a small thing, but it nagged at him. If only he could return to that night, to that moment at the top of the stairs, before he fell asleep. He remembered thinking that he'd entered a new world, or was about to. In his mind he'd imagined something magical, like Neverland. Not *this*. What were the steps he had tried to retrace? The notes and chords the girl had played on the piano, the shape of her smile, the sound of her voice, the swell of his heart. Put them in the right order, like the secret combination to a lock, and perhaps he would wake up again, in his old life, his parents still smiling at him, their bodies unburned, the way they were in all his dreams.

Oh, his dreams . . . At first he had attributed them to the morphine, but they continued even after he came off it. And he remembered them much more vividly than any other dreams he'd ever had. They were not fast-fading mirages but solid new memories. The dreams were his consolation: the one good, sweet thing in his life. He found them so soothing that he tried to sleep as often as he could, to live in that other world instead of this one.

'So . . . that's it!' The nurse had left the room and Frau Schatten could no longer keep the good news to herself. She stood up and clapped her hands. 'Everything has been cleared. We're going to do it.'

He stared at her uncomprehendingly.

'We're going to adopt you! I wanted to from the beginning, of course, but I didn't know if Helmut would approve. But he does, or at least he doesn't object. So as long as you tell the social worker that this is what you want, you will come home to live with us when the doctor says you're ready to leave the hospital.' She looked at him expectantly. 'You do want to, don't you?'

He hesitated. After all his dreams of the Schattens' house – the father's gloomy silence, the son's scowling hostility – this idea filled him with dread. But what was the alternative? As his silence lengthened, Frau Schatten's plump, smiling face started to fall like a soufflé. 'Of course,' he said hastily. 'Thank you.'

'Oh, good!' Frau Schatten looked relieved. 'There's only one condition. For your own safety. You must change your name. From now on you will be Hans Oskar Schatten.'

A voice from the back of the room piped up: 'She wanted Oskar to be your first name, but I said that wasn't right.'

He looked up in astonishment: Herr Schatten was here too, sitting on a chair near the window, a black loupe protruding from his right eye as he examined the innards of a watch.

He turned back to Frau Schatten. 'For my own safety?'

'Yes, dear.' Frau Schatten blushed. 'Because there are . . . certain people . . . who might try to hurt you because . . . Well, like they did with your . . . What I mean is, it can be dangerous . . . in times like these, to be . . .'

'To be what?'

'A Jew,' Herr Schatten said, still staring at the watch mechanism.

'Oh.' He thought of his dead Oma Hannah telling him stories from the Tanakh when he was little. Tales of divine punishments and guardian angels. He had always been vaguely aware that his father was Jewish, but his mother had been a Catholic, neither of them very devout, and he had never thought of himself as anything in particular. Was Frau Schatten saying that somebody had set fire to their house deliberately?

'I'm sorry, dear,' Frau Schatten said, 'but we must live in the real world, as Helmut always says. You'll go to a new school, so nobody will know about your past. And Helmut has a friend at the archives office who can help with the paperwork. Then you'll be Aryan just like us and nobody will— Oh, but you're looking a little tired, my sweet Hans. I know, it's a lot to take in. Should we leave you to get some sleep?'

He nodded gratefully. Yes, let me sleep, he thought. Let me sleep forever.

The bell rang and the teacher shouted something above the sudden din of scraped-back chairs and slammed desk lids. Max's chest felt the way it did in all his dreams: as if something was wrapped tightly around it, constricting his breathing.

He'd been back at school for a whole week now and Josef still hadn't spoken to him. Every time Max smiled at him or tried to start a conversation, his friend stared through him as though he were a ghost. At lunchtimes Josef walked past their usual place in the dining hall and sat next to Karl Schatten at the bullies' table. For the last few days Max's mind had been churning over the past, trying to remember what he might have done or said to upset him.

Now, as the crowd of laughing adolescents flooded through the corridor and into the playground, Max saw Josef walking beside Karl. He called his friend's name. No reaction. Max touched his shoulder and Josef shrugged him off. 'Hey, I'm talking to you!' The voices around them fell silent. Max became aware of a circle of faces, all watching. His throat tightened. 'Why are you being like this?'

Josef hesitated, then kept walking. Karl leaned down and whispered something in Josef's ear. Max ran after him and grabbed his friend's shoulder again. This time, Josef spun around. 'Leave me alone, Jew!' he snarled, shoving Max's face with the flat of his hand. For a second Max was too shocked to react. Then the rage built inside him and, for the first time in his life, he threw a punch. He felt lips, gums, teeth, slimy and then hard against his knuckles. A roar went up around him. A thin line of blood trickled from Josef's mouth. Max felt a rush of euphoria and panic.

'I don't want to fight you,' Max said, his voice shaky with adrenaline. 'But you—'

Josef's fist thudded into his left eye. The edges of Max's vision darkened and blurred and the hopscotch lines on the grey concrete swayed beneath his feet. For a moment he was deafened and then the faces around him were closer, mouths open, a muffled chanting. Hands pushed him from behind and he tripped and fell to the ground. He struggled to his feet and now he could hear what they were shouting. '*Jude! Jude! Jude!*' He saw Karl Schatten smirking at him. Eyes to the ground, Max walked away.

The chanting continued. He stumbled as other hands shoved him. A warm gob of spit hit his cheek and he wiped it away with his shirtsleeve. He began to walk more quickly. To his relief the voices grew more distant. They weren't following him. Then a stone whizzed past his leg and bounced into some bushes. He looked back. Karl, Josef and a few others were standing by the flower beds outside the headmaster's office, bending down to pick up more stones. 'Jude, verrecke!' one of them hollered. *Die, Jew.* Max began to run. A second stone whistled past his ear. A third hit him on the base of his spine. It hurt. He kept running.

Max didn't slow down until the school was out of sight. He glanced behind but the boys were nowhere to be seen. At least he wouldn't have to face Karl Schatten again this afternoon, he thought, because today was the day his family were moving to their new apartment. He took the slip of paper from his pocket and read the address: *Dunkelgasse 16, apartment 4a.* There were directions on the back, in his mother's handwriting.

Max's forehead was throbbing as he walked to Neustiftgasse under a sky of rolling leaden clouds. He caught a number 5 tram. The other passengers kept looking at him. Rain spattered the windows and he saw his reflection through the streaming silver lines on the glass: he looked like he was wearing a patch over his eye. He reached up to brush away a few stray tears and his left eyelid was so swollen that the lashes felt like thick bristle under his fingertips. The tram passed the children's hospital and Max thought about the boy in his dreams. Then it crossed Prinzenstrasse and he felt suddenly sick. Why had Josef said those things? They'd known each other since kindergarten. They were best friends. As the tram crossed the canal into Leopoldstadt, Max remembered the Müller family standing on the pavement that night three weeks ago, calmly watching as their home burned down, and something monstrous began to form in his mind. A realisation. Josef had *known*. His parents too. They'd known about the fire before it started.

Five minutes later, Max found himself in a neighbourhood more run-down than the Vienna he knew, a Vienna without statues or cathedrals, where functional buildings squatted on narrow streets. The Jewish quarter. He got off the tram and started to walk. A web of electrical wires hung above a crossroads. Men with thick beards and strange hats glared at him. Inside number 16 he climbed the stairs to the top floor. The hallway smelled faintly of urine. A toddler whined. From behind a half-open door a radio squawked in a foreign language. Max went into apartment 4a and it was so small and bare that for a second he was afraid he'd got the wrong address. Then his mother appeared in the entrance hall, open-mouthed. 'Max, what happened? Did you get in a fight?'

The three of them ate soup and bread that night, sitting on the floor around an upturned cardboard box. The only light came from a few candles and in the flicker of those flames the apartment no longer seemed quite so bleak or small. 'We should have electricity tomorrow,' his father said. His eyes were weary but his voice was cheerful and he was smiling his reassuring smile. 'I'm sorry everything's a bit of a mess at the moment, Max, but the furniture should arrive by the end of the week and it'll start to feel more like home.'

There was a silence, then Max said: 'I can't go back to that school, Papa.'

'I understand it's frightening, Liebchen, but you can't let the bullies win,' his mother said. 'Franz, perhaps we should talk to the headmaster about this?'

Max shook his head. 'You don't understand . . .'

'Well, the year's almost over anyway,' his father said. 'Max could probably do his schoolwork at home for the next two months. And we could find him a new school before September.'

'Oh, that's a good idea!' his mother said. 'Maybe a Jewish school—'

'No.' Max stood up. 'I don't want to go to a Jewish school.'

'Why not?'

'I don't know anything about being Jewish.'

'Well, that's the point. You'd learn.'

'But I don't want to! I just want to be normal.'

His mother started to protest, but his father patted her thigh. 'It's all right, Ana, I know how he feels. Nobody likes to be different.'

Max remembered his dream from last night: the Schattens adopting him, changing his name to Hans, making him Aryan. Was that what he wanted? Yes, he thought, then immediately drowned the rebellious thought in shame: no, because Hans's parents were dead, while Max's were here and alive and they loved him and he loved them. He was lucky. Max knew this, yet he couldn't help wishing that he could return to his old life: to the apartment in Prinzenstrasse, to Josef being his best friend, to waking up each morning and having only the vaguest memory of his dreams . . .

His mother got to her feet and bent down to pick up the bowls. 'You should be proud of your heritage, not ashamed. There's nothing wrong with being Jewish, you know.'

Max watched his mother disappear into the tiny kitchen. In a voice too quiet for her to hear, he said: 'Then why do they hate us? Why did they set fire to our house?'

His father, still sitting on the floor, looked lost for words.

Hans

'So you get to go home today,' the nurse said. 'You must be excited.'

From somewhere behind, Frau Schatten called out: 'Well, of course he is! Aren't you, Hans?'

The nurse raised an eyebrow. Hans (as he supposed he ought to think of himself now) blushed and said: 'Yes. Of course.' In truth he had grown used to the hospital, to its quiet routines, its safe boredoms. He wasn't sure he wanted to leave.

The nurse squinted in concentration as she started to unpeel the bandages. Hans tensed. Herr Schatten cleared his throat. Frau Schatten muttered what sounded like a prayer. When the nurse had finished, she took a step back and examined him. A brisk smile. 'It's healing very nicely.'

Cautiously Hans touched his face. He began to map the weird topography of his skin. There were rubbery ridges, rough craters, glossy nodules. But the oddest thing was that his fingertips could feel his face while his face could not feel his fingertips; it was like being two people at the same time. He asked the nurse if it looked as bad as it felt. She held out a hand mirror and said: 'See for yourself.'

Hans saw. Only for a second – he dropped that mirror as if it were white-hot – but it was enough. For as long as he could remember, his mother's friends had cooed over his beauty ('Look at those lashes – I'm jealous!') and told him he would be a 'heartbreaker' when he was older, but Hans knew that nobody would ever say anything like that again. The upper part of his face was unchanged: same chestnut hair, same green eyes, same unremarkable nose. But the skin on the lower, right-hand side of his face looked like a partially melted candle – there were actual *drips* of flesh – and the line of his mouth was drawn down in an unchanging scowl. Try as he might to smile, Hans knew he was doomed always to appear sly, sarcastic, cruel.

The nurse bent down to retrieve the mirror.

'It's not broken, is it?' Frau Schatten asked. 'That's seven years' bad luck.'

'The mirror is fine,' the nurse said firmly. 'And so is your face. You just need to get used to it.'

They drove him home and Frau Schatten gave him a tour of the house. He had never been here before, but he recognised it from his dreams: a cramped, stale-smelling place, the walls decorated with gloomy landscapes, the shelves and tables weighed down with knick-knacks. The only new element he noticed now was the number of reflective surfaces: mirrors hanging on walls, ornaments shined to a gleam, brass light fittings . . . Hans's ruined face seemed to be everywhere, mocking him, multiplying his misery.

The last room Frau Schatten showed him was the bedroom he would share with Karl. She knocked but there was no answer. 'Karl, your new brother's here!' she called out. 'Come and say hello.'

'It's open,' said a harsh voice from within.

Frau Schatten turned a sickly smile on Hans. 'Go ahead, dear. It's your room too now.'

Hans opened the door slowly and stepped inside. 'Hello,' he said shyly. Karl was reading on his bed; he scowled as he turned around, but as soon as he saw Hans his expression changed. He dropped his book and, hand over mouth, he half-laughed, half-retched: 'My God! Are you seriously going to look like *that* for the rest of your life?' Hans lowered his eyes and caught sight of the book's sea-blue cloth-bound cover: a small golden eagle carrying a wreath in its talons. And, at the centre of the wreath, a swastika.

That afternoon, desperate for some fresh air, Hans went out for a walk. It was a grey, chilly day. He found himself on Prinzenstrasse, among the crowds. He sneaked glances at the people passing by and saw mouths twisted in revulsion, averted eyes, blank stares. He thought again about Oma Hannah's stories; as a child, Hans had been frightened of God because He always seemed to be punishing people. There was the flood, of course, and the Israelites' forty years in the wilderness, but he also remembered a host of individuals tormented by Yahweh for their sins. But what sins had Hans committed to deserve this hideous mask? Or perhaps it was more like the devil's bargain in *Faust*? Perhaps these scars were the price Hans had to pay not to be Jewish, not to have stones thrown at him . . .

Deep in these dark thoughts, Hans didn't notice the empty space until he was almost level with it. This was the spot where he always used to cross the road, to run towards the shopfront of SPIEGELMAN MUSIKINSTRUMENTE. He tried to remember his life there, thirty feet above the rubble on the ground. His mind conjured the yellow walls of the living room, the black gleam of his mother's piano, the happiness of coming downstairs into morning light and smelling pastries baking in the oven. He even recalled staring out of the window on that last evening as he played 'Ode to Joy', his father in a white shirt, his mother in her pink-flowered dress. All of that was ashes. Memories of another life. Hans crossed the road and stared at the charred bricks behind the wooden barricades. Everyone else walked past without a second glance. Already what had happened had been forgotten, swallowed up by the city's indifference.

Maybe the boy in his dreams believed that he could come back to Prinzenstrasse, that everything could be made whole again, but Hans knew better. There was nothing for him here. He turned around and headed back the way he'd come.

SEPTEMBER

Hans

He wiped Frau Schatten's lipstick from his left cheek and closed the car door behind him. 'Have a wonderful first day at school, darling!' she called through the open passenger window. He looked around. Had anyone seen? Probably not. The pavement was dark with men in hats rushing to their offices and other children suffering embarrassing embraces. He gave a curt wave then ran up the steps and through the main entrance of the elegant, three-storey white building that housed the Musikgymnasium.

It had been a long, dreary summer, spent mostly in the sweltering bedroom he shared with Karl, suffocating beneath the weight of the black dragonfly, remembering his dreams, and waiting for his roommate to leave so that he could practise the violin. Hans had been anticipating this moment for months now with nervous impatience.

Inside, the lobby was full of strange faces. Loud voices echoed off the walls. The air smelled of pencil shavings, sweat, farts and soap. Hans noticed the middle-aged receptionist flinch at the sight of his scars before tracing her index finger down a list of names. 'Ah, here you are!' she said in a falsely cheerful voice. 'Schatten, Hans. Class 1C.' She consulted the timetable and informed him that his first lesson was French at eight o'clock with Monsieur LaRue.

Outside the classroom a group of pupils, most with their backs turned, were talking over one another as they waited for the teacher. Hans leaned against a cold radiator and pretended to check his watch. A mocking, high-pitched voice cut through the din: 'Hey, you! Fleischmütze! What happened to your hair?' Hans looked up at a tall boy surrounded by a crowd of acolytes. Forty eyes were staring past his shoulder; he turned and saw a slender nape, two delicately curled ears and a head covered with a gloss of very short dark hair, like iron filings. Meat Hat: not the most imaginative nickname, Hans thought. Then the boy with the shaved head turned around and . . . it was a girl. An explosion of incredulous laughter.

The girl's face stirred something inside Hans. There was a fierceness to her gaze, a defiance that Hans instinctively admired. He turned back to face the crowd, steeling himself to defend her from their taunts.

'My God, what is this freak show?' the tall boy shrieked. 'That's the worst case of acne I've ever seen!'

Hans frowned as he glanced at the girl again. Acne? Her skin shone with a faint patina of grease and she had a few pimples, but her complexion was clearer than most thirteen-year-olds'.

'Seriously, what happened? No, let me guess. You cut yourself shaving?'

Hans turned back to face the tall boy. Forty eyes staring at *him*. He realised that the boy was teasing him about his scars. He knew he should laugh along or say something to put the others at ease, but he was paralysed, speechless.

'Or you fell asleep too close to the fireplace and melted?'

Hans felt his jaw twitch at this but said nothing.

'Or did you step on a landmine?'

'With his *face*?' asked a shorter boy with red hair, and suddenly a debate erupted over how Hans's right cheek might have ended up that way. In the crossfire of voices Hans was able to retreat, withdraw into invisibility. He looked up at the girl again and she was smiling at him. A smile of sympathy, not pity.

'Shut up! Everyone listen,' the tall boy drawled. 'Landmine here is going to tell us in his own words. What really happened?'

Before Hans could answer, the teacher arrived. '*Ça suffit!* What you are doing to this boy is very unfair,' Monsieur LaRue said in a thick French accent, before unlocking the door and entering the classroom.

The children followed him inside and Hans chose a desk by the wall, near the back of the room. The girl with the shaved head sat next to him. 'That was sickening,' she said under her breath. 'That boy is a real dickhead! I'm sorry, I should have done something.'

'There was nothing you could do.'

'Of course there was! There's always something we can do. You want to know the truth? I was relieved that he was picking on you instead of me.'

Hans shrugged. 'That's understandable.'

'But it's wrong!' Her cheeks glowed pink and when she looked at him he felt his own face flush too. Her eyes were wide and naked-looking, the irises a sort of iridescent grey. For a moment Hans had the feeling he had seen her somewhere before.

'Don't worry about it,' he said. She looked as though she was about to argue with him again, so he added: 'I'm Hans, by the way.'

'Sophie.'

They shook hands. Hers was soft-skinned, cold, surprisingly strong.

'So you're new here too?' she asked.

'Yes. I—'

The teacher clapped his hands until the classroom fell silent. 'Monsieur Arnstein, come here, please.' The tall boy stood up and walked over to the teacher. 'Look at me. Now . . . It is no business of yours how this boy got those scars on his face. Is it?'

All eyes in the room turned to Hans again and he tensed.

'I was just making conversation, sir,' the boy said nonchalantly. 'Getting to know the new kid.'

'Very well then, you may share a desk with him. Monsieur . . . Schatten, is it?' the French teacher asked, checking his list of names.

'Yes, please come to the front and sit next to Monsieur Arnstein.'

Hans sighed, and carried his belongings to the front of the class-room. There, the teacher made him explain, in his halting French, where he lived, what his name was, and what his father and mother did for a living (watchmaker and housewife, he dutifully answered, trying not to think about his real parents). Then, in a voice obviously intended to sound compassionate, Monsieur LaRue asked: 'Et maintenant, voulez-vous nous expliquer ce qui est arrivé à votre visage, Monsieur Schatten?'

Howls of derision. Hans feigned incomprehension. His desk companion translated: 'He wants to know what happened to your face.'

'I don't know how to say it in French, monsieur.'

'Tell me in German,' Arnstein said. 'Whisper it in my ear.'

Hans leaned close: 'I have a rare contagious disease.'

Instinctively Arnstein jerked his head back. Then he heard the roar of laughter behind him and realised that Hans had been joking. Anger flashed in his eyes. Monsieur LaRue dutifully translated: 'J'ai une maladie rare et contagieuse.'

The rest of the day passed with torturous slowness. Hans looked for Sophie at lunch but didn't see her and ended up eating on his own, his gaze riveted to the food on his plate. During physical education, Arnstein had everyone in stitches by inventing two new nicknames for him: Rinderhack (Ground Beef) and Kotzegesicht (Pukeface). Even the teacher chuckled at this, looking annoyed when Hans caught him in the act.

His final class was music. He got lost on the way and arrived five minutes late. The other pupils were lined up in a circle, some sitting on chairs, others standing, all of them staring at him. The teacher smiled kindly and introduced herself as Frau Mayer. She pointed to a space between two girls holding violins: 'You stand there, Hans. We're taking turns to play a little tune of our own choosing. Nothing fancy, just so I can get an idea of your levels. All right? Ingrid, I believe you're next.'

The girl three spots away performed a simple cello exercise. Then a fat boy played *Eine Kleine Nachtmusik*, badly. Hans winced at every missed note, suppressing the urge to correct the boy's fingering. But he was starting to relax now. Next to play was the beautiful blonde girl to Hans's left. Her name was Paula and she had the most perfect skin he'd ever seen. Her technique was a little crude and the tune almost childlike, but it had spirit, Hans thought. He wanted to clap when it was over, but no one else did so he remained silent.

At last it was his turn. He played the first part of Telemann's Fantasia No. 1, one of his favourite pieces. The rendition wasn't flawless but during the final section he felt genuinely swept up by the music for the first time since the fire, transported far from this classroom, until he forgot about his scars and his grief, until he could almost hear his mother playing the piano beside him. When it was over he opened his eyes and Frau Mayer broke into enthusiastic applause. A grin of pride and pleasure crept across Hans's face and he stole a sideways glance at Paula. Her eyes flashed with fury. 'There's no need to mock me,' she hissed, 'just because I'm not as good as you.'

Max

Outside the classroom he leaned against a radiator. 'Hey, you! Fleischmütze! What happened to your hair?' Max looked up. Forty eyes staring past his shoulder. He turned and saw her, and recognised her instantly. That swanlike neck, those soft grey eyes, the bony nose and crooked front teeth . . . Despite the shock of her shaved head, these features matched perfectly with the image in his memory. She looked at him and her eyes widened. Did she recognise him too? Max's heart was pounding. He wanted to say something but the laughter was dying now and Arnstein's taunting voice filled the silence. 'My God, what is it? I can't even tell! A girl, a boy, a hermaphrodite?'

Twenty mouths smirked, tittered, crowed. The girl was staring calmly at her persecutor, only a faint blush hinting at any roused emotion.

'Seriously, what happened? No, let me guess . . . You were shaving your legs and your hand slipped?' This boy, Arnstein, was a few inches taller than Max but rangy rather than muscular. Karl Schatten would snap those skinny limbs like matchsticks, Max thought. He was good-looking in a cruel kind of way: big nose, high forehead, haughty eyes.

'Or are you training to be a Buddhist monk?'

It was the boy's voice that made him the centre of attention. That arrogant drawl. He was the class comedian but also a bully. The others were afraid of him, Max could tell.

Amid the laughter the girl just rolled her eyes.

'Jens asked you a question!' yelled one of Arnstein's disciples, a short, squat, red-haired boy with a squashed-up face like a bulldog's. 'Hey, I'm talking to you.' She glared at him defiantly. Scowling, the dog-boy advanced towards her. 'Are you a he or a she?' he demanded, grabbing her shirt. 'Let's see what you've got down there . . .' A gale of laughter as the girl's face paled and she took a step back.

'Leave her alone.'

Everyone looked at Max and he realised that he was the one who'd said this. The red-haired boy let go of the girl's shirt and turned to face Max. 'Who the hell are you, pretty boy?'

'I'm the one telling you to leave her alone.'

The boy was shorter than Max but heavier and more aggressive. He shoved Max hard against the wall and snarled: 'Make me, asshole!'

Max's first instinct was to punch him in his fat stomach, but he remembered his parents' warning last night – don't get into any fights – and hesitated. In the second that followed, his opponent suddenly whined with pain as his head twisted up to one side. The girl – *Sophie*, Max thought, as if someone had whispered the name to him – was pinching Dog-Boy's ear between her fingernails. When it was level with her mouth she hissed: 'Leave him alone, asshole.' Then she let go, smiling angelically.

The boy's eyes were moist with tears, his ear throbbing blood-red. He gurned at Max and Sophie. 'Oh, are you two freaks in love?' The crowd of teenagers around them made an *Oooooh* sound. Max's eyes met Sophie's and he looked away.

Dog-Boy turned to Arnstein and called out: 'What do you think, Jens? A girl who looks like a boy and a boy who looks like a girl!'

Arnstein shrugged, apparently unimpressed.

'And what is going on here?'

Everyone froze. The French teacher was walking towards them.

'Rien, monsieur,' the girl said coolly. 'We were just getting to know each other.'

'Ah . . . Mademoiselle Strom, c'est ça? Your parents are French, I believe?'

'My mother is, yes, sir.'

The teacher unlocked the door and led the pupils into the class-room.

'Very good. And apparently you have already made the acquaintance of Monsieur Mauser. So why don't the two of you sit together at the front.'

'Sir!' Dog-Boy protested.

'What's the matter, Niklas? Your French leaves much to be desired, does it not? Pay attention to Sophie and perhaps it will improve. Monsieur Arnstein, you can sit next to the new boy, Monsieur . . . Spiegelman?'

Max and Jens Arnstein nodded warily at each other. Sophie was two rows ahead. As Max was arranging the contents of his pencil case she turned and smiled at him. He felt himself blush but by the time he managed to return her smile she was looking the other way.

Max spent the rest of the day looking out for Sophie – he wanted to ask her if she remembered the music shop on Prinzenstrasse six months ago, the duet they were supposed to play together – but she wasn't in any of his other classes and he didn't see her in the cafeteria at lunch. His last class of the day was music with Frau Mayer. Max was tuning his violin when he felt a hand on his arm. He turned to see a pretty blonde girl. She was smiling at him. He nodded politely. 'Hello, I'm Max.'

'I know who you are,' she said hungrily. 'I heard what you did. You're the hero!'

Max frowned. The hero? Was she talking about him saving his parents' lives? But no one at his new school was supposed to know about the fire. 'What do you mean?'

'Come on, don't play dumb. Everyone knows! It's all over the school!'

So they all knew he was Jewish? 'Sorry, I don't know what you're talking about,' he said coldly.

'You punched Mauser! If I was a boy, I'd have done that ages ago.'

'Oh. But I didn't,' Max said, confused. 'It was—'

'It's okay,' she whispered. 'I won't tell anyone if you really want to keep it a secret. I'm Paula, by the way.'

He hesitated, then shook her hand. It was delicate, pale and warm.

When the class was over, Paula congratulated him on being a 'virtuoso', then took him by the arm and marched him through the corridors. She was obviously popular: lots of people greeted her as they passed and she introduced Max to each of them as 'the boy who hit Maus'. A rumour, Max thought, was like a pearl: all it took was the tiniest speck of grit and the most improbable lies could coalesce around it, forming something bigger and brighter than the small forgotten truth trapped within.

Outside on the street, Max scanned the mass of faces for Sophie's. But he didn't spot her until Paula exclaimed: 'Ugh, that bald French girl is waving at you! Come on . . .' She pulled him by the hand until they were around the corner, then breezily said: 'You're welcome.'

'For what?' Max asked.

'Rescuing you from the Freak! You don't want to get too close to her – I heard she has nits.'

Hans

He sat alone in the school cafeteria, chewing the gristly schnitzel and reading his history textbook. They were studying Alexander the Great and in his mind Hans was the young conqueror, discovering new lands, slaughtering his enemies. He'd been at the Musikgymnasium for a week now and still had no friends.

The only other person who deigned to sit at the same table as him was Rudi Schleicher, a good-looking boy whose nickname was Creep and whom the whole school treated like a leper. An invisible cloud of shame seemed to follow Creep around, but even he didn't speak to Hans. The only one to say a kind word to him so far had been Sophie Strom and he hadn't seen her since that French class on his first day. Jens Arnstein and Niklas Mauser, on the other hand, seemed to be in almost all his classes.

Hans heard sniggering behind his back and guessed what was coming. He took another bite of schnitzel, read another paragraph about the Battle of Issus, then clenched his biceps, pectoral and abdominal muscles for five seconds each. He knew he would never be as big as Karl, but he could still be the toughest possible version of himself. His ambition was to be top of his class and strong enough to beat up Jens Arnstein by the time school ended next summer. They were reading Nietzsche's *Götzen-Dämmerung* in philosophy – 'What does not kill me makes me stronger' – and Hans had decided to make this his motto.

'Hey, Rinderhack!' Hans heard footsteps on the tile floor and in the corner of his eye saw Mauser reaching a hand towards his face. The fingers drew slowly nearer then pulled away just before touching the puckered, molten tissue of Hans's scar. 'Ek-el-haft!' Mauser shouted, pretending to vomit. Hans tensed his stomach muscles but said nothing: he didn't need anyone else to tell him that his face was disgusting.

'Go on, Maus!' said another voice. 'I'll give you twenty pfennigs if you do it!' Mauser grinned and reached out again. Hans tensed his chest muscles and gripped his cutlery. As the boy's fingertips touched his face, Hans stabbed at the air with his fork and yelled, 'Get off me!'

Oooooh, said the table behind.

Mauser stared at his hand. 'You stabbed me!' he shrieked.

'He didn't even touch you,' said a girl's voice witheringly. 'And *you're* the disgusting one.' Hans looked up as Sophie sat next to him.

The boy muttered something about leaving the freaks alone so they could have sex. Sophie glanced up and said: 'Yes, please go away.' She smiled at Hans and he started to smile back before remembering what he looked like when he did that.

OCTOBER

He rang the doorbell and Paula answered it. She took his hand and led him into the brightly lit living room. Everything looked brand new and the air smelled of furniture polish. Paula removed her shoes and arranged them neatly against the wall. Max copied her. 'Max, my parents,' she said, gesturing at the man and woman sitting on a leather sofa at the other end of the room. Between them lay an expanse of freshly raked carpet. Max trod on it as lightly as he could but still left footprints behind, as in snow. The man stood up and thrust out his hand. 'Dieter Weiss!' he barked. 'And this is my wife, Emma.' Herr and Frau Weiss, Max noticed, looked much younger than his own parents. There were no bags under their eyes, no furrows on their foreheads, as if life had left less of an imprint on them. Or as if they'd just been raked. 'Please take a seat,' said Herr Weiss. 'So, Paula tells me that you wish to be her boyfriend?'

Max nodded uncertainly. In fact he'd never expressed a firm opinion on the matter – everyone else just seemed to take it for granted that this was what he wanted – but he had a feeling it wouldn't help to point this out. Only four weeks had passed since the start of school but already Max felt trapped in his new role: he was the Maus-slayer, the popular new boy, and now Paula Weiss's latest beau. Of course this was preferable to being a scarred orphan but all the same it made him a little uncomfortable.

'Let me warn you, Max: if I ever hear that you have mistreated my daughter, I will make you regret it for the rest of your life.' This was the kind of thing that Max's father might say as a joke and he waited a couple of seconds for a burst of laughter, a slap on the shoulder. But Paula's father continued to stare at him.

'Of course, sir,' Max said nervously. 'I would never do that.'

'No need to scare him, Liebchen,' said Paula's mother, placing a hand on her husband's forearm. 'Max, why don't you tell us about your family?' Her smile was polite but somehow detached-looking, as if she might remove it and put it in a drawer at night.

'Um, my mother is a piano teacher and my father plays the trumpet . . .'

'In an orchestra?' Frau Weiss asked, looking impressed.

Max nodded vaguely while sipping his tea. He didn't think the Weisses would approve of the jazz club where Franz Spiegelman had been earning his living since the destruction of the shop.

'So you're a musical family, that's nice. And what church do you attend?'

'The Karlskirche,' Max answered. Paula had warned him that they would ask this question. In truth he hadn't been to church in a long time but his mother had taken him to a few Christmas services back when her own mother had still been alive.

What are your hobbies? What do you want to do when you're older? Where do you stand on the issue of a Greater Germany? Slowly and painfully Max made it through the minefield of their questions. He did not tell any outright lies but his evasions, omissions and exaggerations left him shrivelled inside. What would his mother think if she could see him now? What would Sophie think?

During the past month Max had spoken with Sophie Strom only twice. But each time he'd been acutely aware of the looks of surprise and distaste on the faces of those around them, and Sophie, perhaps sensing his unease, had cut the conversation short. He still hadn't asked her if she remembered who he was. He only really knew her from his dreams.

At last Max and Paula were told they could go to her bedroom to work on their biology project. 'You have one hour precisely,' said Herr Weiss, checking his watch.

'And please leave your door open,' Frau Weiss added.

Inside Paula's bedroom Max looked around at the framed photographs of mountains, forests and waterfalls, at the enormous collection of dolls that covered her bed. He turned to see Paula leaning out into the hallway. 'Listen,' he whispered, 'I don't have my books with me. I didn't realise you wanted to work on the project.'

She shushed him, then stood listening. Music came from a radio in the living room and Paula softly closed the door.

Max frowned. 'Didn't your mother—'

'Do you always follow the rules, Max?'

'No, but . . . Well, your father seems quite strict.'

'Oh, don't worry about him – barking dogs never bite. You'd better not mistreat me, though, or *I'll* make you regret it.'

'What do you mean?'

Paula began to inspect her fingernails. 'You know Rudi Schleicher?'

'Creep? Yes, of course. Well, I know who he is.'

'He was my boyfriend once. He hurt me.' Paula paused and her eyes narrowed at the memory. 'So I hurt him.'

Max felt a prickle of fear. 'What did you do?'

'Just started a few rumours.' She smiled and moved closer. 'It's all right, I would never do that to you . . . As long as you're nice to me.' Max started to speak but Paula pushed him onto the bed and pressed her mouth against his before he could make any promises. To Max's surprise, her tongue grazed his lips. She sat up and laughed. 'Haven't you ever kissed a girl?' Max shook his head. 'Really? I'll have to teach you.'

She was a good teacher. Max had never imagined that kissing could be so pleasurable. He'd seen people do it in films, of course, but he'd never guessed what they were feeling as their faces merged and the string section stirred. Kissing was like music, like hearing Mozart for the first time. But it was also intensely physical, Max thought. Like fighting without the pain.

After a while Paula lay back on the bed and sighed. 'Not bad for a beginner . . .' There was a knock at the door. 'Shit.' She jumped to her feet and adjusted her skirt. 'Sit at the desk and pretend to work,' she told Max before calmly opening the door.

'Why was your door shut?' her father demanded.

'Your music was too loud. We couldn't concentrate. But we've made good progress on our biology project. Haven't we, Max?'

Max peered fearfully at the doorway where Herr Weiss stood. 'Uh, yes.'

'What is your project about?' Paula's father asked, still a little suspicious.

'The human mouth,' Paula replied without hesitation. Then smiled, as if waiting for him to leave.

Hans

He knocked on the door – there was no doorbell – and Sophie answered it. She took his hand and led him through the chaotic apartment. Stockings, books and half-eaten plates of food littered the wooden floorboards. The furniture sagged, the sunlit air swirled with dust. Sophie opened the door to a long room lined with windows overlooking the canal, where a woman with short, paint-flecked hair was gouging a pair of eye sockets into a clay skull. 'My mother's studio. Mama, this is Hans!' The woman looked up briefly and gave a curt nod before slipping her thumbs back into the moist holes. 'She doesn't like to be disturbed when she's work-ing,' Sophie whispered.

'She's a sculptor?'

'An artist. She paints and draws too.' Sophie gestured at the studio walls, which were covered with bizarre images. Hans saw a man with bark for skin and tree branches growing out of his ears, a clock with facial expressions instead of numbers, two children playing marbles with human eyeballs. 'She used to be a surrealist but her work is changing now. It's more political.'

'What's a surrealist?' asked Hans, whose knowledge of art was limited to the yellowed Achenbach prints that decorated the walls of the Schattens' house.

'Mama says it's about blurring the boundary between dream and reality. Anyway, let's go to my room. Do you want something to drink?'

They sipped lemonade and sat side by side on Sophie's bed. Hans looked at the posters on her walls – a man and a woman kissing, with sheets on their heads; watches melting in a desert landscape – and felt nervous. Blurring the boundary between dream and reality did not sound like a good idea to him. Hans's feelings about his dreams had changed since the bandages had come off: before, his nightly visions had consoled him; now, they taunted him with all he had lost. A family, good looks, popularity, a girlfriend . . . Perhaps the dreams were part of God's punishment. Or perhaps the Almighty was simply testing him? Yes, the God in Oma Hannah's stories had always been testing people, Hans remembered. Abraham and Isaac. The trials of Job.

Sophie put down her empty glass and smiled. 'So are you ready to start work on our biology project?'

They worked together for the next hour and Hans's confusion faded. Sophie was easy to be around, easy to talk to. She had a way of looking at him – neither consciously avoiding nor insistently glancing at his scars – that made him momentarily forget his deformity. When the project was complete, she lay on the bed with her head on the pillow and patted the space beside her. A little warily, Hans lay down. Sophie looked up at the ceiling, which was painted dark blue and dotted with silvery stars, and said: 'I'd like to get to know you better, Hans. But I've noticed you seem uncomfortable when I look at you, so maybe if we both look at the ceiling or close our eyes it'll be easier for you?'

Hans nodded slightly, his eyes moving from star to star.

'You do need to speak instead of nodding, though, if we're going to do it this way.'

He laughed and some of his nervousness escaped. 'Yes. I think that's a good idea.'

'So do you want to go first or should I?'

'You first.'

'I thought you might say that.' He could hear her smile as she said this. She started to talk and he closed his eyes. 'Well, my name is Sophie Angela Strom and I was born in 1920 in Berlin. But my mother is French, so maybe I should tell you about her first and how she ended up in Germany?'

'All right.' Hans started tensing his muscles as he listened. Pectorals. Triceps. Biceps.

'Her name is Suzanne and she grew up in the French countryside . . . Is this too boring?'

Abdominals. Quadriceps.

'No.' He cleared his throat. 'Honestly.'

'Okay. But tell me if you start dozing off and I'll give you the abridged version. Anyway, she wanted to be an artist, so at eighteen she moved to Paris. This was in the middle of the war, when all French people hated the Germans. But my mother wasn't like everyone else, so when the war was over she travelled to Berlin. And that was where she met my father, Ralf, who was just starting off as an architect. So, you know, they fell in love . . .' – Sophie's voice changed when she said this and Hans tensed his abdominals for longer than usual – '. . . and eventually they got married, even though my mother thinks marriage is a stupid bourgeois institution.'

'So why do it?'

'Because she loved him and his family expected it. She's a non-conformist but she does have a pragmatic side too.'

Hans wasn't sure what either of those long words meant but he didn't want to interrupt.

'And then I came into the world and ruined everything!' Sophie laughed. 'Just kidding. Well, partly. Anyway, I grew up speaking French at home and German at school, so I'm bilingual. I don't like one language more than the other. On the whole I think German is better for arguing and French is better for poetry. What do you think?'

'I don't speak much French.'

'Yeah, I know. I've heard you in Monsieur LaRue's class, remember?' She elbowed him in the ribs and Hans blushed.

'So why aren't your parents together anymore?'

'Politics.' She spat the word out like it tasted bad. 'You know about the new government in Germany, right? Adolf Hitler and the National Socialists.'

Hans thought of the books he had seen on Karl's shelves. 'A little bit,' he said.

'Well, my father's firm won a big government contract so my father ended up working for them. But my mother had just had an exhibition banned. She was on the Nazis' list of degenerate artists. So my parents didn't see eye to eye anymore. And then in March they had this really big fight and in the middle of the night my mother packed our suitcases and she took me in a taxi to the train station. We left for Vienna that morning. I never even had a chance to say goodbye to my father.'

'Oh,' said Hans, trying to sound sympathetic. 'What's he doing now?'

'He's still in Berlin, working for the government.'

'Does he write to you?'

'Sometimes. And we've talked on the telephone.'

'But you miss him?'

'Yes.' Her voice caught in her throat. 'Mama says what he's doing is evil but I don't think he's really changed.'

He turned his head sideways to look at her. 'Do you want to go back to Germany?'

Sophie shrugged. She was looking up at the ceiling. 'I miss my friends, and my dad of course. But I like it here too.'

'Are you still in touch with your friends?'

'Yes. I had one best friend and I write to her every week. But . . .'

'What?'

'I don't know, it's like I can feel her getting more distant. The first letter she wrote to me was twelve pages long. The one I got last week wasn't even a page. Not that I think you can measure friendship in the thickness of an envelope, but—'

'I know what you mean.'

Hans hesitated. He tensed his thigh muscles while trying to decide if he should tell her.

'Why do you keep doing that?' Sophie asked.

'Doing what?'

'Tensing your muscles like that.'

'Oh.' He forced himself to stop. 'I want to be strong. So no one can hurt me.'

'Not everyone wants to hurt you, you know. Sometimes you have to trust people.'

'I trust you,' Hans told the stars.

'Good,' said Sophie. 'So tell me what you were going to say.'

'Just that . . . I lost my best friend too, recently.'

'What happened?'

He could feel her eyes on him now.

'We had a fight.'

'What about?'

Politics, he almost said. Then: 'Just something stupid.' He swallowed. 'Maybe *we* could be best friends? You and me, I mean.'

He looked at her and she smiled. 'I'd like that, Hans.' Then he looked at the stars again, so he could smile without her seeing. 'Now it's your turn,' Sophie said. 'Tell me everything.'

Hans recited the script that Frau Schatten had made him memorise when he first moved to their house. His mother had died in a car crash; the car had caught fire and he'd been taken unconscious from the burning wreck. His real father, Helmut Schatten, was married to another woman – Hans was a bastard, conceived during their affair – but he'd agreed to take Hans in and raise him alongside his legitimate son, Karl. There was more to the script than this, but Hans decided to omit the other details. He felt guilty lying to Sophie.

'So that's how you got your scars? In a car crash?'

'Yes.'

'Really?'

'Yes,' Hans repeated feebly. Could she sense he wasn't telling the truth?

Sophie sat up. Nervously, so did he. Lips quivering, pupils dilated, she looked deeply into his eyes and for a second Hans thought she was about to kiss him. Instead she took his hand and placed it on her head. 'Feel here,' she said, guiding his fingers to a spot behind her ear. Her skull was bumpy there, and the hair – which had grown back a bit since the start of school – was incredibly soft.

'It's nice,' Hans said, his voice barely audible.

'Press harder. Here.' She moved his fingers along a precise route. 'You feel it now?'

There was a hard ridge of flesh in a jagged line about three inches long. A scar. Hans pulled his fingers away. 'What happened?'

'Same as you – I was in a car crash! I was very young, I hardly remember it. A shard of glass got stuck in my head. Apparently I bled like crazy. My mother has a photograph of me somewhere with my head shaved and all these stitches. It's funny, though, isn't it? That we both had the same experience. It's like we're connected somehow.'

He nodded. She was staring into his eyes. He looked away, unable to bear the intensity of her gaze.

'I'm sorry about your mother, Hans.' He felt a surge of gratitude: nobody had said that to him before, not since all those strangers at the hospital. He blinked back his tears while Sophie sat in silence. Finally she asked: 'Can I touch your scar?'

Hans felt disgusted on her behalf: why would she want to touch something so ugly? But she'd let him touch hers. He nodded, closed his eyes. A shock like ice. 'Ah, your hand's freezing!'

'Oh yeah, sorry.' She grinned. 'Cold hands, warm heart, that's what my grandmother says.' She breathed on her fingers to warm them. Then slowly, gently caressed the contours of his face. 'How does it feel?'

Automatically Hans answered that he couldn't feel anything – his scar was completely numb – but as he started to say this he realised it was no longer true. He could feel a sort of deep tingle, like electricity flickering beneath his skin.

All at once there was a slamming noise, so loud that the walls shook, and Hans jerked his face away.

'Don't worry, it's just my mother. She's trying out a new technique.'

They went back to the studio, where they found Frau Strom contemplating the head she'd been sculpting when they came into the apartment. Sophie drew Hans deeper into the room and he felt all those eyes around him – clay and paint, wood and glass – watching as he advanced. Frau Strom stood back from the sculpture and

Hans saw that it was a woman's face: a woman who looked extra-ordinarily similar to Frau Strom herself, except that a meat cleaver had split her skull from crown to chin. The blade was buried in the wooden plinth below, and the two sides of the head were slowly slipping apart, the right half deforming as it crumpled against the wood.

Hans   *Max*

Hans   *Max*

As he lay in bed that night, Hans remembered the conversation he'd had with Sophie, the feel of her fingertips on his scar, and that strange prickling of nerves, as though her touch had awoken something he'd thought dead. He remembered kissing Paula in his dreams and the two girls' faces merged for a moment. He blinked the illusion away. His head spun slightly with tiredness and he turned on his side. Eyes closed, he waited for the waves of sleep to envelop him, for the tide to pull him to the other side. As he sank through black water there was a noise in the room – Karl mumbling in his sleep, perhaps – and Hans resurfaced, half-opened his eyes,

and

turned to see Karl in the other bed then wearily closed his eyes again and felt something stir in the darkness within him as he drifted into sleep and started to dream: the hero with the handsome face, so popular at school, and he felt a spurt of jealousy for that mirror-self, familiar and uncanny, so close now that if he reached out a hand through the warm black water surrounding him, or spoke a word, Max would turn

found himself alone in a smaller room then wearily closed his eyes again and felt something stir in the darkness within him as he slowly started to wake from dreams: the orphan with the twisted face, so intimate with Sophie, and he felt a spurt of jealousy for that mirror-self, familiar and uncanny, so close now that if he reached out a hand through the warm black water surrounding him, or spoke a word, Hans would turn

and he would see the outline of
that face, hear that voice in his
ear whisper . . .

and he would see the outline of
that face, hear that voice in his
ear whisper . . .

'You.'

1934

MARCH

Hans

He stared at his reflection in the wardrobe mirror and wondered who he was now. He was wearing Oskar's old uniform: beige shirt, olive shorts, white knee-socks, thin black tie. The fabric smelled of mothballs, which was how Hans imagined dead things must smell. He peeked at the swastika under the fleur-de-lis armband: the Hitler-Jugend was banned in Austria but it wasn't the illegality that gave him this rush of revulsion and excitement. Shivering slightly, he walked to the other side of the room.

Karl's corner was neat as always. Around Hans's bed was a barricade of broken-spined books and inside-out shirts. His mother always used to complain that it looked like there'd been a robbery in his bedroom. Hans swallowed as he remembered this. Already Ana Spiegelman's face was blurring in his memory: he couldn't picture her the way she'd been when she was alive, only the way she was now in his dreams.

Last Sunday had been the anniversary of the fire. The black dragonfly had squatted on his chest all afternoon and evening as his bedroom walls glowed orange before sinking into gloom. But he'd fought his way through it and he could breathe again. The giant insect had flown away. Nietzsche had been right: Hans had survived and now he was stronger.

A whole year . . . When he looked back over those months of struggle and loneliness, Hans felt as if he'd climbed a mountain. Not that he was at the summit now: he was still ignored by most of his schoolmates, still taunted by Arnstein and his cronies, but his report cards were excellent and sometimes when he caught sight

of his naked torso in the bathroom mirror he could see the out-
lines of his muscles showing under the skin. And then there was
Sophie, of course. His best friend. More than a friend. Hans went to
Sophie's house several times a week to practise music or do homework together. Afterwards they would always lie on her bed and
talk. They hadn't kissed yet, but he felt able to relax in her presence, to open up. Only very occasionally did he find himself tensing
at the fear that she might betray him one day like Josef.

Standing next to Karl's bookshelf, Hans craned his neck to read
the titles on the spines: *The Passing of the Great Race, The Protocols
of the Elders of Zion* . . . *Mein Kampf* by Adolf Hitler. The sight of
that name electrified Hans. He'd gone to the cinema with Sophie
to see *King Kong* a few months ago and had found himself holding
his breath as he watched newsreel footage of the Führer, the man
whose followers had murdered his parents, had tried to murder
him. Those frantic limbs, that furious stare . . . Hans couldn't stop
thinking about him.

Heart racing, he slid the book out and looked again at that sea-
blue cloth-bound cover: the golden eagle, the wreath, the swastika.
Leafing through its pages felt wrong, dangerous, and not only
because it was Karl's property. Karl was not happy at all about
Hans joining the Hitler-Jugend, but Herr Schatten had insisted: it
would look suspicious if he didn't join, when his own half-brother
was a member. To Hans it felt like a logical step, if a strange one:
Max Spiegelman would never have done it, but he wasn't Max
Spiegelman anymore. He was Hans Schatten.

At last he spotted the word he'd been searching for: *Juden*.
He still didn't really understand what it was that Nazis hated so
much about Jews. He started to read and learned that Jews were
foreign-looking and smelled bad, that they were 'false through
and through . . . morally unclean'. Soon he came to a passage that
almost made him drop the book: 'It was always the same gruesome

picture. The names of the Austerlitzes, Davids, Adlers, Arnsteins, Ellenbogens, etc., will remain forever graven in my memory.' Hans read the line again. So his tormentor at the Musikgymnasium was a Jew? From downstairs, Herr Schatten shouted his name and Hans shut the book quickly.

In the entrance hall Herr Schatten nodded approvingly when he saw Hans, and Frau Schatten exclaimed: 'Oh, you look just like Oskar!' By the time he made it outside Karl was already halfway down the street, flanked by three other boys in uniform. 'Wait!' Hans called. Karl ignored him, but the tallest of the four – the only one in long trousers – turned to look. He was about twenty years old and film-star handsome, with slicked blond hair and a rakish moustache.

'Who's this?' the man asked, not unpleasantly.

'My half-brother,' Karl answered grudgingly. 'His name's Hans.'

'Your half-brother?'

'Yes. My father had an affair. This was the result.'

Karl sounded as if he were reading the script aloud rather than acting it out. To Hans's surprise the man seemed to swallow the story. 'Old Helmut? Really?' His neck arched back as he laughed. 'I never would have guessed he had it in him! And this boy's living with you?'

Hans tried to speak but Karl talked over him: 'Yes. His mother died. Car accident.'

The man took a step towards Hans. His face showed more curiosity than sympathy. 'Is that how you messed up your face?'

'Yes, sir,' Hans said. 'The car caught fire. I was—'

The man laughed. 'You don't have to call me "sir"! We're not on the parade ground. I'm Bauer. Heinrich Bauer. I'm one of the leaders of this section. Karl's probably told you about me . . .' Karl had not mentioned him at all – hardly surprising as he'd spoken a grand total of about thirty words to Hans in the past year – but the look on Karl's face warned him not to admit this.

Bauer held out his hand and Hans shook it. Then he was introduced to the other two – Georg and Friedrich Weber: round-faced, curly-haired, obviously twins – and the five of them set off. It was a cold, clear spring evening. They crossed a bridge over the canal before entering the Augarten. 'Tell me, Hans,' said Bauer. 'How much do you know about National Socialism?'

'I just started reading *Mein Kampf*.'

Karl shot a murderous look at him and Hans turned away.

'A masterpiece, isn't it?' Bauer drawled. 'We're so lucky to have the Führer! Men like him come around once in a thousand years . . . I saw him once, you know. In real life.'

'Really?' A shiver ran down Hans's spine. 'Where?'

'In Berlin, the day he became chancellor. When the news came through, it was pandemonium. Thousands of us marching by torchlight through the Tiergarten . . .'

'Sieg Heil!' yelled one of the twins, raising his right arm, and the others mirrored him. Hans followed suit, a second too late. The words sounded odd in his mouth and the movement was awkward, like a new dance step, but he felt an unexpected lightness in that instant. Briefly he remembered his parents the last time he saw them – Papa in a crisp white shirt, Mama in the pink-flowered dress – but he blinked the image away and they started walking again.

Hans heard some shouting in the distance and saw a group of boys playing football on a grass field. One voice rose above the others: 'Penalty kick! He *fouled* me, it's a penalty.' It was Arnstein. Hans stopped dead, remembering all the insults he'd suffered every day for the past six months. Even the dinnerladies called him Pukeface now. 'Hey!' he said to the others, and the strength of his own voice surprised him. They stopped too and turned around. 'I know that kid.'

'So?' Karl said.

'He's a Jew.'

Karl stared at him. In the twilight Hans could make out his features but not the expression they formed. Anger? Disbelief? Warning?

'Which one?' Bauer asked, sounding interested.

Hans pointed out his enemy, who had just scored a goal and was now celebrating. 'His name's Jens Arnstein.'

'Certainly looks like an arrogant kike.' Bauer cracked his knuckles. 'What do you say, boys? Shall we teach him a lesson?' The twins chuckled and Bauer smiled at Hans. His smile was like human sunlight; Hans felt anointed.

'We'll be late,' Karl protested.

Bauer slung an arm around Karl's massive shoulders. 'Come on, Karl! The Jew'll probably shit his pants when he sees you.'

The five of them marched towards the football players, who were now taking a break, facing the opposite direction. Arnstein was leaning on his elbows, boasting to Maus about the goal he'd scored, when Bauer's long shadow crept across his body. He turned around and the smile died on his face. 'Jude!' yelled Bauer, his graceful features transformed by hate.

Arnstein scrambled to his feet. 'Who are you? What do you want?'

Bauer shoved Arnstein in the chest. He was knocked to the ground and the five boys encircled him. When he caught sight of Hans, his eyes widened. 'Schatten, you shit! I'll get you for this.'

'No, you won't,' Bauer said calmly. A kick to the ribs. Arnstein groaned and curled up. 'Not unless you want us to break every fucking bone in your body.'

Bauer nodded at Karl and it rained boots. Hans remembered Arnstein poking his scar with a fork and shouting, 'The bacon's done!' He kicked Arnstein in the spine and felt a rush of triumph and shame. Beside him he saw Niklas Mauser stamping furiously on Arnstein's leg.

'Halt!' Bauer ordered. They stood still, breath steaming. 'Now get up.' Arnstein climbed warily to his feet, shoulders still hunched protectively. He saw his friend and gasped: 'Maus?'

'You never told me you were a Jew!' spat Dog-Boy.

'Look at me, Arnstein.' Bauer was speaking softly now. 'Yes, I know your name. And I've got my eye on you. If you say a word about this to anyone . . .' He snapped open a flick-knife and held it close to Arnstein's throat. 'Got it?'

Arnstein nodded. He was pale and shaky.

'Now fuck off. And don't come back.'

Max

He felt uneasy as he entered the Augarten, but it was a Wednesday evening and he usually played football here with some boys from his school. He soon spotted them, using their coats as goalposts. As he got closer one of the boys called out: 'Max, you're on our team! We're losing – we need you!'

Max didn't really know these boys but he felt a sense of camaraderie when he was with them. Despite being popular, he didn't have any close friends at school and this silent solidarity was the best substitute he'd found. There was Paula, of course, but he couldn't tell her things the way he used to tell Josef. In his dreams he could say anything he wanted to Sophie but in reality their only contact was a half-smile as they passed in the school corridors.

They started to play. After fifteen minutes Max had scored two goals and his team were level. He was happy, his anxieties forgotten. In the distance he saw two figures approaching. He shivered with apprehension when he recognised them: Jens Arnstein and Niklas Mauser.

Max and Arnstein weren't friends but they weren't enemies either. They were both popular, top of the class, good at football. They were rivals. Max sensed that Arnstein would have liked him as a friend, but he was so relentlessly cruel to Hans in his dreams that Max couldn't trust him.

The game restarted, with Arnstein on the opposing team. Arnstein went dancing down the wing and Max dived into the tackle. Arnstein leapt up. 'Penalty kick! He *fouled* me, it's a penalty.'

Max said, 'I got the ball', but even before the words left his mouth he got goosebumps. A floating sense of déjà-vu. He had lived through this moment before.

After that he was on edge, distracted. When they took a break, some of the boys lay on the grass and chatted but Max stood alone, juggling the ball nervously. He monitored the horizon until he saw them. The ball skidded off his knee and rolled away. A group of four boys, no bigger than flies at first, growing larger as they followed their long shadows across the grass. As the boys came closer, Max recognised their uniforms and he turned in a panic. 'Arnstein, go.' His rival looked up at him, confused. '*Run,*' Max hissed.

The man with the moustache yelled, 'Jude!' But when Max turned back he found to his surprise that the Nazi wasn't looking at Arnstein. He was staring straight into Max's eyes. 'I'm talking to you, Spiegelman.' A shove in the chest knocked him backwards; he staggered but regained his balance. 'This park is for Aryans, not Jewish scum.'

Max felt a new emotion rise up inside him. Not exactly anger, not exactly pride. 'I don't see any signs,' he muttered.

'What did you say?'

It was possible the Nazi really hadn't heard him: fear had tightened the muscles around Max's lips and he'd struggled to articulate properly. Another shove, in the neck this time. Max forced himself to look into those pale-blue eyes. He spoke the words slowly and loudly, trying to make the vibration in his voice sound like aggression rather than terror. 'I said I don't see any signs saying NO JEWS.'

'Oh, you want a sign? Here . . .' He slammed the heel of his hand against Max's front teeth. If he does that again, Max thought, I'm going to bite his fucking hand. 'Are you getting the message yet, Spiegelman? We don't want you here.'

Bauer shoved his hand into Max's face again. This time Max caught his right arm in both hands and sank his teeth hard into the index finger knuckle. The hand was soft and salty underneath, with fine hairs on top. Max could feel veins and cartilage giving way beneath the edges of his incisors. The Nazi screamed and flailed his left fist at Max's face, but it glanced off his sweat-slick cheekbone. Max tasted blood. He bit down harder. A thumb dug into his eye socket and he jerked his head back. He saw Karl Schatten gurning at him threateningly. 'Cut him, Bauer!'

Max took two steps back, three, four. Bauer examined his hand for a few horrified seconds – 'You piece of shit!' – then reached into his jacket and pulled out a flick-knife. The next thing Max knew, Jens Arnstein was pushing him in the back and shouting: '*Run!*'

All thoughts fled. He ran. Into the woods. Voices behind. Down dark identical paths. Over a fence and through dense undergrowth. Pulse throbbing in his ears. A tearing in his chest. At last Max bent forward to suck in air, his heart ringing like a bell. He felt a hand on his back. 'I think we lost them.' A few seconds later Arnstein laughed.

'What's funny?'

'I can't believe you *bit that Nazi's hand*.' Max started to laugh too, though it really wasn't a joke: the Nazi knew his name; Karl Schatten knew his family's address. 'Honestly, I've never met any-one like you, Spiegelman. You're either a hero or an idiot, I can't decide which.'

Max looked around: dense forest in every direction, the darkening sky barely visible through the treetops. 'Where the hell are we?'

'I think the nearest exit's that way. Come on, I'll show you.' They walked through clouds of midges. 'I never would have guessed you were a Jew,' said Arnstein.

'I'm not a real Jew,' Max explained. 'My dad says real Jews wouldn't even accept me because my mother isn't Jewish.'

'Yeah, some Jews are strict like that but my family isn't. Anyway, to bigots like *them*' – here, Arnstein gestured backwards with his thumb – 'you're exactly the same as me. And bigots like them could be running this country soon. You know what's happening in Germany, don't you? They're persecuting our people, boycotting our businesses, burning our books.'

Max couldn't help feeling sceptical of these claims. Arnstein was Arnstein, after all, and his father was a journalist on the *Neue Freie Presse*, which Max's mother refused to read because it was 'too extreme'.

'If you think it's wrong to persecute people, why do you do it to other kids at school?'

'Oh, come on! It's hardly the same thing, is it? I just mess around. This is serious.'

'You pick on the weak and humiliate them,' said Max. 'Seems like the same thing to me.'

Arnstein stopped walking. They were near the park gates now. 'You weren't exactly friendly yourself, Spiegelman.'

'Only because you bullied Sophie.'

'That wasn't me, it was Maus. Which reminds me: where is that little prick?'

'I don't think Maus is going to be your friend anymore. He doesn't like Jews.'

Something like shock flashed in Arnstein's eyes before he looked away and muttered: 'Good riddance, then.'

Max felt a brief swell of sympathy. He had lost Josef to the same disease.

Arnstein rallied. 'Anyway, Sophie and I are friends now. And I'm not sure your girlfriend is all that keen on Jews either.'

Max bristled at this, then realised that Arnstein was probably right. Paula had made him flinch on several occasions with casual references to 'people like that'. He had never challenged her about it, just changed the subject. 'All right, point taken.' He stared at the ground as he said this, depressed by the prospect of being picked on at the Musikgymnasium just as he had been in his old school.

To his surprise, Jens Arnstein put a thin arm around his back and, in a voice drained of his usual sarcasm, said: 'Listen, Max, I know I can be a dick sometimes, and I'm sorry. It's probably a defence mechanism. That's what Freud would say.'

'Who's Freud?'

Arnstein laughed. 'Don't you know *anything?*'

Offended, Max shrugged him off. 'Apparently not. I should go.'

'Max, I was joking.'

Max sighed and closed his eyes, and for an instant he saw Hans kicking Arnstein in the back. His anger quickly cooled. 'Could you teach me?' he muttered. 'About Freud and all that?'

'I'd be honoured. And maybe you could teach me to fight?'

'I don't know how to fight.'

'Could have fooled me.' Arnstein held out his hand and Max looked at it. 'To shake, not to eat.'

Max smiled.

MAY

Hans

The upright piano in the Schattens' living room did not have a single speck of dust on it. It had belonged to Oskar, and Frau Schatten kept it immaculate as a sort of shrine to her dead son. Today, however, marked the first time it had been played since his death. Frau Schatten stood watching Sophie with tears of joy rolling down her cheeks until Hans politely asked her to leave because he was finding it hard to concentrate.

Hans and Sophie had always practised at her mother's apartment before this, but Frau Strom was frantically preparing for her new exhibition, which opened in two days' time. The vernissage was to take place directly after the Musikgymnasium's spring concert. This was their penultimate practice before the big night.

'Shall we try again?' Hans asked, standing next to the piano bench where Sophie sat.

'I feel bad for your stepmother,' Sophie whispered. 'I wish you'd told me this was Oskar's piano.'

'Sorry, I didn't think about it. You made her happy, though. I mean, I know it didn't look like that, but—'

'I understand. It's like the music brought him back to life for a minute.'

'Exactly,' he said. Sophie always understood. 'Ready?' She nodded and they began.

Hans loved playing music with Sophie. Something pure flowed between them when they performed together. In fact he felt a quiet joy whenever he was with her, whatever they were doing: reading books, listening to music, walking, talking. A conversation with Sophie was like a duet, all harmony and interplay, all effortless glide, so different to the boxing matches, chess games and dripping taps that he had with other people. As they played, the murky green-and-brown leaf-motif wallpaper and the stale tobacco smell of the Schattens' cramped living room dissolved to reveal a forest glade, tall trees and a river, the scent of grass and wildflowers. The last note sounded and Hans opened his eyes. Sophie was grinning at him. 'I think we'll be good on Friday,' she said.

She patted the bench. Hans put his violin in its case and sat down beside her. They looked at each other in silence and Hans wondered if she was waiting for him to kiss her. Instinctively he turned towards the door to make sure that it was closed and that Frau Schatten hadn't sneaked back into the room. Sophie started messing about on the keyboard, playing a series of simple pieces. Hans recognised 'Chopsticks' and 'Clair de Lune' and Brahms's 'Wiegenlied', and then she played another song that stirred something in his memory. Jaunty, repetitive, half-familiar . . . He was transported to the top of the stairs in the Prinzenstrasse apartment. Was this the song his mother had been playing when he fell asleep that night? The descending melody and then the chord he hadn't been able to remember. It all came back to him in a rush of images and the hairs on the back of his neck stood up. Then his vision telescoped and he saw himself outside his father's shop, looking through the window at the girl with the ponytail and the pretty ears, her hands skipping quickly over the keyboard. The same hands, he felt sure, that were moving in front of him now. For the first time, he believed that what Max recalled of that night had truly happened. Sophie was the girl and this was the song, two parts of the secret combination that had brought him into this strange new world. Hans wished he could ask her about that afternoon, but he knew it was impossible. Herr Schatten had warned him of what would happen if he revealed his true identity to anyone. Still his thoughts rushed onward as she kept playing the song, faster and faster. In almost every respect, Max's life was better and luckier than his, but Hans was the one sitting close to Sophie now. She was *his* best friend, not Max's. Sophie lifted her hands from the keyboard and exhaled, laughing. Her cheeks were pink as she turned to Hans. Then she noticed the look on his face.

'Hans?' she asked shyly.

He just stared into her eyes.

'Ich auch,' she murmured, as though he'd spoken. And she closed her eyes and leaned in.

Hans was glad he knew how to kiss, thanks to his dreams. This kiss was nothing like the ones Max and Paula had shared, though. Physically it produced the same sensations, but he felt a euphoria, a relief, a deep happiness that Max, he knew, had never experienced.

He opened his eyes for a second and saw that Sophie's were still closed. The expression on her face was blissful and sincere. The moment was perfect until the door crashed open and Karl came in. Face screwed up as if there was a bad smell in the room, he barked: 'Get ready. We're leaving in ten minutes.'

Hans nodded, embarrassed. When the door banged shut, he muttered: 'Sorry. But I do have a meeting . . .'

'That's all right. I should be going anyway. I have to help Mama get ready for the exhibition.'

There was a silence then, but it wasn't awkward. Sophie held his hands and smiled, and Hans smiled back, unworried for once about how it made him look. He wasn't sure why he still hadn't told Sophie about the Hitler-Jugend, nor about what had happened with Jens Arnstein in the Augarten two weeks earlier. It wasn't that he was ashamed, just that the right moment hadn't come up yet. I'll tell her on Friday, he thought, after the concert.

'Hello Max, dear! You'll stay for dinner, won't you?' Jens's mother called from the kitchen as he walked through the hallway of the Arnsteins' townhouse. At the dining-room table Jens's willowy younger sister Charlotte looked up from her Latin homework and said, mock-solemn: 'Salve amicus', then grinned as he ruffled her hair. And in his armchair in the living room, Herr Arnstein lowered his newspaper. Jens's father was a distinguished-looking man – steel-grey hair, oval glasses, neat beard – and when he wasn't smiling he looked like the kind of man who never smiled. But when he saw Max he beamed and said: 'Ah, there you are, my boy!'

The infectious riff to 'The Crave' seeped through the half-open door to the music room. Jens glanced up from the piano and shouted, 'Maximus!'

'It's sounding pretty good now,' said Max. 'You'll be playing at my dad's jazz club before you know it.'

Jens stood up to wrap him in a bear hug. 'Oh, ask him to bring his trumpet tomorrow night! We can get a little concert going after dinner.'

Max smiled. The two of them were in remarkably high spirits considering they had just endured yet another day of being shunned and insulted at the Musikgymnasium. Paula had dumped Max as soon as she found out about the incident in the Augarten and since then she had kept her promise to transform him into a pariah. Not that she'd needed to invent any rumours; the fact of his and Jens's Jewishness had been enough to make all the popular boys and girls turn away whenever they walked past, and for Niklas Mauser and his fellow thugs to jeer 'Juden' like a herd of mooing cows. It wasn't pleasant, but for Max it was nothing like as harrowing as it had been at his previous school, not least because he had his best friend – and his best friend's family – to support him.

His downfall at school had also coincided with a distinct upturn in morale at home: after more than a year of wrangling with insurance companies, his father was about to open a new musical instruments shop. The change this news had wrought in Franz Spiegelman was spectacular. After months of looking pasty and dishevelled, of coming home from the jazz club in the middle of the night smelling of alcohol and other women's perfume, of waking at noon with bad breath and a short temper, his father was himself once again. Which meant that his mother was *herself*, no longer the brittle, grey-faced, angry stranger she had been. Max wasn't entirely sad to have broken up with Paula either. Particularly since Jens had told him that Sophie would be at the Arnsteins' post-concert dinner party. He remembered the kiss she and Hans had shared in his dream last night, and felt an odd mix of jealousy and hope.

'Shall we get started?' Max asked, opening his violin case.

'In a minute,' said Jens. He walked over to the door and quietly shut it.

'What's the matter?'

'Nothing. I . . .' Jens hesitated then said: 'Sit down. Let's have a drink. There's something I want to say.'

Max stared at him, astonished. He couldn't remember Jens ever looking so serious before. 'A drink?'

Jens went to his father's bar in the corner of the room and called over his shoulder: 'What do you want? Gin, brandy, wine?'

Max had never tried alcohol, apart from the odd mug of Glühwein at Christmas, and he wasn't at all sure it was a good idea to start when they were about to practise for the biggest concert of their lives. But Jens seemed intent, so Max said: 'Um, whatever you're having.'

Jens poured two glasses of a golden-brown liquid and sat next to Max on the battered old leather sofa. 'To you, Max Spiegelman!' he said, knocking his glass against Max's.

They both took a swallow and Max's face curdled in disgust. He put his glass down and said: 'So what's wrong?'

Jens downed the rest of his drink. Exhaling with a shudder, he said: 'Nothing's wrong, I just . . .' He sighed. 'Today, when Maus was calling us filthy stinking Jews, I thought about how that prick used to be my friend. Probably my best friend, as ridiculous as that sounds.'

Max shrugged. 'You didn't know what he was like then.'

'I did, though,' Jens said. 'I didn't know he was an anti-Semite, but I knew he was a bully. And it got me thinking about what a shit I used to be too. To you, to everybody. So I wanted to say—'

'You don't have to apol—'

'Let me finish!' Jens shouted.

Max held out his palms in surrender.

'Sorry,' said Jens in a gentler voice. 'I'm not good at this sincerity stuff. Anyway, I'm sorry I was such a prize dickhead before, and I'm really glad and grateful that you're my friend.'

Touched, Max said: 'Ich auch.'

'This is the first time in my life that I've felt comfortable being myself with anyone outside my family. It's like I don't have to perform when I'm with you. I don't have to play the part of Jens the Joker or Jens the Asshole, and believe me that is such a relief. So, yeah . . .' His voice wavered a little and he cleared his throat. 'I just wanted to tell you that you're my best friend and I love you.' The look in Jens's eyes was so intense that Max wondered if his friend was about to lean forward and kiss him. 'I mean it, Max.'

'Um, yeah, I can tell.'

Jens laughed and the tension evaporated. A little nervously, Max opened his arms and Jens fell into them and hugged his friend tightly. Their embrace lasted slightly longer than Max was expecting, and he felt Jens's sandpapery chin in the crook of his neck. In the end he patted his friend's shoulders a few times to bring him back to normality. Jens pulled away, reached across to Max's glass and swallowed the contents in a single gulp. Wiping his eyes, he said: 'My God, how do people function without sarcasm? It's fucking exhausting.'

Hans

Cradling his violin, he took deep breaths. He was sitting in a chair on the stage of the Vienna Konzerthaus listening to the velvet rumble of the orchestra pit, the murmur of voices. The audience was lit up while Hans remained in darkness, so he let his gaze sweep the front rows.

He spotted several familiar faces. His enemy Jens Arnstein, more subdued since the beating they'd given him in the Augarten; his new friend Niklas Mauser, who had been inspired by Hans to join the Hitler-Jugend; Paula Weiss, who'd recently started being more friendly; Frau Strom, impossible to miss with her short hair, crimson lipstick and dramatically pencilled eyebrows; and Frau Schatten, pointing out something in the programme (Hans's photograph?) to her husband, who nodded vaguely. A few rows behind he could see Bauer looking smooth in a tuxedo and Karl dressed in one of his father's suits. Briefly Hans imagined his parents in the audience too but that was like staring into a bottomless abyss. He blinked, swallowed. It's better this way, he told himself. Besides, they would see him perform tonight in his dreams.

The house lights dimmed, someone coughed, silence fell. His breathing thickened. Two spotlights poured down from above and Hans turned to see Sophie sitting at the piano. She smiled at him and he felt suddenly confident. Facing the glare, he picked up his violin and bow. The light was hot on his scars, which he imagined burning hideously red, but no one gasped or laughed. Hans closed his eyes, heard the choir of steel wires inside the piano, softly scraped his bow over the violin's strings and let the melody sweep him along in its current.

Max

The silence was burst by applause. Max opened his eyes and Jens joined him in the middle of the stage. They bowed and the applause grew louder, then they left the stage and walked through the wings and into the audience. Max kept his head down as they passed Maus, Paula, Karl and Bauer, who sneered and whispered to one another.

Max's father was the first to congratulate them. Looking dapper in a suit and tie, Franz Spiegelman wrapped his arms around both their necks and boomed: 'Bravo! Bravo!'

Max's mother was wearing the dress with the pink flowers – the first time she'd worn it since the night of the fire – and she looked younger. 'I'm so proud of you, Max,' she murmured in his ear.

Soon they were joined by his father's young shop assistant Helena, whom Franz had invited on an impulse that evening. Then the Arnsteins came over with a short-haired woman and amid the clamour of voices Herr Arnstein said: 'Franz, Ana, may I present Suzanne Strom? We'll be going to her new exhibition in a minute . . .'

Across a sea of faces, Max saw Sophie smile shyly at him.

Hans

He walked hand in hand with Sophie through the mild May night, the mizzle wetting their foreheads as they talked. Sophie was telling him how thrilled she was that he would finally be able to see her mother's new art. Hans looked back at the entourage trailing along the street behind them. He wanted to be alone with her, to taste her soft mouth again, to bask in the shared glory of their performance, to catch her up on all the things he hadn't yet got round to sharing with her. 'Tell me again why the Arnsteins are here,' he said, trying not to sound annoyed.

'Jens's father is writing a piece about my mother for the newspaper, remember? I've been meaning to tell you, actually: I think we may have misjudged Jens. He's not so bad once you get to know him. He's quite sweet, in fact.' Hans stared at her, speechless. It was true that Jens Arnstein seemed a much nicer person in his dreams, but surely Sophie didn't expect him to just forget all those months of bullying and humiliation. He was about to say this when she gripped his arm. 'Hans, look! We're here.'

Inside the bright gallery she pulled him by the hand through the elegant, wine-sipping crowd. 'Come on, I want to show you my favourite pieces!' She took him to see a series of paintings of Vienna viewed from the air. In the first, the edge of a shadow was just visible in one corner; by the fifth, it stretched almost all the way across the city, covering the streets and buildings in darkness. From the other side of the room, Hans heard Sophie's mother talking loudly to Herr Arnstein: 'No, I am not a prophet, simply a seismograph. The things I see and feel are already here around us. Those who are unaware of them lack sensitivity. Or they prefer ignorance.'

'But my favourite series is over here,' Sophie said, leading him into an adjoining room filled with sculptures. 'You recognise this one?'

Hans looked down and saw the clay head split in two by a cleaver, mounted on a white plinth. 'Rift #1, 1933', said the label. On the wall next to it was an ink drawing of a girl playing a grand piano, except that the right-hand side of the instrument was falling, like liquid, onto the ground. Even parts of the girl's hair and dress were pouring sideways. Hans thought of Sophie playing the Bösendorfer in his father's shop window hours before it went up in flames. One day I will tell her the truth, he swore, vaguely imagining the two of them as adults together, perhaps even married, the secrets of his past out in the open. 'Is that you?' he asked, pointing to the drawing.

But she didn't respond because Jens Arnstein sidled up beside her just then and gushed: 'Your mother's a genius, Sophie.'

'Thank you, Jens,' she replied politely. 'I'm glad you appreciate her work.'

Hans whispered: 'Sophie.' But she was talking to Arnstein now, her back turned to Hans, so he moved on to the next sculpture. This was a clay figure, about three feet tall, of a man whose torso divided into two necks and heads. The head on the left looked angry and its arm was making a Nazi salute, while the head on the left recoiled in terror. Hans read the label: '*The Other*, 1934'. Was the Nazi's face scarred or was he imagining it? He examined it more closely. The moulding was so crude that it was impossible to tell, but even so the idea disturbed him.

Sophie was still deep in conversation with Jens Arnstein. Hans said her name again, touching her arm. She turned towards him, about to speak, but Hans and Arnstein's eyes met at that moment.

'Schatten,' his enemy said, turning suddenly pale.

At the same moment a tray of canapés went flying. It clattered metallically to the floor as tiny squares of ham and pastry rained down. 'What is this shit?' someone yelled angrily. The hubbub of voices fell silent, as if the needle had been lifted from a gramophone record. 'You call this art?' Hans turned. It was Bauer, still dressed in his tux and bow tie. Suzanne Strom recoiled as Bauer yelled insults at her, spittle flying from his mouth. 'This isn't art, you bitch. It's filth, it's poison!'

Sophie looked as though she was about to faint. Hans put his hand to the small of her back, ready to catch her.

Two large men in suits approached Bauer. He raised his arms and said: 'Yeah, yeah, I'm leaving. I have no desire to keep breathing this decadent bourgeois air. You lot will be first against the wall when the Führer takes Vienna, mark my words.' His gaze strafed the faces in the room. When he saw Hans his expression changed instantly. In a relaxed, affable tone, he called out, 'Hallo, Hans! See you at the rally next week!' before nonchalantly walking out of the gallery, accompanied by the hulking figure of Karl.

Amid the frowning murmurs and nervous laughter that rose up in his wake, Sophie turned to Hans and said accusingly: 'You know that man?'

Hans withdrew his hand from the small of her back.

Max

He sat next to Sophie at the Arnsteins' long dining-room table. Jens was on the opposite side, deep in a philosophical debate with his sister Charlotte.

'I think you have an admirer,' Sophie whispered to him as he sipped his leek soup.

Max frowned. 'Who?'

'Jens's sister. Surely you've noticed? She can't keep her eyes off you.'

Max looked up. Charlotte, who was staring at him, blushed a deep red and looked down at her plate. 'She's probably just remembering all those times she thrashed me at chess.'

'She's pretty,' said Sophie.

Was this true? If it was, Max had never paid attention. Jens's sister was boyish and brainy, not to mention almost three years younger than him. 'I think you're just imagining things,' he said.

There was a shriek of laughter from the far end of the table where the adults were sitting. Max's father was running through his repertoire of jokes. Frau Arnstein and Helena the shop assistant were hanging on his every word while Max's mother, who had heard all these lines a hundred times before, smiled indulgently. Sophie and Max listened to the next one and Sophie gave a throaty laugh. 'He's a charming man, your father. I remember him now . . .' Max looked at her, surprised, and she moved her chair closer to his. 'And you. I thought it was you when I saw you on the first day of school, but you didn't seem to recognise me so I—'

'I did recognise you,' Max cut in. 'And I was going to say something about it, but . . .'

'Paula Weiss happened?'

He rolled his eyes, laughing. 'Yeah. But that's over now. She—'

'I heard.' Their faces were inching closer together as they spoke, as though their words were a string of spaghetti that they kept sucking between their lips, finishing each other's sentences, their voices growing quieter. 'It was horrible, what those Nazis did to you in the Augarten! Jens told me about you biting his hand, though. That was really brave.'

'Stupid, more like,' muttered Max.

'Stupid . . . brave . . . Same thing, really.'

They both smiled, then seemed to realise how close they'd grown and looked around guiltily at the other guests. Across the table, Jens raised an eyebrow while Charlotte appeared to have discovered a fly in her soup. Sophie shuffled back in her chair to a more respectable distance and said: 'I was shocked when I went back to your father's shop to see you and it wasn't even there. It's lucky none of you were hurt.'

Max thought of Hans. 'Yes, it could have been worse.'

'So, maybe we can finally play a duet together?'

'I'd like that,' he said with a smile.

The rest of the evening passed swiftly and sweetly. There were several toasts – to Suzanne Strom's new exhibition, to Franz Spiegelman's new shop, to the Arnsteins' warm hospitality – and a magnificent meal of roast chicken with potatoes and figs, followed by Kaiserschmarrn. The conversation went over Max's head at times but he enjoyed it all the same. At one point, during a discussion of Jung's concept of individuation, Frau Strom said: 'What he's saying is we cannot be fully human until that shadow, that inner darkness, is brought into the light of consciousness.'

'You know,' said Herr Arnstein, sucking on his pipe, 'a wise man once told me that no one is fully human until they've had their heart broken, lost a loved one, and become a parent.'

'Oh come on, Papa, you made up that line yourself, didn't you?' drawled a loud voice from across the table.

Herr Arnstein shook his head. 'You're so cynical, Jens.'

'So, wait, are you saying that *we're* not fully human?' Charlotte asked.

'Well, in the sense of being wholly developed, of understanding life and the world, then no, probably not. But you are only twelve, Liebchen.'

'According to the Nazis, most of us here aren't fully human,' said Jens. 'They think we're Untermenschen.'

'*They're* the ones who aren't human!' Sophie said savagely.

And, to her evident pleasure and embarrassment, everyone applauded.

Hans

He knocked but nobody answered so he sat outside her door and waited. He had barely slept last night and his whole body ached now. Twelve hours earlier Sophie had left the gallery with her mother and the Arnstein family, refusing to even look at him. He understood why she was angry but he felt sure he could explain if only she would listen. He didn't want to lose her. He couldn't. Surely they weren't going to let *politics* drive them apart . . .

The lift door clattered open and Sophie's mother emerged. A cold glare. Hans struggled to his feet, clumsy as a puppet. 'Frau Strom, do you know where Sophie is? I need to talk to her.'

'I'm here,' said Sophie. She was still standing inside the lift, as if the sight of him had frozen her to the spot.

Suzanne Strom said something stern in French and Sophie replied, conciliatory. Her mother sighed, then went into the apartment. Hans and Sophie stood facing each other. Hans took a breath. 'Listen, I'm sorry, I had no idea he was going to—'

'Hans, we can't be friends anymore.'

'What?' He felt like he was falling and had to put his hand to the wall to steady himself.

Sophie's face looked small and pale. 'How can we be? After what you did to Jens? He told me all about it.'

'Oh come on, Sophie. I know you like him now but he's a bully.'

'But you didn't attack him because he was a bully, you attacked him because he was a Jew.'

'That's not the point!'

'Oh, it's not?' she said icily.

'If you'll just listen to me, you'll understand . . .'

She crossed her arms and stared at him fiercely. 'Go on. I'm listening.'

'I wanted to tell you last night. About the Hitler-Jugend, about Arnstein, but . . . not with all those people around.'

'All those *Jews*, you mean?'

'No, it's not like that! National Socialism isn't about hating Jews, it's about being part of something bigger . . . building a better future . . .' He began to stammer. He'd heard these arguments so many times at HJ meetings, spoken by authoritative men, and they'd always seemed to make sense. Now, in his own mouth, they were just words, rolling around meaninglessly like the beads of a necklace with the string cut.

'You don't even believe it,' she said. 'I might have more respect for you if you did. You're just doing this because the others are doing it, because you're afraid of what they'll say if you don't. Because you want to *fit in*.'

'What about your father? He joined the Party, he works for the Führer. You still love *him*.' Hans felt his face turn hot. Sophie said nothing and for a moment he wondered if he might have won her over. 'You said it yourself: he hasn't really changed. Well, that's true for me too, Sophie. I—'

Suddenly her cheeks were red. 'My father designs office buildings, he doesn't beat people up in parks!'

Hans felt winded, as if he'd been punched in the stomach. 'But . . .'

'I have to go,' she said coldly, turning away.

He put his hand on her arm. 'Sophie, wait.' Only three days ago they had kissed for the first time and Hans had believed that she was God's reward to him for all the suffering he had endured. He wanted to tell her the truth about himself – that he was the boy in the music shop that afternoon, that he was Jewish and his parents had been killed by Nazis. If only the words would come out of his mouth then surely she would forgive him, understand, not turn away. But in the end all he managed to say was: 'I love you.'

'Please let go, Hans,' she said in a quiet, shaky voice, staring down at the floor. 'This is hard for me too, you know.'

He let go. She stepped inside and closed the door behind her. Hans stared at the blank wooden rectangle in disbelief. He couldn't have lost her. He couldn't.

JUNE

Water lapped the sides of the rowing boat. A hawk circled the blue sky. It was mid-afternoon, the air so hot that even the birds had fallen silent. Max and Sophie sat close together on the bench while Jens rowed them towards the shade of the tree-lined shore. He rested the oars in their rowlocks and the ripples in the lake faded to a glassy lull. Jens pulled a bottle of strawberry wine from his rucksack and took a swig, then passed it to Max. 'I stole this from the icebox this morning,' he said. 'I've got some bread and cheese too.'

Max and Sophie grinned at him and they spent the next half-hour contentedly eating and drinking, dipping their hands in the lake's cool water, hardly speaking for a change. 'This is perfect,' Sophie sighed, and Max nodded. He and Sophie had been staying at the Arnsteins' house in the Wachau Valley for the past seven days and Max wished they could stay here forever.

A ladybird landed on Sophie's left thigh and Max put his hand close to lure the insect onto it. Sophie pressed her leg to his fingertips. The bare skin was smooth and warm. He glanced at her and their eyes met: a brief, silent electric shock. Then the ladybird flew off in a flash of red and black and Max reluctantly moved his hand away. He forced himself to keep breathing. Sophie passed him the bottle of wine. He drank some, then passed it to Jens.

Sophie cleared her throat. 'So, what was your favourite book when you were a child?' They had been asking each other questions like this all week, opening up their pasts and hopes and fears, and Max could feel their friendship growing more closely woven with each conversation. He suspected Sophie was just trying to erase the tension of the last few minutes, but the question interested him all the same.

'*Emil and the Detectives*,' Jens said quickly. 'Although I reread it recently and it seemed a bit sinister to me, probably because I was imagining Emil and his friends as members of the Hitler-Jugend hunting down some poor Jew. It's banned in Germany now, though, so apparently the Nazis don't see it that way.'

'Max, what about you?' Sophie asked.

'*Peter Pan*. I loved the idea of being able to fly, being taken to another land.'

'Ich auch!' said Sophie. 'I used to read fairy tales all the time when I was little. Just that idea of a door opening in reality and leading you through to a place where magic happened . . .'

'Jung says fairy tales are expressions of the collective unconscious,' Jens said.

'Still ploughing through his essays, then?' she asked teasingly. Jens had asked her yesterday if she was 'still ploughing through' *War and Peace*, after she'd insisted on reading it despite his warnings about its length and dullness.

Jens sighed. 'Jung isn't boring, just hard to understand.'

'What about you, Max?' Sophie asked. 'Are you still reading Freud?'

'Yeah . . .' Max had begun *The Interpretation of Dreams* earlier that week and was now close to the end. It was fascinating but its conclusions had left him perplexed, and slightly anxious. If dreams were wish fulfilment, what exactly was his subconscious wishing for? That his parents had died in a fire? That Paula was still his girlfriend? That he and his friends were Nazis? He stared into the haze of golden-haloed leaves above them and shuddered as he remembered last night's dream. And to think he had once felt sorry for Hans . . .

'My dad's met Freud a few times,' Jens offered. 'Says he's a bit of an oddball. But brilliant too, of course.'

'Aren't all brilliant people considered oddballs?' Sophie asked.

'Like your mum, you mean?'

She kicked him and the boat tilted.

'I had a horrible dream last night,' Sophie said. 'Hitler was the headmaster in our school.' Max watched her as she spoke. In profile, with her high cheekbones and long slender neck, her dark bobbed hair, she struck him at that moment as almost regal. 'And everyone around him was being so obsequious. All our teachers, all the parents and students. They would beam with pride whenever he paid them a compliment and rush to put his orders into action. It was sickening.'

'What about me?' Jens asked. 'Was I in it?'

'Yes, you and Max were just like the others. I was the only one who hated him.'

'What?' Jens looked outraged.

Sophie shrugged. 'I can't control my dreams.'

'I would never bow down to that bastard in real life – I hope you know that.'

'I don't think anyone can say that, really,' Max said. 'What if we'd grown up with different parents? We might be Nazis now, all three of us.'

'Horseshit! There's good and evil and that's all there is to it.' Jens downed the last gulp of wine, then flung the bottle as far as he could across the lake.

'Calm down, Jens,' Sophie said. Turning to Max, she frowned. 'What makes you say that, Max? I'm not saying you're wrong, but . . .'

Max hesitated, but not for long. Jens and Sophie were his friends and he trusted them completely. Besides, it didn't seem such a momentous step, out here on the lake in the endless afternoon, so unmoored from reality. So he told them everything, from the dream that had saved his parents on the night of the fire to the most recent ones about a Hitler-Jugend summer camp. He gazed at the horizon while he spoke, avoiding their eyes. Then he fell silent and looked up to find them staring incredulously.

'Are you serious?' Jens barked. 'Every night?'

Max nodded.

'I can't believe you never told me this before. And . . . you're saying it feels real?'

'It *is* real,' Max said quietly.

Jens laughed. 'What do you mean?'

A shrug. Max was beginning to wish he'd never said anything, but it was too late now. 'I know things I shouldn't know. That I couldn't possibly know if . . . if Hans wasn't real.'

Silence.

'You don't believe me.'

'I *do*,' said Sophie earnestly. 'I really do, it's just—'

'Oh, come on!' Jens scoffed.

Max looked at Sophie. 'I know about the scar on the back of your head,' he said in a monotone. 'I know about the car crash and the photograph your mother took of you with your head shaved when you were a little girl. I know she told you that you bled like crazy.'

Sophie was pale, open-mouthed. 'How could you . . .'

'Because you told *him*. In my dreams.'

Jens stared questioningly at Sophie. She nodded.

'Seriously?'

She took Jens's hand and pressed it against the back of her head. He looked shocked. 'And you never told Max any of that?'

'No. I swear.'

A pause. 'Oh, you two are pulling my leg!'

Sophie, silent, shook her head.

Jens looked at Max. 'What do you know about me?'

'Nothing. He hates you, remember? You used to bully him and

now you're scared of him. But *he* knows about you. Things he shouldn't know.'

There was a silence. The blop and thunk of water on wood.

'But why would that happen?' Jens asked, the shape of his mouth showing a refusal to accept this impossibility. 'Why would your life suddenly split in two?'

'I don't know. But . . . I could feel it coming, somehow, that evening.'

'Maybe you just realised, subconsciously,' said Jens, 'that your so-called friend hated you because you were a Jew and his parents were planning to burn their own house down to kill you. I mean, you said he was acting strangely that day.'

'Yeah, Josef was part of it, but it wasn't just that. I mean, that was the afternoon I met Sophie, and now she's . . .' Max looked at her, unsure what to call her.

'Your friend,' she said.

'Yeah.'

Jens sighed. 'Okay, but—'

'And there was a song. Sophie was playing it on the Bösendorfer, I think, when I first saw her. And when I fell asleep that night, at the top of the stairs, my mother was playing it.'

'Which song?' Sophie asked.

'I don't know.'

'Can you hum it?'

Max closed his eyes and tried to remember. The descending melody he'd heard in his dream, on the evening that Hans had kissed Sophie. Another clue to their shared destiny, he thought, but he couldn't tell her that. Not yet. 'I can't remember. It was something simple, though.'

Sophie looked thoughtful. '"Clair de Lune"?'

Max shook his head.

Abruptly Sophie turned to face him, her knees brushing his

thighs, and water slapped the boat's hull. 'Wait, was this it?' She started to sing. The melody was jaunty, repetitive, half-familiar, the words in a foreign language.

> *Row, row, row your boat*
> *Gently down the stream*
> *Merrily, merrily, merrily, merrily*
> *Life is but a dream*

'That's it!' Max said. The notes echoed hauntingly in his mind. He was at the top of the stairs again, falling into another world.

Jens pulled a face. 'Okay. But so what? I mean, what does it even mean?'

She translated the words and Max felt a jolt in his chest at that last line. *Das Leben ist nur ein Traum.*

'You think this song has something to do with what happened to you?' Sophie asked.

Max blinked sweat from his eye. He felt uncomfortably hot all of a sudden. 'I don't know. You or the song. Or both.'

'Wow,' Jens said sarcastically, 'it's like you two were fated to find each other or something. Star-crossed lovers!'

'We're not lovers,' Max said, just as Sophie said: 'We're not star-crossed.' They looked at each other, both blushing.

'I'm going for a swim,' Sophie said suddenly. Max watched as she took off her shorts and vest, revealing a one-piece red bathing suit that showed her naked back. He had seen her in her bathing suit every day for the past week but his Adam's apple still seemed to swell up too large for his throat as she bent over the side of the boat and dived into the water. The rowing boat rocked from side to side.

He and Jens sat in silence for several minutes, watching Sophie swim in circles around the boat before diving down under the water. Jens had a strange expression on his face, as though he was about to start crying. Finally, he said: 'I'm sorry, Max. I didn't mean to sound facetious, it's just—'

'I know, don't worry. I probably wouldn't believe me either.'

Jens put a hand on Max's shoulder and squeezed. Max flinched and pulled away. 'What's the matter?' Jens asked, looking hurt.

'Sunburn,' Max muttered.

A few seconds later, Sophie broke the surface of the water. She breathed in loud gasps as she trod water about ten feet away, then called out: 'Jens, how deep is this lake?'

'No idea. Deep.'

Sophie took a breath, dived down again, and a minute or so later came sputtering to the surface. 'It's really dark down there!'

'Did you reach the bottom?' Max asked as she swam towards them.

'No. It's quite scary, actually. How still and cold it is.' She was shivering as she climbed inside the boat. Max passed her a towel and she wrapped it around her shoulders. Her lips were bluish and her teeth were chattering. 'I had an idea, though, while I was down there.' She looked at Max as she said this.

'What?'

'I think you should write to Freud and tell him about your dreams.'

'That's actually a good idea,' said Jens.

'Maybe not the part about Hans being real, though,' Sophie added, embarrassed. 'I mean . . .'

'He'd probably have me committed?'

'No!' She slapped Max's arm. 'That's not what I meant at all – and you know it!' As she said this, she dug her fingers into his ribs, making him squirm. There was a look of manic excitement on her face. 'I never knew you were so ticklish!'

'Put him down, Sophie,' said Jens in a cold voice. 'You'll capsize the boat if you're not careful.'

'Sorry,' she said, looking sheepish.

There was a long, strained silence as the boat grew still again. Jens gazed moodily out at the diminishing ripples on the surface of the lake.

'Um, do we have any more water?' Max asked.

Jens tossed him the bottle, which was almost empty, and Max poured the last few drops of lukewarm liquid into his mouth.

'We should probably head back to the shore,' Sophie said. 'I'm thirsty too.'

'Someone else can row, then,' Jens replied in a surly voice. 'I'm going to take a nap.'

The two boys swapped places and Max rowed them back to shore in silence, wondering what had happened to their afternoon idyll. Halfway there, Jens opened his eyes and, sounding more cheerful, said: 'I like Sophie's idea about Freud. He might even write a paper about you. Let's talk to my dad about it tonight.'

'All right,' said Max, unwilling to disturb this new truce by expressing his reservations.

As they were tying up the boat, Jens, still a little drunk, slipped on a slimy rock and fell into the water, so the three of them lay on the grass for an hour and waited for the sun to dry his shoes and shorts. Sophie lay between the two boys in her red bathing suit and read Tolstoy, while Jens quickly fell asleep. Max dozed and half-woke in another body, on another shore. Paula was lying next to him in a blue bathing suit, eyes closed against the sun. He blinked and she vanished, the lake changed shape, the sun disappeared behind some trees. Sophie sat up and looked intently at him. Next to her, Jens was snoring open-mouthed.

'Did you fall asleep?' she whispered.

'A little bit.'

'And you dreamed?'

'Sort of.'

'Was he there? Hans?'

Max sat up too, wrapping his arms around his knees. He looked out at the lake. '. . . Yes.'

'Did you try talking to him?'

'Talking to him? No. What would I say?'

She shuffled closer. Max watched her hand as it scooped up sand and she let it pour through her fingers. 'Maybe you could persuade him that what he's doing is wrong . . .'

'I doubt it,' said Max. '*You* couldn't.'

'What do you mean?'

'The other you.'

Hans was in love with you and he still wouldn't give up the Hitler-Jugend for you, Max thought. But he didn't say this. It felt like dangerous territory.

'Oh! I hadn't even thought about that.' Sophie leaned in and he smelled the strawberry wine on her breath. Ripples of light caressed her face. 'What's she like, the other me?'

'Same as the real you.'

'She's not different at all?'

Max shrugged. 'I don't think so.'

'That's strange.'

'Although . . . I don't know you as well as I know her.'

'That's even stranger!' Sophie gave a crooked smile. 'We'll have to do something about that.' Her face was close to his as she said this and Max wondered if they were about to kiss. But then Jens snorted himself awake and the moment was over.

The three of them walked slowly home across the fields, their shadows lengthening behind them. Cutting through the woods near the Arnsteins' house, they heard a strange humming in some bushes. Jens pulled aside a branch and they saw a dead rabbit caught in a hunter's trap, flies buzzing around its body. 'Poor thing,' Sophie said. 'Do you think rabbits have souls?'

'I'm not sure *humans* have souls, never mind ickle bunnies,' said Jens.

Sophie looked slightly shocked. 'So what do you think happens to us when we die? We just get eaten by flies and that's it?'

'Pretty much.'

They started to walk again and came to the edge of the woods. The setting sun blazed red and gold above the hills behind the house.

'So you don't believe in an afterlife at all?' Sophie asked.

'Even devout Jews don't really believe in that,' Jens told her.

'Really? Jews don't believe in heaven and hell?'

'No, just this underworld called Sheol. A bit like Hades in Greek mythology.'

They climbed the fence at the bottom of the back garden as the shadow of the house consumed grass and trees and flowers. Max felt an undertow of melancholy; he didn't want the day to end.

'What about you, Max?' Sophie asked. 'What do you think happens when we die?'

'Max is an atheist too,' Jens answered for him.

'Hans isn't, though,' Max said.

The other two stopped and looked at him. 'What do you mean?'

Max shrugged. 'He believes in God. He thinks his dreams are God's way of punishing him or testing him or something.'

'But why would Hans believe in God if you don't?' Sophie asked.

'I don't know,' Max said. 'Maybe because his parents died?'

'Yeah, religion's basically a crutch for people who can't accept mortality,' said Jens.

Sophie, looking annoyed, said: 'It's not mortality I can't accept, it's injustice. Good people should be rewarded and wicked people should be punished, don't you think?'

'Isn't that what the legal system's for?'

'It doesn't seem enough,' Sophie said. 'The idea that someone can commit murder and all that happens is they get sent to prison. Killing people isn't just a crime, it's a sin.'

Jens sniggered. 'Does your mum know you're a Fatherland Front supporter?'

'I'm *not* a—' When Sophie realised that Jens was making fun of her, she began to tickle him hard in the ribs.

'Sorry, doesn't work on me,' Jens said, holding his hands above his head. 'You'd better save that for your boyfriend here.'

Just then, Frau Arnstein appeared at the open French window of the living room and called them in for dinner, sparing Max and Sophie further embarrassment.

All through the meal Max felt edgy, aware that Jens was going to speak to his father as soon as Sophie, Charlotte and Frau Arnstein took the dishes back into the kitchen. He was so quiet that Frau Arnstein asked him if he'd caught sunstroke. He said no and Herr Arnstein gave him a complicated smile: 'You know, I don't mind you drinking our wine, Max, but you need to be careful not to overdo it. Especially when you're out on the lake. Your parents would never forgive me if you got drunk and drowned.'

When the women had left the room, Jens told his father that they needed to talk in private. Herr Arnstein took the two boys into his office and closed the door. A soft breeze was blowing through the open window. Cicadas thrummed from the dark garden. Herr Arnstein lit a pipe and asked what all this was about. Jens looked at Max, who shrugged. Jens told his father about their conversation on the lake. Herr Arnstein puffed away, nodding, his expression serious. He asked Max several questions. 'Well, I'm no expert, but that does sound interesting,' he concluded. 'And I'd be surprised if Dr Freud didn't think so too.'

'You think I should write to him, then?'

'Absolutely. I'll deliver it myself.'

Max nodded. He was nervous now. The box was open, but what

exactly had he let out? He remembered the definition of 'unheim-lich' that Freud had quoted in one of his essays: *What ought to have remained secret and hidden but has come to light.*

That night, in the bedroom he shared with Jens, Max wrote the draft of a letter. Around midnight, Jens turned out the lights and was asleep within minutes. Max used his torch under the sheets and began reading the last chapter of *The Interpretation of Dreams*. He wanted to finish the book so he fought against tiredness and focused on the words in front of him – *Is it not carelessness on the part of this guardian to diminish his vigilance at night?* – but as his eyelids drooped, the letters started to crawl across the yellow page like ants, rearranging themselves, the words inside his head trans-forming into the sound of a girl's voice – *Is it not wake up on the part of the forest while no one's looking?* – and the insides of his eyelids glowed bright pink.

Hans

'Hans, wake up! Let's sneak into the forest while no one's looking.' Paula was whispering into his ear. He opened his eyes: some ants were crawling across the yellow earth, close to the towel on which he lay. 'Come on, the coast is clear!'

He looked up. She was squatting next to him in her blue bathing suit, shoulders freckled, face in shadow as the sun set through the trees behind her. Hans stood up, still a little groggy, and stabbed his feet into his sandals. He followed her away from the lakeshore and into the woods. They stopped in a small clearing and kissed until the straps of her bathing suit were down by her elbows, his hands on her breasts. Paula slid the costume over her hips and stepped out of it. The newly exposed skin was bright white against the pale brown of her limbs.

Hans gaped. This summer camp had been everything he could have wished for. For seven days there had been football matches, running races and tug-of-war contests. There had been marching, chanting and singing drills, lazy afternoons spent swimming in the lake, beer and free-flowing discussions in Bauer's tent at night. There had also been some slightly dull lectures about the perfidy of the Jews and the genius of the Führer, but – most memorably of all – there had been Paula. He just wished Sophie could see him now, with his suntan and his muscles and his pretty girlfriend. At the thought of Sophie he felt a flash of black nausea. The door banging shut on him. The coldness of her voice. How *could* she?

Paula pulled his swimming trunks down and stroked the underside of his erection with the backs of her fingers. Hans held his breath and his mind was once again filled by the present moment. 'Touch me here,' she said, pulling his hand between her legs until his fingertips encountered a new sensation. It was like liquid origami: a complex series of folds, lips within lips, and then the smooth hot slide inside. Her tongue flickered wildly in his mouth. She gripped his shaft and slowly rubbed her hand up and down. Hans went cross-eyed, the pleasure so intense it was almost painful, and he ejaculated seconds later. Paula knelt down to lick him like an ice cream and he shivered.

'Now it's my turn,' she said, standing up. She parted her legs then ordered Hans to kneel in front of her. 'Kiss me here. Move your tongue here. Side to side. Yes . . .' The taste of warm oyster. 'Faster . . .' Hans obeyed until his neck ached and he lost all feeling in his tongue. 'Don't stop!' Paula begged him. At last her knees buckled and she groaned and pinched his sunburned shoulders and the two of them collapsed onto the forest floor, twigs and dust glued to their sweat-slick bodies. Hans imagined Sophie suddenly materialising here in the woods and seeing them, her eyes wide with hurt.

'There's that look on your face again!' Paula said, yanking him from his reverie.

'What look?' Hans asked guiltily.

'You looked like that when you were asleep by the lake too. Sort of sad and hopeful, like a puppy-dog or something. What were you dreaming about?'

Sophie's face caressed by ripples of light. 'I was— I don't remember.' Hans sat up, suddenly self-conscious about his nakedness. 'We should be going, don't you think?' He found his trunks and put them on, then passed Paula her bathing suit.

In an uncharacteristically thoughtful voice she said: 'The strange thing about dreams is . . . it's like watching a film, or hearing a story. You never know what's going to happen next, do you? It's always a surprise.'

'Uh-huh,' said Hans as Paula's small breasts disappeared under blue fabric.

She stood close to him and looked into his eyes. Hans willed her not to notice his scars. Paula was so beautiful and blonde, so perfectly Aryan, it was hard to believe that she actually liked him. 'But if . . . if *you're* not the one telling the story . . . then who is? It's like there's someone else living inside you. But who?'

Hans felt a reckless urge to share the secret of his dreams with her, like Max had done. He held her hands and gazed tenderly at her soft lips. 'Well, Freud would say it's your id . . .'

'Freud? Isn't he that Jew?'

'Yes, but—'

'And you believe what he says?' She took a step back and let go of his hands, as if what he'd said might be infectious. 'You should *never* trust a Jew, Hans! Haven't you learned anything from this camp?'

He saw himself reflected in her ice-blue eyes and felt soberness drench him like a bucket of cold water. 'You're right. I . . . I don't know what I was thinking.'

'I'm going fishing. Anybody want to come?' Jens's voice sounded distant, probably because he was standing up. The insides of Max's eyelids throbbed red against the late-morning sun and the breeze from the lake grazed his skin.

'No, thanks,' murmured Sophie. 'I'm just going to stay here and sunbathe.'

'Max, are you coming?'

Max slowly opened his eyes. Through the morning dazzle of sunlight on water, he saw Jens standing on the beach, holding a fishing rod and watching him expectantly. Max shook his head – 'Maybe later' – and Jens gave a brisk nod, lips pursed.

'Lotte, what about you?'

'I'm going for a swim,' his sister said, taking off her shorts.

'You can swim at the fishing pond,' Jens said.

'No, I'm going to stay here. The pond's too shady and small.'

Jens sighed irritably. 'Suit yourself,' he grunted, and began walking towards the forest. They all watched him leave.

'What's wrong with him today?' Charlotte asked.

Sophie shrugged. 'He's probably hungover. Too much strawberry wine.'

'Ah,' said Charlotte. 'So you don't want to come swimming, Sophie?

'No, thanks. The sun is just so nice at this time of day. I'll go this afternoon if you like.'

Max closed his eyes and breathed slowly.

Charlotte's voice shook a little as she said, 'Max, do you want to come with me?'

He watched the kaleidoscope of shapes and colours inside his eyelids.

'I think he's fallen asleep,' Sophie whispered. 'When he wakes up, I'll tell him where you've gone.'

'All right. I'll see you later, then.'

'Have a nice swim.'

Max drifted off and for a long time he was kissing Paula under a giant, billowing swastika. When the kiss ended, she looked into his eyes and called him Hans and he startled awake. With a sigh, Max turned onto his side. Sophie was lying on a towel only a few inches away, eyes closed. He saw an ant crawl across her red bathing suit and reached out to pick it off, crushing it between thumb and forefinger. Sophie opened her eyes. 'Oh, you're awake! Charlotte has—'

'Gone swimming. Yeah . . . I heard.'

Sophie looked puzzled for a second, then a smile spread hesitantly across her face.

'You had an ant,' said Max. 'On your bathing suit. That's what I—'

'Thanks.'

Their faces, already close, began to move slowly towards each other, as if magnetised. A drop of sweat gleamed in the hollow of Sophie's upper lip and Max felt a visceral urge to taste it. He looked into her eyes, which in this light were not merely grey but flecked with bright blue and green and violet, like slivers of sun-kissed sea. Her expression softened and she leaned her face over his. Max's heart was thudding. He was breathing her breaths. If she came any closer she would feel his cock hard against her body. Suddenly they heard a muffled cry, very distant. Sophie frowned. 'What was that?'

Max sat up. He looked out at the smooth, glimmering lake. 'Where's Charlotte?'

He saw a splash, heard another cry.

Sophie jumped to her feet. 'Max, she's in trouble!'

He ran to the water's edge and started to swim. The lake was cold and his erection shrank quickly. A couple of times he looked up and couldn't see Charlotte and fear rushed through him. But he kept ploughing through the water, heading towards the brightest part of the lake, concentrating on keeping his strokes and breaths regular. At last he spotted her, thirty feet to his right: a flailing arm, a shock of blonde hair, then nothing . . . only ripples. He swam as hard as he could. His hand touched something solid beneath the surface. He grabbed hold of Charlotte's body and lifted her above the water. Her skin was slippery and she was so heavy – was she dead? No, he could feel her arms clinging to him, could hear her cough and sob. 'Hold tight . . . I've got you . . . It's okay.' His voice came in short gasps. Max felt suddenly aware of the vast depths below them, his cramping limbs, his wheezing lungs. He struggled back towards the shore, alternating between sidestroke and backstroke, readjusting his position to keep Charlotte's face out of the water. Her eyes were closed. Don't die, he begged her silently. He thought she was breathing but he couldn't be sure because his own face kept sinking underwater. There was no strength left in his body. The blue sky dimmed and frothed above him and he thought how easy it would be to just let go, to drift downwards into the deep. He closed his eyes and somewhere inside him a voice whispered: *Wake up. Breathe.* With one last surge of effort, Max kicked his feet and his head rose above the surface.

An explosion of colour and noise. Jens, treading water beside him, yelled: 'I've got her, Max! You can let go.'

Charlotte was safe. Max let go. He sank with relief under the water, too tired to swim another yard. As everything was turning dark, a hand grabbed his arm and pulled him up. He saw Sophie looking drawn and pale. 'Max, come on! You're nearly there. Swim. Don't give up.' Max could hear the fear in her voice. She was struggling to stay above the surface herself. He blinked in the dazzle and forced himself to kick his legs. But he was still very weak and he swam like a drunken frog. His eyes kept closing and opening again as the voice inside whispered harshly.

'Come on!' Sophie begged. 'Please, Max . . .' At last the water was shallow enough that he could stand. He crawled the last few yards through muddy sand before collapsing. Max contorted his body and looked further up the beach. He saw Charlotte lying motionless, Jens beside her.

'Jens, is she—'

'She's fine!' Jens called back. 'She just threw up half the lake. I reckon she caught more fish than I did.'

Max exhaled with relief and heard Sophie laugh beside him. Then her back convulsed and he realised she was crying. 'Sophie, what's the matter?'

She shook her head and covered her face with her hands. 'I was scared,' she said. 'I thought I'd lost you.'

'You saved me.'

'And you saved Charlotte.'

She held him tight, her body still trembling, and he felt a swell of emotion: pride, relief, gratitude, happiness and . . . something else. Something he'd never felt before.

Hans

It was the last night of the camp and Bauer's tent was crowded. A crate of bottled beers stood in the centre. The air was fetid with belches and farts. 'Hans, you made it!' Bauer shouted as Hans zipped the tent shut behind him. 'I won't ask where you've been all this time, you dirty bastard. Is that a love bite on your neck?' Hans touched his throat and there was a roar of laughter, a few lewd remarks about Paula. 'All right, lads, that's enough. Hans, sit next to your brother. Karl, shift up to let him in.'

Grudgingly Karl made room and Hans sat between him and Maus. All Bauer's favourites were here and from the shine in their eyes Hans guessed that this was not the first crate of the night. Karl leaned forward to open another bottle and two or three conversations restarted at once. Bauer was leading a debate on the rights and wrongs of last week's Night of the Long Knives while the Weber twins argued over what the future held for Vienna's Jews. Karl's voice rose above theirs: 'They *have* no future here. Haven't you read *Mein Kampf?*'

'So what's the plan? We just cart them all off to Poland?'

'I heard Palestine.'

'Sounds expensive . . .'

'Oh, we'll make them pay their own way. They're all rich bastards.'

'It's not enough,' grunted Karl. 'We need to get rid of them permanently.' His elbow was digging into Hans's ribs as he spoke.

Bauer eyed Karl soberly. 'Are you talking about all the Jews in Germany and Austria?'

'All the Jews everywhere! I'd wipe them off the face of the fucking planet.'

Bauer smiled condescendingly. 'Well, I admire your gusto, Karl, but—'

'It's unfeasible,' Hans cut in.

'What's *un-aus-führ-bar?*' Karl asked, stretching the long word out to mock Hans for his clever-dick vocabulary. 'Should've known *you'd* defend the Jews . . .'

A splinter of ice in Hans's chest. Karl wouldn't, would he? 'I'm not defending them.' The tent fell silent. All eyes were on him. He was walking a tightrope and he had to keep his balance, hold his nerve. 'But what you're suggesting is a practical impossibility. You realise there are millions of Jews in Europe alone? Who would do the killing? Who would pay for it all? Consider the logistics . . .'

'Fuck the logistics,' Karl growled.

A heavier silence. Hans saw drunken hate in Karl's eyes and looked away.

'So how would *you* do it, Hans?' Bauer asked conversationally.

'I don't know . . .' Hans saw his parents screaming in the flames. He closed his eyes until the image faded. Karl's elbow dug even harder against his ribcage. Hans wanted to drop the subject. He thought about making a joke of it or asking Bauer what *he* would do. But Bauer was waiting patiently for an answer and Hans wanted to impress him. He tried to drain the question of emotion, consider it as a maths problem. 'The simplest thing might be just to dig a lot of big holes and make the Jews walk into them. Then bury them alive.'

He could feel Karl's eyes boring into the side of his face.

'And they'd just obediently walk to their deaths?' Bauer asked sceptically.

'Well, you wouldn't tell them the truth. You could say it was a queue for food or something.'

Bauer raised his eyebrows. 'That's pretty smart. You know, Karl, I reckon your little half-brother will be giving you orders a few years from now.'

Hans swallowed and muttered a quiet 'Danke'.

Later, when the others had gone back to their own tents, Hans enjoyed a long, optimistic talk with Bauer about his future while Karl slept in a corner. Now and then Karl would mumble something in his sleep and the other two would cover their mouths and laugh. He finally slurped himself awake at two in the morning, and Bauer said perhaps it was time they all got some sleep.

Outside, the air was cool and the tents loomed black in the deep-blue darkness. Karl, swaying as though he were on a storm-tossed ship, tripped over a guy-rope and collapsed to the ground. Hans rushed over and tried to help him up. Karl swung his elbow, narrowly missing Hans's head, and slurred: 'Get your filthy hands off me.'

Hans felt relieved: it was always safer being shouted at. It meant that Karl's rage was being released, little by little, that it wasn't building up like a roomful of gas.

They walked a little further – Karl unsteadily, Hans warily, a few feet behind – until Karl lurched sideways and vomited.

'Karl, are you all right?'

Karl said nothing. His back quivered, his head jolted and another gush of puke came from his mouth. 'It's not far to your tent,' Hans whispered after a minute. 'Let me help you.'

Karl slowly stood and turned to face him. His breath stank but he was clearly less drunk than before. 'I don't need your help, Jew.'

He was not speaking loudly, but his voice sounded alarmingly clear in the silence of the night. 'Don't call me that,' Hans said quietly. 'I'm a National Socialist.'

Karl snorted contemptuously. 'Do you have any idea how much I hate you? The way you've wormed your way into my life. Bauer, my mother, even my father . . . None of them can see you for what you really are. But I can. You're just like Oskar used to be: the smart-arse, the goody-goody. Everyone's fucking favourite.'

Hans edged backwards. He was watching Karl's hands as they swung by his sides, surveying the roll and sway of those burly shoulders.

'Scared?' Karl whispered. 'You should be. You know what happened to Oskar, don't you? A shove in the back by the side of the road . . .'

Hans realised he was holding his breath. Had his half-brother just confessed to murder? 'I never meant to—'

A massive force knocked him off his feet. He fell hard, banging the back of his skull against the sun-baked earth. His spine hurt, his head spun. Karl climbed on top of him, invisible in the darkness, the weight crushing him into the ground. 'I will kill you before I ever take orders from you, little brother.'

Max

At home, the atmosphere was strange. Max's mother was silent and thin-lipped, his father exaggeratedly cheerful, whistling as he poured hot water into the teapot and talking about how Max had caught the sun. The two of them had driven out to the countryside that morning to cut short his idyll with no explanation and Max had sulked all the way home, wishing desperately that he was still lying on the sand with Sophie. Now, though, he felt a hollow foreboding as he watched his mother serve slices of Sachertorte with trembling hands. His father said: 'Oh, Max, by the way, did I tell you what happened at the shop?'

'Enough!' Mama snapped. 'Tell him now. Or I will.'

'Ana, this isn't how I—'

'It doesn't matter. You can't always arrange everything to suit yourself. Just tell him.'

His father took a deep breath. 'I know you're going to be shocked by what I have to tell you, Max, but I honestly believe that everything is going to turn out fine.'

A long silence. Max's fingers went numb. He had a feeling he was going to remember this moment for the rest of his life.

'I just want you to know that this is not your fault,' his father said at last. 'I love you. With all my heart. And so does your mother. But . . . we don't love each other anymore. So I'm going to move out. Your mother and I are getting a divorce.'

Max exhaled. So his mother had finally grown tired of her husband's infidelities . . . The few times Max had visited his father's jazz club, he had seen the way the waitresses and dancers looked at him and had known without really knowing that his father slept with other women. 'Mama,' he said, swallowing the tears that rose to the back of his throat. 'Can't you forgive him? Please?'

'Max,' his father said, 'you don't understand. This is my choice. I fell in love with someone else. You met her, actually,' he added with a nervous smile. 'Helena, my assistant?'

The visible happiness on his father's face made Max feel even sicker. His mother glared stonily into her tea.

'I know this is going to be hard for you, Max,' his father went on, making a steeple with his fingers. 'But I do think, one day, when you're older, when you fall in love yourself, you'll understand. Love is—'

'Oh, shut up!' Mama screamed, rising to her feet. 'Shut up! Shut up! Shut up!' She grabbed a piece of cake and threw it at Max's father. 'I hate you!' she shrieked. She ran to her room. They heard the door slam, then Mama weeping behind it.

Another long silence. Max stared at the table.

'You should drink your tea, Max,' his father said in a thick voice. 'Before it goes cold.' Obediently Max sipped the lukewarm liquid. 'And eat some Sachertorte. It might make you feel better.'

Max spooned some cake into his mouth but it tasted like soil. It stuck to his teeth and palate. He tried to swallow it but coughed it back up and finally spat the brown mess into his napkin. Drops of water fell onto his plate and Max realised he was crying.

His father put a hand on his shoulder. 'Max, this isn't the end of the world. I'm not dying. We'll still see each other.'

'Where will you live?'

'In the room above the new shop, on Spaltgasse. I hope you'll come to visit us.'

Max nodded slowly. He wanted to ask his father to drive him back to the Wachau Valley so he could talk to Sophie and Jens about all this, but he could hear his mother sobbing inconsolably.

'I'm going to see Mama.'

JULY

Halfway down Spaltgasse, Max saw the sign hanging from a brass rod: SPIEGEL MUSIKINSTRUMENTE. Not for the first time, he wondered what had happened to the 'man' in the family name; in all the turmoil of the past few weeks, he kept forgetting to ask his father. The shop was closed, so Max rang the bell and his father answered the door in his dressing gown, a bottle of champagne in one hand. Max frowned. 'You're celebrating?'

'Observant as ever, Max!' Papa laughed and slapped his shoulder. He called upstairs: 'Helena, darling, Max is here. Would you make yourself decent?'

Max tried to hide his embarrassment. He had met Papa's girlfriend twice before and on each occasion had spent the whole day wishing she would go away, staring disapprovingly whenever she put an arm around his father's neck or a hand on his thigh, and then feeling guilty at the guilt he saw on their faces.

'I meant: what are you celebrating?'

'Everything!' Franz spread his arms wide. 'Life, love, a beautiful morning . . . Oh, and the small fact that the Nazis failed to take over Austria last night! Didn't you hear?'

'I heard that the chancellor was murdered.'

Franz had the decency to look a little abashed. 'True, a man lost his life. Several men, in fact. But all I've heard for the past year is how the Austrian police is riddled with Nazis, the nation is divided and weak, blah blah blah . . . And look what happened. The police stood firm. The army stood firm. The putsch failed, and Hitler ends up looking like a bumbling fool. Come on, I think it's probably safe to go upstairs now. Have you had breakfast yet? I was about to fry some eggs.'

An hour later Max said goodbye to his father and walked to the Café Viktoria, at the corner of the Volksgarten, where he'd arranged to meet Sophie and the Arnsteins. For the first time since hearing the news about his parents' divorce, Max felt happy. This morning his father had been his old ebullient self. He had even used the old code at one point: when he got to the top of the stairs and presumably found Helena still half-naked, he gave Max the hand signal for *Come back in five minutes*. And five minutes later, when Max went upstairs, Papa was cooking eggs on the camping stove, as he'd promised, not smooching in bed with his girlfriend. Even Helena had looked pleased to see him. Admittedly she had also been a little drunk, but still . . .

And now he was about to see Sophie for the first time since the day they almost kissed, the day she saved his life.

Max spotted Charlotte waving to him from the packed terrace of the Viktoria. 'We've saved you a seat!' she called brightly. As he approached, he noticed how gloomy all the people at the other tables looked. And the orchestra on the bandstand, which usually played waltzes in the summer to entertain tourists, was droning its way through Chopin's 'Marche Funèbre'. Even Jens and Frau Arnstein, he could see now that he drew close, wore grave, anxious expressions.

'What's the matter?' Max asked Jens as he sat down in the vacant chair. 'And where's Sophie? And your father?'

'They'll be here soon. But what do you mean, "What's the matter"? The chancellor's just been murdered by Nazis.'

'But I thought you hated the Fatherland Front . . .'

'Keep your voice down, Max,' Frau Arnstein murmured. 'And don't speak ill of the dead.'

'Dollfuss was a fascist,' said Jens, not making any particular effort to keep his voice down, 'but at least he was *our* fascist.'

'And he died to save Austria, right? And our country held firm, so maybe we're not as weak and divided as—'

'Good morning, Max.' A man's voice behind him. Max turned and saw Herr Arnstein. He, too, looked weary and drawn. 'I take it you've just been talking to your father?'

'Yes. How did you know?'

'From your ludicrously optimistic view of the political situation.'

'Shall I get you a chair, Papa?' Charlotte asked.

'No, don't worry, I have to get to work. The new chancellor's about to give a press conference. I just brought someone to see you.'

Herr Arnstein stepped aside and Max saw Sophie. She was wearing a white cotton summer dress and black eyeliner. His heart leapt and she smiled at him sadly. The others all looked away. 'What's going on?'

Sophie touched his hand. 'Come with me, I have something to show you.'

She held his hand tightly as they walked away from the café and through the crowded Volksgarten. Max kept glancing sideways at her, but her eyes were lowered and her expression gave nothing away. He had so many things to tell her – and he'd missed her so much – but something in the atmosphere of the morning was all wrong. 'Where are we going?'

'Somewhere quiet.'

In a shady corner of the park Sophie sat at the foot of an oak tree and patted the ground beside her. It was a still, muggy morning. Some bees hovered lazily around a clump of lavender. Max sat facing her and said: 'Sophie, what is it?'

She gave him that sad smile again. 'First the good news. This came for you yesterday.' She handed Max a sealed envelope. It was addressed to *Max Spiegelman c/o Gerhard Arnstein*, and the sender's name was *Dr S. Freud*.

'What's the bad news?'

'Open your letter, Max. Sigmund Freud wrote to you.'

Impatiently Max tore open the envelope and extracted the single sheet of paper. He unfolded it – both sides were covered in a dense, slanting, spidery handwriting – and read:

Dear Max,

Thank you for your letter, which I read with interest. So far as the first, 'prophetic' dream is concerned, I am afraid I cannot believe anything of the kind. Not that I doubt your good faith, but in such circumstances it is only natural for our memory and perceptions to be distorted, and I think the simplest explanation is that you have confused the order of your dreams: that you dreamed of your parents dying <u>after</u> you had, in reality, saved them.

And yes, although – like all my patients – you resist the idea that such a dream could be a form of wish-fulfilment, I can assure you that that is precisely what it is. To be clear, I am not suggesting that you wish either of your parents dead <u>now</u>, merely that you did so at some point in the past, probably during your early childhood.

I am more interested in what you tell me about this perennial dream of your (Nazi) alter ego. I am not in a position to give a full interpretation of this dream, as that would require analysis, and while you kindly offer to answer any questions I might have, my current schedule, coupled with my uncertain health, does not permit me to accept any new patients. However, your account reminds me of a story by Rosegger about a man who was a successful poet but dreamed every night of being a poor tailor. Admittedly, that was fiction, but I have had certain dreams of my own that allow me to accept such a possibility, and, in addition, to offer an explanation. I see no objection to regarding such dreams as <u>punishment dreams</u>.

Above all, you have no reason to feel guilty for anything that this 'other you' might do in your dreams. As Plato wrote: the virtuous man contents himself with dreaming of that which the wicked man does in actual life. I am therefore of the opinion that dreams should be acquitted of all evil.

Below this was Freud's signature. Max folded the letter and inserted it back in the envelope.

'Well?' Sophie asked. 'What did he say?'

Max tried to compose his face. He didn't know how he felt, really: disappointed and relieved in equal measure, perhaps. 'Nothing much. I'll show you later.'

'But—'

'Sophie, please tell me what's going on.'

She sat cross-legged, facing him, her bare knees touching his, and looked into his eyes. 'My mother and I are leaving for Paris this afternoon.'

'Oh. For how long?'

She sighed and he noticed a watery gleam in her eyes. 'For good, Max.'

'What are you talking about?'

'Mama's received death threats. Because of her art. She's been talking about leaving all summer, but I kept persuading her to stay. I didn't want to leave, Max. I *don't* want to leave . . .' Sophie took his hands in hers as she said this and Max felt his heart dilate with love. Yes, he thought, that's what I've been feeling all this time. Why had it taken him so long to recognise it? 'Yesterday's putsch was the final straw. We were spared this time, but during the hours when we thought it might succeed . . . Mama was terrified. I knew I couldn't talk her out of it. I'm sorry.'

Max looked away, then said with a savagery that took even him by surprise: '*You* could stay. With me. With Jens's parents. The

Nazis don't care about you, just your mother. Why do you have to go with her?'

When he looked at her again there were tears rolling down her face. 'She's my mother,' Sophie said helplessly.

Max closed his eyes. He knew he was being selfish, unfair. But his father had just abandoned him, his mother was sunk in a dark rage, and now the thought of Vienna without Sophie was unbearable. He wanted to howl with pain but instead he just mumbled: 'Everybody's leaving me, Sophie.'

She leaned forward and put her arms around him, her forehead nestled in his neck. 'I'll write to you,' she whispered. 'Every week. And you still have Jens. And at least you still see both your parents, even if they're not together.'

Max remembered how much Sophie missed her father. He stroked her hair.

She pulled back so she could look into his eyes. 'You still have me too, you know.'

Max shook his head. 'How?'

'In here.' She tapped his chest. 'And you're in mine. Always.'

'I love you,' Max said without meaning to, and she kissed him on the mouth. The kiss was salty with their mingled tears. It lasted a long time and the earth seemed to slow in its orbit, the morning to become eternal. If only we could live here, in this golden now, hidden in this fold in time, Max thought. He and Sophie could be together, love each other, marry and have children, grow old hand in hand, and look back serenely over the course of their life knowing they had found the one soul in the world who fitted perfectly with theirs. They could have been so happy . . . But, in the end, time cleared its throat. Their lips parted and she said: 'I have to go.'

They held hands as they walked back and Sophie said: 'So I suppose this means Jens was right. We really are star-crossed after all.' Max didn't have the heart to laugh.

By some tacit agreement, their intertwined fingers slowly detached as they drew near the Café Viktoria, where the Arnsteins were preparing to leave.

'There you are!' Jens called. 'So what did old Sigmund have to say?'

Hans

From the depths of sleep Hans groaned: 'No . . . No . . . *No* . . .' The sound woke him and he sat up straight, heart pounding. Last night he'd been disappointed that the Nazi putsch had failed, but now he didn't care about that at all. Sophie was leaving. He might never see her again.

He dressed in haste, his feet getting stuck in his trouser legs, his shirt buttons fastened in the wrong holes, as Karl sniggered. Ignoring him, Hans ran across the room, through the hallway, down the stairs and out of the front door. 'Hans? Aren't you going to eat breakfast?' Frau Schatten called after him. He ran to the tram stop and waited there nervously, unsure where to go first. The city centre tram came before the Leopoldstadt tram, so he rode it to the Volksgarten and ran to the Café Viktoria.

He was greeted by the same scene he'd witnessed in his dream: the orchestra playing Chopin, the gloomy faces, the anxious conversations. He moved closer and saw the Arnstein family drinking coffee and eating pastries, but there was no sign of Sophie. In desperation Hans went to their table and asked Jens if he'd seen her. Jens just glared incredulously.

'Do you know where she is? Tell me! I have to speak to her.'

Frau Arnstein whispered something into her son's ear and Jens answered coldly, without taking his eyes off Hans: 'He's a Nazi, Mama. He probably wants to stop her leaving.'

– 117 –

Hans heard a few mutters and jeers from the nearby tables, but he didn't look around. 'Sophie's my friend. I just need to talk to her.'

Jens sneered. Frau Arnstein stood up and in a rigidly polite voice announced: 'I think you should leave now.'

Hans looked at his watch – not yet noon – and decided to head for Frau Strom's apartment in Leopoldstadt. But by the time he got there the front door was wide open and removal men were carrying her artworks to a van idling on the pavement. Hans darted inside the apartment and went to Sophie's room. It had been stripped bare. Only the stars on her ceiling remained.

He caught another tram to the train station. When he reached the concourse he ran to the departures board and scanned the names of cities. *Paris*, he read: *Platform 11*. The train was leaving in fourteen minutes. He ran, legs shaky, and went all the way along the carriages, scanning the windows, searching for Sophie.

At last he saw her, reading *War and Peace*. He banged on the glass. She stared at him, perhaps in shock, perhaps only embarrassment. He mouthed: 'Please come out! I have to talk to you!', though he had no idea if she could tell what he was saying. She said something to her mother, who looked at him in distaste and grabbed hold of Sophie's arm to prevent her leaving. Sophie spoke again, calm and reasonable, and finally her mother let her go. Sophie checked her watch as she emerged from the train carriage.

'What do you want?' she asked coolly. 'How did you find me?'

'No time to explain.' Hans was still breathing heavily. His hair was dripping sweat and his shirt had dark stains beneath the armpits. 'Sophie, I have to tell you . . . how sorry I am . . . for everything that happened.'

'All right. But I'm moving to Paris now, so it doesn't really matter.'

'It does! It does matter. Sophie, you're the best friend I've ever had.'

Her expression softened for a second. Then she closed her eyes and said: 'You ruined everything, Hans.'

'I know. And I regret it. I miss you so much.'

'How did you know I would be here?' she asked again, an edge of suspicion in her voice.

'I dreamed you were leaving Vienna. Last night. I came here as soon as I—'

'You dreamed it?'

'Yes. But listen . . .'

'Someone talked, didn't they? You and your Nazi friends are trying to stop us leaving.'

Hans shook his head desperately. 'Nobody talked, I promise. It's nothing like that.'

'Good.' Sophie glanced at her watch. 'I should go. The train will be leaving soon.'

'I love you.'

She opened her mouth. Her cheeks flushed scarlet. Silence, then: 'What about Paula?'

So she knew. Hans had thought he would feel triumphant at this but all he felt was regret. 'I'll leave her, Sophie. I'll leave the Hitler-Jugend too, if you stay. Please don't go.'

'I have to,' she repeated. But she was looking at him differently now. She reached out to stroke his scar and Hans realised he was crying: she was wiping away his tears.

'Sophie,' he said, his voice hoarse.

'I have to go, Hans.' She kissed him on the lips. Softly, lingeringly. He could smell her scent, though he couldn't tell what flowers or herbs it contained: it was just *her*. He nestled his face into her neck but a fist thumped the window next to them and they were startled apart. Sophie looked up to see her mother pointing theatrically at her watch. Sophie nodded before turning back to Hans. She held his hands for a moment. Gently, smiling sadly, she freed herself and walked away. On the steps of the train, she called out: 'I'll write. I promise.'

I will too, he wanted to say, but he had no voice left.

The doors closed. Sophie returned to her seat. She waved from behind the window. The train started to move away and she covered her face with her hands. Was she crying? Hans couldn't tell. Everything was a blur. He started running alongside the carriage, waving to her, until he was outside and the sun was blinding him. The train was moving too fast now and Sophie was disappearing into the horizon, leaving him behind.

1934–1938

Sophie

*Max, I am writing you this postcard from the train station at Kehl,
where we have stopped for fifteen minutes. The image on the front
is* Fulfilment *by Gustav Klimt. I love the look on the woman's
face, don't you? That's exactly how I felt this morning. Mama says
it's sentimental (i.e. bad) art, but I think she's wrong. It's nearly
three in the morning as I write this and I haven't slept a wink. I
can still feel your kiss on my lips. Today (which is how I think of it,
even if it's tomorrow already) was the sweetest, saddest day of my
life. Oh, why did we ever stop kissing? I am going to miss you SO
much! I already do. Love, Sophie*

*29 Rue Jacob, Paris
Sunday, 5 August 1934*

Dear Max,

*We've been in Paris for ten days now, and I'm starting to fall in
love with this city. I'm sorry it's taken me so long to write you a
proper letter, but we were staying in hotel rooms, moving around
constantly, and I didn't have an address to give you where you
could write to me. Now I do (so you'd better write!) – Rue Jacob
is a charming street in the heart of Saint-Germain-des-Prés, only
a short walk from the Seine. I spend most of my days exploring
the city on foot. Mama is busy with her art, so I'm always on my
own, but I don't feel too lonely because in my mind you are with
me. I show you the bouquinistes by the Seine and we explore the*

Louvre. We stroll through the Jardin du Luxembourg together and sit on a bench to eat a picnic of bread and cheese and fresh purple figs. Then we spread our blanket on the grass and I rest my head on your chest and we both read for hours on end! I finished War and Peace *on the train, and I'm now almost done with* Anna Karenina. *The next book I read will be Hemingway's* A Farewell to Arms, *because I managed to find a German translation. So I was thinking . . . Perhaps you could get hold of a copy in Vienna and we could read it together? I love the idea of us reading the same sentences, thinking the same thoughts, experiencing the same emotions even though we're eight hundred miles apart.*

Will you come and visit me here next summer? Or even sooner if you can? I know things are complicated with your parents' divorce, but I hope you'll find a way. I would love to go back to Vienna, but Mama has already made it clear she won't allow that.

I've decided that I want to be a writer when I'm older. In fact, I've already started sketching a few poems at night in my bedroom. I write in French because it seems to me more naturally poetic than German. So I want you to concentrate in M. LaRue's class because one of these days I'll probably send you something I've written.

I don't suppose Jens will bother writing to me – you know what he's like – but perhaps you can show him some of the letters I send you. Not this letter, though, or any of the postcards! I feel like I've smeared my poor little broken heart all over them.

I can't stop thinking about that week we spent with Jens and his family in the Wachau Valley. Was it really only a week? It seems like it must have been longer than that, to take up so much space in my memory.

I also keep thinking about your dreams. I know you told me that you hated Hans, that you felt cursed because you had to dream of a Nazi every night, but maybe you're looking at this the wrong way, Max. Remember the dream that saved your parents? That was Hans, wasn't it? I feel like you're going to scoff at this, but I do sometimes wonder if that's why he came into existence. To absorb all your misfortune, to make all your wrong choices for you. In a strange way, I think he could be your guardian angel.

But it's past midnight now, so I will stop here and send this to you first thing tomorrow morning. Please, please, please write back to me as soon as you can. Tell me everything. What's happening in your life . . . and in your dreams. I can't wait to hear from you, Max.

All my love,
Sophie

29 Rue Jacob, Paris
Wednesday, 12 June 1935

Happy birthday, Max!

I know it will be in the past by the time you receive this, but I'm thinking of you right now, imagining you celebrating, and hoping you have an enjoyable day. I have sent you a gift in the post too. Hopefully you will already have received it. I remember you telling me how much you loved that book when you were young, and how your copy was destroyed in the fire. Do you think Peter Pan could be the next book we read together? Or are you too grown-up for it now?

Thanks so much for the photograph of you and Jens by the lake! It brings back so many good memories. I've had it framed and it sits on my bedroom desk next to the photo of my father.

I'm trying really hard not to be sad that you won't be able to visit me this summer. I know you told me all along that you

*thought it would be difficult, but I clung to hope anyway because
I wanted to see you so badly. I can't help feeling a little despairing
that we will soon have been apart for a whole year, and who
knows when we will see each other again. But don't worry, I'll get
over it. I have a few trips planned with my friend Elise over the
summer, including a two-week stay at her grandparents' house
on the Breton coast. I love the sound and smell of the sea, so I'm
really looking forward to that. We're also going to be attending
a few psychology lectures at the Sorbonne. I didn't tell you that
before, because I was hoping to surprise you during your visit. Oh
well . . .*

*Anyway, I hope you have fun at Jens's parents' house. I wish I
could be there with you. Please give my love to the whole family.*

*A birthday kiss
from your best friend,
Sophie*

*29 Rue Jacob, Paris
Saturday, 4 April 1936*

Dear Max,

*I attended a lecture last night that I'm sure you would have found
interesting. It was given by Dr Édouard Kahn – you know, the
young psychologist I told you about last summer? – and it was all
about recurring dreams. (By the way, what is Hans up to these
days? It's been a long time since you've mentioned him.) Elise
and I stayed to talk with Dr Kahn afterwards, but Elise was so
embarrassing. She has a crush on him and all she could do was
simper and giggle. She even told me that she wants to marry him
and have his babies! I don't understand that at all. There's so
much I want to do before I settle down: write a book, travel the*

world, improve my English . . . Anyway, I don't think Édouard was too impressed. He kept wrinkling his nose and frowning.

Some of the girls at school have stopped talking to me since Germany invaded the Rhineland. They call me the German Bitch behind my back, which is ironic given that I was known as the French Freak when I was in Vienna. I don't really care what any of those imbeciles think, but I do feel very alone sometimes. I wish you were here.

I miss my father quite badly too at the moment. I love Mama, but she can be hard to live with sometimes. I know your mother is moody too, but at least she cooks dinner for you and keeps the apartment clean.

Of course you can tell me about your friend Annamaria. I get the feeling from your last letter that you're falling in love with her, but you don't want to admit it because you're worried about how I will react. Please don't ever think that, Max. You're my best friend and you can tell me anything. Besides, surely she can't be as bad as Paula Weiss!

love,
Sophie

29 Rue Jacob, Paris
Sunday, 21 February 1937

Dear Max,

I was sorry to hear about you and Klara. You don't sound too broken-hearted, though, so I'm sure you'll be fine. It seems like you always have dozens of girls lining up to go out with you. What about Jens – has he found anyone yet? Tell him he needs to be less picky or he'll end up a grumpy old bachelor!

I went out to dinner with Dr Kahn one night last week – I suppose I should start calling him Édouard, now that we're friends.

I don't think his intentions are romantic, but I must admit it was very nice to go out to a restaurant and eat such wonderful food, to have cloth napkins and silver cutlery, to drink real champagne and listen to a string quartet . . . It made me feel special. I very rarely feel like that at home or at school these days – at least, not in a good way.

My mother is slowly driving me crazy, Max. She seems to disapprove of everything I do and say these days. She insults me as a 'bourgeois conformist' even as I'm cleaning up the cigarette ash that she drops all over the floor. Her last exhibition was not a success and she's been drinking more lately. I tell myself that it's the alcohol talking, not her, but in the end it doesn't make much difference. I still want to get away from her. All my poems recently have been about birds, wings, empty cages.

Did I tell you I've started keeping a dream journal? I mentioned that to Édouard and he asked to read it. I'm not sure how I feel about that. There's something so intimate about dreams. Then again, he is a professional. It's like taking off your clothes to be examined by a doctor, I suppose. Not sure why my mind suddenly skipped to getting naked just then . . .

Anyway, write to me, you idler! I want to know how everybody is: Jens and his family, your father and Helena, your mother and her new husband (did you tell me his name?), even your bête noire Hans. Or don't you dream about him anymore?

Sophie x

Doctor and Madame Kahn
are delighted to invite
Monsieur Max Spiegelman
to Hôtel Le Bristol
112 Rue du Faubourg Saint-Honoré
at four o'clock
on Saturday, 9 April 1938
for a reception in celebration of
the marriage of their son
Dr Édouard Kahn
and
Mlle Sophie Strom

Please do come, Max – my father is boycotting the wedding because Édouard is Jewish, my mother disapproves because he's a conservative, and Elise is sulking because she's jealous. And you're the only person in the world I really want to be there (apart from Édouard himself, of course!)

1938

JANUARY

Max

'Drei . . . zwei . . . eins . . . Frohes Neues Jahr!' People cheered. Confetti swirled. Jens pounded his back, Frau Arnstein kissed him on the cheek, Herr Arnstein shook his hand vigorously, and then Max found himself face to face – or, more accurately, chin to forehead (he'd had a growth spurt in the past year) – with Charlotte Arnstein. She too had changed quite a bit since the day he fished her from the lake: she was sixteen now, almost a young woman, her curves accentuated by the satin ballgown she was wearing. Charlotte was still intimidatingly intelligent, but two glasses of slivovitz had made her tipsy. She'd been tripping over her words all evening and blushing sweetly each time. She leaned against him now and turned her face up to his. Max kissed her on the lips. She put her arms around his neck. The kiss went on for quite a long time. When Max came up for air he saw Charlotte gazing rapturously at him, her parents watching with raised eyebrows and delighted smiles. 'Well!' said Frau Arnstein. 'I wonder what 1938 will bring . . .'

Jens grabbed Max by the elbow and dragged him through the party to the toilets. The cream of Viennese society was here in this vast ballroom, on the second floor of the Palais Albert Rothschild. The orchestra had just finished playing the *Radetzky March* and the murmur of voices lapped loudly from the walls and ceiling. Waiters in white jackets pirouetted smoothly between guests, carrying trays of champagne, spirits, appetisers. As he half-stumbled, half-floated behind his friend, gazing up in wonder at the painted ceilings, Max realised that Charlotte was not the only one who'd had too much slivovitz.

They stood side by side in front of the gleaming urinals and Jens said: 'I take it you got the wedding invitation, then?'

'Yes . . . Uh, why?'

'Oh, you don't see any connection between that and what you just did with my sister?'

'Relax, Jens, it was only a kiss.'

'With Charlotte! In front of our parents!'

'They didn't seem too upset about it.'

Jens gave a strangled laugh. 'No, they're fucking thrilled, you idiot! My mother was mentally planning the wedding before you'd even got your tongue out of Charlotte's mouth. But is that really what you want? You're eighteen, Max! Just because Sophie's doing something mind-numbingly stupid doesn't mean you have to.'

'Sophie? What does she have to do with—'

'Oh, give me a break. I know how you feel about her.'

They walked over to the sinks to wash their hands.

'She's my friend,' said Max. 'That's all. I'm happy for her.'

'Yeah, yeah, whatever. Look, my point is you can do better than Charlotte. She really isn't that interesting, you know. Maybe you imagine she's going to be just like me with tits and a cunt, but you're sorely mistaken. She's a nice enough girl, and academically brilliant, of course, but she's bland. Boring.' To Max's surprise, Jens sounded not only serious, but almost angry. Max turned to face his friend and Jens's eyes flickered away evasively. 'Hang on,' he said in a thick voice, 'I'm dying of thirst here . . .'

Jens put his head under the tap and drank while Max examined himself in the mirror. His cheeks were a little pink and there was a hint of dormant hilarity in his eyes, but otherwise he looked normal, he thought. Of course, he'd changed quite a lot since the summer of 1934. His face was narrower, more angular, his cheeks hollowed, his chin covered with a light down, his long throat deformed by the anvil of his Adam's apple. His chestnut hair hung down over his shoulders now. Jens said it made him look like some sort of laudanum-sipping dandy and Max's mother complained that it was scruffy. But Sophie, back in the summer of 1936, had seen a photograph of him with long hair and written that it suited him, and since then he had refused to let anyone go near him with scissors. Perhaps he would shave it all off tomorrow?

Max still couldn't quite believe that Sophie was going to get married. She'd barely even mentioned her fiancé until last September, when she described him as the most brilliant man she'd ever met, a thirty-year-old Freudian psychologist who also happened – she revealed a few letters later – to be six feet two and devastatingly handsome. 'I'm sure you'll like and admire him as much as I do,' she wrote. Max doubted it somehow. He'd shown that letter to Jens, who'd remarked: 'Doctor Édouard Kahn? Sounds like a cunt to me.' Jens always knew the right thing to say.

And now she was inviting him to their wedding in Paris. Did she seriously expect him to go? Max sighed. He knew he was being unreasonable. Notwithstanding all the girls he'd gone out with over the past few years, he'd somehow always imagined that he and Sophie were destined to be together. But the truth was that they had only really been close for a few weeks before she moved to France – and more than three years had passed since then. It was inevitable that they would drift apart, meet other people . . . He just hadn't expected it to happen so soon, to be so final.

Jens stood up straight and gave a loud belch.

'Feeling better?' Max asked.

'Yeah, sorry about that. Don't know what got into me. Anyway, it's your life.' Jens waved his hand in a vague gesture of dismissal. 'Do what you want. Just don't say I didn't warn you.'

Three hours later, standing in the entrance hall of his stepfather's house, Max closed the front door behind him with exaggerated slowness. There was a light on in the kitchen. He took off his shoes and crept towards his bedroom, only to find Herr Oberhuber standing in the kitchen doorway. 'Good evening.'

'Good evening . . . uh, morning. Sorry, I tried to be as quiet as I could.'

'You didn't wake me. I waited up for you.'

Max started to open his bedroom door. 'Thank you, sir.'

'Ernst,' Herr Oberhuber reminded him.

Ernst Oberhuber had married Max's mother nearly a year ago, but Max still regarded him as a stranger. Despite living under his roof, Max had formed no real opinion of him, except that he was nothing like Max's father. In fact he seemed almost the exact opposite of Franz Spiegelman: reserved, reliable, serious, charmless, dull.

'Thank you, Ernst, but there was really no need.' Max spoke slowly, trying not to slur his words. 'The Arnsteins brought me to the car in their door. I mean—'

'It wasn't your safety I was concerned about. Well, not your immediate safety. Let's go to your room.'

Max turned on the desk lamp and perched on the edge of the bed. Herr Oberhuber sat on the desk chair in penumbral gloom. He had strong, bony hands and watchful eyes sunk deep in his bald head.

'It was in fact the Arnsteins that I wished to talk to you about. That family . . . and their acquaintances.'

Herr Oberhuber was speaking as if he had an unpleasant taste in his mouth. Max felt his blood leap in anger. 'Jens is my best friend! And Charlotte—'

'Yes, I know. Therein lies the problem.'

'Problem?'

'I am well aware of what your father is, and consequently what you are. But it is not only a question of blood, it is also a question of behaviour. Connections. Associations.'

'What is?'

'Your safety.'

'Are you . . . threatening me?'

Herr Oberhuber sighed and leaned forward. 'Quite the contrary, Max. I am offering to protect you. But you must meet me halfway or I will be powerless when the time comes.'

'What are you talking about?'

'You must cut your ties with the Arnstein family. No more Jewish cocktail parties. No more private concerts for the Rothschilds.'

Max choked. 'How did you . . .'

'It doesn't matter how or what I know. What matters is what *they* know.'

'They?'

'I think you understand me. You are running out of time, Max. You should make some new friends.' Max watched speechless as his stepfather stood up and walked to the door. 'You should get a haircut too,' Herr Oberhuber added before leaving.

Max lay in bed and thought about his stepfather's warning, about Charlotte's kiss, about Sophie's wedding, about the growing threat of a German invasion, and a slew of emotions swirled inside him: anger, excitement, sadness, anxiety. The alcohol distorted and magnified them, but when he woke in the morning he would write them down and they would be manageable again. Normally he would have poured all his feelings into a letter to Sophie but that was impossible now, so he would start a journal, he decided. Not a dream journal, though. He didn't want to make Hans seem any more real than he already was.

There was something Max hadn't told his friends. Something that had slowly altered over the past three years, creeping across his life like a stain. Something he hardly even wanted to admit to himself now, as the bed spun slightly in the darkness and he began the long slide into sleep. He closed his eyes and the dizziness worsened. He opened them and saw flickering lights, heard voices. *No, not yet.* He closed his eyes again, wishing hard against the rising vertigo.

Hans

His eyes startled open. The room stopped spinning. Paula squeezed his knee. Had he nodded off for a second there? He'd been somewhere darker, colder. He scanned the faces around the candlelit table. The Schattens' dining room. A family gathering. An expectant silence. Paula whispered: 'It's your turn, Hans. What's your wish for the coming year?'

They had already gone most of the way around the table. Frau Schatten had wished for good health for everyone she knew. Herr Schatten had wished for prosperity. Frau Weiss had wished for a new Vorwerk vacuum cleaner, Herr Weiss for good snow in the mountains during their skiing holiday in Kitzbühel. 'What did you wish for?' Hans asked Paula.

She tutted. 'Weren't you listening? I wished that you and I would pass our final exams.'

'Oh. Well, I wish that Austria will become part of the greater German Reich,' Hans said, glancing at Karl in the hope of an approving nod.

'Who could doubt it?' said Karl, a giant of a man now, before adding acidly: '*I* wish that the Jews will get what's coming to them.'

'Which is what exactly, in your opinion?' Herr Weiss asked conversationally.

'Well, let's ask the expert.' Karl looked at Hans. 'What do *you* think will happen to Vienna's Jews once the swastika is hanging from the Ballhausplatz?'

All eyes turned to Hans. He felt his face grow warm. He thought of various pithy answers – 'Nothing good', 'They will pay the Jewish price', 'They'll be rounded up and shipped out' – but for some reason his tongue was tied.

At last, looking alarmed, Frau Schatten stood up. 'Well, I'm going to get the Apfelstrudel from the kitchen. Max, would you fetch the pieces of lead from the cupboard under the stairs? They're in a box labelled *Christmas and New Year*. It should be on the top shelf.'

Hans stood, then froze. *What* had she called him?

'You mean Hans, Kat,' said Herr Schatten.

Flustered, Frau Schatten lifted her hands to her face. 'Yes, Hans – of course! Oh dear, I must be losing my marbles.'

Karl snorted and Hans walked shakily out of the room. As he was leaving, he heard Paula answer Karl's question in a matter-of-fact voice: 'What will happen to the Jews? That's obvious, isn't it? They will leave. Or they will perish.'

Hans opened the cupboard door and turned on the light. The air here was cold, a relief after the warmth of the dining room. Standing on a stepstool, he looked through the labels taped to the tins on the top shelf. The casting of the lead was a yearly tradition: Frau Schatten would melt the little pieces one by one in a spoon over a candle and pour the molten metal into a glass of cold water. Then she would inspect the resultant shape and tell each guest's fortune. Hans couldn't find the tin he was looking for but there at the back another label caught his eye. *Hans*, it said, in Herr Schatten's precise handwriting. Curious, Hans picked up the rectangular biscuit tin and removed the lid, expecting to find papers relating to his adoption or his name change. Instead he discovered a stack of unopened envelopes, each addressed to him. He turned the top letter over to see the sender's name: *Sophie Strom, 29 Rue Jacob, Paris, Frankreich*. The stepstool wobbled.

'You're taking a long time, Hans. Can't you find them?' It was Herr Schatten, who came into the cupboard smiling. 'Katharina sent me to help you . . .' He fell silent as he saw the open tin. His smile faded.

'What is this?' Hans demanded.

Silence.

'Tell me.'

Herr Schatten lowered his eyes. 'It was to protect you. Karl said that girl was a bad influence.'

'*Karl* said? Why didn't you talk to me about it? Sophie was my best friend.'

This was not something Hans had believed for a long time. In fact, until just now, he'd felt certain that he despised Sophie. She'd promised she would write to him – on the train station platform after that kiss – and then he'd never heard from her. For a few months he'd clung to the idea that God was testing him, but in the end he believed that God, like Sophie, had simply abandoned him. That this was his punishment for some forgotten sin, some imagined slight. An unjust punishment. Every week at Hitler-Jugend meetings Hans was told that God was dead and every week he had to read the letters that the other Sophie wrote to Max, but not once did the girl he loved or the God he worshipped spare a thought for him. Over the years Hans's hurt had curdled, hardened. He'd come to hate Sophie, to lose all faith in God. Yet the truth was that she *had* written to him. Hundreds of pages without receiving a single word in reply. He felt a sharp stab of shame: what must she think of him? What must God think?

'I can't believe you did this.'

'I'm sorry. Perhaps it was the wrong thing to do.' Herr Schatten's voice was stiff but sincere.

Hans rushed upstairs, tin in hand, and closed the bedroom door. He sat on his bed and opened the first envelope. The pages shook in his hands.

Dear Hans,

We have been in Paris for ten days now, and I am starting to fall in love with this city. I'm sorry it's taken me so long to write, but we were staying in hotel rooms, moving around constantly, and I didn't have an address to give you where you could write back to me. Now I do – so you'd better write!

Rue Jacob is a charming street in the heart of Saint-Germain-des-Prés, only a short walk from the Seine. I spend most of my days exploring the city on foot. Mama is busy with her art, so I'm always on my own, but sometimes I imagine that you are with me. I do miss you, you know. I missed you even in Vienna, after what happened at the gallery. You were my best friend, more than a friend, and I felt betrayed, but I never stopped caring about you. In fact, I would often have conversations with you in my head. I don't think I've ever felt as close to anyone as I did to you. So, yes, since I've been here, I've taken you – the old you, the boy I still hope and believe you truly are – to visit the Louvre and the bouquinistes by the Seine. I walk through the Jardin du Luxembourg and sit on a bench to eat a picnic, and in my mind you are with me . . .

Hans felt his heart thaw as he read. Suddenly there was a loud knock on the bedroom door and Paula burst into the room. He stuffed the letter under his blanket and sat in front of the biscuit tin. 'What are you doing?' she said. 'Come on, hurry up. Your mother's about to tell our fortunes!' She grabbed his hand and pulled him from the bed. 'Oh, I hope I get the Slipper . . .'

'What does the Slipper mean?' Hans asked distractedly, glancing back at the tin with his name on it.

'That we'll be married before the year is out, of course.'

1935–1938

Sophie

Happy birthday, Hans.

I know it will be in the past by the time you receive this, but I'm thinking of you right now and hoping you have a good day. I wonder if you received my previous letters. I suppose it's silly of me to keep writing to you when I haven't heard back, but you seemed so sincere that day in the train station that I have to assume there's a good reason why you aren't replying.

I've decided I want to be a writer when I'm older, but as yet I haven't written anything I've wanted to keep. The wastepaper bin in my bedroom fills up daily with discarded poems and story beginnings. My French teacher, Mlle Gopin, told me that the most important quality for any writer is <u>empathy</u>: the ability to put yourself into the thoughts and feelings of another person, even – or especially – someone whose thoughts and feelings you don't understand.

So, if I don't hear from you soon, I'm going to start writing myself replies from you, imagining what you would say if you did write to me, imagining your life in Vienna. I'm even going to try to imagine all the things you don't want to tell me because you think I would judge you for them. Mlle Gopin says that writers should not judge their characters, only depict them as they are. So if you do ever write to me, Hans, I want you to know that you can tell me anything, and I won't judge you.

Please write. I miss you.

Sophie

29 Rue Jacob, Paris
Saturday, 4 April 1936

Dear Hans,

This is the ninth letter I've sent you since I moved to Paris and I still haven't heard back from you (apart from the letters I wrote myself). I do sometimes wonder why that is. Perhaps your parents moved to a different house and you never received my letters? Perhaps they went missing in the post? Perhaps you consider me an undesirable friend? Perhaps you are dead. That last possibility is the one that haunts me. Please don't be dead, Hans.

In your last letter to me (from me), you told me about how your feelings for Paula have changed, how you have come to truly love her. I'm glad about that. Obviously Paula Weiss was never my favourite person, but I hate to think of anyone loving somebody who doesn't feel the same way, somebody who is only using them.

I attended an interesting lecture last night. It was given by Dr Édouard Kahn – the young psychologist I told you about last summer – and it was on recurring dreams. I haven't told you this before but, since moving to Paris, I've had a recurring dream about you. In the dream you are lying on my bed next to me, talking to me about your life, but I can see us both from above. And . . . you remember those paintings by my mother where a shadow moves slowly across Vienna? Well, in the dream your face is gradually eclipsed by darkness and the same thing happens to your voice. At first I can hear and understand you perfectly, but as the dream goes on your voice becomes muffled and in the end it's like you're speaking a different language (or maybe I've just forgotten all my

German?) and I have no idea what you're saying. Do you ever dream of me, Hans? I think I'll answer that question in your next letter to me . . .

love,
Sophie

29 Rue Jacob, Paris
Friday, 22 October 1937

Hans, something has happened and I don't know what to do. Tonight, at dinner in a romantic restaurant, Édouard asked me to marry him! I was flattered and terrified and embarrassed all at once. He looked so crestfallen when I didn't say yes straight away. I told him I would think about it and give him my answer soon. But what should I say?

I'm only seventeen, and I'm not one of those girls who has dreamed of marriage all my life. I always imagined I would travel the world first, that I would be <u>free</u>. Yet there is a kind of freedom in Édouard's proposal. Because it means I would no longer have to live with my mother. Is it wrong of me to want to live in a clean house, with a housekeeper and nice food and a piano? It all sounds so petty now I set it down in writing. I have to admit I am also very lonely here. The girls at school all hate me because I'm German and cleverer than them, and even Elise isn't speaking to me anymore since I started going out with Édouard. And then there's the final, most important question: Do I love him?

Oh, Hans, I have so many thoughts and feelings about this that writing it all down is like trying to catch a waterfall in a teacup! The only time I've ever felt truly in love with anyone was . . . well, with you, when I was fourteen. But that was different. My love for you was more complete, somehow. It encompassed my whole being. With Édouard, my body and my mind are engaged but my heart feels slightly detached, I don't know why. Perhaps because you broke it and it's never quite healed? And he's older than me – he's a <u>grown-up</u> – and we never laugh together the way you and I used to. On the plus side, as Jens said, at least he's not a Nazi. (Sorry, I know I promised not to judge you.)

I probably shouldn't admit all this, but you'll never read it anyway, so I may as well write the truth here . . . You are the only person I ever imagined marrying. Édouard is handsome and brilliant, but he doesn't <u>listen</u> like you did. He's always trying to analyse me, to fix whatever's wrong. He means well, of course, but with you I could just be myself. Which is why I feel compelled to keep writing these letters, I suppose. Oh, but who am I fooling? It's so long ago now, and I don't even know if you're alive.

I wish you were here, Hans, so we could talk it through together. But the only you I know now is the one I've invented. And I can't take advice from a ventriloquist's dummy.

Doctor and Madame Kahn
are delighted to invite
Monsieur Hans Schatten
to Hôtel Le Bristol
112 Rue du Faubourg Saint-Honoré
at four o'clock
on Saturday, 9 April 1938
for a reception in celebration of
the marriage of their son
Dr Édouard Kahn
and
Mlle Sophie Strom

I know you won't come, Hans, but I wanted to send you this invitation anyway. Am I doing the right thing?

10 Rue des Princes, Paris
Sunday, 9 January 1938

Dear Hans,

I can't believe I finally heard from you! Thank you so much for the long, open-hearted letter you sent me – it makes up for all the years of silence, particularly as I now know that you are alive and well. It's sad that your father tried to keep you from reading my letters, but I'm so happy that he didn't destroy them and that we're back in touch at last.

I feel embarrassed when I think back to some of the things I wrote to you. I don't remember the details, but I have a feeling that I used you as a sort of journal, confiding doubts and desires that I ought to have kept to myself. Hans, would you please burn those letters? You can keep the first one, because that was written to <u>you</u>, but all the others should be destroyed.

Thank you for telling me about your feelings towards Paula and National Socialism. I feel sorry for Paula, and yes, you should probably find a way to end the relationship as soon (and as gently) as you can. I know it won't be easy, but it's obvious from what you wrote that she is very much in love with you and the longer you stay with her, the more upset she'll be when you break things off. And of course, as you say, it's best not to go into a marriage if you don't feel sure that this is the person you want to spend the rest of your life with. As for the politics, I'm relieved that you don't seem as fanatical as some of your fellow Nazis, but please continue being honest with me, Hans. I meant what I said about not judging you. I feel as if there's a gulf in our society between people with your beliefs and people with mine, and I don't

want us to be caught on opposite sides of that gulf, growing more
and more distant as it widens. I want us to find some way to meet
in the middle. Let these letters be a bridge.

Lastly, thank you for all the incredibly sweet things you wrote
about me. I had no idea you still felt that way and I'm very
touched, Hans, truly. And of course I still have feelings for you.
You're a dear friend and there will always be a place for you in my
heart. But I will be a married woman soon and I would like to be
able to correspond with you without the feeling that I am betraying
my husband in any way. I hope you understand.

With love,
Sophie

MARCH

Max

When the announcement was over, the radio started playing a cheerful tune and someone turned it off. Herr Arnstein went to make some telephone calls. Frau Arnstein prepared sandwiches. Jens played melancholy jazz-blues on the piano. The sky outside grew black. Max sat on the sofa next to Charlotte and she rested her head on his shoulder. 'I'm so sorry,' he whispered.

'Don't say that! It's not your fault.'

But it was and Max knew it. The Arnsteins had been ready to leave weeks ago and he'd insisted on trying to persuade his father to go with them. Now it was too late: the German army would be in Vienna by tomorrow morning.

'I'm sure Papa will find a way out,' Charlotte said. 'He knows people.'

'True,' said Jens, breaking off from 'St James Infirmary'. 'Unfortunately none of them are Nazis.'

'Oh, shut up, Jens,' Charlotte snapped.

There was a silence. Jens turned back to the piano.

'And stop playing those miserable blues songs!'

Jens muttered: 'Yeah, long anxious silences, that's what we need right now . . .'

Finally Herr Arnstein came back into the room, grey-faced. 'I'm afraid it's impossible to get out of Austria at the moment.'

'What should we do, Papa?' Charlotte asked.

He took a breath. 'I think we should pray.'

'*Pray?*' Jens brayed, incredulous.

But they did it anyway, standing in a circle and closing their eyes as Herr Arnstein read from the siddur in his faltering atheist's voice. Max peeked at them between his eyelids: Charlotte solemn, Frau Arnstein anxious, Herr Arnstein frowning with concentration. Max's gaze passed on to Jens, who winked at him, but he couldn't muster a smile in response. If they'd been reduced to praying, the situation must really be desperate.

'So what happens next?' Frau Arnstein asked. They were sitting around the dining table, each with a plate of egg salad sandwiches in front of them, although nobody other than Jens felt like eating.

'Things will probably calm down after a few days,' Herr Arnstein replied. 'But we may be stuck here for a while. I'll need time to get to grips with the new bureaucracy, sort out exit visas and so on. There's a chance we'll lose all our money, but—'

'But what's happening *now*?' Max demanded impatiently. 'In the city centre?'

'Well, it sounds pretty awful. They're beating up Jews, destroying their property . . . Max, what is it?'

Max scraped his chair back and got to his feet. His heart was pounding. 'My father! I have to make sure he's all right.'

'You can't go out there now. I'm sure Franz is fine. But if you're worried you can call him.'

They went to the entrance hall and Max dialled the number. He let it ring for more than a minute but there was no answer. 'I have to go,' Max repeated, turning towards the front door.

'No!' Herr Arnstein blocked his path. 'You'd be throwing yourself to the wolves. I can't allow it.'

Alerted by their raised voices, the others came into the entrance hall. Jens volunteered to go with Hans. Charlotte said she would go too. Herr Arnstein bellowed: 'Listen to me!' and everyone shut up. Herr Arnstein never shouted normally; even when he was angry, he always spoke in the same quiet, measured tones. But he wasn't angry now, Max could tell. He was frightened. 'Listen to me,' he repeated in a whisper that shook with emotion. 'No one is going anywhere. We stay here, together. I won't risk losing any of you. And that includes you, Max Spiegelman.'

'But my father—'

'Your father would agree with me, you know he would. I'll take you into town tomorrow morning. I have to go to the office anyway. In the meantime, we should all get some sleep.'

That night Max lay in the darkness of the spare bedroom, shifting restlessly on the iron cot. Whenever he closed his eyes, he felt adrenaline rush through his veins. Max was exhausted but he didn't dare let himself fall asleep: he was afraid of what he might do in his dreams.

Hans

Hans got dressed in his new grey uniform and combed his wave of hair back into place with styling wax. Paula came up behind him and stroked the close-shaven stubble at the back of his head. 'You look very handsome, Liebchen,' she said. He studied his reflection. Was it true? Hans had thought of himself as ugly ever since the fire but his scars no longer made him cringe. In the last four years they had faded from blood-red to bone-white and he thought his deformed face looked subtly disturbing now, like Reinhard Heydrich's. He straightened his tie and took a deep breath.

An hour later a Luger P08 pistol hung heavy from his belt and Hans was marching through the Heldenplatz with the 89th Standarte. The sky was dark, the air cold. Broken glass crunched under his boot heels. He did not know any of the other men in the unit; one of the soldiers had dropped out at the last minute, and Bauer had used his connections to have Hans take his place. Now here he was, at the cutting edge of history.

The square was packed with people, their bodies pressed close. A gigantic swastika flag bellied from the windows of the Ballhausplatz. Right arms rose rigid like sentry barriers and '*Sieg Heil!*' was shouted from so many mouths, syllables overlapping, that the words fused and lost all sense. 'Make way!' the soldiers at the front of the wedge called out as Hans felt himself propelled forward, the mass of bodies closing up behind the Standarte's ranks, pushing it ever faster. The roar of voices grew so loud that it distorted Hans's hearing; it sounded like radio static, the howl of a hurricane.

At last the wave broke, the physical pressure slackened. Hans had time to look around: behind him at the sea of heads and hands he had just crossed and ahead at the government guards staring blankly from beneath their helmets. Hans watched Bauer walk over to the gate to speak with one of the guards. Nearly four years had passed since the failed putsch; now was the hour of their redemption.

The order rang out in the darkness and Hans's body stiffened. As he and his comrades saluted and marched forward, as the government guards parted to let them through, Hans imagined Sophie walking beside him, watching him proudly, not judging him, thinking how handsome he looked in his uniform, how wrong it would be for her to marry someone else . . .

Max

It was nine in the morning when Herr Arnstein parked the car at the end of Spaltgasse. Max felt weak from lack of sleep, and still troubled by the dreams that had tormented him when he did finally surrender to exhaustion. He got out of the car and politely thanked Herr Arnstein for the ride. An alarm was ringing in the distance and two drunks were carrying a leather sofa from a vandalised furniture store, but otherwise the street looked deserted. 'I'm going to the newspaper office now,' Herr Arnstein said. 'I'll meet you there at noon. You remember where it is? On Schauflergasse?' Max nodded and started to walk away, but Herr Arnstein called him back. 'Max . . . Please be careful. This is not a good day to go around biting Nazis' hands.'

Max smiled, then saw the look on Herr Arnstein's face. 'I'll be careful,' he promised.

When he reached SPIEGEL MUSIKINSTRUMENTE he found the display window smashed, the metal shutter hanging from a single hinge. His pulse beat like a drum in his neck. Shakily, Max ventured inside. The shop had been stripped bare, the word JUDE scrawled in yellow paint on the back wall. Upstairs, the bedroom was empty, pillows, sheets and blankets on the floor, the mattress slashed. There were still a few feathers hovering in the air, illuminated by a beam of sunlight. But no blood. No bodies. There was still a chance that his father was alive.

He walked to his father's jazz club but a sign on the door said The Black Cat was closed until further notice. He tried the cathedral where he had once gone to Mass with Helena and his father, but the doors were locked. After that he just wandered aimlessly, hoping he might spot them somewhere. He heard a hum of voices in the distance and headed towards it. When he reached the Heldenplatz, he stopped dead. It looked as if the entire population of Vienna was crammed into the square. And how happy they all were! He saw children laughing as they scrambled to catch little swastika flags tossed into the crowd from loudspeaker vans. He saw policemen in swastika armbands drinking beer and singing. Pushing his way through the crowds, he began to notice people staring at him. He told himself he was being paranoid but the looks became too frequent, too persistent. Max glanced down at his clothes: surely these grey trousers, these nondescript black shoes, this ordinary white shirt couldn't give him away? Should he have taken Herr Oberhuber's advice and got a haircut? He accelerated, shouldering his way past a woman holding a baby in front of a camera, past more and more pairs of eyes that turned, probed, accused, marking him out instinctively as an uninvited guest, an enemy.

As Max entered the Volksgarten someone shouted, 'Hey, you!' – cheerfully or aggressively, he couldn't tell. He kept moving forward. He saw the tree where he and Sophie had kissed: a lighthouse of love in a sea of fear. Church bells rang out, tolling the hour. He passed a squadron of young Nazi soldiers drinking outside a bar and heard the voice again. '*Hey, you!*' Louder now, closer. Horribly familiar. Max felt a hand on his shoulder. He turned and saw Karl Schatten towering over him.

Hans

A hand slapped his back, hard, between his shoulder blades. 'How're you feeling?' Hans turned. Bauer was grinning at him. 'Quite a night, eh? Hair of the dog?' Without waiting for an answer, Bauer handed him a stein of beer, fingers of foam dripping down its sides. 'Prost!'

Hans drank some and almost retched. It was ten in the morning and they were standing outside a bar in the Volksgarten, all forty of them in uniform. Hans had got less than an hour's sleep last night and he was perilously light-headed now. Bauer had his arm around Karl's shoulder and they were singing the 'Horst-Wessel-Lied'. Drowsiness throbbed through Hans's body, but every time he closed his eyes he felt a raw terror; swastikas took on a sinister aspect. He put the glass down on the bar.

'Hey, you . . .'

Hans looked up. He thought it was one of his comrades urging him to drink. Church bells rang out and the voice re-emerged through the bronze din. Louder, closer.

'Fang ihn – er ist Jude!'

A boy ran through the crowd. Karl shoved past Hans and into the mass of bodies. Bauer dropped his glass on the ground and set off in pursuit, followed by half of the Standarte. Hans stood at the bar, heart racing under his uniform. For a second he'd thought they were after *him*.

Max

He bolted.

'Catch him – he's a Jew!'

He ran through the open gates of the Volksgarten and into the crowds that blackened the Heldenplatz. The nearest street was at least a hundred yards away; he was surrounded by enemies. I'm going to die, Max thought. He felt like he had when he'd grabbed hold of Charlotte's sinking body in the lake all those years ago: abruptly aware of the dark depths beneath him, of his own weakness and exhaustion. But he kept running blindly, crashing into people, pinballing from group to group, sending glasses smashing to the ground, soaking his sleeves in beer. A pigeon flapped in front of his face and he stumbled. 'Catch him!' A hand grabbed his shirt and Max felt a sudden pain in his ribs. He turned and saw a policeman beating him with a truncheon. As the heavy wooden stick smashed into his hip, his thigh, Max spotted Karl and Bauer coming closer. He elbowed the policeman in the nose and dragged himself free. The policeman yelled. A cacophony of voices rose behind Max. Mouth open, eyes bulging, throat scorched, he ran for his life.

He escaped the Heldenplatz and started taking streets at random. The yelling behind him grew quieter, the streets narrower. He found himself in a small marketplace and looked around. Had he lost them? When no one was looking, he dived under a butcher's stall and hid behind a brown tarpaulin draped over the wooden table. His breathing was ragged, loud in his ears. Trickles of pig's blood crept near where he squatted. The air smelled close, metallic. His white shirt, he noticed, was filthy and torn. He peeked through a gap in the tarpaulin and saw a small blonde girl staring at him. She couldn't have been more than four or five. Max flashed her his most charming smile and slowly put his finger to his lips. The girl smiled back, then tugged at her mother's hand. A woman bent down and peered under the butcher's stall. She frowned. Footsteps, raised voices. Max sprang to his feet, knocking the stall over, shouldering the woman aside, and ran again. The dome of a church loomed through a side street. Some policemen on horseback at the end of the road. He kept going, finding it harder to breathe, to run. Had that truncheon cracked his ribs? He darted through an archway into a cobbled courtyard and crouched behind a fountain, sweat dripping from his forehead into his eyes. He was thirsty and he needed to piss. He waited, staring at his watch as the second hand crawled slowly past all the Roman numerals. He looked around: the courtyard was deserted, shadowy. No sound but the gurgle and splatter of the fountain and a caged bird singing on a balcony. Perhaps his pursuers had given up? Max's hip was throbbing: he undid his belt, pulled his trousers down a couple of inches and saw a bruise forming, the shape and colour of a storm cloud.

After ten minutes he emerged from the archway and began limping in what he hoped was the right direction. He had no idea where he was. At last he came to a crossroads, half-familiar. He stopped and saw Karl and Bauer standing together on the other side of the street, deep in conversation, their eyes scanning the crowds around them. Max focused his gaze on the ground and forced himself to walk slowly away. His heart was banging so violently that he worried they would hear it.

He didn't look up again until he reached Schauflergasse and heard someone call his name. His father was standing in a doorway with Helena and Herr Arnstein. 'Max! Are you all right? My God, what happened?'

Max opened his mouth to speak but no words came out.

APRIL

Max

'Where did they come from, Jens? All those *Nazis* . . .'

Max and Jens were sitting with their backs to the old apple tree in the garden of the Arnsteins' country house, sharing a bottle of homemade plum brandy. A cool spring night. It had rained that afternoon and the earth was damp beneath Max's backside but everything smelled sharp and true: the earth, the stones, the rosemary bushes by the garden shed.

Max was remembering the day of the Anschluss, three weeks ago. 'They were just ordinary people, that's the scariest thing, the kind of people you see every time you walk down the street or go into a shop . . . Were they always like that? Did they always hate us? Even when they were smiling and giving us our change and wishing us a good evening?'

'Who knows,' Jens slurred, taking a swig of the brandy. 'Most of them are probably just cowards. What was it Jesus said? *The sheep shall inherit the Jews' possessions?* Something like that.'

'When they set fire to our house, I thought it was just some fanatics,' Max said. 'Now it's the whole country.'

Max was spending the spring in Wachau with the Arnsteins, in defiance of his stepfather's wishes. Jens and his family had nowhere else to live since their townhouse had been confiscated. Even their country house was not what it used to be: Herr Arnstein had lost his job at the newspaper so they'd been forced to sell their jewellery, books, gramophone records, even their instruments. The last three weeks felt like they'd lasted about three years.

Jens squeezed Max's knee. 'It'll be all right,' he said. 'My dad should get the visa for Switzerland in a few days. And then all this will be behind us.'

Max sighed heavily.

Jens handed him the bottle. 'Why do I get the feeling you're not too thrilled by the idea of coming to Zurich with us?'

Max drank some brandy and said: 'It's just . . . I don't know, things with Charlotte are . . . Recently it's been . . .' He shook his head at his inarticulacy.

Jens chuckled softly. 'I knew you'd get bored of her.'

'I didn't say I was bored!'

Normally Jens would have imitated Max's high-pitched, out-raged tone but tonight he just smiled sadly. 'You didn't have to say it.'

Max groaned. 'I feel so guilty. I keep hoping my feelings will change, that they'll go back to the way they used to be.'

'You can't stuff a genie back in the bottle. And by "bottle", I obviously mean my sister's vagina.'

'Ugh, you're so cynical about love,' Max said. He waited for another glib one-liner but it didn't come. When he looked at Jens, he was surprised by the earnest expression on his face.

'I'm not cynical about love. I just don't think that was ever what you felt for Charlotte.'

'What are you talking about? I wrote poetry for her. She was all I thought about. For two months we—'

'All lovers are like that for two months. Then the spell wears off. Be honest: you never really loved her.'

'Then I've never loved anyone,' Max said gloomily. He drank some more brandy and noticed that his upper lip was going numb.

In a quiet voice Jens said: 'You loved Sophie. I think you prob-ably still do.'

'But she's *married*.' Max had received the announcement – and a photograph of the happy couple – earlier that week. 'So what's the point in having feelings about her now?'

'What's the point? Our hearts don't listen to logic, Max.'

'Oh, what would you know? You've never loved anyone in your life.'

Jens said nothing.

'Have you?' Max insisted angrily.

'Yes.'

'Who? You've never kept a girlfriend for more than a few weeks. And you ridiculed every single one of them.'

Jens stared straight ahead. 'I wasn't talking about them.'

'Then who? And don't say your parents because that's not—'

No more words came out of Max's mouth. It was suddenly stoppered. Max could feel Jens's large, strange tongue against his, the stubble around his lips scraping Max's skin, his long fingers gripping Max's shoulders. He was so shocked that for several weird moments he didn't react at all. Jens finished up the kiss by sucking on Max's numb upper lip and holding Max's face in his hands. 'I love *you*, Max. I've always loved you.'

After a second or two of stupefaction Max jumped to his feet, banging the top of his head on the tree's lowest branch. 'Shit!' he said, rubbing it. 'Shit.'

Jens carefully stood and put his hand to Max's hair. 'Are you bleeding? Let me look.'

'Don't touch me.'

'Calm down, I was just—'

Max pushed him away and stalked off through the garden. He couldn't believe it. All this time he'd thought they were friends and Jens had just been . . . He tripped over a tree root but kept walking towards the house. Jens ran after him. 'Max, I was joking, you idiot! Come on, I was just kidding.'

Max went into the house and closed the door behind him. With the back of his wrist, he tried to rub Jens's kiss off his mouth. The disgust faded quickly and he was left staring into a deep well of despair. His best friend. He'd lost his best friend again.

Hans

Burlesque music blared from the orchestra pit and women with long, stockinged legs high-kicked on the stage in front of them. Bauer watched them avidly while Hans sipped his beer. This place – The Black Cat – was Bauer's new favourite hangout. Hans remembered coming here as a boy when his father used to play trumpet in the band, but it had changed since then. A swastika flag hung above the bar and most of the employees were new. The old ones must have been Jews or communists, he supposed.

At last the band stopped playing and the dancers trooped off stage to loud applause. Bauer sat back in his chair and beamed at Hans. 'Gorgeous, aren't they? What do you say we buy a bottle of champagne and invite two of them to sit with us?'

Hans shook his head wearily. 'I think I'll just finish my beer and get an early night.'

Hans was still in uniform, the armpits of his shirt sticky with sweat after a long day working as an SS guard on the railways. But that was only temporary. In August he would start work at the Central Office for Jewish Emigration, processing visas for Jews who wished to leave Austria, and at the same time ridding his homeland of unwanted elements.

'What's the matter, Hans? Worried your girlfriend will find out? I can keep a secret, you know.'

Hans grimaced slightly. 'Actually, it's over between me and Paula.'

'Really? Did the bitch dump you?'

'No, it was my choice.' Hans had finally given Paula the bad news by telephone last night. It had been unpleasant and he'd felt guilty, but the relief afterwards had been almost euphoric. 'We'd been together so long that I realised I had to either marry her or break things off. And the truth is I didn't truly love her. She wasn't The One, you know?'

'The One?' Bauer scoffed. 'I never knew you were such a romantic.'

Hans looked around at the other tables: the men were mostly older, laughing, dressed in suits or uniforms, the women younger, smiling tightly, wearing lingerie and stilettos. It was not the ideal place for a heart-to-heart. And although Bauer was his best friend, Hans knew he could never tell him about his feelings for Sophie. So he just shrugged and gave a self-deprecating smile.

'Although I must admit,' said Bauer, 'I always had a soft spot for old Paula. She fell for you after we beat up Jens Arnstein in the Augarten, after all, so I felt a little bit like your matchmaker.' Bauer grinned, then lit a cigar and blew a plume of white smoke over Hans's head. 'Talking of Arnstein, I have some news that might interest you . . .'

Hans frowned. 'What news?'

'He and his father were just arrested.'

'For what?'

'*For what?*' Bauer exploded with laughter. 'Oh, you mean were they arrested for being commies or for being Jews? Good point. I'll have to check on that . . . Why don't you look happy?'

'I am happy,' Hans said, though in truth he felt almost guilty. Years had passed since the days when Jens Arnstein used to bully him at school, and after the incident in the park his old enemy had been visibly frightened whenever Hans looked at him. That power was satisfying, of course, but . . . perhaps it was enough. The idea of the Arnsteins in a prison camp made him feel slightly sick. He wondered if his dreams were making him soft.

Bauer laid his cigar in the ashtray and fixed Hans with a serious look. 'You can't let yourself be weak with people like that, Hans. I mean it. They'd take advantage of your good nature. You know Arnstein would stab you in the back the first chance he got, right? Honestly, you make me question whether I'm doing the right thing, asking you to come with me to Berlin . . .'

Hans looked up. 'What?'

'Oh, didn't I mention that? I'm being transferred to SS head-quarters. Heydrich asked for me himself.'

'My God.' This was the most glamorous thing Hans had ever heard. 'Congratulations, Heinrich! But . . . why would you ask me to come with you?'

Bauer was smiling now: not one of his white-toothed charm-ing smiles but a lopsided curve of the lips that seemed to indicate some private amusement. 'You know, for someone so brainy, you can really be quite dense at times. I want you to be my deputy.'

A wave of excitement swept through Hans's body, followed by a backwash of panic.

'Your deputy? But I've got no experience, no qualifications.'

'Heydrich's given me carte blanche to recruit my own men. And I've always had a feeling about you, Hans. You're the smartest per-son I know. You just need to toughen up a bit and you could be a great man.'

'But . . . I'm supposed to start at the Central Office for—'

'I know, but that's Vienna. I'm offering you Berlin. More money, more responsibility. And you'd be at the heart of things. Eichmann will be annoyed, of course, but who cares? This is your destiny, Hans.'

Hans thought back to those history lessons about Alexander the Great, to his dreams of conquest and glory. Bauer was right: this was his destiny. So why was he fighting it? He closed his eyes and felt fear. Something deep inside holding him back . . . What would happen if he and Max were in different cities? Over the past four years the two of them had grown closer. Too close. They repulsed each other – Hans wanted Max gone from his life and Max felt the same way about Hans – but their days and thoughts were so inter-twined now it was like they were Siamese twins.

'I . . .'

'Just say yes,' said Bauer impatiently.

Besides, how would Sophie feel if he moved to Berlin, to work with Bauer of all people?

'Let me think about it, Heinrich. Please.'

Just then the band started up again. Bauer rolled his eyes and yelled over the din: 'Fine, think about it! I'll give you two weeks. You'd be a fool to say no, though.'

'I know,' said Hans. 'I know I would.'

A woman came on stage dressed only in a fur coat. Bauer cheered and sat forward in his chair. Hans closed his eyes and heard a ring-ing noise.

Max

He held the receiver to his ear and listened to the *brnng-brnng* on the other end. His stomach was tight with apprehension, but he had to warn them. Max, of all people, knew how pro-phetic his dreams could be. He imagined the family eating lunch together, arguing over whose turn it was to answer the telephone. He imagined Charlotte and Frau Arnstein standing at the door, sobbing helplessly as Jens and his father were taken away by the Gestapo.

'Hello?'

Jens's voice. Max's knees weakened with relief. He almost called out his friend's name. Then he remembered how he had fled the

Arnsteins' country house the day after the kiss in the garden, without even saying goodbye. His mouth closed silently.

'Hello?'

'Jens, it's me.'

'Max?' He sounded surprised, and a little guarded. 'Is everything all right?'

'No,' Max said. He heard a floorboard creak somewhere in the corridor behind him and he moved closer to the wall, covering the telephone's mouthpiece with his left hand. 'Listen, you need to leave Austria. As soon as you can. I . . . I had a dream.'

'Ah.' Max could hear other voices in the background. 'Actually, we received the visas today. I think my sister was about to call you. Yes, she wants to talk to you now.'

'Wait, I wanted to tell you . . . I'm sorry, Jens. For how I reacted when—'

'Here she is,' said Jens, as though he hadn't heard a word Max had said.

'Max?'

His heart sank at the sound of her voice. 'Charlotte, listen . . .'

'We've got the visas! We can leave tonight. Pack your bags and we'll—'

'Charlotte, stop. Listen to me.'

'Yes?' she asked anxiously.

'There's something I have to tell you.' Silence. He swallowed. 'I don't know how to say this.'

'I think I know what you're going to say.' Her voice sounded suddenly different: sadder, older.

'You do?'

'You left your journal in my room the other night.'

'Oh. But that wasn't what I—'

'I read it, Max.'

Her words stole the air from his chest. So she knew: how he

felt about her, about Jens, about Switzerland, about Sophie. Briefly Max wondered if he had left the journal there deliberately.

'You're not coming with us, are you.'

It wasn't really a question but it demanded an answer. It took him a long time to speak, but finally Max said: 'No.'

Silence.

'I'm sorry,' he added. 'Please tell your parents that I—'

There was a click and the line went dead. Max hung up. He breathed in guilt and breathed out relief.

'Ahem.' The sound of Herr Oberhuber clearing his throat. Max turned around and saw his stepfather standing only a few feet away.

'Were you listening to my call?'

'I was waiting for you to finish. We need to speak.'

'Not now, I have to go and see my father.'

'Now,' Herr Oberhuber insisted. 'Come with me.'

Max followed him through to the living room, where he found his mother sitting on the sofa, waiting: his stepfather sat down next to her, straight-backed, and stared at him, while his mother sat with her hands on her knees, eyes lowered. A wooden stool had been placed in front of the sofa. Ignoring it, Max slumped in an armchair. 'What's this about?'

'It's time you left Austria,' said Herr Oberhuber.

'We wouldn't say this unless we thought it was important, Max,' his mother added. 'I will miss you so much, but . . .'

'Your mother would rather you were in another country than in a prison camp. That is your choice, as things stand.'

Max said nothing. At last he was face to face with his fear. He knew Vienna was no longer his home, that he should have left long ago. But the Arnsteins were about to leave for Zurich without him and he had no other plans. And when he closed his eyes, he felt the thrum of a deeper dread.

'Max, we're trying to help you,' his mother pleaded.

Max opened his eyes. He'd just had a thought. 'Where would I go?'

'I spoke to an official at the Central Office for Jewish Emigration this morning,' said Herr Oberhuber. 'An acquaintance of mine. He's willing to do me a favour. He can get you a visa for China or France. He recommends China as it's faster. You could be in Shanghai by the end of the month. If you choose to go to Paris, you may have to wait several—'

'Paris.' Max felt himself smile, for the first time in a long time. 'I choose Paris.'

Herr Oberhuber exhaled. 'Suit yourself. I'll arrange it now.'

'Wait! What about my father?'

'What about him?'

'Could you get a visa for him too?'

'I *could*,' Herr Oberhuber said coldly. 'Why would I?'

'What?'

'I am helping you because your mother is important to me, and you are important to her. Your father, on the other hand, is not.'

Max noticed that his hands hurt; he looked down and saw his fingers writhing like a nest of white snakes. He looked imploringly at his mother.

She said quietly: 'He *is* Max's father, Ernst.'

Herr Oberhuber gave an irritated sigh. 'I'll see what I can do.'

'Thank you, Ernst.' Ana looked expectantly at Max.

'Thank you, Herr Oberhuber,' Max said dully, staring at the carpet.

This time Herr Oberhuber didn't remind Max to call him Ernst. He said, 'Bitte' and left the room.

'Max, if it wasn't for Ernst . . .' his mother whispered.

Max leapt to his feet and shouted: 'If it wasn't for people like him, I wouldn't be forced to leave my homeland like a criminal.' His mother stood up too and frantically pressed her palms down again and again, pleading with Max to lower his voice. He fell silent, then said more calmly: 'I remember you telling me once that I should be proud to be Jewish.'

Something flickered briefly across his mother's face. Pain? Shame? Regret? 'The world has changed, Max.' She reached out to touch his hands. 'But I haven't. You're my son. That's why—'

'I know,' Max said wearily. All at once he saw how vulnerable she looked. Her eyes were wet with tears. He put his arms around her shaking back. 'I know, Mama, it's all right.'

Later that afternoon, Max left the house. He wanted to see his father, to persuade him to leave Vienna. He had not managed to convince him last time, but this was more urgent. If necessary, Max would even tell him about Hans, about his dreams.

Franz and Helena lived in a tiny rented apartment near the Danube. Max caught a tram, and as he stared through the windows at the familiar buildings rumbling past he daydreamed that he was in the French capital already, on his way to see Sophie. Even in the midst of all this horror, the thought left him elated.

Walking along Spaltgasse, Max noticed some figures on the street standing next to a car. As he got nearer, he was surprised to see that one of them was his father. Max waved. He began to walk more quickly. His father had seen him. He was lifting his right hand. Max was about to yell 'Papa!' when he noticed that his father wasn't smiling. He wasn't waving either. His hand was motionless in the air, his fingers twisted into some odd configuration. Then the shape of his hand changed. Was it their old code?

Max slowed down and looked more carefully at the two men beside his father. Friends of his? For some reason Max didn't think so. They didn't look like the kind of people who would enjoy jazz or cocktails. They wore identical grey suits and blank expressions. Max kept walking, but more slowly. His father was staring at him, his face blank too. His hand hung down by his side now but at last Max could see the O shape made by his finger and thumb. He'd guessed right: it was the code. That shape meant: *Silence*. Now his father's right hand curled into a fist and his left hand reached across to cover it. Max frowned. What did *that* mean? He used to know all the code signals the way he knew the alphabet, but it had been so long since they'd practised.

One of the other men had seen Max and was staring at him with what looked like suspicion. The third man was ushering Franz Spiegelman towards the car. The man who was staring at Max opened the back door. As his father looked away and got into the car, Max finally remembered what the code meant: *Hide*.

He crossed the road and walked past the car, hardly breathing, not looking at it until the engine growled and it sped away in the opposite direction.

Hans   Max

As Hans drifted into sleep that night, he found himself thinking how angry he was that Max was going to Paris. He was sinking down through black water as Max rose towards the surface. In a moment they would be together, souls intertwined, face to face. Hans's thoughts came out as words, and he knew Max could hear them. He did not want to have a conversation, but how could he stop himself thinking?

Why are you angry, Hans?
I thought you wanted to get away from me.

You know why.
What if it kills us?

Is that really why?
Not because you're jealous?

Of course I'm jealous.
You know how I feel about Sophie.

                              I don't think it'll kill us.
You don't know that.
                    I know what will happen if I stay here.
                    You saw them take my father today.
Yes, and I hated it.
He was my father too, you know.
At least yours is still alive.

                                   If I stay in Vienna,
                              your friends will arrest me.
                    Do you really want to spend your nights
                                   in a prison camp?
They're not my friends.
You blame me for everything, but—

                                   I'm going to Paris.
                         Be glad – you'll see her again.
Max, wait . . .

                                   Goodbye, Hans.

MAY

Hans

'Papers!' Hans barked, and the four people in compartment 49 hurriedly took out their passports. Three of them were fine; he returned each with a nod. The fourth had a large J stamped on it. Hans examined it closely as the man in question – forties, bald spot, round glasses – eyed his own shoes. 'Look at me,' Hans ordered. The man obeyed and Hans compared his face with the photograph on the passport. He asked for his final destination. 'Paris,' the man said with a nervous smile. Hans asked to see his French visa and Unbedenklichkeitserklärung. Both were in order. Irritated, Hans searched his suitcase, checking every item against the handwritten list on the inside of the lid then tossing it aside. When the suitcase was empty, its contents scattered over the floor, he told the man to tidy up the mess. Without a word he did as he was told. The other passengers sat there watching: one elderly woman looked sympathetic but the others could hardly contain their glee.

'Why don't you all mind your own business?' Hans shouted. The passengers looked up in alarm, and he left the compartment feeling shaken. He stood by the window and pressed his forehead against the cool glass. What was wrong with him tonight? His nerves were frayed. It was partly exhaustion, of course, after working seven nights in a row. But there was something else. Why had he felt such rage towards those strangers? He replayed the scene in his head, and then it came to him. *Paris* . . . Max was going there tonight.

As the train rounded a curve, Hans grabbed a ceiling strap. His body swayed one way, then the other. Christ, he was tired . . . He closed his eyes then opened them again with a gasp. Stay awake, he told himself. Only another five compartments to go and he could stop in the restaurant car for coffee and a sandwich.

Max

Max opened his eyes and watched dark fields roar past the window. Another three hours until they reached the French border. It was cold in compartment 50 and everyone else was asleep. He was sitting by the window, opposite a prim, middle-aged woman who had eyed him suspiciously when he first sat down and was now nodding, face slack, a thread of saliva trickling from the corner of her mouth. Two businessmen in dark-grey overcoats faced each other on the middle seats and took turns at snorting themselves awake, mumbling something, and falling back asleep. At the far end of the compartment a young woman slept, legs crossed, her skirt riding up as she slumped deeper in her seat. Max envied them all their unconsciousness. He was tired, but he knew he mustn't fall asleep until they'd passed Kehl. In fact he didn't even dare close his eyes again after what he'd just seen.

'Papers!' a voice barked as the door swung open.

Max reached into his inside pocket and took out the passport, visa and Unbedenklichkeitserklärung. The prim woman, waking up and surreptitiously wiping her chin on her sleeve, stiffened at the sight of the red J on his passport. Max covered the offending letter with his thumb and glanced around the compartment as the others emerged from their dreams. The businessmen sat up, coughing and stamping their feet, while the young woman pulled her skirt down and frowned before delving into her handbag. The businessman next to Max was the first to offer his passport. A leather-gloved hand took it from him, then handed it back. The young woman handed the guard her passport. Max held his breath and looked up: long black leather overcoat, grey SS jacket, grey SS cap. The guard was turned towards the young woman so Max couldn't see his face.

His heart was beating loudly now, or was that the vibration of the train? They entered a tunnel and the shriek was deafening. The lights flickered off and on again. Max gripped his papers even tighter. He saw the prim woman hand her passport to the guard and the gloved hand return it. He didn't dare look up. He stared at his shaky reflection in the window.

'Papers!' the voice repeated, shouting over the howling of the train.

Hans

'Papers!' Hans repeated, glancing down at the last person in the compartment. A man. Young. Thin. Cheap suit. Brown hair. Hands tightly gripping a pile of documents. The man looked up.

The train screamed through another tunnel and suddenly Hans felt faint. A sharp bend. He stumbled, had to grab hold of a luggage rack to stop himself falling. The floor jerked and plunged beneath his feet. 'Excuse me,' he said. 'One minute.' He turned and barged his way out of the compartment. The train emerged from the tunnel and the howling ceased. Sweat was pouring down his face. He ran to the nearest toilet and locked the door behind him. He removed his cap and placed it next to the sink before vomiting into the toilet bowl.

Impossible, it can't have been, he told himself as he splashed water over his face. It must be lack of sleep. The face in compartment 50 flashed in his memory and he blinked it away. It wasn't real, it was a dreamed face, drawn from the depths of his subconscious. Or perhaps he'd just seen his own face reflected in the window as the train went through the tunnel? Yes, that must be it . . . The handle twisted and someone banged on the bathroom door. 'It's occupied!' Hans yelled in his harshest SS voice.

'Sorry, sorry,' came the timid response.

Hans took a deep breath. He examined himself in the mirror. A young man with a white scar looked back. SS-Scharführer Hans Schatten. Soon Max would be in Paris and Hans would be free of these strange fears. And with Max leaving Vienna, there was no reason not to take Bauer up on the offer to be his deputy in Berlin. Hans had thought that helping Jews emigrate from Vienna might be the kinder option, that he might sleep better at night, but that struck him as absurd now. At least in Berlin he wouldn't have to *see* all these pitiful victims. At least their names would mean nothing to him. There would be no Jens Arnsteins in Germany. Yes, Hans would call Bauer tomorrow and give him the good news.

He left the bathroom and walked calmly, steadily, past the closed door of compartment 50. Then he opened the door of compartment 51 and barked: 'Papers!'

Max

The train came to a stop in Kehl. Steam hissed outside as the prim woman left, shooting one last mistrustful glance at Max. She hadn't slept at all after the incident outside Vienna. None of the others had for a while, and the compartment had been filled with low murmurs, suspicious frowns. Max had put his papers in his jacket pocket and pretended to stare out of the window, though all he could see was the dark, fractured reflection of the compartment and its whispering passengers.

He was alone now. The young woman had left the train at Salzburg, the two businessmen at Stuttgart. He looked through the window but all he could see was another line of tracks and then the empty platform, a sign reading KEHL dimly illuminated by a single bulb. He checked his watch: two forty-six. The second hand took an eternity to tick its way around the full circle.

Two forty-seven.

He tried to distract himself by imagining the moment when Sophie would open the door of her Paris apartment to him: the look on her face, the warmth of her embrace, the broken thread made whole again. But then he glimpsed her husband, Dr Édouard Kahn, standing behind her in the hallway . . .

How long was the train supposed to remain here? Was this normal? Max started to imagine that the prim woman had alerted the police when she got off and that an SS squadron was on its way to arrest him now. It was an agonising thought: to be less than a mile from the French border, yet still inside the Reich. His papers were all in order, he reminded himself; theoretically, he had nothing to fear. But he remembered the morning of his father's arrest. The blank looks of the men who'd put him into that car. A Jew in the Reich had everything to fear. Would Max ever see his father again? Three weeks had passed since that harrowing day and still not a word regarding his whereabouts . . .

'Papers!' a voice barked as the door swung open.

Max tensed. He swallowed. He reached into his pocket and took out the passport, visa and Unbedenklichkeitserklärung. Without looking up, he held them out to a leather-gloved hand. The hand took them; they disappeared from sight. Max stared at a balled tissue on the floor of the compartment. He listened to the whisper of shuffled pages and glanced at his watch.

Two forty-eight.

'Look at me!' the voice barked.

Max took a breath and looked up to see a young SS guard. A perfect stranger.

The guard's eyes snapped from Max's face to the photograph on his passport and back again. 'Max Spiegelman – that's you?'

'Yes.'

Five minutes later the train crossed the Rhine. Max was safe at last.

He was free.

When Hans awoke the next morning, after vague dreams that vanished from memory with the daylight, he felt different. Lighter, somehow. As if he'd been carrying a burden on his shoulders all this time and now that weight was gone. And as he lay there alone on the narrow single bed in the room that he shared with Karl, he remembered that Max was far away now, in another country, and he breathed a sigh of relief. He was still whole; still himself. Good riddance to Max Spiegelman! thought Hans. Good riddance to those blurring, merging dreams. Soon he would be with Bauer in Berlin, where he could get on with the rest of his life, cut loose from his clinging shadow . . .

When Max awoke the next morning, after vague dreams that vanished from memory with the daylight, he felt different. Lighter, somehow. As if he'd been carrying a burden on his shoulders all this time and now that weight was gone. And as he lay there alone on the narrow reclining seat in the train that sped through France, he remembered that Hans was far away now, in another country, and he breathed a sigh of relief. He was still whole; still himself. Good riddance to Hans Schatten! thought Max. Good riddance to those blurring, merging dreams. Soon he would be with Sophie in Paris, where he could get on with the rest of his life, cut loose from his clinging shadow . . .

PART TWO
PARIS

1940

JUNE

Max breathed in the smell of warm bread and listened to the murmur of conversation. In the bakery queue all the talk was of the
German army's swift advance and the lovely warm June weather.
He found himself tuning out the other customers' words. After
two years in Paris, he spoke French fluently but he did miss the
range and ease of communicating in his native language; it was like
composing for a string quartet after years in command of a full
orchestra. It was possible he would soon be hearing German every
day, of course, but that was hardly a consolation.

His turn came at last and he ordered two baguettes. When the
woman behind the counter heard his accent, her smile soured. Sullenly she wrapped the baguettes in paper and handed them to him.
Max noticed that the bakery had fallen quiet. He thanked the woman
and dropped his coins in the saucer on the countertop before hurrying
from the shop. Out on the street he inhaled the blossom-scented air
and walked towards Rue des Princes. Swallows soared and swooped
joyously above the rooftops and he started to forget his unease.

He passed a car parked outside an apartment building with
two double mattresses tied to its roof, yellow stains showing, sides
sagging over the open windows. Two boys raced around the car
while a little girl whined to her mother that she didn't want to
leave Paris. The exodus had begun but Max had no intention of
joining it. Not even the might of the German army could drive him
away. He turned onto the street where he'd lived for the past nine
months and was still deep in his reverie when he found himself
standing across from number 10. He stared at the red front door

and red shutters. He'd haunted this spot when he first arrived in Paris, coming here night after night to stand unseen and watch the silhouettes move behind glass in the brightly lit rooms. Standing there, he remembered . . .

SEPTEMBER 1939

Max crossed Rue des Princes to the door of number 10 and steeled himself to ring the bell for apartment 3a. His fingertip hovered over the black circle. Why was he such a coward? He swallowed his shame and reminded himself he ought to be happy: he was going to see her again at last. He pressed the bell. Silence, then a distorted male voice. 'Oui, allô?' In his best French, Max explained that he was a friend of Sophie's. He gave his name and asked if she was home. 'Oh, Max? Of course, I've heard so much about you! Come in, come in!'

Before he was even halfway up the second flight, he heard Sophie's voice above him in the stairwell. 'Max, is it really you?' she called down in German. 'Where have you *been*?' Footsteps, a speeding heart, and then she was there, standing in front of him. For several seconds they held hands and simply stared at each other. Max had time to take in the changes in her appearance since that kiss in the Volksgarten five years ago: she was a few inches taller but seemed shorter to him because he'd grown so much; her figure was fuller, her features smoother; her hair was shoulder-length and fashionably cut, her dress chic, her skin scented, and her face subtly made-up. What struck him most, though, were the elements that hadn't changed: her voice, her smile, the spark in her eyes. Beneath all the Parisian sophistication she was still the girl who'd pinched Maus's ear and called him an asshole. She laughed with joy, kissed Max several times on the cheeks and hugged him tight. Then she took his hand and pulled him upstairs. 'Come on! Come and meet Édouard . . .'

Édouard Kahn was waiting for them at the top of the stairs. Max saw an imposing and very adult-looking man with sideburns, oval glasses, a bulging waistcoat. Black hairs curled from under his shirt-sleeves and a thick gold ring gleamed dully on his finger. When he leaned down to kiss his visitor on both cheeks, Max got a musky whiff of cologne. He turned to Sophie and caught a glimpse of her own wedding band. She saw him looking and smiled, though Max couldn't decipher the emotion behind that smile. Was it apologetic? Pitying? Amused? Or was she just sharing his incredulity? Yes, crazy, isn't it? Married at nineteen!

They went inside the apartment and Sophie said she would fetch them something to drink. Max and Édouard sat across from each other at the dining-room table and made small talk. Soon they were absorbed in a discussion of Freud's *Moses and Monotheism*, which Édouard had not yet read because no French translation was available. Max was in the middle of summarising the book when Sophie came back with a bottle of champagne in a bucket of ice and three glasses on a tray.

'Champagne?' Édouard protested. 'France has just declared war on Germany and you want to celebrate?'

'No, I want to celebrate because I've just found out that my best friend is alive.'

'Yes, chérie, I know, but—'

'Will you open this, please?' Sophie interrupted, handing her husband the bottle. Then she sat next to Max and squeezed his hand. 'Tell me where you've been!' she said in French. 'I was afraid you'd been arrested.'

Édouard frowned as he tore off the foil and twisted open the wire around the bottle's neck. 'But Max was just telling me about Freud's new book. Let him finish first and then—'

'You can't be serious.'

The psychologist sighed. 'All right. But, Max, you must promise to continue your account later.'

'Of course,' Max said. He took a deep breath and turned to Sophie. 'I wasn't arrested. My father was, though.'

'Yes, I know, you told me. He's not . . . ?'

The cork popped loudly and Édouard poured the champagne into the first glass.

'No, he's alive. He was released just after Kristallnacht. I think the camps were full.'

'I'm so glad! Max's father is the funniest, most charming man, Édouard.'

'I know, chérie, you've told me many times.'

'How's your mother?' Max asked.

'Oh, the same as ever,' Sophie said, rolling her eyes. 'She didn't talk to me for about six months after the wedding, but we speak on the phone every few weeks now. She's living on a farm near the Pyrenees.'

'What about Jens?' Max asked guiltily as Édouard handed out glasses. 'Have you heard from him?'

'Not since he first moved to Switzerland. He was never a great letter-writer, though, was he? Anyway . . .' Sophie raised her glass. 'Here's to you finally making it to Paris, Max!' Her cheeks glowed pink; she looked radiantly happy. 'I can't believe it took you five years to visit me. So when did you get out of Austria?'

'Just over a year ago.'

She stared at him, uncomprehending. 'A *year*? But where did you go?'

'I went to Paris,' Max said, turning away from her raw gaze.

'What do you mean? I don't understand.'

'It's hard to explain,' Max answered in German. He wanted to tell her that he'd stood and watched her from the other side of the road on so many evenings like this one, that he'd almost rung the doorbell a hundred times, that he'd desperately wanted to see her but had been afraid things wouldn't be the same between them, that it had seemed somehow preferable to keep intact the memory of their perfect friendship even at the cost of never communicating again, but he knew it would be too strange to say any of this here, now, in front of her husband, so instead he just mumbled: 'I've been busy.'

Sophie looked shocked. 'Too busy to write me a letter, so I knew you were safe? Too busy to call me?'

'Would you mind speaking French?' Édouard asked politely.

'I kept meaning to,' Max said, still in German. Then, in French: 'I'm sorry.'

'I don't believe this.'

'Chérie, please speak French so I can understand what you're saying. I know you're excited to see your friend again, but it's simple courtesy.'

Sophie sat back in her chair and closed her eyes. 'It doesn't matter. Nothing important. You can talk about Freud now if you like.' She put her glass on the table, untouched.

'Oh, really?' Édouard said, then started enthusiastically peppering Max with questions. Max, though still shaken, concentrated on trying to answer them. The next time he looked up, Sophie had left the table. She returned ten minutes later, her eyes a little puffy, and sat next to her husband. Max felt as though he might throw up. 'Fascinating, fascinating,' Édouard said, passing his wife her champagne glass. 'I really wish I could read it myself. Not that I have any reason to mistrust your summary, Max – you clearly have a strong grasp of psychoanalytical principles – but as you know, with Freud, the devil's in the details. Do you have any idea when the French translation will be published?'

'I don't know, sorry.' Max was looking at Sophie, whose eyes were lowered. He wanted to reach out, touch her hand, tell her that he loved her.

'Where are you working at the moment, Max?' Édouard asked.

'Well, I had a job in a restaurant.'

'A restaurant! With a mind like yours? What a waste!'

'But it's closing,' Max went on. 'So I'm unemployed now. It's an Austrian restaurant, you see. My colleagues are planning to turn themselves in. They think they'll be able to convince the authorities that they're loyal to France.'

'Hmph, good luck with that! I read today that all enemy nationals will be put in internment camps.'

'Yes, exactly. So I was wondering . . .' He looked at Édouard, who waited, eyebrows raised, apparently clueless as to what Max was trying to ask. He cleared his throat. 'Um, I wondered if I might stay with you? If you could protect me.'

'From the authorities?' Édouard asked, recoiling.

'Of course we will,' Sophie said. 'You can have the spare room.'

'Chérie, it's not that simple. If anyone were to find out that we were harbouring—'

'Then we must keep it a secret, mustn't we?'

'You don't understand, this is serious.'

Max sensed that they were on the verge of an argument, that he should absent himself for a moment. 'Could I use the bathroom?' he asked, getting to his feet.

'Through the hallway over there,' Édouard said in the same grave tone, gesturing with his chin but not looking up.

Max left the kitchen and closed the door behind him as their voices grew louder.

'It's nothing personal,' he heard Édouard saying. 'The rules are there for our safety.'

Then Sophie's voice: 'You should hand *me* over to the authorities too, then. My father is German, after all. And unlike Max, I'm not Jewish, so it's not completely absurd to suggest I might be loyal to the Nazis.'

Max closed his eyes, then walked to the bathroom. With the door shut, he could no longer hear what they were saying. He splashed water on his face and looked at himself in the mirror for a few seconds, breathing in the scents of the married couple's toiletries. It had been so good to see Sophie again after all these years, but if his presence was going to be a source of disharmony he should probably make his excuses and leave. The thought made his chest ache, but he knew it was the right thing to do. He flushed the toilet, despite not having used it, then walked back through the corridor to the kitchen door. He stood listening for a second, but they were speaking in murmurs now. At least they weren't arguing . . . Should he knock?

In the end he coughed quite loudly before opening the door, and when he caught sight of them Sophie was sitting in Édouard's lap, stroking the back of his neck, and they were smiling at each other. Max felt suddenly nauseated. Édouard looked up at him and said: 'Ah, there you are. Listen, I've changed my mind. You can stay here for a while, Max, but you will have to be very discreet.'

'Of course,' he said. 'There is one thing, though. I'm afraid I can't pay you rent until I find another job. I realise that's not ideal, but . . .'

'Actually,' Édouard said, 'Sophie had an idea that I think will work out rather well.'

JUNE 1940

Hans

He saw golden sunlight staining a parquet floor, felt a breeze blowing through the French window, tasted warm bread, smelled real coffee, heard birdsong, glimpsed her smile. Abruptly the birdsong was drowned out by a harsh ringing noise. He opened his eyes to the dim, drab shapes of his apartment in Berlin – the closed blinds, the desk piled with paperwork, the uniform hanging from the door of his wardrobe – and reached out with one hand to silence the alarm clock. In the quiet that followed, Hans thought about his dreams.

For the past two years they had been like a radio signal blocked by mountains or forests or simply fading over the expanse of miles. To his relief he often found that they vanished the moment he woke, like breath from glass, the way his dreams always used to before the night of the fire. The intertwining of his life and Max's had stopped too: if he closed his eyes in the middle of the day he would see nothing but the red-and-black screen of the illuminated lids, and the only voice in his head was his own. For months this new inner emptiness had seemed like a blessing; as if he'd been locked in a cage with someone he hated and finally his cellmate had left him in peace. But, as time passed, that silence had expanded to fill the space left behind by Max's absence. He was still in a cell, after all, only now he was alone. Solitary confinement. Did he *miss* Max Spiegelman? Hans shook his head to rid himself of these aberrant thoughts.

He got dressed and opened the blinds. Five storeys below, the city was coming to life: tiny cars gliding through the dawn murk, trams creaking, hats swarming. He ate breakfast alone at his desk and reread the last letter he'd received from Sophie, dated 27 April. He examined her words every day, hoping to detect traces of love in the dry accounts of her daily activities, the reproachful allusions to German aggression. He still wrote to her every week but her replies had grown less frequent and more guarded since war had been declared last September. It was not only a question of her avoiding subjects that might draw the ire of the censor; it was as if she were trying to back out of their friendship, to empty herself of memories and feelings, to slowly fade from his life.

But something was changing. Was it the Western offensive, bringing Paris within reach? Or was it Sophie herself, the way she looked at him each night? Either way, Hans found he could remember his dreams much more vividly these days. There they were, gleaming and solid, when he opened his eyes every morning, and they haunted his waking hours with a sort of secret joy. What wouldn't he give to lie on his bed with her now, to look up at the ceiling and open his heart? He wondered if the invasion of France was God's way of rewarding him for his patience and faith by bringing Sophie back into his life.

'Do you know if there'll be any positions up for grabs in Paris?' he asked Bauer as they walked along Prinz-Albrecht-Strasse to the Reich Main Security Office later that morning, boot heels clicking on the pavement.

'I'm sure there will. The French aren't going to police themselves, are they?'

They strode past a window and Hans watched their reflections: an Oberscharführer and a Sturmbannführer, both tall and broad-shouldered, in identical death's-head caps, belted grey jackets, grey riding breeches, knee-length black leather boots . . . Two young gods marching towards their destiny. He breathed in petrol fumes, shouted over the noise of horn-blare: 'How would I go about applying?'

Bauer stopped and turned. He looked almost hurt. 'You want to leave Berlin, Hans?'

'I'm just curious.'

A raised eyebrow, a wry smile, and they started walking again. 'Well, I don't blame you. They say the women in Paris are the most beautiful in the world! Anyway, Dannecker's the man you need to see. I should warn you, though: he's a miserable bastard. Always looks like someone's just pissed in his beer. He hasn't figured out who it is yet but he's already planning how he's going to get revenge.'

The guards on duty saluted as they entered the lobby. Abruptly the ambient noise levels decreased. Now they could hear the slap of their boot soles on the marble floor. Bauer lit a cigarette as they waited for the lift. 'I don't suppose you speak the language, do you?'

'A little.' Hans had never actually tried speaking French but he'd noticed recently that he could follow the conversations in his dreams.

'Really? Go on, say something.'

Hans looked around. They were out of earshot of the guards and he felt certain that Bauer would not understand anything he said. 'Je rêve chaque nuit d'un autre moi qui te déteste.' To his surprise he liked the way the words felt in his mouth: smooth, velvety, almost liquid.

Bauer looked impressed. 'What did you say?'

Every night I dream of another me who hates you.

The lift doors opened and the two men stepped inside. 'I said, "Do you want me to teach you how to speak French?"'

Bauer snorted smoke through his nostrils. 'God, no, I'm far too lazy to learn another language! I'll just join you there in a year or two. The Frogs will all be speaking German by then.'

Max

He jogged upstairs, carrying the baguettes. Sophie and Édouard were in the dining room and a breeze was stirring the linen curtains at the open French window. Flickers of golden summer sunlight stained the parquet floor. Sophie gave a brisk smile and said, 'Bonjour' while Édouard glanced up from some papers. 'Max, there you are! Please cut the bread – I'm starving.'

His tone was peremptory but Max was used to it after nine months as Édouard's dogsbody. To start with he'd been given room and board in return for translating *Moses and Monotheism* into French. Sophie had revised the translation for him, polishing his sentences, correcting his mistakes. They'd spent an hour together each day working on the book, and every so often a look would pass between them that seemed to burn through the mist of years. To Max's disappointment such moments had been fleeting. Each time, Sophie would retreat behind her wall of hurt, unable to forgive him for having lived in Paris all that time before coming to see her. They had lost their old closeness and it was all Max's fault. Max was studying psychology in the evenings now, while in the daytime he worked as Édouard's full-time assistant; consequently he spent more time talking with his employer than he did with his best friend.

Édouard dipped a hunk of buttered bread into his bowl of coffee and spoke as he chewed. 'Funny thing, Max. Six of my eight patients yesterday described their recent dreams as sinister or ominous. That's highly atypical. And revealing, don't you think? The Germans aren't even in Paris yet but they have already invaded our collective subconscious.'

'Ernest Jones says that nightmares arise from a clash between the id and the ego,' Max remarked.

'Not a view endorsed by Freud,' Édouard said, frowning. 'I think it more likely that the people of Paris are secretly wishing for a German invasion.'

Max tensed at this but said nothing. He remembered last night's dream – the first he'd been able to recall clearly in more than two years – and wondered if he would describe that as 'sinister or ominous'.

Sophie said: 'Mama says nightmares are warnings from the animal inside us, which senses danger long before our minds can conceive of it.'

Édouard gave a dismissive snort. 'Anyway, I was thinking of writing a paper on this phenomenon: dreams in wartime. But I would require a larger sample in order to give the findings real weight. I thought the two of you could help me by interviewing people. Out on the streets, you know?'

'The two of us?' Sophie asked.

'All right,' Max said eagerly.

'Good, that settles it,' said Édouard. 'You can start this morning.'

Max stole a glance at Sophie, who gave a brief, nervous smile.

They went downstairs after breakfast but there was nobody around to interview. Rue des Princes was deserted, while on Avenue Foch there were no pedestrians, only a slow-moving line of cars trying to escape the bottleneck of the city. The exodus was in full spate. Sophie said she knew some cafés in Saint-Germain-des-Prés that were always busy, so they decided to cycle there. Thirty minutes later, pink-faced and panting slightly, they locked their bicycles to a metal fence and walked along Rue Jacob. 'I haven't been here in ages,' Sophie said, raising her arm to point at a shuttered window. 'That's where I used to live with Mama. I walked these streets with you so many times when we first moved here. In my imagination, I mean.'

'I remember.' Max hesitated, then added shyly: 'I came here too, when I first moved to Paris.' It was true, if embarrassing: he'd tempered his loneliness by following the itineraries that Sophie had described to him four years earlier in her letters, imagining that she – the she that he'd known back then, pre-Édouard – was with him.

For a second Sophie looked shocked. Then her face closed up like a flower at night and she said: 'Let's find a café.' Inside, they drank cold Perrier in silence as Sophie looked around at the other customers. Max thought back to their bike ride – the sun on his face, Paris flashing past, Sophie by his side – and cursed himself. Why had he mentioned his early days in the city? 'Let's go and talk to that old man at the bar,' Sophie said, getting to her feet.

Max followed her.

'Monsieur, may we speak with you?' Sophie asked in a loud, clear voice, perhaps afraid that the old man might be deaf. 'We're interviewing people on behalf of the psychologist Dr Édouard Kahn, who is writing a study on dreams in wartime. Would you mind if we asked you a few questions?'

The man's eyes glittered from under his beret. 'Salut, ma jolie! Sit down, sit down. Who's that, your beau?'

'This is my colleague, Max. He's going to write down what you say, if that's all right?'

'That's just fine, mademoiselle. So you're single, then?'

Sophie smiled and held up her ring finger. 'Do you remember what you dreamed last night?'

'Actually, I do. It was a strange one. Not erotic. Many of my dreams are erotic, you know.' He gave a lascivious wink. 'But the one last night was . . . eerie.' The man described his dream: cockroaches crawling over the floorboards of his bedroom, up the legs of his bed and between his sheets, until his naked body was covered in them – 'I always sleep naked, my dear!' – and he woke in darkness, clawing wildly at his arms and chest, trying to scrape the repulsive creatures off his skin. He spoke so theatrically that they were soon surrounded by a crowd of other customers, all eager to share their own dreams. Most of them reported nightmares. Max thought about his own dream again. The strange thing was how serene it had felt at the time. Even after waking, Hans's excitement had felt a little like it could have been his own. It was not until he'd looked at the morning newspaper headline – GERMANS ONLY 20KM FROM PARIS – that the anxiety had started to churn inside him.

By the time they'd questioned everyone in the bar, it was almost noon: Max's notebook was full and Sophie looked happy again. They went outside. Rue Jacob was resplendent with sunlight. Max started walking towards the bicycles but Sophie stopped in the middle of the street and said in German: 'I don't want to go home yet.'

'Isn't Édouard expecting us for lunch?'

'Oh, he can make himself a sandwich or something. I'm sure he'll forgive me when he sees how many dreams we've got. In fact, if you think about it, recording this many would normally have taken us all day. We just got lucky, finding them all in that café. But Édouard doesn't have to know that . . .'

She shot him a small, sly smile.

'What do you want to do?' he asked.

'I want to take you on a walk, like I used to when you were just a figment of my imagination.'

Max swallowed. Don't say the wrong thing, he reminded himself. 'I'd like that.'

'But it'll be lunchtime soon, we should buy supplies.'

They bought cheese from a fromagerie, a baguette from a boulangerie, fresh figs from a primeur, a bottle of wine and a corkscrew from a caviste, and two copies of the same book from one of the three remaining bouquiniste stalls by the Seine. Apparently the other booksellers had all fled Paris. As the man handed them each a matching leather-bound hardback edition of Hugo's *Notre-Dame de Paris* – the only book he possessed in more than one copy – Sophie asked him if he remembered what he'd dreamed last night. 'I dreamed that all the books I was selling were in German,' he said.

After that, Max and Sophie walked across the bridge to the Île de la Cité. They admired the cathedral, then she led him to the end of the island, where they sat on the grass in the shade of a weeping willow to eat their picnic. 'I often used to bring you here,' she said. 'It was one of our favourite spots.'

Max watched a barge float past, silver ripples spreading in its wake, and took a bite of bread and goat's cheese. 'Mmm, this is the best food I've ever tasted.'

She laughed. 'Because this is our last day of freedom before the tanks roll in?'

'Because it's our first day of freedom,' he said, and she frowned. 'Oh shit, did I say the wrong thing again? Sophie, please don't go silent on me. I'm an idiot, just ignore everything I say.'

'No, you're right. It does feel like our first day of freedom. The first time we've truly been friends again since you came to Paris.'

'But not the last?'

'I hope not.' She smiled at him. 'No, I think Édouard will be very pleased with our treasure haul for today. Maybe he'll let us spend the whole summer doing this?'

'Even if the streets are full of tanks?'

Sophie looked around. 'Why would anyone drive a tank to the end of this island?' She drank some red wine from the bottle and handed it to him, then wiped her mouth on a paper napkin. 'Doesn't this remind you of that day on the lake?'

'Yes,' Max said. He'd just been thinking the same thing. He thought about Jens and drifted into regret about the way their friendship had ended. He had told Sophie about the kiss in a letter, and she had predicted that they would be friends again in no time, but apparently she had been wrong. 'I miss Jens.'

'Ich auch. No one could make me laugh like he could.'

'Do you think the three of us will ever be together again?'

'I hope so,' she said. 'To be honest, though, at the time, I just wanted to be alone with you.' Max glanced at her but she was staring across the river. She took the two copies of *Notre-Dame de Paris* from her bag. 'Now lie down so I can rest my head on your chest . . .'

They read as small clouds drifted slowly across the sky, the two of them dwelling in the same imagined world. Sophie read faster than Max and she took a pencil from her pocket every so often to underline a phrase. A few hours later, as the sun shone through the leaves of the willow, painting the pages of his book green with glowing shadows, Max came across a sentence that struck him so powerfully that he sat up and asked to borrow Sophie's pencil. She sat up too, handed it to him, then watched as he discreetly drew a pencil mark next to the three lines of text, folding the top of the page so he'd be able to find it again. 'Can I see?' she asked.

Max pulled a face, embarrassed.

'Please? I bet I marked the same passage.'

'It's on page one hundred and twelve,' Max said.

Sophie leafed back through her book and found that page. 'Oh!' She blushed. 'The lines about love?'

'About friendship,' Max said, then read the sentence out loud: '*It means being brother and sister, two souls touching but not merging, two fingers of the same hand.*' Oddly, reading it again, he found himself thinking of Hans.

'Ah, yes.' Sophie smiled, her cheeks still red. 'I underlined that too. Can you lie back down, Max? I need my pillow.'

Max lay down and started reading again, wondering what she'd meant by the 'lines about love'. In the next paragraph he found out. '"*Oh, love!*" *Esmeralda said, her voice trembling and her eyes radiant. "That is being two and yet only one. A man and a woman fusing into an angel."*'

Max tried to keep his breathing under control, but his heart was thudding so hard against his ribcage that he felt sure Sophie must be able to feel it on the back of her head. He wondered if she'd been thinking of Édouard when she underlined that passage. They continued reading in silence until the sun was low over the Seine.

Hans

In Berlin, at a table on a restaurant terrace bathed in evening moonlight, Hans raised his champagne flute to the same height as Bauer's. 'To Paris!' Bauer bellowed.

'To Paris,' Hans echoed.

The meetings with Dannecker had gone well, he'd aced all his language tests, and this afternoon he had been told he would be flying to the French capital in two days' time. His heart fluttered at the thought.

'May you rid that beautiful city of all its Jews! Though I'm sure it won't be all work and no play.' Bauer leaned close, face twisted in a leer. 'Did you hear the Führer's warning about Parisian degeneracy? Negro singers, strip clubs, the finest bordellos in Europe . . . Ah, Hans, how I envy you.' Bauer snapped his fingers as the waiter passed and told him to bring them more champagne. 'Watch out for Arnstein, though,' he added casually.

Hans frowned. 'Arnstein?'

'Yes, apparently your old school pal escaped from Dachau. I told you he was slippery. I read a report from one of the prison camp officers saying that Arnstein had wormed his way into their trust through good behaviour and then betrayed them. Their fault for trusting him in the first place, of course . . .'

Bauer fell silent as the waiter arrived to uncork the bottle and fill their glasses, and Hans wondered at the feeling of lightness that filled his chest. Was he *relieved* that Jens had escaped? No, it was probably just his indestructible good mood. Bauer could have told him that every prisoner in the camp had escaped and Hans would still have been happy, as long as it didn't prevent him flying to Paris.

When the waiter had gone, Bauer added: 'So anyway, the rumour is that Arnstein fled to France.'

'Well, it's a big country, Heinrich. I doubt I'll bump into him.'

'Yes, you're probably right. You've been right about most things over the past two years. So here's to you, Hans Schatten: the best deputy a man could wish for.'

'Thank you.'

They clinked glasses again and drank. Tipsy and ecstatic, Hans sat back in his chair and looked up at the darkening summer sky. He remembered a fragment of last night's dream: Sophie, standing on the balcony of her apartment, glass of kir in hand, gazing at the large, yellowish evening moon. The same moon that shone down on him now. That moment in his dream had been so alive, almost as if he could have reached out and touched her . . .

He noticed that Bauer was looking at him with a strange expression on his face. 'Did you say something?' Hans asked. 'Sorry, I was miles away.'

Bauer smirked. 'Yes, I guessed that when you didn't react to what I just told you.'

'What did you just tell me?'

'That I hired your replacement today.'

'Oh, good. What's his name?' Hans took a sip from his glass.

Bauer waited until Hans was looking at him, then said: 'Karl Schatten.'

Hans spat champagne all over the tablecloth.

'Ha, now that's the kind of reaction I was expecting!'

Max

He stood beside Sophie on the balcony of the Kahns' apartment, sipping kir and gazing at the moon. It had been another glorious day and the evening was, if anything, even more beautiful, a play of blue shadows and golden glimmers on the building opposite. A warm breeze caressed their skin. Inside the apartment Édouard was greedily reading through the reports of Parisians' dreams they'd brought back from their latest day in the city. Max thought about his own most recent dream and felt his heart start to speed: whether with fear or excitement, he couldn't quite tell.

'Max, are you sure?' Sophie said in an undertone. 'I could always interview people on my own, you know. You could stay here, in hiding.'

They'd seen their first Nazis today, seen swastikas hung triumphantly from the Eiffel Tower and the Arc de Triomphe. At the end of the afternoon they'd sat on a bench in the Jardin du Luxembourg and talked about how dangerous it would be in Paris for an Austrian Jew. Max knew Sophie was trying to protect him but even so her words stung. How could she suggest that after their last few days together?

'I don't want you to interview people on your own.'

'I don't either, but—'

'Sophie, I'm not going to let the Nazis drive us apart again.'

Hans

He stood at the end of Rue des Princes, looking up at the silhouetted figures on the third-floor balcony, and shivered. He couldn't believe he was here at last.

He'd arrived in Paris this afternoon and hadn't even unpacked yet. He had left his suitcase on the bed of his hotel room and walked straight here through the deserted city. To the place where she lived. To the place in his dreams. Was that Sophie he could see now, standing on the balcony, a wine glass raised to her lips? And who was that beside her? For an instant his heart leapt at the impossible thought. But no, it was just her husband, of course.

Hans took a few steps forward. The figures on the balcony moved inside and closed the French windows. Lights came on in the living room. He kept walking until he was standing across from number 10. He stared at the red door, the red shutters. The yellow glow of her home, his future. Hans's heart was pounding. He could cross the road now if he wanted, ring the doorbell. He could be with her in less than a minute. But he didn't move.

No, not yet, he decided. Not while he was in uniform. He'd written her a letter from Berlin, telling her he was coming to Paris, but had not received a reply. Perhaps it had arrived after he left the city? He would write her another letter tonight, telling her he was in Paris, and wait for her to invite him. In the meantime it was enough to be here, breathing the same air, standing under the same moon, dreaming of her every night.

JULY

They sat in the shade of a parasol and sipped their cold Perriers. The lunch hour was over, the café terrace deserted. In front of them rose the Montmartre hill. They'd come here because Sophie said it was usually packed with sightseers, but they'd walked its steep streets all morning and found almost nobody to interview. And the few people they'd seen had been reluctant to answer questions. Finally a soldier had walked over to ask them what they were doing. Sophie had explained the situation and the soldier's suspicions had quickly given way to curiosity about her fluent German. He'd flirted with her a little bit before she made her excuses and left. It was all fine in the end but Max – who stayed silent throughout – had been shaken by the incident. What if the soldier had asked to see his papers? It had made him realise the precariousness of what they were doing, the likelihood that it would all come to an end soon.

'Sophie?'

She looked at him keenly, alerted by the tone of his voice. 'Yes?'

'I'm glad we've been able to spend this time together.'

Sophie smiled without taking her eyes off him. 'Ich auch.'

'And . . . I wanted to tell you that I'm sorry. About before. About being in Paris all that time and not getting in touch.'

Her smile froze; she lowered her eyes. 'It's all right.'

'No. It's not. It was wrong of me. Stupid. I know it hurt you. But you have to understand: it wasn't because I didn't want to see you.'

Sophie sighed as she sat back in her chair. The parasol shifted in the breeze and the sun caught her face for an instant. She shaded her eyes. 'Why, then?'

'It was the opposite, if anything. Things were so perfect between us before, especially that week in the Wachau Valley, and . . . I think I was afraid that, seeing each other again, it might not live up to our hopes, that we'd be disappointed, and those memories . . . You remember the ladybird?' he asked as the image blinked in his mind. Sophie said nothing. He took a breath. He felt like he was floundering. Staring at the frantically spurting bubbles in his drink, he said: 'What I'm trying to say is . . . those memories mean so much to me and I was worried that they'd be . . . That the present might not live up to them.'

A deeper sigh. 'I know what you mean. But you're my *best friend*, Max. I was so excited to see you.'

'So was I. Almost too excited. It was overwhelming. And . . . things were different, more complicated. You were married.'

'I'm still married,' she reminded him.

'I know.' It was Max's turn to lower his eyes. 'Why are you?'

Sophie laughed, frowning. 'What do you mean?'

'Why did you marry him?'

'I don't know. I told you all this in the letters, didn't I? Because he was brilliant. And handsome. And charming. And he asked me to. And my mother disapproved. And I didn't think I'd ever see you again. How many reasons do you need?'

Max caught his breath. 'What did not seeing me again have to do with it?'

Sophie's gaze was transparent. 'You were my first love, Max. Surely you know that?'

'You mean the summer of thirty-four? When we were staying at Jens's house?'

'Long before that. I liked you the first time I ever met you, in your father's shop. And then I thought I'd lost you. So when I saw you outside Monsieur LaRue's classroom, it just felt fated to me. Not that you noticed, of course. You were too dazzled by Paula Weiss at the time.'

'Ugh, don't remind me!' said Max, and they both laughed.

'I was in love with you even after we came to Paris,' said Sophie. 'For an embarrassingly long time.'

'There's nothing embarrassing about it.'

'Easy for you to say,' she said with a grimace. 'You had about six different girlfriends while I was pining over you!'

Max leaned forward and said in a low voice: 'None of them meant anything compared to you.'

A polite smile. 'It's sweet of you to say so.'

'I'm not trying to be sweet!' said Max, frustrated. 'I'm being honest. You're the only person I've ever loved.' He sounded almost angry and he couldn't look at her. He sipped his Perrier. There was a silence, broken only by birdsong. Eventually he asked: 'So when did you stop feeling that way?'

'I don't know.'

He waited for her to say something else but she didn't. Had he upset her? He couldn't tell. She poked the lemon slice in her glass with a spoon and bubbles buzzed to the silver surface. The silence lengthened. The waitress came out to ask them if they wanted to order anything else. Max looked questioningly at Sophie.

'Better not,' she said in French. 'Édouard's been complaining about my spending recently.'

Max already knew this: the walls in the apartment were thin and he'd overheard a few rows. When the waitress had moved away, he said quietly: 'He doesn't seem all that charming, to me.'

Sophie gave a wry smile and looked up at the white domes of the Sacré-Cœur. 'He was definitely more charming *before* we were married. Since then he's . . .'

'Taken you for granted?'

Sophie shrugged. 'Perhaps. But aren't all married couples like that?'

We wouldn't be, Max thought. Without looking at her, he said: 'I don't like it when he shouts at you.'

'No, nor do I.' There was a silence, then she leaned forward and added more brightly: 'Édouard's not a bad person, Max. He's just worried about our finances. He really wants to publish this paper soon. He thinks it could make his name.'

She sat back, face offered to the sun. Max noticed the waitress hovering in the shadows, waiting to take away their glasses as soon as they were empty, and moved his chair closer to Sophie's so they could speak without being overheard. 'But if nobody will talk to us about their dreams, what are we going to do?'

'Well . . .' The edge of her lips curled mischievously. 'We could just invent them.'

'Are you serious?'

Sophie smiled, eyes closed against the glare. 'We already know the general pattern. All we'd have to do is continue it. I think it'd be fun. The dreams could be like short stories. Vignettes.'

'But what about Édouard's paper? Wouldn't it make the whole thing meaningless?'

'It's not really scientific in the first place, though, is it? Anybody could lie about their dreams. There's no way of knowing. Our guesses might be more accurate than what people tell us.' She opened her eyes, sat up, looked around. 'Take that woman over there, on the other side of the street.' Max saw a straight-backed, grey-haired lady walking briskly along the opposite pavement, a white poodle scurrying ahead of her at the end of a leash. 'If she had a romantic dream about a German soldier, do you really think she'd admit it?'

'Do you lie to Édouard about your dreams?'

'No. Do you?'

Max laughed. 'Of course! He'd write a book about me if he knew the truth.'

Sophie's eyes grew wider. 'Wait . . . You're still dreaming about your alter ego? The Nazi? What was his name again?'

'Keep your voice down,' Max whispered. He leaned closer to her, so that his lips were brushing the lobe of her left ear. 'Yes, I still have the same dreams. His name is Hans.'

'Hans, that's right.' She turned to face him and their lips almost touched. Max pulled his face back slightly. Sophie was wearing a skirt and her bare knees were pressed against his, although he didn't think she was even aware of it. She was just eager to hear more about Hans. 'So you still dream about him even when he's hundreds of miles away?'

'Yes, although less vividly.' He hesitated. 'He's here now, though. In Paris.'

'Really? Why?'

Max bit his lip. 'He came for you.'

'For me?'

'He . . . loves you.'

'Oh.' Sophie blushed so violently that Max could almost feel the heat radiating from her cheeks. She pressed the Perrier glass to her face. 'Am I married to Édouard in your dreams?'

'Yes.'

'And does the other me love Hans?'

'The other you won't even answer his letters. He's a Nazi.'

Sophie looked thoughtful. 'I suppose so. He's still you, though.'

Max desperately wanted to lean forward and kiss her then. But he was aware of the waitress watching them from inside the café. And anyway, what if Sophie recoiled? Or just turned her face away? In a few seconds he might ruin everything.

She finished her drink and put her glass on the table, then looked him straight in the eye. 'I do remember the ladybird. I didn't want it to fly away either.'

Hans

Édouard Kahn's office was located directly below his apartment. Hans rang the bell for 2a and was buzzed into the building. He climbed the stairs slowly, savouring the sense of déjà-vu. The play of light on the marble steps, the muted sounds, the sultry air, the smell of French cooking . . . It was all exactly as it had been in his dreams.

On the second-floor landing he knocked at the door, his senses electric with the knowledge that Sophie was just upstairs at this very moment, probably in bed taking her afternoon nap. Hans yearned to see her again – for the first time since she'd kissed him goodbye on that train station platform six years ago – but he knew he had to be patient. He'd been in Paris over a week now and had written her two letters. She had not replied to either. He felt a little guilty at what he was about to do but what choice did he have? God had brought them back together, so he couldn't simply do nothing. Hans's presence in Paris was his reward for all those years in the wilderness, those hidden letters. It would be wrong not to grasp the opportunity he was being offered.

Édouard Kahn answered the door himself. He used to have a secretary, Hans knew, but he'd let her go recently because most of his clients had left Paris. He looked exactly like the man in Hans's dreams but he acted very differently, the bland condescension replaced by deference. 'Monsieur Schatten, please come in!' he said, ushering Hans into his consulting room. 'Tell me, how are you enjoying Paris and this magnificent weather that you and your countrymen have brought with you?'

'It's a pleasure to meet you, Dr Kahn,' Hans said in his best French. 'And everything I heard about Paris is true: it really is the most beautiful city in the world.'

Édouard Kahn reacted as though Paris were his own personal creation. 'Thank you most humbly. And may I compliment you on your excellent command of our language?' Once he was sure that his patient was comfortable on the leather couch, Dr Kahn sat in a chair near the window and said: 'Now, Monsieur Schatten, tell me about your dreams.'

Max

'So you didn't take a nap this afternoon?' Édouard asked his wife. It was early evening. The three of them were at the table eating apple tart.

She answered quietly: 'Yes, I did.'

'Oh? I didn't receive your report. Did you forget to write it?'

Sophie took a sieste every day after lunch and this was generally when she experienced her most vivid dreams. Édouard was in the habit of noting down all his wife's dreams, just as he noted down his own, but he had a particular penchant for her afternoon dreams. They were, he claimed, 'extraordinarily precise and revealing'. When he was feeling affectionate, instead of telling his wife that she had beautiful legs or beautiful eyes, he would tell her she had beautiful dreams.

'No, I didn't forget.'

'Then why—'

'Let's talk about it later,' she said. 'I'm tired.'

Édouard laughed then: an odd, shrill sound. 'Chérie, you're displaying every textbook sign of repression. You know perfectly well that I can't let you go without talking this through.'

Sophie shook her head. 'It's not that.'

'Oh no? Then what?'

In a murmur she said: 'I'm afraid you'll be hurt, that's all.'

'Please be assured that no dream has the power to hurt me. My viewpoint, as you know, is a purely clinical one.'

Sophie shot an anxious glance at Max. 'I'll tell you in private,' she said to her husband.

'Don't be absurd. Why shouldn't Max hear? He's my assistant. So, please, enough resistance: tell me what you dreamed.'

Sophie sighed. It was so quiet in the apartment that Max could hear the ticking of the living-room clock. He cut a small slice of tart and speared it on his fork, then raised the fork to his mouth. Sophie joined her hands on the table and stared at them as she spoke. 'It was daytime in the dream and I was in our bed . . . with Max.'

The piece of apple tart was held suspended before Max's open mouth.

'Go on,' said Édouard.

'We were naked, and we were kissing. I think we were about to . . .'

She left a silence. The piece of tart fell from the end of Max's fork and landed on the cream tablecloth.

'Have intercourse?'

'Yes.'

Max picked up the piece of tart and noticed the brown stain it had left.

'But before we could start, you knocked on the door and called my name. The two of us jumped out of bed and got dressed. I asked you to wait. You knocked on the door again, harder, and twisted the handle, but the door was locked.'

Max put the piece of tart in his mouth and chewed. His mouth was dry so he sipped some water and glanced at Sophie over the rim of the glass: her gaze was focused on the backs of her hands, as if she had written her report there.

'When we were dressed, I opened the door and you came in and started lecturing me about how dusty your desk was. You were trying to stay calm but I could tell you were upset, that you suspected something. But you just kept talking about the dust, and then you took me by the hand and showed me your desk. And it was covered, not with dust, but with sand, like a beach.'

For a moment nobody spoke.

'And the dream ended there?' Édouard asked finally.

'Yes.'

'Hmm . . .'

Another silence. Max looked at Sophie, who was very pale. Her eyes met his for a second, then she stood up, excused herself and hurried out of the dining room.

Édouard turned to Max. 'What do you make of it?'

With an effort Max suppressed the quaver in his voice. 'I don't know. The, um, sand is interesting. I read somewhere that sand can be a symbol of the border between the conscious and the unconscious.'

'Yes, symbols can be useful interpretative tools, and Freud did not dismiss them entirely, but let us be methodical about this. The latent dream-thoughts are usually to be found in the events in waking life that directly preceded the dream. You were with Sophie this morning. What happened? Whom did you meet? What was said?'

Max gave as detailed an account as he could of the various people (mostly imaginary) they had interviewed that morning. He told his employer about those people's dreams (mostly invented) and the bottles of mineral water he and Sophie had drunk on the café terrace. He did not tell him how they'd spent part of the afternoon lying in the grass in the Jardin du Luxembourg reminiscing about Vienna, or about the silent look that had passed between them there, like an ellipsis of longing in the midst of all their words. He didn't tell him that he and Sophie had finished reading *Notre-Dame de Paris* and begun *Bel-Ami*, so that they could be together even when they were apart. Max was still speaking when Sophie returned, her face just as pale as before.

'Well, we haven't got to the bottom of your dream yet,' Édouard told his wife, 'but don't worry, we will.'

Max began clearing the table so he wouldn't have to look at either of them.

Hans

Carrying a package emblazoned with the logo of a famous Parisian department store, Hans nodded at his colleagues in the Judenreferat and headed towards the door. 'Leaving already, Schatten?' sneered the man at the next desk, a fellow Hauptscharführer named Dieter Geier. Hans ignored him. Geier had a ratlike face – small mouth, sharp nose, piercing eyes – and a personality to match, and Hans had known from his first day in the office that they would never be friends.

In truth, Hans didn't really have any friends, apart from Bauer. He'd been promoted to the rank of Hauptscharführer at a much younger age than was usual and this had stirred up quite a lot of resentment and suspicion. He felt sure that his colleagues were whispering about him now behind the closed door of the Juden-referat. Not that he cared. Since coming to Paris, since sharing a city – a life – with Max again, his loneliness had evaporated. And then, of course, there was Sophie.

His heart was pounding as he descended the broad stone stair-case and exited the building onto Avenue Foch. Tonight was the big night. She would be getting ready at this very moment, he thought, putting on her make-up and dabbing scent in the hollow of her throat, only a few hundred yards from where he now stood. Hans let his gaze travel along the wide, tree-lined avenue. Unmarked black sedans were parked along both kerbs. A heat haze rose from the empty concrete, blurring the enormous swastika flag that hung from the Arc de Triomphe in the distance. Sweat trickled down the back of his neck. Calm down, he told himself. Everything will be all right once you're together again.

It worried him that Sophie still hadn't replied to any of his letters. What would he do if she were hostile towards him at dinner? To soothe his anxiety, Hans recalled a moment from a recent dream – the tenderness in the other Sophie's voice when she'd said: 'He's still you, though' – and allowed himself a more optimistic vision of what lay in store for them this evening. First, though, he had to go back to his apartment on Rue Orphée and change his clothes. He did not want to be in SS uniform when Sophie saw him for the first time in six years.

Max

He set the table while Édouard read the newspaper. 'Anything interesting?'

'Not really,' Édouard said. 'Life goes on as normal. Or it would have done, if all those stupid people hadn't fled Paris. What do they think is going to happen here that won't be happening in the rest of the country? The Germans seem perfectly civilised, anyway. Perhaps they will bring some discipline and order back to this country.'

Max held his tongue. He'd made the mistake of mentioning the fate of the Jews in Vienna once before and Édouard had accused him of fear-mongering. Édouard was Jewish too but his family had been in France since the Revolution and he considered himself a patriot.

Sophie came in, carrying a terrine of pâté and a basket of bread, and sat down opposite Max. 'Oh, I forgot the bottle of wine. Édouard, would you fetch it from the kitchen?'

Édouard sighed. 'Let's just drink water.'

'Never mind, I'll get it,' she said, rising to her feet.

'Sit down!' her husband snapped. His face was red. Sophie froze, then slowly sat down again. The colour faded from Édouard's cheeks and his lips twisted into an expression of vague bitterness. 'We need to tighten our belts anyway, now I have fewer patients.'

Max glanced up and saw Sophie blinking furiously but neither of them said anything and a heavy silence blanketed the table as they finished the first course. The timer began to ring and Sophie stood up. 'I have to take the lamb out of the oven.'

'I'll help you,' Max said, picking up the empty plates and following her into the kitchen.

When Sophie opened the oven door a puff of steam rolled over her face, scenting the air with rosemary and roasting flesh. 'Well, at least the lamb looks perfect,' she said, her voice shaking slightly. She reached for the metal tray.

'Wait!' Max called. But it was too late: Sophie's bare fingers touched the burning steel. She cried out and pulled her hands away.

'What an idiot!' she said. 'How could I have forgotten to wear oven gloves?'

'Show me your fingers.'

'I'll be fine, don't worry.'

But Max had already turned on the cold tap in the sink and now he took hold of Sophie's left hand and examined the fingertips. 'They're red. Put them under the water.'

'I should take the roast out of the oven.'

'I'll do that. Give me your other hand.'

She did. The middle fingertip was a darker red than the others. Without a thought Max lifted it to his mouth and sucked. Sophie stared at him, lips parted. He stared back, as surprised as she was. After a few seconds he removed her finger from his mouth. 'Saliva is good for burns.'

'Yes . . .' She looked away. 'I know.'

Their bodies touched as he moved past her to get to the oven. Had the kitchen shrunk? Max put on the oven gloves that were hanging from a hook on the wall and removed the lamb. 'It's supposed to rest for five minutes,' Sophie said thickly.

'Okay. How are your fingers?'

She turned off the tap and examined them. 'They'll be fine.' A silence. 'Thank you, Max.'

He glanced up at her. 'For what?'

'For looking after me.' She was gazing straight into his eyes.

'I'll always look after you,' he said, then wondered if he'd gone too far. He watched as she spooned the potatoes into a serving bowl. The air was dense and humid.

The silence stretched on until, without turning around, she finally said: 'I think it's probably been five minutes.'

He stood next to her at the countertop, where the shoulder of lamb was sweating pink blood into the moat around the wooden chopping board. As she stirred the flageolet beans and he picked up the carving knife, their hands accidentally brushed and all the hairs on Max's forearm pricked up. He thought he could see goosebumps on Sophie's arm too, the tiny hairs rising in unanimous salute: a forest of static, flesh drawing flesh, atoms magnetised, longing to merge.

Hans

The door opened and once again it was Édouard Kahn who stood there smiling, this time inviting Hans into his home. 'Come in, my dear Monsieur Schatten, so good to see you again!'

'Call me Hans, please.' Hans looked around for some sign of Sophie's presence.

'Sophie's just getting ready. Perhaps I should hurry her along?'

'Please don't,' Hans said hastily. 'I've waited six years to see her; I can wait a few more minutes.'

Édouard laughed at this, but there was something forced about his manner. 'Very true, very true.'

He showed Hans around the apartment. It was all exactly as he remembered it: the kitchen where their arms had touched, the dining room where they exchanged secret glances, the balcony where they drank wine together under the ivory moon. After so many dreams about this place, it felt uncanny to be here in real life. It was warm even with the breeze blowing through the open French windows, so Hans took off his jacket.

'Here, let me hang that up,' said Édouard. 'And may I take those bags for you?'

'Actually, they're gifts.' Hans lifted up the department store package. 'For you and—' He saw Sophie standing in the doorway looking at him and his words dried up.

'Ah, there you are, chérie! Come in, what are you waiting for? Your friend Hans is here. And he brought us presents!'

'Hello, Hans,' Sophie said coolly. She was wearing a sleeveless midnight-blue evening dress and her dark hair was pinned in a chignon. 'You really shouldn't have.'

Hans took a step towards her. 'Sophie, it's so good to see you again.' She held out her hand and let him shake it briefly. He wanted to hug her and breathe in the smell of her skin, the way Max had done with his Sophie when they'd met again on the stairs. But her face was blank, her body taut and self-contained, as if she were wearing an invisible suit of armour. There was an awkward silence as Édouard stared imploringly at his wife.

'Why don't I give you your presents?' Hans said, opening the package.

Édouard oohed and aahed as Hans handed out pipe tobacco and

cognac for monsieur, silk stockings and chocolates for madame. Sophie just gave a thin smile.

After opening the bottle of cognac and sniffing it approvingly, Édouard exclaimed: 'But how rude of me. I haven't offered our guest a drink. Sophie, why don't you take Hans out to the balcony while I fetch the champagne from the fridge?'

'Champagne? I thought we had to tighten our belts.'

'Sophie . . .'

'Anyway, I need to check on dinner. I'm sure our guest can wait a few minutes while you open the champagne.'

'Yes, of course,' said Hans. 'Would you mind if I looked at your library? I noticed you have an impressive collection of novels.'

'The novels are mostly Sophie's, the reference works mostly mine,' Édouard explained. 'But feel free to browse. And if anything catches your eye, you're welcome to borrow it.'

'Thank you.'

Hans went through to the living room, which was lined on two sides with fitted bookshelves. Straight ahead were the opened French windows and the balcony. Hans could hear the dusk chorus of birds perched on telegraph wires and rooftops. From behind him came the muffled duet of a conjugal row: the bass throb of Édouard's voice, soothing and reasoned, answered at irregular intervals by Sophie's piercing high notes. He rolled up his shirtsleeves as his gaze wandered over the shelves. He'd read several of these books through Max's eyes. Hans immediately searched out M for Maupassant and his finger traced the spines. Just then, Édouard entered the living room, holding two flutes of kir royale, one of which he handed to Hans. Sophie followed behind like a chastened child. They went out onto the balcony, where Édouard noticed the book in Hans's hand. 'Ah, what do you have there?'

'*Bel-Ami.*' The book that Max and his Sophie were reading

together. 'I was wondering if I might borrow it, Sophie?'

She shrugged. 'Help yourself.'

Hans nodded his thanks.

Inside the apartment, the telephone rang. 'I'll answer that,' Édouard told his wife. 'You stay and entertain Hans.' A look passed between them but Sophie didn't protest. Édouard went inside and Hans and Sophie were left alone on the balcony.

He couldn't stop staring at her. The lineaments of her face, her slender neck, her pretty ears, her bare shoulders: every part of her made his heart swell uncomfortably inside his chest. She turned to the primrose sky and Hans noticed her elegant hands tensed around the guardrail of the balcony, as though she feared he might try to push her off.

'Sophie, I'm sorry,' he said softly in German. 'Perhaps I shouldn't have come.'

For the first time her mask of hostility slipped and he glimpsed a hint of regret in her eyes. 'I'm sorry too. As I said in my letter, I would have—'

'Your letter?'

'You didn't receive it?'

'What did it say?' he asked, half-dreading the answer.

She took a breath. 'Just that you're right: you shouldn't have come. You were my friend before, Hans, and maybe one day you'll be my friend again. But things have changed.'

'But . . . I'm still me,' he murmured, echoing her words in his dream.

She ignored this and looked at the street below. Hans remembered standing down there a couple of weeks ago, imagining himself up here on this balcony, in her presence. It was not going the way he'd hoped. He took a sip of his drink then put the glass down on a table inside the apartment and stood next to her at the guardrail. 'Sophie, do you remember what you once wrote about building a bridge across the chasm that was opening between us?'

She rolled her eyes. 'We're not two teenagers writing letters to each other anymore, Hans. You're here—'

'I'm here because I want to protect you.'

She looked startled. 'To protect me?'

'And to see you again.' He turned to face her and reached out as if to touch her shoulder, before letting his hand drop to his side. 'I've missed you so much, Sophie. It's been a long time.'

'Six years,' she said, nodding. 'I remember it clearly, our last parting. You told me you'd leave the Hitler-Jugend.'

'I would have done to make you stay.'

'But you knew I couldn't, so it was an empty promise.'

'No, I meant it. I'd have done anything for you.'

'Instead you joined the SS.'

Hans sighed. 'What happened to not judging me?'

'*Judging you?*' she hissed. 'Like your Nazi friends judged Jens and his father? They're in a prison camp, did you know that?'

'I heard, yes.'

He wondered if Sophie was in touch with Jens now. She made it sound like she thought he was still a prisoner, but perhaps that was only for Hans's benefit.

'And what about Édouard? You do know my husband is a Jew? How can you—'

'Shhh.' Hans put his hand up. He'd heard something.

Down on the street below, an elderly couple were peering up at them curiously. Looking queasy, Sophie moved away from the edge of the balcony.

They heard Édouard's heavy tread across the living room and both looked away.

'So what have you two been chatting about?' he asked cheerily. 'Catching up on old times?'

'Something like that,' said Sophie.

'By the way, chérie, I didn't receive your report today. Did you forget to write it?'

Sophie's eyes flickered briefly towards Hans before she answered her husband. 'Yes, I must have forgotten. Sorry.'

'That's all right, you can tell me now.' Turning to Hans, Édouard explained: 'Sophie's afternoon dreams are always so lucid and revealing.'

'I don't remember,' Sophie said.

'Think! I'm sure it will come back to you. How did you feel when you woke? Were you angry? Sad? Excited?'

'I told you, I don't remember. The lamb must be ready by now. I have to go.'

'I'll help you,' Hans said.

It was hot in the kitchen and when Sophie opened the oven door a puff of steam rolled over her face, scenting the air with garlic and roasting flesh.

'You dreamed about *me*, didn't you?' he said in a gentle voice.

She turned on him, eyes raw with fury. Or was it shock? Perhaps he'd guessed right. 'My dreams are none of your business,' she said, reaching out to pick up the metal tray.

'Wait!' Hans called, and he grabbed her wrists before she could touch the burning steel. For a moment their bare forearms were entwined, moist with steam and sweat, all the hairs rising in a forest of static. Their eyes met. Hans swallowed. 'You forgot your oven gloves.'

NOVEMBER

Hans

Outside in the darkness, rain lashed the windows. Inside, Hans and Sophie sat side by side on matching chairs in front of the fireplace and talked about *The Red and the Black*. They'd both finished it the night before and now they were comparing notes, arguing about the reason for Madame de Rênal's death. 'I'm confused,' said Sophie archly. 'I thought her shoulder was healing nicely. I mean, surely she didn't die of a broken heart . . .'

'Of course she died of a broken heart!' Hans protested, feigning outrage. 'My God, you're so unromantic.'

'How can I be unromantic? I'm a woman.'

Sophie crossed her legs and Hans made an effort not to stare. She was wearing the burgundy wool dress he'd bought her last week and the silk stockings he'd given her on his first visit. 'Women aren't always more romantic than men,' said Hans. 'Anyway, I love Madame de Rênal. She was so sweet and devoted. Julien didn't deserve her.'

'Well, I agree with you there. I thought Julien was despicable.'

'Despicable?' Hans laughed. 'That's a little harsh.'

'You're right, I shouldn't be so judgemental.' Hans sensed that their exchange had lost its flirtatious, bantering tone. He searched her face for clues. 'Sitting here in front of a coal fire with a member of the occupying forces while my husband is asleep. Who am I to call anyone else despicable?'

Hans sighed. 'Sophie . . .'

'Sorry, did I ruin things again? If only I could just forget about the real world out there.' She gestured at the blackness beyond the

French windows. He couldn't tell if she was being sarcastic or sincere.

The fire was dying. Hans got out of his seat, knelt in front of the hearth and added a few lumps of coal from the scuttle.

'Don't waste it,' said Sophie. 'I need to go to bed soon anyway.'

'Not yet,' Hans murmured to the fire. 'And it's not a waste. I can bring you more coal next month.'

He felt her hand touch his shoulder. He held very still. 'I'm glad you're here, Hans. It's just . . .'

'You feel guilty. I understand.' He turned and raised an eyebrow. 'I *am* the Serpent, after all.'

Sophie smiled, embarrassed. Back in August, after a spiky discussion of *Bel-Ami* had mutated into an argument about the precise nature of their friendship, she had shown Hans a poem she'd written about him. It was quite long, and not all of it was openly hostile, but a few lines had imprinted themselves on Hans's memory: *you are the serpent/ slowly coiling itself/ around my life . . ./ will you puncture my skin/ with your venomous fangs/ or gently strangle me/ till I resist/ no more?* He'd been shocked by this image. Who did she think he was, the devil? But the following week he'd made her laugh by reciting the poem in a sinister voice and Sophie had admitted that it was perhaps a little overwrought. The Serpent had been a running joke between them ever since.

Hans stood up and took the half-empty bottle of wine from the dresser. He went over to fill Sophie's glass but she placed her hand over it. 'No more for me, thank you. There's something I have to tell you.'

'Sounds serious,' said Hans in a light-hearted voice.

'It is.'

'All right.' He cleared his expression of all traces of amusement. 'Why don't we lie on the rug and look at the ceiling, like we used to.'

'We used to lie on my bed,' she said, although she got off her chair and lay down next to him anyway.

'I know, but I didn't think you'd want me to—'

'You were right.'

He gazed up at the ceiling, where glimmers of orange firelight flickered in the gloom. 'I'm so glad you're back in my life, Sophie. I've never been able to talk with anyone else the way I talk with you.' Hans waited in the lengthening silence. He hadn't planned to say any of that and now he was wondering if he had overstepped the mark. He didn't dare glance sideways so he had no idea of the expression on her face.

At last, in a low voice, she said: 'Ich auch.'

Hans exhaled with relief. He moved his right hand until the back of it brushed against the back of Sophie's left hand. The cold pressure of her wedding ring against his skin.

'I took part in that protest march today at the war memorial,' she said.

'Oh, Sophie . . .'

She moved her hand away from his. 'You sound as disapproving as Édouard.'

'I'm not disapproving, just concerned. I don't want you to get hurt.'

'It was a peaceful demonstration. We were there to honour the young men and women who died in the last war. And in this one.'

'Not many have died in this one,' Hans pointed out. 'They had the good sense to surrender.'

'Your colleagues arrested people at the march, did you know that? They took them away in their vans. For waving French flags and singing the "Marseillaise".'

'I didn't know, but—'

'What will happen to them, Hans?'

'I imagine they'll be released, if that's all they did.'

'Really?' Her voice sounded so full of hope. She turned to face him and he looked into her eyes. He could fall into that soft, bare gaze of hers . . .

'Yes, really,' he said. 'We're not monsters, you know.'

Max

He took the violin from its case and cradled it on his shoulder. Max hadn't played since being forced to sell his Klotz in Vienna more than two years ago, yet it was only now that he realised how intensely he'd missed it. The instrument belonged there, he thought, nestling his chin against the rest; it was as if a missing part of his body had been restored.

The violin was an old Lupot. Max had found it by chance at a brocante in the sixth arrondissement and had known as soon as he set eyes on it that he had to possess it. Prices had gone up dramatically since the occupation, and he had not been able to bargain the vendor down to less than a thousand francs. This had meant asking Édouard to give him an advance on next month's wages, an indulgence that had embarrassed Max and clearly pained his employer. Still, it was all worth it now, he thought, stroking the bow over the strings.

A loose shutter banged in the wind. Max blew on his fingers to warm them. He was wearing his coat over two sweaters and a shirt. The only time he ever felt warm these days was in his dreams.

He put the violin on his bed and leafed through some sheet music. He chose a simple Bach sonata and began to play. He'd forgotten what a relief it was to pour his emotions through those recurring patterns of minims and semiquavers, the music rising like a cloud around him.

Throughout August, September and October he and Sophie had

spent every morning together, sitting on café terraces and inventing dreams, lying side by side in parks and talking about books, constantly almost but never quite kissing. Then, two weeks ago, Édouard had told them he had all the dreams he needed: Sophie could return to her domestic duties while Max helped him analyse and interpret the data. So for the first time in months Sophie and Max hardly saw each other all day and were never alone together for a moment. Her absence from his life was a hollow ache. But as his right hand swayed and caressed, as the fingers of his left found their marks with growing fluidity, Max sensed the sadness slowly melting, flowing outward, leaving him lightened.

When it was over, he looked up and saw Sophie standing in the doorway. Her eyes were wet, the pupils magnified. 'I wish I had a piano so I could play with you again.'

'Ich auch,' Max said.

She sat on the bed next to him. 'Remember the duets we played at Jens's house?'

'Yes. We were good together.'

'We still are.'

Their eyes met, vertiginous, electric.

'I love you,' Max said without meaning to, and she kissed him on the mouth. Miraculously, it was the same kiss as before, under the oak tree in the Volksgarten, before the Anschluss, before Édouard Kahn, time spiralling back in on itself, restoring them to that lost paradise.

'Sophie? Sophie! Where are you?' Édouard's voice boomed from the hallway. 'I can smell something burning in the kitchen!'

With a sigh Sophie withdrew her lips and pressed her forehead against Max's. 'J'arrive,' she called out, her breath warm on his chin. She pulled away just in time.

The door opened and Édouard stepped inside. 'There you are.' He eyed them curiously. 'What are you two doing in here?'

Max's mouth opened but no sound came out. His throat was tight with guilt.

'Max was showing me his violin,' Sophie said calmly.

'Hmph. Seems like a waste of good money to me.'

'You should hear him play before you say that.'

'Yes, yes, I'm sure you're right. But please come to the kitchen, chérie! I would rather not eat ashes for dinner.'

Édouard stomped away. Sophie and Max stood up. He started towards the door, but she put a hand on his chest to stop him. 'Listen,' she whispered. 'I have an idea. For how we might be able to see each other.'

Hans

The Konferenzraum was almost full. Uniformed men sat in rows of wooden chairs, smoking cigarettes and chatting. Hans took a seat in the third row. A fist thumped the lectern and he looked up. Obersturmführer Dannecker opened the meeting with a detailed account of the protest march. He talked in a dry monotone and Hans found himself stroking the folded piece of paper inside his jacket pocket. He wished he could take it out now to see Sophie's familiar handwriting. He hadn't yet memorised the entire poem but he knew the final stanza by heart: *last night I dreamed/ that you being here/ was only a dream/ and I should have been relieved/ but when I woke/ I felt bereaved.* She hadn't even mentioned the poem to him: he'd found it in his pocket when he got home from Rue des Princes. She must have slipped it in there as she was handing him his jacket.

'I propose, therefore,' Dannecker said, jerking Hans back to the present, 'that we execute twenty of the ringleaders. Your opinions, gentlemen?'

There were a few murmurs of assent. 'Why not all of them?' shouted Geier, prompting a burst of laughter.

Before Hans knew what he was doing, the words were out of his mouth. 'Is that really necessary, Obersturmführer?'

A hum of surprise filled the Konferenzraum. Dannecker glared at him. He had a bland face, its only notable features being the sour mouth and frowning brows, but when he was irritated those two elements combined to produce a remarkably unpleasant expression.

'Pipe down, Schatten, you Schlappschwanz!' Geier jeered.

'No, no, it takes guts to question one's superior,' said Dannecker, although the look on his face suggested more annoyance than admiration. 'Tell me, Schatten, why you think it unnecessary to punish insurrection.'

'With respect, Obersturmführer, it was a peaceful march in honour of the nation's war dead.'

Geier intervened again: 'They waved French flags and sang the "Marseillaise". It's obvious we can't tolerate that kind of thing. It would only embolden them.'

His words were met with a few grunts of agreement. Hans thought about backing down but he didn't want to face Sophie without having at least tried to save those men's lives. Heart racing, he stood up. 'My point is that we've worked hard in the last few months to win the trust of the French. I'm afraid that, if we execute people for such a mild infraction, we risk losing that goodwill.' Hans could hear jeers from behind but he noticed that Dannecker was nodding thoughtfully, so he went on: 'The Führer himself has said that Paris must be treated with respect because the eyes of the world are upon us. We have an opportunity here to show that we are civilised men, not monsters.'

Hans sat down and the room erupted in debate. Dannecker thumped the lectern again and the men fell silent. 'That was well argued, Schatten,' he said graciously. 'I propose therefore that we execute only ten of the ringleaders. Thoughts?'

Suddenly Hans felt unwell. He shuffled past several pairs of grey-trousered, outstretched legs and escaped into the corridor. Sweat was pouring from his temples. In the sanctuary of the bathroom he took deep breaths and splashed cold water over his face. A few minutes later Geier came in.

'That was not a clever move,' he said to Hans's reflection. 'You know, there were rumours about you, Schatten, even before this incident.'

'What rumours?'

Geier went to the urinal and began to piss. 'One person told me that you got your scars when you were tortured by the Gestapo for being a queer,' he shouted over the sound of the splashing water.

'Horseshit!' Hans scoffed. 'I was in a car accident. Is that the best you can do?'

Geier, buttoning up his fly, smiled mockingly as if acknowledging the absurdity of this story. 'I also heard a rumour that you're a Jew,' he said, walking over to the sink to wash his hands. After a horrifying silence Geier laughed and Hans forced himself to laugh too. Thankfully Geier wasn't looking at the mirror so he didn't see how white Hans's face had turned. 'Frankly, though, Schatten, if you keep taking the enemy's side, people will start to believe shit like that.'

Max

At nine o'clock Max crept through the corridor and knocked lightly three times on the door. It opened with a click and he found himself in a candlelit storeroom. Sophie had told her husband she was going to the storeroom to knit the sweater she would be giving him for Christmas, but as far as Max could tell the room was devoid of wool and needles. The only objects he could make out in the gloom were the bicycles leaning against the far wall, a small cupboard in one corner, and a radio set buzzing and squawking senselessly on a low table in front of a love seat. Sophie locked the door again and sat down. 'Come on, quick, he's already started.'

'He?'

'Churchill. And he's speaking French!' Sophie pulled a blanket over their legs and nuzzled the top of her head into the crook of Max's neck. 'The enemy try to jam the signal but you can still make out quite a bit usually.'

Between blizzards of static and electrical whirs and squeals, Max gradually began to discern the Englishman's slowly spoken, strangely pronounced words.

'. . . at home in England, under the fire of . . .'

Sophie's hand squeezed his then guided it between her knees.

'. . . London, which Herr Hitler says he will reduce to ashes . . .'

His fingertips climbed a ladder in her stockings.

'. . . are waiting for the long-promised invasion. So are the fishes . . .'

Sophie laughed, very quietly – he felt it more than he heard it, her lips vibrating softly against his collarbone, her breath warm on his skin.

'. . . how Napoleon said before one of his battles . . .'

He caressed the skin of her inner thighs, soft as sifted flour, and heard her sigh.

'. . . never will I believe that the soul of France is dead . . .'

Her body twisted round, her dress hitched up, her right leg stretched across his left. The blanket fell to the floor as she kissed him on the mouth.

'. . . we shall never stop, never weary, and never give in . . .'

Her tongue lapping his, two flames in blackness, a gasp as his fingers parted silk from wet flesh.

'. . . seek to beat the life and soul out of Hitler and . . .'

Her fingers unbuckling, unzipping, gripping, stroking, and his fingers inside her, thumb rubbing the swollen nub of her clitoris and the radio blaring a hurricane of shrieks and sizzles and howls, a crescendo of white noise as they came in unison and Sophie said his name over and over again into his ear: 'Oh Max, oh Max, oh Max, oh Max.'

And then a long silent sighing fall. 'Good night, then,' growled Churchill as the buzzing faded, the German censors apparently tired after their jamming exertions. 'Sleep to gather strength for the morning.'

Sophie wiped her hands on a handkerchief then handed it to Max. She leaned down to turn off the radio and in the silence they kissed again. Eventually she pulled away. 'I should probably go to bed.'

Why did we ever stop kissing?

'Yes. I know.'

She stood up and smoothed her dress down while Max buckled his belt.

'If the coast is clear, I'll knock twice.' She blew out the candles and all he could see of her was a reddish silhouette in the black.

'Sophie . . .'

She stepped closer and whispered, 'Yes?'

'I don't want it to be like this. I want—'

'I know,' she said gently.

'Then why don't you tell him? Tell him how you feel about me. You could leave him, we could find an apartment somewhere.'

She crouched down beside him. 'But how would we pay for it, Max?'

'I could get another job. We'd manage. It might not be easy, but—'

'Édouard would report you to the authorities. You'd go to prison.

He's already told me he suspects you of being a résistant. He thinks we should evict you and tell the Gestapo about you.' Sophie said all this in a soft, mournful voice but Max felt the words like punches. He had thought Édouard liked him. He couldn't speak.

She squeezed his hand in the darkness. Seconds later, he heard the door click open and shut.

Hans

The two men sipped their digestifs in silence. It had been at least fifteen minutes since Sophie had excused herself to visit the bathroom. Édouard looked nervously at his watch. 'I'm sorry, Hans, I can't imagine what Sophie's been doing all this time.' Hans could but thought it wiser not to say so. 'I would also like to apologise for her rudeness towards you this evening. I'm afraid she overreacts to the news sometimes.'

So she'd heard about the executions; Hans had feared as much. 'Perhaps you'll let me talk to her alone when she comes back? If we speak German, I might be able to explain things more easily.'

'Of course, my dear Hans, if that's what you want. I fear she's very stubborn, though.'

'Sophie is principled,' Hans said. 'I admire her for that.'

When Sophie returned, Édouard duly made his excuses and went to bed. She stared coldly at Hans across the table. He sighed. 'For what it's worth, I didn't agree with the decision to execute those protesters. In fact I spoke out against it.'

'I'm sure that will be a great comfort to the dead men's families.'

He wanted to tell her the truth – that he'd saved ten men's lives, at some cost to his reputation in the office – but he knew it would make no difference. Ten men had been killed, that was the reality. 'My boss showed me the files of the people they shot, though, and they weren't quite as innocent as you seem to imagine.' This, too, was true. Hans had gone to see Dannecker to ask him privately if the death sentences might be commuted and Dannecker had shown him the mug shots, the police records, the Communist Party membership cards. Of course Dannecker could have been lying or exaggerating, but . . . 'They were criminals, Sophie. Extremists, ex-cons.'

'You sound like the Nazi newspapers.'

'You shouldn't believe everything you hear on the BBC.'

She flinched, then looked defiant. 'How did you know?'

'About the BBC?' Hans shrugged. 'I didn't. But the last two times I've been here, you've disappeared around nine o'clock, so it seemed likely.'

'Will you report me?'

'Of course not. I'm your friend. Don't you know that?'

She looked down at the table and shook her head. 'Friend or foe? It's not that simple anymore, Hans. Nothing is.'

He leaned across the table and kissed her, furiously, passionately. She started to kiss him back. Then he stroked her face and she jerked away as if he'd slapped her.

'Please leave.' She eyed him with an intensity that might have been love or, just as easily, hate. When he didn't move, she said: 'You have to go.'

His heart was still fluttering, cartwheeling madly from the kiss, and he found it impossible to process what she was saying. 'But—'

'I can't do this anymore. Leave, Hans. Now.'

'I love you, Sophie.'

'*Go.*' It was almost a scream: loud enough to alert her husband, to wake the neighbours. He stood up, shaking slightly.

'All right,' Hans said, defeated. 'If that's what you want.'

And he left.

DECEMBER

Max

Small blue sparks crackled as Sophie pulled the wool dress over her head. She was naked underneath, her body all shadows and gold in the candlelight. The static made her hair rise in odd shapes then fall over her face. She leaned down to kiss Max, who lay naked on the love seat, while beside them the radio hissed: 'Ici Londres. Les Français parlent aux Français . . .'

They had done this almost every night for the past three weeks, bringing each other to orgasm with their fingers or tongues as news of the war mingled with wails of interference and the little gasps and moans that escaped their joined mouths. Afterwards Max would go to his room and play the violin, to articulate his longings and fears and – every Thursday and Sunday, regular as clockwork – to drown out the sound of the conjugal bedframe banging against the wall. God, he hated that sound. Sophie assured him that she hated the act too, that she didn't want her husband to touch her or even share her bed. 'But if we stop having sex, he'll know something's wrong. He'll suspect us and that will ruin everything. You understand, don't you, Max?'

Max told her he understood but he didn't really. He would watch Édouard Kahn every day – in the mornings, taking his copy of *Le Matin* into the bathroom so he could read the latest Vichy propaganda while he took a shit; in the office, idly picking wax from his ear as he asked Max to translate the latest issue of the *Zentralblatt für Psychoanalyse* – and feel only repulsion, wondering how Sophie could even bear to breathe the same air as this man. When he and Sophie had first started kissing behind her husband's back, Max had felt sorry for Édouard. But that was before he learned that his employer wanted to hand him over to the Nazis. In Max's dreams, Édouard was fawning and submissive, all too eager to leave his wife alone with Hauptscharführer Schatten, and as Sophie pressed her lips to Max's neck, his collarbone, his nipples, his tensed stomach muscles, as Max held his breath to stop himself making any noises that might betray them, he found himself wishing *he* was a Nazi officer, with the power to act as he wished.

Just then, the door handle rattled. Max and Sophie froze. They peered through the darkness at the door. A few seconds later came a flurry of loud knocks and Édouard bellowed: 'Sophie, let me in! I know what you two are up to in there. I won't allow it in my home.'

Sophie and Max sprang apart and began getting dressed. Max wondered if Sophie's dream about the sandy desk had been prophetic.

Édouard hammered at the door again. 'Sophie, open this door! I know you're in there.' She pulled the dress over her head as Max frantically buttoned his shirt. 'Open up this instant or I swear I'll—'

Sophie opened the door and Édouard nearly fell into the room. He stared wildly at his wife standing in front of him, at his employee sitting nervously on the love seat, and finally at the radio set still burbling away on the coffee table. 'Turn that damned thing off!' he barked. 'How dare you? Listening to the BBC is against the law. I said turn it *off*!' Sophie twisted the knob at the front of the radio and it fell silent. Édouard picked it up in both hands and carted it out of the room. Max and Sophie looked at each other incredulously, then laughed with relief.

A minute later Édouard returned and ordered Sophie to give him the key to the storeroom door.

'Édouard, I'm sorry,' she said. 'It won't happen again, I promise.'

'The key,' he repeated, holding out his hand.

Sophie handed it to him.

'Now get out,' he said contemptuously.

Max felt a flare of anger. Édouard shouldn't talk to Sophie like that. He got to his feet and said: 'Hang on a—'

Édouard turned to Max and said coldly: 'You too. Out of this room now or you can find a new place to live.'

Max and Sophie filed out like two naughty schoolchildren. They watched as Édouard locked the door and pocketed the key.

Hans

Three weeks had passed since Sophie had ordered Hans to leave her apartment, two since he'd sent her the gift, and still he hadn't heard from her. Of course he'd told her in the letter that he did not expect anything in return, that he just wanted her to be happy, and that was true. But deep down he had hoped for something. A thank-you note. A telephone call. A kiss.

Life might be easier if he could give up hope, Hans thought, but it clung to him no matter what he did. Every evening he walked from the office on Avenue Foch to his apartment building on Rue Orphée and as he unlocked the door to the lobby he told himself there would be nothing from Sophie in the letterbox. And every time he opened the box he felt hope expand to fill the hollowness inside him, then turn to dust as he found the box empty. That night, the same thing happened: he warned himself not to hope, he hoped, he opened the box, and . . .

A letter lay inside the metal container. He pulled it out and examined the handwriting on the envelope. *Her* handwriting.

Hans ran upstairs and let himself into his apartment. It was cold, small, impersonal. He went to the living room, sat on the couch. And with trembling fingers he opened the envelope and unfolded the single page.

Dear Hans,

I have written this letter so many times, only to throw it away. I've never felt so torn in my life. The gift you sent me is beautiful, the most thoughtful thing anyone has ever given me, and I wanted to thank you as soon as it arrived. I wanted to hold you, kiss you, tell you how much I love you. Which is why I made myself wait. Because I didn't trust my emotions. Nothing had really changed, after all.

So what has changed now? Time, I suppose. Three weeks without hearing from you, seeing your face, being able to talk to you. Hans, I can't stop crying. I've told Édouard that it's 'women's problems', which is usually enough to send him running in the opposite direction, but I think even he is growing suspicious. I try to read books but it's not the same, knowing that I won't be able to share my impressions with you.

Can you forgive me or have I waited too long? Perhaps you've found somebody else by now. I would be heartbroken if you had, but it would also be a relief: to know that this love of ours truly is impossible.

If you still want to see me, come to my apartment at seven o'clock tomorrow evening. Édouard is staying with his parents in Neuilly-sur-Seine for a few days so I'll be alone. If you don't come, I will know that everything is over between us. If you do come, bring your violin.

S.

Hans read the letter three times, lingering over that miraculous phrase 'this love of ours', then closed his eyes with relief. Tomorrow. He would see her again in twenty-four hours. It seemed an eternity.

The day after the confrontation in the storeroom, it was as if nothing had ever happened. Or perhaps that wasn't true. It was more as if Édouard, having triumphed over his wife and employee, had decided to act magnanimously. During dinner he praised Sophie's cooking and Max's latest translation, and when the meal was over he told Sophie: 'I have a surprise for you, chérie. That Bavarian major I've been analysing gave me some coal, so we can sit by the fire tonight. How does that sound?'

'It sounds nice,' Sophie replied stiffly.

'Perhaps Max could play for us?' Édouard said. 'You keep telling me how good he is.'

Max went to fetch his violin while Édouard lit the fire. As Max tuned the instrument, Édouard announced that he was going to open a bottle of 1933 Bordeaux that the major had given him and he went to the kitchen to find it. As soon as he was out of earshot, Max hissed: 'What's he playing at?'

'I don't know.' Sophie stepped close to Max and touched his arm. 'Let's just go along with it.'

'I feel like he's luring us into a trap. Do you think he knows?'

'I don't think so.' She frowned. 'Just do what he asks and stay calm, okay?'

Édouard was whistling a popular tune as he re-entered the living room. It took Max a few seconds to recognise the song. It was 'Wishing (Will Make It So)' by Glenn Miller and His Orchestra, from the film *Love Affair*. Max tensed as he realised this. It could be a coincidence, of course, but . . .

'What are you going to play for us, Max?' Édouard asked, sitting on the couch by the stove. He patted the seat beside him and Sophie obediently sat down. He put his arm around her and pulled her close.

'Mozart,' Max said. And he played the first part of the same violin sonata that he and Jens – and, in his dreams, Hans and Sophie – had played at the spring concert six years earlier, trying not to watch as Sophie's husband smirkingly fondled her.

'Bravo!' cried Édouard when it was over.

'It's better as a duet with piano,' Max said sullenly.

'Nevertheless, it was very good.'

Max nodded and put his violin back in its case.

'And what will you do now?' Édouard asked.

'Go to my room and study, I suppose.'

'Don't you think you deserve a night off? You've been working so hard recently.' Was he being sarcastic? 'You know, when we first met each other, Max, you used to go out and seduce a new girl every week. What happened?'

In fact there had only been three girls. At the time Max had hoped they might cure him of his obsession with Sophie, or at least sting her into jealousy.

Max shrugged. 'I wanted something more meaningful.' He looked at Sophie as he said this but she wouldn't meet his eye.

Édouard adjusted his glasses. 'What you need, my young friend, is a wife.'

Yes, Max thought. Yours.

'Wives are wonderful things,' Édouard added, pressing his mouth against Sophie's neck. Was he drunk? This display of public affection – or *possession*, rather – was not like him at all. Or perhaps he was simply torturing them. Sophie closed her eyes as her husband kissed her on the mouth. She didn't struggle or complain. And it was a Thursday, so tonight, Max knew, he would again have to listen to Édouard Kahn doing to his wife what she had never let Max do. Meanwhile the other Sophie had invited Hans to her apartment while her husband was away. And why? Because he could afford to buy her nice things? Jaw clenched, Max put his violin back in its case and slammed the lid shut. 'Maybe I will go out,' he said.

'Excellent!' said Édouard.

Sophie stared pleadingly at Max but he turned away. As he put on his coat in the entrance hall, he heard Édouard say: 'We have the apartment to ourselves at last, chérie . . .'

Hans

It was snowing as Hans made the short walk to Sophie's apartment. A pair of dim, blue-tinted headlights moved through the almost silent darkness. On the corner of Rue des Princes a gendarme stopped Hans and asked to see his papers. Hans flashed his SS badge and the gendarme saluted respectfully. Outside the red door of number 10 he pressed the bell for 3a.

Hans climbed the marble stairs, adrenaline flooding his chest. The apartment door had been left off the latch. He went inside and heard piano music. Walking through the dining room, he recognised the tune: it was the same Mozart sonata they'd played together at the spring concert all those years ago.

In the living room the stove was lit and Sophie was wearing a sleeveless, backless dress. A dozen candles burned in different parts of the room, and in the flickering dimness Hans felt as if he were about to step inside a painting. Her hair was in a chignon and she was sitting at the piano he'd bought for her, fingers travelling lightly across the keyboard. Hans admired her naked back, her swanlike neck. She knew he was there, he could tell, but she continued playing. He took off his jacket, hung it on the back of a chair, and took his violin from its case.

Hans began to play, a smooth stream flowing over a pebble bed. The tendons in Sophie's neck fluttered beneath her skin and he watched as a few dark hairs slipped loose and curled over her exposed nape.

Max

Rue Lepic sloped up ahead of him, a thin strip of neon in the Paris dark. A dense crowd filled the street. Bars and clubs on either side spilled saxophone blare, snare-drum rattle, double-bass throb. In the falling snow it was hard to tell at first, but Max tensed as he got closer and saw grey uniforms, heard German voices. Evidently the street was a Nazi hangout.

He almost turned back but he couldn't stand the thought of returning to Rue des Princes and hearing the woman he loved having sex with a man he hated. Seeing Sophie in Édouard's arms had put Max in a reckless mood. What did it matter if he was arrested? At least it would make her realise what she'd let slip through her fingers.

Towards the upper end of the street the crowds thinned out and Max found a bar that suited his mood: the Café Bleu, a gloomy little place with no more than a dozen clients, none in uniform. On stage a band was playing mournful jazz under a blue spotlight. There were four musicians: a pianist and a drummer, invisible in the shadows, a tall black man on double bass, and a young white trumpeter. Max didn't recognise the song but there was something oddly familiar about the way the pianist played, something almost classical in his phrasing. Max ordered a glass of red wine at the bar and took a seat at one of the tables near the stage.

For the next hour he sat there sipping his wine (supposedly a Bordeaux, although it tasted more like vinegar), nodding his head to the music and thinking about Sophie. He was starting to worry that he'd been unfair, leaving her at the mercy of her husband. The band played 'St James Infirmary' and the bass player sang the words in a voice like Louis Armstrong's. Max remembered Jens playing this song on the night of the Anschluss and felt a pang of loneliness.

When the song was over, the bass player announced in American-accented French that they were going to take a break, and Max decided it was time to leave. But when he saw the pianist walk across the stage, something about his gait caught Max's attention. The man was tall and thin, dressed in a cheap suit, his hair cut short. He was hurrying after the trumpet player, calling: 'Hé, Benoît, c'était nul, ton solo!' That accent. That voice. It was so dark in the club that he could hardly see the man's face. Max stood up as he approached and peered at him through the gloom. The pianist noticed and scowled back: 'What are you looking at?'

'Jens?'

The pianist stopped dead. His scowl vanished. 'Max? Oh my God!' He was speaking German now and Max sensed a few faces turning in their direction. He put a hand on Jens's arm and muttered in French: 'Let's go somewhere quieter.'

Jens nodded and led him over to a booth on the other side of the room. The drummer and the trumpet player were there too. 'An old friend,' Jens explained to them in an undertone. 'Could we have a moment? Oh, and ask Yvette to bring me a drink . . .' Without a word the two musicians headed towards the bar.

'It's so good to see you, Jens. You haven't changed a bit!'

'You have,' said Jens, eyeing Max curiously.

They fell silent for a moment as the waitress placed a glass of amber liquid in front of Jens. When she'd gone, they clinked glasses.

Max wanted to tell his friend how much he had missed him, how deeply he regretted his reaction after the kiss, but he felt inhibited with all these other people around. In the end, sounding ludicrously formal, he just said: 'So tell me, what are you doing in Paris?'

Jens shrugged. 'Playing jazz, as you can see.'

'But you were going to Zurich the last I heard. Surely it's safer there . . .'

'True, but it was also more boring. I think jazz might actually be illegal in Switzerland.'

'You made it out of Austria without any problems, then?'

'Yeah. It wasn't the most joyous escape, though. I think Charlotte cried most of the way. Nine solid hours of sniffling and sobbing. Thanks for that, by the way.'

Max smiled sadly and said: 'I'm sorry, Jens. For everything. I—'

'Don't get maudlin on me, Max. It's all in the past. You could have ignored me tonight, but you didn't. That's enough for me.'

There was a silence. Max drank some wine. 'How is Charlotte now?'

'She's married.'

'*Married?*'

'To a complete bore, obviously. I think she chose the most boring man she could find so there'd be no possibility of him getting bored of her! Oh, and she's studying for a physics degree, although she's going to have to take a year off because she's just found out she's pregnant.'

Max shook his head incredulously. So much had happened in such a short time. 'Is she happy?'

'Yeah, she's over you now, don't worry. She and I had some good talks after your break-up. She became almost interesting for a while. But it was never going to last.'

'And your parents, how are they?'

'My mother's fine. My father is . . . not the man he used to be. Health problems.'

'I'm sorry to hear that. He's a good man. Do . . . do they ever talk about me?'

Jens laughed then, hard and loud. 'Oh, Max! You really don't want to know what they said about you.' Max looked distraught and Jens laughed even harder. 'I'm kidding!' he said. 'Well, mostly. They were angry for a while, of course, but they still love you. Honestly, they'll be thrilled when I tell them I've seen you. They were afraid you might not get out in time. So how *did* you get out? And how are things now?' He peered into Max's eyes, like a doctor examining a patient. 'You're in love, aren't you?'

'How did you know?'

'I don't know, you seem . . . sadder. Almost fully human, in fact. Don't tell me you got your heart broken?'

'I—'

'You found Sophie.'

'What, are you a mind-reader now?'

Jens smiled. 'It wasn't that hard to guess. No one else ever had that effect on you. So I take it she's still married to Dr Édouard Kunt?'

This time Max could barely muster a smile. He poured his heart out to Jens about everything that had happened since he first rang the doorbell of the Rue des Princes apartment at the start of the war: his estrangement from Sophie, their growing closeness, their secret assignations, and the most recent developments.

'Yeah, love's a bitch,' Jens said after Max had described the hollow, black melancholy he'd felt walking up Rue Lepic. 'Now you know how Charlotte and I felt.'

He said it in his usual ironic, offhand tone, but Max guessed at deeper sufferings below the surface. He wanted to touch Jens's shoulder or squeeze his leg in sympathy, but he was afraid his friend might take it for pity. Then something occurred to him: 'Hang on, how come *you* didn't find Sophie? You had her address, didn't you?'

Jens looked sheepish. 'I thought about it, but it wouldn't have been the same. We'd have just ended up talking about you all the time, making each other miserable. And if you *had* been in Paris, well . . . I thought it might be awkward, seeing you again.'

'I'm glad it's not,' Max said.

'Ich auch.' Jens glanced at the bar. His bandmates were finishing their drinks and standing up. 'You'll stay for our last set, won't you? I play a solo on "Summertime", which is obviously the highlight of the night.'

Afterwards Jens invited him to a back room where a carafe of (more drinkable) wine and a plate of bread, cheese and saucisson was laid out for them. 'Gérard, the owner, always feeds us after a performance,' Jens explained. 'I told him I needed a little privacy tonight.' An uncertain look passed between the two friends and Jens burst out laughing. 'Don't worry, I'm not trying to seduce you! I've learned my lesson on that one. Have some saucisson, it's not bad. Gérard's parents have a farm in the Zone Libre.'

'Mmm, that *is* good. I'd almost forgotten what real food tastes like.'

'Yeah, the Germans have really ruined French cuisine. If there's one thing I miss from Zurich, it's my mother's cooking.'

'Ah yes, her Sachertorte . . .'

They began reminiscing. For Max it was overpowering, seeing Jens again, reliving all those long summers spent at the country house, the intimate conversations in the dark of the garden, the casually magnificent meals, the endless sunlit afternoons on the lake . . . It made him ache with nostalgia, remembering all he had lost and would never know again.

When the food and wine were gone, Jens gave a contented burp. He looked at his watch. 'Shit, it's two in the morning! You should stay here tonight. You don't want to be walking down Rue Lepic after curfew, believe me.'

Jens spent a few minutes cursing the Nazis, then recalled the night he and Max became friends, in the Augarten, after being chased by Bauer and his Hitler-Jugend comrades. The two of them laughed hysterically as Jens imitated the look on Bauer's face after Max bit his hand. 'I still can't believe you did that. You're the bravest bastard I've ever known in my life, Max Spiegelman.'

'No, just the most stupid.'

Jens's expression grew sober. 'Actually, there's something I wanted to talk to you about.' He leaned across the table and spoke in a whisper. 'I belong to a group of people here who are fighting against the regime. We call ourselves the Knights of Liberty . . .'

Max, who was still in a state of mild hysteria, collapsed into giggles at this. 'The Knights of Liberty!'

Jens rolled his eyes. 'It sounds better in French.'

Max pounded the table and howled.

Jens gripped his arm and stared into his eyes. 'Max, listen, this is serious. Someone has to stand up to those cunts. You and I know that better than anyone. Eventually, if we stay here, they'll round us up and kill us. So what do we have to lose? And we could use a brave idiot like you . . .'

Hans

They played the last phrase together and the chord slowly faded to silence. Hans put his violin down and moved towards her. She sat motionless on the piano stool, arms by her side, her bare back facing him. Hans touched the backs of his fingers to her neck and gently ran his hand down her spine, a descending scale on the vertebrae. Sophie shivered but didn't turn around.

In a few seconds or minutes they would kiss again. Hans thought about their first kiss, all those years ago, after practising their duet at the Schattens' house. Remembering the nursery rhyme Sophie had played that day, he leaned his chin lightly on her shoulder and picked out the simple notes on the keyboard. Her cheek lay cool against his and he felt her smile. She started to sing – 'gently down the stream, merrily, merrily, merrily, merrily . . .' – and Hans remembered a beautiful dream he'd once had: sunlight, a lake, strawberry wine. He remembered seeing Sophie's hands skipping across the Bösendorfer's keyboard, making the same shapes that his were now, hearing this melody muffled by the shopfront window. He remembered falling asleep at the top of the stairs, listening to his mother play this tune, and he caught a glimpse of something: a meaning, a trajectory. A way to close the circle. The song, the girl, and . . . death. Hans had actually been glad to have Max back in his life during the past six months – that presence inside had made him feel less lonely, more complete – but what if Max had to die before Hans could fulfil his destiny? Was that why God had sent them both to Paris, why Max had agreed to join a resistance net-work? Hans and Max; Abraham and Isaac. It would also explain why things were going wrong between Max and his Sophie while – suddenly, joyously, finally – everything was perfect in his own world. Hans felt a twinge of pity, but not for long. God knows he had earned his victory. He had suffered while Max glided painlessly through life. Now the spoils were his.

They kept playing the song together, Hans speeding up the tempo each time, Sophie breathlessly trying to fit all the words into the compressed measures. Eventually he started hitting wrong notes and gave up, laughing. He put his hands on her soft, bare shoulders and pressed his mouth against her neck, inhaling her scent. She slowly stood up and turned around, her face caressing his. Hans saw desire flash in her eyes, and they kissed. It was not the same kiss as before, however; it was more reckless, more carnal. Her fingertips undid the buttons of his shirt, her nails grazed the skin beneath. On the piano bench in the Schattens' living room six years ago, when Hans had sneaked a look at Sophie's face, her expression had been like the woman in Klimt's *Fulfilment*. Now, half-opening his eyes, he was startled to find her staring at him like she wanted to eat him alive.

Max

It was six in the morning when Max emerged from the Metro station at Porte Dauphine. The air was cold on his eyeballs; he felt viscerally alive. He walked across Avenue Foch and under the silent chestnut trees. He'd barely slept at all last night, just an hour or two curled up on Jens's floor before the alarm clock rang. The ghost of a melody circled his head and then with a jolt of bitterness Max remembered his dream. Hans and Sophie were lovers. He and Sophie were merely star-crossed. And to top it all he was going to die . . .

Because, despite the clumsy grandiosity of their name, the Knights of Liberty were clearly risking their lives. Jens had told him about two comrades who'd disappeared inside the Gestapo's headquarters months earlier and had not been seen since. 'I hope they're dead, for their sakes and mine,' Jens had said, showing Max the pea-sized cyanide pill he kept in his cigarette packet. 'We'll probably all be caught in the end. What chance do we have? We're like ants trying to bring down a mammoth.'

Max glanced at the facade of 84 Avenue Foch as he walked past, the doorway guarded by uniformed sentries who watched him from under their helmets. He held his breath and kept walking, wooden soles echoing in the silence.

Inside the apartment he took off his shoes and tiptoed past Sophie and Édouard's bedroom. He opened the door to his own room. It gave a little creak as he pushed it shut.

'You're alone?'

Amazed, he turned and saw her. Lying in his bed, under the sheets. 'Sophie? What are you doing here?'

'Waiting for you. So you didn't bring a girl back?'

'No . . .'

'But you stayed the night at her place?'

He almost told her then. But Jens had made him swear not to breathe a word to anyone. 'Not even Sophie. I mean it, Max. I'd love to see her again, but it's safer for all of us if she doesn't even know I'm in Paris.'

'There was no girl.'

'Good.'

She was almost invisible in the shuttered darkness but her presence was palpable as body heat, desire, elation.

'But you spent the night with your husband, so what right do you have to—'

'I know, Max,' she said softly. 'I have no right. But I can't help the way I feel.'

He knelt down next to her, disarmed. 'What do you feel?'

She shrugged. 'I love you and I'm in love with you and I want you. We're in an impossible situation and I can't see a happy ending, but I don't want to hide from the truth anymore. To love and be loved – that's all anybody wants, isn't it? I'm lucky. We both are.' The plainness with which she said all this undermined Max's carefully stored anger.

'Do you mean it?'

Smiling, she lifted up the covers and he saw that she was naked.

Max rubbed his eyes and laughed, light-headed, suddenly feeling the effects of his sleepless night. 'So what exactly would you have done if I *had* brought a girl home?'

'Scared her away! Now take off your clothes and come to bed.'

Hans

Standing at the top of Rue Lepic, Hans had the feeling he could fly if he just held out his arms. His body was light as air. He and Sophie had made love last night and he would see her again in a few hours. First, though, there was something he had to investigate.

Ever since his dream about Max finding Jens Arnstein, Hans had been anxiously wondering just how symmetrical their worlds were. Bauer had told him that the real Arnstein had fled to France: was it possible he was working at the Café Bleu too? Was he part of a resistance network? And, if so, what did that mean for Sophie? Hans knew she was sympathetic to their cause and he had no doubts about her courage. He also knew that she and Jens had been close friends back in Vienna. What if he'd led her astray, put her in danger? She hadn't mentioned Jens since Hans had arrived in Paris, but she wouldn't, would she, if they were comrades? In all likelihood he was worrying about nothing, but he had to make sure.

The Café Bleu was exactly as it had been in his dream: the painted indigo outline of a trumpeter on the window, the lugubrious jazz oozing, muted, through the door. Hans opened it and the music engulfed him, haloed with a reverberation of voices. The door banged shut and the waitress, Yvette, looked up. She'd been speaking to the owner but she fell silent when she saw Hans. He was in full uniform: death's-head cap, long leather coat, knee-length jackboots. Around him conversations hushed and eyes glanced furtively from the darkness. Now he could hear the music in all its purity. The brush of a snare drum, the low tug of a bass string, the wail of a trumpet . . . and the smooth wanderings of the pianist's fingers.

Hans took off his cap and behind the bar a fat man with a small beard hurried over to greet him. 'Monsieur, I'm Gérard Blanc, the owner of this establishment. May I offer you something to drink?'

Hans smiled to himself. What did that politeness signify? That the man was a collabo, eager to please the Germans? Or a résistant, eager to allay suspicion?

'A glass of red,' Hans said. 'How long until the band takes a break?'

'Ten, fifteen minutes. You don't like the music, monsieur?'

'It's not bad. But I'd like to speak to your pianist.'

Did the man flinch? It was hard to tell in this light. 'Of course, monsieur. You can have the back room.' He poured wine into a glass and pushed it across the bar towards Hans. 'Something to eat?'

'Just some bread and charcuterie.'

The owner nodded. Hans took out his wallet but the man waved it away. 'On the house, monsieur.'

Hans stood by the bar. He could hear the waitress muttering to someone behind his back. He heard the word 'cicatrice' and the word 'Boche'. He thought he also heard something that sounded like 'Jens' but he could have been mistaken.

He sipped his wine and watched the band. As in his dream, the only two people visible under the blue spotlight were the trumpeter, a tough-looking teenager with impressive technique, and the bass player, who was in his forties, well over six feet tall, with skin the colour of a shadow. In a voice quivering with emotion the Negro sang foreign, incomprehensible words into the microphone.

The song ended to scattered applause and then all four musicians were walking towards the bar. Hans zeroed in on the tall, thin pianist. Jens Arnstein? No, this man walked with a limp, head hung low, and when he reached the bar he sat on a stool, alone. Hans watched as the owner approached him and the young pianist jerked his head up, first at the man behind the bar and then at him.

He got a shock. It *was* Arnstein, although it took Hans a second or two to recognise him. Because he too was maimed now, an ugly scar running from his hairline down past the side of his left eye.

Arnstein tensed. He looked as though he was about to make a run for it. But the owner touched his forearm and whispered something and he sat back down on the barstool.

Hans felt suddenly nauseated – the sheer improbability of his old enemy's presence here was making his head spin – but he composed himself and walked over. How many times had he fantasised about this scenario? Having the power to torment his childhood tormentor. All those hours of clenching his muscles, all those evenings spent working late, they had all been worth it. God was rewarding him now, like Job. And yet – seeing the fear in Jens Arnstein's eyes; the nerviness of his gestures, like a cornered rat – Hans felt an undertow of some darker emotion, deep in his gut. A mélange, he thought, of guilt and dread. He had always thought of himself as the good one, the victim, and Jens Arnstein as his evil oppressor. Now, for a moment, he glimpsed a different viewpoint.

'Good evening, Landmine,' he said in German. He smiled broadly and spoke loudly, to drown out his qualms. Arnstein glanced at the bar owner then reached into his jacket pocket. Hans's gloved hand snapped around the pianist's wrist before he could complete the action. 'I don't think your boss would like it if you shot an SS officer in his bar. Might lose his licence, you know.'

A contemptuous snarl. 'I was getting a cigarette.'

Hans quickly patted him down. Apparently he was telling the truth: the only thing in his pockets was a battered, almost-empty packet of Gitanes. Hans pulled the packet out and examined it while Arnstein watched him anxiously. This was, he knew, where the other Jens kept his cyanide pill. 'French cigarettes? They smell like old socks to me.' He tossed the packet back to Jens, who pocketed it, apparently having changed his mind about wanting to smoke. The owner motioned for them to follow.

They were led to the same back room as in his dream, with the same food on the table. 'I'll leave you in peace,' said the owner, nodding respectfully at Hans and flashing an unreadable look at Arnstein. 'Got your papers on you, Jens, or do you need me to fetch them from your room?'

'It's all right,' Hans said. 'I don't need to check his papers. Jens and I are old friends.'

The owner looked surprised by this but he nodded and closed the door. There was a long silence. Hans, who was already help-ing himself to saucisson, signalled for Arnstein to sit down. After a brief hesitation, he did.

'You should eat,' Hans said, trying to keep the nervousness out of his voice. 'You look thin.'

The ghost of a sneer hovered on Arnstein's lips, but he attacked the food anyway. He ate like a wild animal: chewing and swal-lowing rapidly, pausing every so often to scan his surroundings for danger.

Hans remembered Bauer's warnings not to trust Arnstein because he was 'slippery'. But he also remembered the Jens of his dreams, so honest and open-hearted with those he loved. He decid-ed to be as frank as he could.

'I'm not here to arrest you, Jens, if that's what you're worried about.'

Arnstein froze. 'Arrest me for what?'

'I know you escaped the camp.'

There was a moment of absolute stillness, and then Arnstein's hand moved towards his jacket pocket.

'Don't do anything rash,' Hans warned him quietly.

'I need a cigarette. Is that all right?'

Hans nodded. 'Go ahead.' He watched as Arnstein took a slight-ly misshapen Gitane from the packet and inserted it between his lips with a trembling hand. Hans took the silver-plated SS lighter – a birthday present from Bauer – from his own coat pocket and spun the wheel, concealing the engraved lightning-bolts logo with his palm. The flame appeared, thick and yellow, and Jens's cheeks grew briefly gaunter as he sucked the cigarette. A glow of orange, a cloud of smoke, and Jens's face relaxed. He closed his eyes, then looked up at Hans.

'What do you want, Schatten?' he asked calmly. 'And how did you know where to find me?'

There was no way Hans could answer the second question honestly, so he chose to ignore it. 'I just want to talk. It's been a long time. So . . . how's your family?'

In a voice of contained anger, Arnstein said: 'My father is dead. He was killed in a Nazi prison camp.'

A jet of acid in Hans's stomach. 'I'm sorry. I didn't know. But you and your mother and sister all escaped Vienna?'

Arnstein frowned. 'My sister died six years ago. My mother is safe – you bastards can't touch her.'

'Your sister died?'

'She drowned when she was twelve,' Arnstein said impatiently. 'Just tell me what this is about.'

'She drowned . . .' Hans repeated to himself. 'In the lake near your country house? She went out swimming and got cramp, is that right?'

Arnstein was eyeing him with a mixture of loathing and incredulity. 'How the hell should I know? We didn't find her body until the next day.'

For a moment Hans was too stunned to think, then his mind began to leap from question to question. 'What happened to your face?'

'Ask your colleagues in the SS.'

'And your limp?'

'Enough! What do you want, Schatten? I haven't seen you since my last year at the Musikgymnasium, and we weren't exactly best friends then. Now you show up to where I'm working in Paris and start asking me about my family. Why are you here? Are you going to report me or not?'

Hans remembered kicking Jens's spine in the Augarten. He remembered the fear on his face that night in the gallery. He thought about his father and his sister Charlotte, both dead; in Hans's dreams they had been loving and kind. Perhaps Jens Arnstein was dangerous and untrustworthy, and perhaps the safest thing – for himself and for Sophie – would be to arrest him now, or report him to the Gestapo. But how would Sophie react if he did that?

'No,' Hans said quietly. 'I'm not going to report you, I promise. You've suffered enough.' He meant every word, yet somehow he couldn't rid his voice of its sardonic edge. As if his uniform, and Arnstein's opinion of him, had infected his personality.

Arnstein glared. 'I've suffered enough? Oh, how fucking magnanimous of you!' He was shouting now. 'Am I supposed to be grateful? Bow down and lick your jackboots for not arresting me? Well, fuck you.'

Hans felt a reassuring flicker of the old hostility. Oh well, he told himself, at least he had tried being pleasant.

'No, I don't expect you to be grateful. But you must promise me something in return.'

'What makes you think I—'

'Don't let Sophie do anything dangerous.'

Arnstein's eyes opened wide. His half-smoked cigarette dropped to the floor. 'Sophie? What are you talking about?'

Hans leaned forward and grabbed the collar of Arnstein's shirt. 'If anything happens to her, I will personally bring down your entire network.'

Arnstein pulled himself free. There was panic all over his face. 'I have no fucking clue what you're talking about.'

'I know about the Knights of Liberty,' Hans said in a low voice. 'And I love Sophie. So I'm warning you: keep her safe.'

From the shocked expression on Arnstein's face, Hans guessed that his message had hit home. He stood up, crushed Arnstein's smouldering cigarette under his boot heel, then opened the door and strode out through the bar, stopping at the counter to compliment Monsieur Blanc on his excellent saucisson.

1941

JUNE

Hans

He sat with Bauer at a corner table in a dark little café near the train station, both of them in SS uniform. Two old Frenchmen eyed them morosely from the counter while the waiter ignored Bauer's finger-snapping and calls of 'Garçon! Ici!' Bauer grinned at Hans and slapped him on the shoulder. 'It's good to see you, Hans! You look different. Tanned, healthy, a sparkle in your eye . . . Have you got a French mistress?'

Hans blushed but said nothing. He and Sophie had been lovers for six months now and he fell more deeply for her every day. As happy as he was to see his old friend again, he couldn't help wishing that Bauer had come to stay for only a day or two, not two weeks. Fourteen days without Sophie – how would he survive? But he couldn't risk Bauer finding out about her. 'Ah, here comes the waiter,' he said, relieved to have an excuse to change the subject. 'Let me do the talking, Heinrich.'

'I am not a dog, monsieur,' the waiter hissed at Bauer.

'What did he say?' Bauer asked.

'He asked what we want to drink. Beer?'

'Not champagne?'

'I doubt they'll have anything very drinkable in this place.'

'All right, then, a glass of French rat's piss.'

Hans ordered two beers and the waiter gave an icy nod before walking back behind the bar. 'You'd better stop calling him garçon or you'll end up with French waiter's piss in your beer.'

Bauer looked doubtfully around the poky, damp-smelling café. 'So this is Paris, eh?'

'Not the most salubrious part of it, but yes. So how are things in Berlin?'

'Oh, things are going well.' Bauer's smile was secretive, almost shy.

'What are you hiding? You're not in love, are you?'

'Ha ha, no, better than that!'

'You're being transferred to Paris?'

'You're not going to guess.'

'Tell me, then.'

'I met the Führer.'

For a moment Hans was too shocked to speak. 'My God. Really? What was he like?'

'Surprisingly small. And slightly ill, I think. But when he looked me in the eye—'

'He looked you in the eye?'

'—it was a bit like meeting God. You know, if God actually existed.'

Hans nodded; he kept his religious beliefs to himself where other Nazis were concerned. 'Did he speak to you?'

'Not directly. But he shook my hand. And I got to listen to him talk about his plans for the war.'

'Find out anything interesting?'

Bauer grinned. 'I'm not supposed to tell anyone. But if you promise to keep it secret . . .'

'Of course.'

Their beers arrived then with a smack on the marble tabletop and foam dripped down the sides of the glasses. Bauer glared at the waiter but said nothing.

'The pact with Stalin is over,' Bauer whispered when the waiter had disappeared back behind the bar. 'We're going to invade Russia.'

'You're not serious?'

'What's the matter? It's glorious news, don't you think?'

'But Russia's so . . . vast.'

Bauer rolled his eyes. 'I know what you're going to say: Napoleon failed so we might too. But Napoleon didn't have a Luftwaffe, did he?'

'Hmm, true.'

'Besides, the vastness of Russia is precisely why we need it. All that oil and Lebensraum. And it gives us somewhere to send the Jews. Apparently they're going to have their own homeland in Siberia.'

Hans felt strangely relieved by this news. So the five thousand foreign Jews he'd helped to target and list over the past three months – and who were due to be arrested in the next few days – were going to be relocated, not executed. It would be so much easier to explain it to Sophie that way. 'Karl won't be pleased,' Hans remarked. 'He wanted a more permanent solution, remember?'

Bauer chuckled at this, then moved his chair closer to Hans's and said in a low voice: 'Actually, I wanted to warn you about Karl.'

Hans could feel the pulse in his thumbs as he gripped the edge of the table. 'Warn me about what?' he asked in a hollow voice.

'He's a Sturmbannführer now, like me.'

'Shit, that was quick.'

'Yes. He's one of Heydrich's favourites. It's annoying, because I was on to a good thing there. I think Heydrich and Eichmann see him as a sort of human weapon that they can send out into the world to express their displeasure.' He glanced around and lowered his voice. 'And I suspect this place might be next on their list.'

'Paris?'

Bauer nodded. 'The deportation rates here are the lowest in Europe.'

'It's not easy, you know, dealing with the French.'

'Don't waste your breath, Hans. They've heard the excuses. All they care about are the numbers. If those don't improve soon, Karl will be sent to Paris.' Hans shuddered. Bauer put his arm around Hans's back. 'No need to panic. I'm going to have a little talk with Dannecker. I'll tell him Eichmann's thinking of sending him east if things don't improve. That should focus his mind. Anyway, that's enough doom and gloom . . .' He picked up his glass and Hans raised his own to meet it. 'Prost!'

They drank and Bauer pulled a face.

'Christ, I think the waiter really did piss in this.'

Max

There was only one bed and they sat on it together, shirtless in the heat, backs to the wall. Each of them held a half-empty tin mug of eau de vie. Their names, according to the papers in their pockets, were Clément Dubois and Jean Carpentier, while in the network they answered to Franz and Freud.

Max and Jens were hiding in a safe house – or a safe room, to be more precise: a tiny attic space in Rue de Milan – because French gendarmes would soon be knocking on doors all over the city, handing out green slips of paper. Those green slips ordered the bearer to report to their local police station the next morning so that the authorities could 'examine their situation'; in reality they would be ushered onto buses and driven to internment camps. Max knew this because Hans knew it. He'd told Jens and the order had been given for all the network's Jewish operatives to go into hiding.

Today was the first time since their reunion at the Café Bleu that Max and Jens had been able to get drunk and speak German together. Since then there had been six months of perilous missions and clandestine meetings, lingering colds and insufficient food. Jens was even thinner than he'd been back in December: his ribs were clearly visible through his blue-veined skin. Max's face was gaunt, his eyes bulging and alert. But he was also quicker and sharper than before: mind, feet, senses. He was like a wild rabbit, tensing and fleeing at the slightest hint of danger, leaving his pursuers grasping at shadows.

The network was called Liberty now and it had become more organised, more professional. Its cells were structured so that nobody knew more than a few of their comrades. Other than Jens, the only operative Max had met was a gruff, barrel-chested Frenchman codenamed Danton. Max guessed that Danton was the network's leader, though this had never been made clear. Max was paid a thousand francs per month (half of which he handed over to Édouard in rent) and he'd been supplied with false papers, a cyanide capsule, a hand grenade and a Modèle 1935 pistol. It all sounded very impressive but Max knew from his dreams that the Germans were not particularly disturbed by their activities. When Jens had first told him about the network he'd described them as ants fighting a mammoth. Well, now maybe they were more like flies: irritating and harder to kill, but not actually dangerous. They needed to become more like wasps or mosquitoes, he thought. Max took the pistol from his knapsack and stared down the barrel.

Jens looked wary. 'Put it down, Max, it's not a toy.'

'It may as well be.'

'What do you mean?'

Max dropped the gun onto the bed. 'Those bastards are putting five thousand Jews into prison camps and all we can do is hide from them! Are we just going to let them get away with it?'

'We can't save everyone.'

'But we're not saving anyone except ourselves, are we? What exactly *are* we doing?'

'Our best,' Jens said testily. He sipped his drink, then added: 'What do you suggest?'

'Well, we could kill some Nazis. We all have guns. Why can't we use them?'

Jens was silent for a moment. 'Actually, we've been thinking along the same lines. Not that a few deaths would really make any difference to the Germans' strength, but it might make them lash out.'

'Lash out?'

'I hear it all the time, don't you?' Jens propped himself up on one elbow. '*The Germans aren't so bad . . . Life hasn't really changed that much . . .* Maybe we need to enrage the beast so people can see what big, sharp teeth it has. So they'll understand the choice we face: resist or die.'

Max wasn't entirely sure he liked the sound of that. 'So are you saying I can kill one?'

'Pick a target and put together a plan. But don't strike until you receive the order.'

'All right,' Max said. Now he had permission, the prospect daunted him.

Jens poured them both some more eau de vie and leaned back against the wall, eyes half-closed.

'The Germans are going to invade Russia, by the way,' Max announced casually.

Jens sat bolt upright, spilling half his drink. 'What? But how could— Oh. Hans?'

Max nodded. Jens knew about his dreams, of course, but only recently had he come to trust the information they contained. He was still sceptical about anything remotely supernatural, but Max's dreams had saved lives.

'Anyway, it's good news, don't you think?'

'I don't know,' Jens said. 'The Russians have enormous resources – gas, oil, iron. If the invasion succeeded—'

'They'd win the war, yeah.' They were silent for a moment, contemplating this bleak possibility. 'What will you do, Jens, when the war's over?'

'Rest in peace, I imagine.'

'Be optimistic for a minute. If the Allies win the war and we survive, what do you want to do with your life?'

Jens shrugged. 'I haven't thought about anything like that in a long time. I mean, I love playing in the band, but . . . I do still wonder about psychology sometimes. Maybe I could go to university, become an analyst.'

'Where? In Vienna?'

'I think Paris, actually. It's a beautiful city. Or it will be if we ever get rid of all these Nazis. What about you?'

'Same as you, I think. Hey, we could go into business together.'

'I would love that,' said Jens, suddenly sincere. 'I could babysit your children while you and Sophie go to the opera or whatever. They'd call me Uncle Jens and I'd let them do whatever they wanted. They'd probably love me even more than their own parents.'

'I bet they would.' Max imagined himself with Sophie, a baby in her arms, a little boy standing between them smiling at his Uncle Jens behind the camera. It was a sweet vision: a photograph from the future. He wished he had a few of those to give him courage through the dark days to come.

'I really wish I could tell Sophie you were here so you could see each other again.'

'Me too, Max. But the rules are there for a reason. The more she knows, the more danger she'd be in.'

'I know,' Max said miserably. 'I know.'

Hans

It was a warm summer night, nobody on the streets. Hans rang the buzzer and waited, hoping against hope that it would wake Sophie but not her husband. He was debating whether to ring it again when she appeared on the steps behind him, key in hand. 'Sophie! What are you doing out so late?'

She shrugged. 'Just seeing friends.'

Hans frowned. This was not the first time he had gone to see Sophie when she wasn't expecting him and she had been 'out with friends'. He strongly suspected that those friends were part of a resistance network, but what could he do? He had warned her many times about the dangers of getting involved in forbidden organisations. Having spent the past few days supervising the transfer of thousands of foreign Jews to the internment camp in Compiègne, Hans sympathised more than ever with her views on the occupiers, but the idea of switching sides was unthinkable. It would be treason, not to mention suicide. The only way he could hope to protect Sophie was to stay in his post and remind her not to take any stupid risks.

'But what about the curfew?'

'You're not going to report me, are you?' she asked.

'Of course not!'

Sophie smiled; she was teasing him. Had she been drinking? Her eyes shone in the moonlight and his blood leapt with lust.

'It's nice to see you, Hans. I thought you couldn't come while your friend was in Paris.'

He took her hands, the skin so soft in his, and lowered his mouth to her ear, breathing in her scent. 'I couldn't stand another night without you.'

She moved her face across his and whispered: 'Really? How much have you missed me?'

'I'm addicted to you.'

'Ich auch.'

Their faces touched every time they spoke, lips brushing cheek, ear, neck, sending frissons of desire through his body.

'Where's your friend?' Sophie asked.

'Asleep, at my place. Too much to drink. I wanted to come earlier but he wouldn't stop talking.' Hans's hand slid down from the small of her back to the cleft between her buttocks. She was wearing a thin summer dress and he could feel the silk underwear he'd bought her through the fabric. They kissed.

'Bravo! Bellissimo!' a voice blared from the shadows nearby. Bauer emerged, clapping his hands. 'What a romantic little scene!'

Hans stood protectively in front of Sophie, who turned away and started unlocking the door. 'What the hell are you doing, Heinrich?'

'I wanted to see your secret mistress! Aren't you going to introduce us? Mademoiselle, enchanté. Je m'appelle Mur-syur Bauer!'

'Keep your voice down,' Hans growled, nodding to Sophie as she slipped inside the apartment building and closed the door.

'Why? What's the big mystery? She's not a Jew, is she?'

Hans closed his eyes and breathed out, exasperated. 'She's married. And her husband's asleep upstairs. So please shut up.'

'Hans, you devil!' Bauer said in a stage whisper. 'A married woman! And her old man doesn't suspect?'

'Go home, Heinrich.'

'Will do.' Bauer had to grab hold of Hans's shoulder to stop himself falling. 'Very pretty girl,' he said wetly into Hans's ear. 'Maybe she could visit me when you're done? I don't usually like sloppy seconds but I'd make an exception in her case.'

Hans clenched and unclenched his fists. He exhaled slowly as Bauer staggered away, letting the anger drain out of him. His friend was drunk: there was no sense in taking him seriously when he was like that.

As soon as Bauer was out of sight, Hans knocked lightly on the door and Sophie opened it.

Max

After five days and four nights in the attic room, Max decided it was safe to return to Rue des Princes. He was halfway up the third flight of stairs when he heard a German voice on the landing. He held his breath and listened but all he could make out was a man's intonation and accent, not his words. Max took off his shoes and carried them in one hand. He crept close enough to see the legs and torso of a uniformed Nazi outside Sophie and Édouard's door.

'I see you in the street yesterday,' a voice was saying in mangled French. 'And I think: very pretty girl.'

It was Bauer. Max's hand slipped into his jacket pocket and touched the cold steel of the Modèle 1935. But he couldn't shoot a German here, outside his lover's home. Max let go of the weapon and listened.

'So I search you. Not easy, mademoiselle! But now I find. Therefore, I want to ask. Come you with me to dinner tonight? I pay, of course! Very nice restaurant. Yes?' Bauer kept swaying as he talked.

'No, I'm sorry,' Sophie replied. 'That's impossible. It's so late and—'

'No problem. Restaurant open for me.'

'And I'm a married woman.'

Max moved to the side until he could see her: lightly tanned calves, cream silk kimono. She was standing in the doorway with her arms crossed tight to her chest. He crouched down so he could see her face. Sophie was doing a good job of concealing her fear, but Max could hear it under the formality of her words, could see it in the lines around her eyes and mouth.

'It's not important,' Bauer said complacently. 'Your husband is home? He is Jew, no? I explain. Very good for him if you with me.'

'My husband's asleep. I'm sorry, the answer is no.'

'Not tonight?'

'No.'

'Therefore . . . tomorrow?'

'No, sorry.'

'You are busy tomorrow?'

'Yes.'

'When you are not busy, mademoiselle?'

'Madame,' Sophie corrected him.

'Yes, madame! It's true. I am sorry. I speak bad French, I know.' Bauer took a step towards Sophie; Max saw her recoil slightly. 'But you are young and pretty, you look like mademoiselle. Therefore, when you are free? Next week?'

'I don't know.'

'Perhaps next week?'

'Perhaps, I don't know.'

'Good! I come back next Saturday and we go to nice restaurant.' He bowed then, ignoring Sophie's protests, and hurtled downstairs. Max barely had time to stab his feet into his shoes and pretend to tie his laces before the Nazi passed him. Bauer was wearing a strong, sweet aftershave and particles of that odour seemed to stick to the back of Max's throat as he climbed the staircase.

Hans

He withdrew from Sophie and lay next to her on the love seat as she wiped herself between her legs. They were both layered with sweat. In the candlelit storeroom, Hans felt like he was floating in a sea of love. 'What's your friend's name?' Sophie asked.

Hans looked at her, surprised. 'You don't remember him? It's Bauer.'

'The one who ruined my mother's exhibition?'

'Yeah, but he's not usually like that, he's—'

'A nice guy?' she asked sarcastically. 'Yes, I'm sure. I mean, he was perfectly charming tonight.'

Hans sighed. There was no point trying to win Sophie round when it came to Bauer. 'He'll be gone soon.'

Abruptly Sophie got up and started gathering her clothes, which were scattered over the table and the floor. Sex, he noticed, seemed to have sobered her up. 'When?'

'Third of August. Honestly, I can't wait. I hate it when anything comes between us.'

She smiled wryly. 'Like the war, you mean?'

'The war will end one day, Sophie.'

'But one of us will be on the losing side,' she said as she fastened her bra. 'What will happen then?'

Hans pulled her close to him and kissed her belly button. 'Nothing will happen to you. I won't let it.'

'And what if my side wins?'

His lips moved down to the soft V of her pubic hair. He shrugged. 'It doesn't seem very likely, does it?'

Sophie freed herself from his embrace and bent down to pick up her knickers. 'What does he do during the day while you're at work?'

'Who, Bauer?' Hans watched as her bottom disappeared under cream silk. 'Sleeps in my apartment or goes out drinking, normally. But he's coming to the office with me tomorrow.'

'Why?'

'He has to talk to my boss.'

She picked up her cornflower-blue dress and pulled it over her head, then sat next to him on the love seat. Hans was still naked. 'About you?'

'No.' Hans hesitated. He was used to Sophie's questions by now and resigned to the idea that they were prompted by more than mere idle curiosity. But why was she so interested in Bauer? And how would she feel if he told her the truth about the reason for Bauer's meeting with Dannecker? Then again, if he were honest with her, perhaps Sophie would be honest with him too. Perhaps they could exist together on a neutral borderland between two enemy camps. 'About the number of deportations from Paris.'

With her fingertips she traced the ridged lines of his stomach muscles, then placed her hand on his inner thigh. He shivered. 'Your hand's freezing.'

'Deportations of Jews?'

She was looking straight at him.

Hans held her gaze. 'Yes. Berlin wants us to move faster.'

Her hand tensed on his thigh. 'Is Édouard at risk?'

'Yes, but not immediately. For now, it's only foreigners.'

She removed her hand from his leg and crossed her arms over her stomach. 'Will you protect him if the worst comes to the worst?'

When, Hans thought, not if. 'I'll try, Sophie. I can't promise anything.'

There was a silence. Then she said: 'Thank you for being honest, Hans.'

He put his arm around her. She was shaking slightly.

'I'll tell you whatever you want to know,' he murmured into her hair. 'Just promise me you won't get involved in anything dangerous.'

She made a movement with her head and shoulders. A nod or a shrug? He couldn't tell.

Moonlight poured like milk through the open shutters. Max and Sophie lay next to each other in bed. When their breathing had slowed, Sophie sighed sleepily and lay across him, lips touching collarbone, breasts against ribs, her right thigh draped over his. 'We fit perfectly together,' she whispered.

'I know.' Max had just been thinking the exact same thing.

She took a breath, as if hesitating. 'It was lucky, wasn't it, you being away when the gendarmes came?'

'Yes. Very lucky.'

'And I shouldn't ask where you were, I suppose?'

'It's better if you don't.'

'And that Nazi who came to the door tonight?'

'He won't come back, I promise.' He stroked her arm and she flinched. 'What's the matter?'

'Nothing,' she said, moving her arm away.

Max caught a glimpse of a dark mark on her skin. 'What's that?'

'It's nothing, just a bruise.'

Max turned the bedside light on and examined the mark more carefully. It was purplish-black, just above her biceps, in the shape of two fingers, one thumb. He sat up and looked at Sophie's other arm. Another bruise, almost identical. He imagined Édouard grabbing and shaking her in a fit of jealous anger. 'He did this to you?'

'He felt terrible afterwards. Édouard's not a violent man. I'm hurting him more than he's ever hurt me.'

'Does he know? About us?'

'I don't know. He hasn't said anything, but . . . he must realise I have feelings for you. I can't hide it anymore.'

Max stared at the wall that separated him from the sleeping Édouard Kahn. 'If he ever does this again . . .'

'Don't, Max. He could fire you, evict you. Report you.'

'I can't just let him hurt you.'

'Shhh.' She stroked his face, gently pushing him back against the pillow. 'It'll be all right. Let's get some sleep.'

She shifted slightly and rested her head on his chest. Almost immediately her limbs started to twitch, her teeth made quiet clacking noises. Seconds later she was a dead weight. Max snorted incredulously. For Sophie, falling asleep was like blowing out a candle: a puff of smoke, the burnt wick glowing, then everything went black. For him, the day's memories and emotions would swirl in a long spiral, like water slowly draining from an overfilled bathtub, and it might be hours before sleep took him. His heart was still speeding now as he thought about the bruises on Sophie's arms, about Bauer propositioning her, threatening to return. He thought about his own powerlessness and a strange dark rage stirred within. He had a gun, he had muscles and fists. He saw that gun pointed at Bauer's head. He saw those fists pounding Édouard's soft flesh. He saw the fear in their eyes, the complacent superiority fleeing their faces, he saw himself in uniform, felt taller in those black leather boots, and without realising it he had already crossed over to the other side. He'd fallen asleep.

Hans

He walked furiously to Rue des Princes. He entered the apartment building, using the key that Sophie had copied for him, then hammered his way upstairs. He knocked, hard and repeatedly, on the door of 3a and shouldered his way in as soon as Édouard unlatched it. The kitchen smelled of coffee – coffee that Hans had bought for them. The psychoanalyst was still in his pyjamas. 'Hans!' he said, shaken but relieved. 'What is it? What's the matter?'

Hans glared at Édouard Kahn. At his chubby, hairy fingers, at the thick gold wedding band. 'Where's Sophie?'

'In the bedroom. Has she done something wrong?' He raised his hands. 'I swear, I knew nothing about it.'

'Silence!' Hans pushed past him and went through to the bedroom.

Sophie stood in her underwear, a skirt and blouse laid out on the bed. She looked up at Hans, surprised at first, then horrified as she noticed his uniform. 'What are you doing?'

'Show me your arms.'

'What? Hans, what's wrong with you? Why do you look like that?'

'Show me your arms!'

He moved towards her and she took a step back, her face pale with fear.

Hans exhaled slowly through his mouth, forcing himself to calm down. 'Sophie, I'm not going to hurt you. I would never do that. Please let me look.'

She froze as he caressed her shoulders. 'Why do you want to see my arms?'

Hans examined each one in turn. They were perfect, not a mark on them. He closed his eyes and sighed, nestled his face in the hollow of her neck. 'I had a dream . . . that your husband had hurt you. You had bruises on your arms, I . . . It seemed so real.'

Sophie laughed softly. 'Édouard would never hurt me. He might want to sometimes but he'd never dare.'

'What makes you so sure?'

'Isn't it obvious? He's terrified of you.'

JULY

Max

He stood in a doorway across the street from 84 Avenue Foch and waited. He'd been here over an hour already; his feet ached and he needed to piss. In the real world, Bauer was not visiting Paris – he lived here. He worked for the Judenreferat and inhabited the flat on Rue Orphée that, in Max's dreams, was occupied by Hans. For the fiftieth time this afternoon Max slid his hand into his jacket pocket and lightly touched the pistol, checking that the safety was on. It was. He withdrew his hand and wiped the sweat on his trousers. He had not been given orders to carry out this killing: he'd wanted to ask Jens's permission but there had been no way of contacting him at such short notice, and Bauer was supposed to visit Sophie again tomorrow evening. It had to happen tonight.

It was six o'clock when Bauer left work. Max slung his knapsack over his shoulder and followed the Nazi at a distance as he walked to his apartment, then waited another forty minutes before he came out again, still in uniform. He followed him for the next hour and a half, until the July light began to fade and their shadows grew long. Several times he could have pulled the trigger. He was close enough, there was nobody else around. But he kept delaying the act, telling himself to wait until dark, until Bauer was drunk, until his heart had stopped pounding, his hands had stopped shaking. Each time he did this Max felt a rush of relief that quickly turned to guilt and fear: what if he didn't have the guts to go through with it?

At quarter past eight Bauer complicated things by entering La Porte Noire in Pigalle, where four other SS officers were already seated around a table. Bauer joined them amid much backslapping while Max picked up a copy of *Paris-Midi* from the newspaper rack and sat at a table in the corner. He thought about drinking alcohol to settle his nerves, but in the end he decided a clear head was more important and ordered a coffee.

Max watched over the top of his newspaper as the five Nazis guzzled beer and ate frites and talked and laughed. Max recognised Geier from his dreams: the rat-faced Hauptscharführer who hated Hans. Another man had a voice that sounded familiar but he was facing the wrong direction. Max peered at the man's broad shoulders, his thick neck, his blond hair. It couldn't be, could it? At last the man got up to go to the toilet and Max caught a glimpse of his face. He jerked the newspaper upward to cover his eyes and the sheets rustled like leaves in a strong wind. He was shaking so hard that he feared he would draw attention to himself. *Calm down*, a voice inside him urged. *If he sees you, you're dead*. The big blond man was Karl Schatten.

Max ordered a cognac and a sandwich. The alcohol helped him breathe more easily, the food took the edge off his nausea. He spent thirty minutes reading that newspaper and didn't absorb a single word. When he ate he turned away from the Nazis' table, but was able to watch them in a mirror on the wall. The mirror was painted with the image of a red-haired woman in a purple dress – a Pernod advertisement – but Max could still see enough through the unpainted fragments to know that Bauer and the others were just behind him.

He could hear them too, of course. At one point Karl began to sing the 'Horst-Wessel-Lied' and the others joined in, thumping the table in accompaniment. Two young women stood up to leave and Bauer shouted: 'Ladies! Why you go? Come back, we buy you drinks! We buy you real stockings!' His comrades exploded with laughter at that; the Frenchwomen had black seams painted down the backs of their calves.

Max had a grenade in his knapsack. He could easily roll it under the Nazis' table and run away. Nobody would ever catch him in all the confusion. But what if the explosion hurt an innocent bystander? What if Bauer survived? Max told himself he had to be sure. He told himself it wasn't fear making him hesitate, just uncertainty. He waited for them to finish their drinks and followed them as they walked around the corner to a nearby cinema.

The Nazis got in for free, of course. Max had to hand over ten francs. He hadn't been inside a cinema since the war started: the last film he'd seen was *The Wizard of Oz*. This time, he didn't even look up to see the name of the movie. Already he was thinking about the logistics. It would be dark outside by the time they emerged from the cinema, but there was no guarantee Bauer would separate from the others. What if they went out for more drinks? It could be midnight or later before Max was alone with him, and he absolutely had to finish this business tonight. A cinema was not ideal. But at least it was dark.

The place was about two-thirds full, but when the Nazis chose to sit in the fourth row everyone in the vicinity moved discreetly away. Max sat alone in the sixth row, positioned directly behind Bauer. It was easy to tell which one he was from the silhouette of his cap and the arrogant way he threw his arms over the backs of the seats. Karl sat beside him, towering over all the others.

There was a newsreel. There were advertisements. Clouds of cigarette smoke drifted up through the projected light. At last the main feature started. The title appeared: *Le Juif Süss*. Max had heard about this movie. It was a German propaganda film, a huge hit in the Reich. The images flickered on the giant screen, black and white, dramatic. The story unfurled – about the rise and fall of an avaricious Jew in eighteenth-century Württemberg – and Max found himself sucked into the story even as somewhere in his brain he made calculations, argued feverishly with himself, even as his heart squelched sickeningly inside his chest. It was not until an hour and a half later, as the film reached its climax, as the Jew Süss was locked in a cage and a noose placed around his neck, as a drumroll began and the cage was lifted by ropes high above the good people of Württemberg, as the cowardly Jew pleaded for his life and Bauer and his comrades roared at the screen . . . it was only then that Max took the pistol from his pocket, leaned over the row of seats in front and took aim at the back of Bauer's head. He lowered the safety.

The drumroll intensified. Max took a breath and held it. His arms were tensed, hands trembling. *Aim to the right*, the voice inside him whispered. On the screen the people of Württemberg watched, solemn-faced. *Aim to the right. Kill Karl, not Bauer.* Finally Max realised whose voice it was. Tired of the suspense, the mayor gestured. The executioner yanked the rope. Max wrapped his index finger around the trigger. *Aim right!* The silhouettes directly in front of him suddenly lurched upward. Karl's voice yelled out: 'Jude – verrecke!' The cage floor dropped. The Jew choked. All five Nazis were on their feet. Max stood up, arms shaking. *Kill Karl*, the voice hissed. Max glanced at the giant beside his target. His aim wavered. But Karl Schatten was not the one trying to seduce Sophie. Max forced himself to remember Bauer's handsome face curdled with hate in the Augarten all those years ago. He forced himself to picture those leather-gloved hands pawing Sophie's thighs. He pointed the gun at the back of Bauer's head. *Please*, said the voice. At last Max breathed out, involuntarily shouting 'Die!' as he squeezed the trigger. Probably no one heard him, though, because the gunshot was deafening. His hands jerked back and up. For an instant all Max could hear was the calm, sweet music of the film's happy ending muffled and distorted by the ringing in his ears. Then the screaming started. Max dropped the gun, ducked behind the seat. The Nazis turned and started shooting into the darkness.

All around was chaos, people running, shrieks of terror. Max picked up his knapsack and crawled along the floor towards the side aisle.

On the screen the mayor was giving a speech. It was inaudible amid all the screaming but Max looked through a gap between two seats and read the French subtitles: *All Jews must leave Württemberg within three days.* The Nazis were shouting again now. They were ordering the projectionist to stop the film, turn on the lights, lock the doors, but none of them spoke enough French to make themselves understood. When Max reached the aisle he got to his feet and was swallowed up in the flood of panicking cinemagoers rushing through the dark towards the exits. One of the Nazis – Max thought it was Geier – tried to block their path. He shouted 'Arrêtez!' and fired his pistol in the air. Plaster dust rained down from the ceiling but the crowd kept surging forward, propelled from behind. Max's feet hardly touched the floor as he was swept past the yelling Nazi. The credits were rolling now, the music swelling. The lights came on just before Max reached the exit. He had time to see Karl's blood-splattered face and the horror in his eyes as he looked down at his friend's dead body. *You shouldn't have done that*, said the voice inside him. But by then Max was outside in the cool night air. He was free.

Hans

He woke from his afternoon nap covered in sweat. A small electric fan whirred beside him. 'Heinrich?' he called, but there was no answer. Remembering the strange symmetry of finding Arnstein in the Café Bleu, Hans felt the first stirrings of panic. He got out of bed and went into the living room: empty. He tried the bathroom: also empty. Eventually he found a handwritten note on the kitchen countertop: *Didn't want to wake you, but really need a drink so going out now. Will probably head to Black Door later if you want to meet up? Au revoir mon Ami!* Hans checked his watch: half past seven. He put on a clean shirt and a jacket, slipped the Luger into his shoulder holster and went out.

He walked to the Victor Hugo Metro station and caught a train to Pigalle. But it stopped between stations for no apparent reason and then the lights went out, the engine shut down. Hans cursed under his breath. He slammed the train's windows with the heel of his palm and shouted in German. Alarmed, the other passengers sneaked through to the next carriage. When the train finally crawled into the Monceau station, a voice announced that it would terminate there for repairs. 'All passengers must leave the train now. We apologise for the inconvenience.'

Hans climbed the stairs to street level and walked quickly along Boulevard de Courcelles. At Place de Clichy he saw that it was nearly eight thirty and broke into a run, pushing past pedestrians on Rue de Douai before breathlessly entering La Porte Noire. Three men in SS uniform were sitting at a table in the centre of the room but all three had their backs to him. 'Heinrich!' he called out.

Dieter Geier turned around and raised an eyebrow. 'Schatten? What are you doing here?'

'I'm looking for Bauer. Have you seen him?'

'He was here a few hours ago.'

'Where did he go?'

'Hunting for pussy, I think.'

Sniggers from around the table.

'What makes you say that?'

Geier sighed impatiently. 'He tried it on with some Frog girl in the bar and she told him where to stick it. I was all for teaching the bitch a lesson but Bauer said he had a better idea. And he went off with a gleam in his eye.'

'He didn't say where he was going?'

'No, but I'm guessing he won't appreciate it if you interrupt him.'

Hans heard Geier say something sarcastic to his companions. He heard the word 'Schwuchtel' followed by a roar of laughter. 'I'm not a fucking queer, Geier,' he said coldly. 'I think someone's trying to kill Bauer. Does any of you have a car?'

Geier opened his mouth as if to make another joke, then changed his mind. 'Are you serious, Schatten?'

'Deadly.'

'All right. I'll drive you myself.'

In Geier's car they sped through the empty boulevards and Hans managed to compose himself. 'Thank you for doing this,' he said.

'What makes you think someone's trying to kill Bauer?'

'I'll explain later. I might be wrong. I hope I am. I just—'

'Are you sure you're not queer, Schatten?'

'Of course I'm sure.'

'It's just that I've never seen a man care *this* much about another man before.'

Hans gritted his teeth, but he stayed silent. He needed Geier's help; there was no point getting into an argument. Besides, he could hardly admit the truth: not only was Bauer his best friend, he was his only friend. If Bauer were to die, who would shield Hans from the wrath of Karl? But there was another reason too, one he could certainly not reveal. He had not forgotten the lecherous remarks Bauer had made about Sophie. If he was with her now . . .

Hans watched as the buildings rushed past in a blur and kept checking his watch. It was nearly nine already. What time had Bauer been killed in his dream? Five minutes later they entered Rue Orphée. 'Stay here,' Hans said. 'I'll be back in a minute.' He jumped out while Geier was parking the car and rushed to unlock the door of the building. He ran upstairs, holding his key, ready to open the apartment door.

But it was already open.

Hans's heart thudded. He pocketed the key and took out his Luger. He released the safety and began to edge inside. He saw Sophie standing in his living room, looking down at something on the floor. He said her name. She didn't react. Hans lowered his weapon and walked towards her. She was wearing a white blouse and a beige skirt, clutching a brown leather handbag to her chest with both hands as if trying to protect it. He noticed two wine glasses – one of them standing half-full on the coffee table, the other broken and empty on the floor by Sophie's feet – and as he passed the end of the couch he tripped over something. Glancing down at the carpet, Hans half-gasped, half-screamed, like someone waking from a nightmare. He had tripped over Bauer's feet.

Bauer was lying in the space between the couch and the coffee table, his best white shirt stained crimson. At first Hans thought he was dead, but then he heard him groan, saw red spit bubble from his open mouth. Hans moved closer to Sophie. He expected her to be shaking but she was almost unnaturally still: as white and frozen as a marble statue. Only her rapid breathing gave any clue to her emotional state.

'Sophie, you have to get out of here,' he told her. 'There's another man coming – he could be here any minute.' She seemed to wake from her trance then. Hans led her towards the balcony. He slid the bolt to open the glass door and they went outside. 'Use the fire escape. Cut across to Avenue Alphand.' He pointed to where she should go. 'Be careful.' Sophie nodded and began climbing down the iron steps. She didn't look back.

Hans went back into the apartment and bolted the balcony door. His heart was speeding but he felt oddly calm. Bauer was still moaning and panting on the floor. Hans took a handkerchief from his pocket and began wiping door handles. He wiped the stems and bowls of both wine glasses, the broken shards of glass.

Then he heard footsteps coming up the stairwell. If Hans used his Luger now, Geier would hear the gunshot. He knelt beside Bauer, pinched his nose and held his mouth shut. The muscles in Hans's forearms twitched and bulged as he kept Bauer's airways closed. The way his friend stared at him was unbearable so Hans looked away. Bauer's legs kicked, his head jerked from side to side, his hand gripped Hans's sleeve. At last the grip loosened. Hans grimaced as the smell of shit filled the air.

Seconds later the apartment door creaked open and Geier called out: 'What the hell's taking you so long, Schatten?'

Hans bent down and pressed his mouth to Bauer's bluish lips. He blew air into his friend's mouth, then pounded his chest with both hands. They were, he noticed, stained with blood.

'Schatten, what are you . . . Oh Christ.' Geier came closer and stood watching in horror as Hans clamped his mouth to Bauer's again and exhaled, as he shoved down so hard on Bauer's chest that a rib cracked. In the end, Geier grabbed Hans's shoulders and pulled him away. 'Stop, Schatten. Stop! It's too late. He's dead.'

Max

Sophie stroked his arm and whispered to him soothingly. It was nearly midnight and she'd just managed to escape the conjugal bedroom. They were standing on the balcony together under a black sky. Max had barely spoken a word since coming home that afternoon. He'd spent the previous night in the safe house on Rue de Milan, and as soon as he got back to the flat he'd taken a long shower that used up all the hot water, sending Édouard into a rage. But he still didn't feel clean. Sophie kept asking him what was wrong and finally, when he felt able to control his voice, he confessed.

Max couldn't see her face in the darkness, only the whites of her eyes. But he felt her fingers tense on his shoulders for a second.

'You're shocked. Aren't you?'

'A little,' she admitted. 'But mostly I'm relieved that you weren't caught.'

She moved close, kissed his neck. Max pulled away.

'What's the matter?'

'I'm a murderer, Sophie.'

Sophie put a finger to his lips. 'You don't know who's listening.'

Max sighed. Summer lightning flashed soundlessly across the sky.

'It's not just a crime, it's a sin,' he whispered. 'I remember you saying that once.'

She took his hand. 'This is different. You did it to save me. The man you killed was probably a murderer.'

'Then how am I any different?'

'You're on the right side.'

Only by chance, he thought. Had it not been for his dream on the night of the fire, he would be fighting for the other side.

He noticed that his teeth were chattering. Sophie wrapped her arms around him and held him tight. 'You're torturing yourself for no reason, Max. Please stop. God knows they'll do it to you if they ever catch you, so don't do it to yourself.'

Hans

Geier stood chatting amiably with the doctor as the prisoner was attached to a wooden plank. Jens Arnstein was naked, his thin white body shivering in the cold basement room. Two guards secured his arms and legs then covered his head with a sort of grey wool balaclava with no holes for the eyes or mouth. The guards carried the plank to the bathtub, which was filled with cold water. The base of the plank rested on the edge of the tub. The guards held the top of the plank on either side, their hands close to the prisoner's covered face. One of the guards nodded at Geier, who said: 'Ready, Schatten?'

'Yes,' said Hans.

But was he? Dannecker had warned him not to take part in the interrogation unless he was sure he could control his emotions, and Hans had assured him that he would be fine. In truth he'd been a mess for the past twenty-four hours. The Gestapo had questioned him after Bauer's body had been removed from the living room and his apartment dusted for fingerprints, and when they asked him if he had any idea who could have committed this atrocity, it was Arnstein's name that he gave them. It had been an impulse: he had warned Jens to keep Sophie safe, after all, and he had needed a name to draw suspicion away from her. But thinking about it now, he felt sick with regret. Sophie might never forgive him if she found out what he'd done, and what if he had inadvertently put her in even more danger?

It had been Hans, too, who had warned the Gestapo agents that the suspect kept a cyanide capsule hidden in a packet of cigarettes in the inside pocket of his jacket. When they arrested him, they were able to confiscate it before he could commit suicide. Why the hell had he done that? If Jens had killed himself, that might have been the end of the story. Alive, he threatened everything.

The doctor – a tall, urbane-looking man in his fifties – walked over to the end of the bathtub. He was there to observe, and to ensure that the interrogation did not result in cerebral impairment or death. Having made his inspection, he nodded. 'You may proceed.'

Hans had not been involved in the initial interrogations but Geier had shown him the transcripts. Arnstein had confessed to Bauer's murder but he was obviously lying: more than a dozen witnesses placed him on stage at the Café Bleu between the hours of seven and eleven that night. Who was he protecting? It was Hans's job to find out.

Hans crouched close to the prisoner's head. 'Can you hear me, Arnstein?'

No sound or movement came from the grey wool head. Arnstein's body was still trembling.

'Can you hear me?' he asked in a louder voice.

Silence.

'He can hear you,' growled one of the guards.

'Who killed Heinrich Bauer?' Hans asked. 'Tell me now and you won't have to go through this.' Still no response. Hans felt awkward. It was like having a conversation with a sofa cushion. The guards looked at him expectantly. His voice hardened: 'Last chance, Arnstein. Who was the killer?'

Another silence. The prisoner's Adam's apple slid up and down like a guillotine blade. Hans nodded and the guards plunged the grey head underwater. They held him there for a few seconds. The prisoner resurfaced, choking and spluttering. The greenish-blue veins in his hands bulged alarmingly as his fingers clung to the edge of the plank. His scrotum shrank and wrinkled.

Hans could sense Geier's cool, sceptical gaze evaluating him. Geier stepped closer and said: 'I heard a rumour that the killer is a woman. Is that true?'

Hans stifled a gasp.

Arnstein coughed and spat. His body jerked.

'Give us an answer or you go under again,' Geier barked.

'No.'

'No, the killer is not a woman?'

'Yes.'

'So the killer is a man?'

Silence.

'Is the killer a man? Yes or no?' Geier demanded.

'Yes.'

Geier glanced at Hans. 'Good. We're finally getting somewhere. Now tell us his name.'

After an agonising silence, Arnstein mumbled something.

'What did you say?'

'I . . .'

'Tell us his name or you're going under.'

'I don't know!'

Geier nodded at the guards. The grey head was plunged beneath the water. The plank shook as the prisoner's body convulsed. Yellow piss sprayed suddenly over his bare legs. 'Enough,' Geier said, and the plank was raised.

This time the noises that the prisoner made sounded inhuman: a sort of gurgling, squealing cackle that reminded Hans of a jammed radio signal or a stuck pig. The doctor intervened, lifting up the balaclava for a moment and helping to expel water from the prisoner's airways.

'Let's try again,' said Geier in a wearily patient voice. 'What is the killer's name?'

'I don't know his name. Only his—' Arnstein coughed until he started retching. 'Only his codename.'

'What's his codename?'

Arnstein shook his head. Hans held his breath.

'What's his codename?' Geier shouted.

A second. Two. Three. Hans was moved and impressed by Arnstein's refusal to speak but every man had his breaking point. Hans needed to end this before he revealed the truth. 'Put him under,' he ordered the guards.

They obeyed and the prisoner's body started to spasm again. *Don't do this*, whispered the voice inside Hans. *You're killing him!* As the guards waited for Hans's signal to raise the plank from the water, as Geier eyed him suspiciously, as the doctor frowned and started forward, as Hans stared furiously at the grey balaclava under the water, at the thin hands frantically flapping against the sides of the plank, he began to feel the water filling his own nostrils, scorching his throat, swelling his brain, flooding his lungs.

'Stop!' shouted the doctor, and the guards lifted the plank.

Max

Max spluttered awake. It took several seconds to rid himself of the sensation that he was drowning. He sat up and gulped the good, dry air. Dawn light filtered through a crack in the shutters. Sophie was out of bed. She was hurrying towards the window. 'What is it?' he asked.

She peered through the shutter's crack, then said: 'Oh God.'

Max jumped out of bed and took his turn looking through the window. Uniformed figures were pouring from an unmarked van outside the apartment building.

'Don't panic, they might not be here for me.' But Max was packing his belongings into his knapsack even as he spoke. It was the Gestapo – or the SS, he couldn't tell in this light – and he had to get out as quickly as possible. And it was vital that he leave behind no clue to his presence because that could incriminate Sophie.

The doorbell buzzed. 'What should I do?' Sophie asked.

'Don't answer it,' Max said, continuing to pack. He kept very few clothes in the apartment for precisely this reason. The rest were in the safe house on Rue de Milan.

The doorbell buzzed again.

'Sophie? Sophie?' A muffled voice on the other side of the dividing wall. The doorbell had woken Édouard.

'Go and calm him down.'

'He'll want to answer the door. You know what he's like.'

'Just buy me as much time as you can.'

His knapsack was ready now. The room looked uninhabited. Except for the bed.

Max took her hands and spoke as calmly as he could. 'Tell them you slept here last night because of your husband's snoring. The sheets smell of you anyway and—'

Behind him, the door opened. Sophie's face froze. Max turned around and saw Édouard standing there in his pyjamas, blinking behind spectacles. His eyes swept the spare room, taking in his wife in her nightdress, his lodger with his bag packed, the two of them holding hands, the crumpled sheets and dented pillows on the bed. Édouard's facial expression hardened. He stared coldly at Max, as though seeing him for the first time as he truly was. Half-ashamed, Max let go of Sophie's hands and took a step towards the door. 'Édouard, listen . . .'

'You snake,' Édouard hissed. 'I welcome you into my home and this is how you repay me.'

Max closed his eyes for a second. He felt sick, and then – abruptly, incongruously – like laughing.

The doorbell buzzed again and three floors below fists beat urgently on the outside door.

Édouard calmly announced: 'I'm going to let them in.'

'Don't!' Sophie begged. 'They'll kill him.'

Édouard glanced at her with contempt and turned away. He went into the hallway and pressed the intercom button. 'Entrez,' he said in a neutral voice. Turning to face Max again, he said: 'Do not resist. It will be better for everyone that way.'

Heart pounding, Max watched as Édouard opened the apartment door and picked up the newspaper that lay on the mat outside. Without a word, he pushed past Max and went into the bathroom for his morning shit. The sound of the bolt sliding into place. The percussion of heavy footsteps below. Max and Sophie exchanged a panicked look. 'The storeroom cupboard,' she whispered.

Max nodded and ran through the hallway. He closed the storeroom door behind him and opened the small cupboard in the corner. There was nothing inside it but a stack of blankets; if he climbed into that tiny space and covered himself with the blankets and kept perfectly still, there was a chance the Nazis wouldn't notice him. But as he bent down to peer inside the suitcase-sized cavity, he knew he would not be able to do it. Claustrophobia tightened his chest: Max had been afraid of enclosed spaces ever since those dreams of the black dragonfly, when he would wake up feeling like he couldn't breathe. He could hear a man's voice inside the apartment now. He heard Sophie say something in reply, the sound of a door slamming shut. In a panic, Max climbed onto the love seat and opened the back window. The rusty shutter hinges groaned as he pushed them outward.

He was about to climb down the fire escape when he heard someone cough below him in the gloom. He froze, listened. Then he spotted two SS guards, submachine guns hanging from shoulder straps, patrolling the courtyard behind the house. Max looked left, he looked right. He looked up. It was his only chance. He stepped onto the top of the fire escape, closed the window behind him and then, very slowly, the shutters. Another rusty groan. He held his breath but the guards below did not look up.

Taking off his shoes and socks and stuffing them into his knapsack, Max placed one bare foot on the windowsill and hoisted himself up to the edge of the roof. It was slate, gently sloping, slick with dew. With infinite care he crawled, inch by inch, up towards the ridge. The roof felt as if it were swelling like the sea. He manoeuvred his body so that it straddled both sides. He tried not to look down. He could hear the Germans moving around inside the apartment now, hear their barked commands. It was only a matter of time, Max guessed, before the storeroom shutters creaked open and armed men in uniform came out to arrest him. And then what? Shoot as many as he could before they shot him? No, that would only make trouble for Sophie. Perhaps Édouard was right: he ought to go quietly. But what if he talked? Every man had his breaking point. The cyanide pill was sewn into his jacket. But the jacket, he realised, was at the safe house. Max lifted his head to the side and stared down the long grey slope of the roof. All he had to do was let go. The fall would kill him. His heart sped as he imagined plunging over the edge of the roof, the ground rushing up to meet him. He wasn't a hero, he understood that now. He wasn't as brave as Jens imagined. He clung even tighter to the metal ridge.

After a while Max noticed he could no longer hear voices. Car engines throbbed and faded on the road below. Still he waited. At last he heard it: the squeal of the shutters. And then Sophie's voice. 'Max? Are you there? They've gone.'

Max slowly edged down the roof and she helped him in through the open window. The two of them hugged for at least a minute while Sophie sobbed quietly. 'It's all right,' he whispered. 'I'm safe, it's all right.' They sat next to each other on the love seat and he asked her what had happened. 'Édouard didn't tell them I was here?'

'He did, but they didn't listen.'

Max stared at her in amazement. Her lips quivered oddly.

'They weren't looking for you.'

'What do you mean?'

She hiccupped then started to cry again. There was something faintly hysterical about her expression.

'Sophie, what do you mean? Why were they here, then?'

'They came to arrest Édouard.'

'What? But they were only supposed to arrest foreign Jews.'

Sophie gestured at something on the floor. Max looked: a newspaper, its pages fanned out as if it had been thrown there. He picked it up, pushing the pages together, and examined the front page. It was today's copy of *Le Matin*. THE JEWS MUST PAY, read the headline above a photograph of the cinema that had been showing *Le Juif Süss*.

Fifteen minutes later he was sitting in a Metro carriage, reading the newspaper article. It contained a lurid account of the 'cowardly' murder of a German officer at the cinema and offered a reward of fifty thousand francs to anyone providing information leading to the culprit's arrest. Ambassador Abetz was quoted as saying that the Gestapo believed the murderer to be a 'Jewish terrorist' and that until he was caught the Jews of Paris would 'suffer the consequences' of his actions. As the train came into the Censier-Daubenton station, Max folded the paper and stuffed it into his jacket pocket.

It took him another ten minutes to walk to the doorway on Boulevard Port-Royal. This was where he usually met Danton. As on his previous visits, Max took the stairs up to the fourth floor and rang the bell: two short buzzes, one long. He waited. Silence. 'Come on, come on, answer!' he muttered.

Eventually Max gave up and left the building. He walked down the street, hardly even aware of the warm grey summer haze, the teeming faces, the fragments of conversation. While he worried, frantically and guiltily, about Édouard, about Jens, about the thousands of other Jews his actions had imperilled, someone bumped into him. 'Excusez-moi,' Max said automatically.

'No, Franz, excuse *me*,' a man in a fedora mumbled. Max looked up. That thick black moustache, those melancholy brown eyes. It was Danton. 'Follow me,' the Frenchman said, and Max trailed him around the corner into a dark alleyway. The two men stood behind a skip filled with stinking rubbish and spoke in low voices.

'You shouldn't have come.'

'I know, but I had to talk to you. We must warn all the Jews in the network before it's too late. They—'

'It's already too late.'

'What do you mean?'

'They have Freud.'

Max closed his eyes and groaned. 'This is all my fault.'

'It's also too late for this kind of remorse,' Danton said. 'What you did was rash but it was an act of heroism. And it provoked a response. Now the people of France will see these monsters for what they are. Anyway, don't worry: Freud has his cyanide capsule. I'm confident he won't talk.'

Hans

Sophie opened the door and Hans gaped at her in shock. Her head was shaved, her beautiful long hair gone. Without a word she went back into the apartment. Hans followed her. She continued into the living room and sat on the sofa. She was wearing a long black dress and no make-up. The rims of her eyes were red. 'Sophie, what have you done?'

She looked at him blankly. 'You know what I did. You were there.'

Hans knelt in front of her and placed his hands on hers. 'I mean your hair. Why did you do this to yourself?'

Sophie laughed almost soundlessly. 'I thought you liked my hair like this. Doesn't it remind you of when we were young, before everything went wrong?' There was a hint of mockery in her voice, a manic quality that disturbed him.

'Yes, but that's not why you did it. Tell me what happened.'

She closed her eyes. 'Édouard was arrested this morning.'

'Yes, I heard.'

She eyed him sharply. 'You said you'd protect him.'

'There was no time. They were only supposed to arrest foreign Jews, but at the last minute they expanded the order.'

'Why did they do that?'

Hans sighed and looked away. Keeping his voice as gentle and steady as he could, he said: 'Because a senior member of the Judenreferat was murdered.'

Sophie stared at him in horror. Her shoulders sank and she started to sob.

'Listen, you've had a shock. I'll pour you a drink.'

She shook her head, but Hans went to the cabinet and found a bottle of brandy. He poured a generous amount into a glass, then took it over to where she was sitting. He sat next to her and put one arm around her shoulders. She was taut as a bowstring. 'Drink this.' Again she shook her head, but Hans insisted, raising the glass to her lips and tipping it so that the brown liquid flowed into her mouth. She swallowed and coughed, and Hans wiped her chin then raised the glass to her lips again. This time she did not protest.

There was a long silence before Sophie muttered: 'What have we done?'

'It will be all right,' Hans said soothingly.

'I never loved Édouard the way a wife should, but I didn't want anything bad to happen to him. He's a good man.'

No he isn't, Hans thought. He's an arrogant, cowardly bully. He imagined saying this, imagined Sophie's fierce eyes, imagined her spitting in his face, imagined himself slapping her hard across the cheek. He could practically feel her saliva trickling down his chin, see the red hand-shaped mark on her skin. He decided not to say anything.

The minutes passed and slowly the alcohol took effect. She leaned into him. Hans felt her muscles relax as she lay her head on his shoulder; her breath was warm on his neck. He stroked her soft suede hair. He could see the pale scar that ran across her scalp.

'Let's go and lie down,' Hans said. He took her hand and led her to the spare bedroom. He'd never been there before in real life, although Max and Sophie had made love there many times. The wallpaper was older than it was in Hans's dreams and one corner of the floor was cluttered with cardboard boxes. The linen curtains were drawn, the air stale and muggy. Hans opened a window and a gust of wind billowed the curtains. Outside, the last of the daylight was fading. From the street below came the sound of a woman's laughter. Hans and Sophie lay down on the bed side by side. They held hands and stared at the ceiling.

'Tell me,' he said.

For a long time Hans listened to Sophie breathing in and out, in and out, before she finally started speaking. 'He came here while you were asleep yesterday afternoon. He was trying to persuade me to go out with him. He said he wanted to get to know me better.'

Hans grimaced. 'Did he—'

'I kept saying no,' she continued tonelessly. 'And he started to get angry. He grabbed my arms and shook me. He said if I didn't do what he wanted he'd tell my husband about you.'

'What did you say?'

'I told him I'd do what he wanted, but not here.'

Hans swallowed. 'But—'

'I'd already decided what to do by then,' Sophie said. 'I didn't want a dead Nazi in my apartment.' Hans nodded but said nothing. 'I keep the pistol in my handbag, so I went to fetch that while he dialled your number. He let the phone ring for a long time. When he was sure you weren't home, he told me to follow him. We went down to his car and he drove us to your apartment.'

Hans dreaded what was coming next. Sophie took a long, ragged breath before continuing. Hans couldn't see her face but from the sound of her voice he guessed that she was crying now.

'He poured two glasses of wine and told me to sit next to him on the couch. He drank some and tried to make small talk, as if we'd just gone out to dinner together. I was holding the handbag tightly in my lap. He tried to push it out of the way but I wouldn't let go.' Hans could feel the bed vibrating slightly from her sobs. He gently squeezed her hand. Another ragged breath. 'In the end he lost patience. I think he was worried about you coming back and finding us. He put his glass down and shoved his hand between my knees. He . . . he started kissing me. His teeth were banging against mine. I managed to put my hand inside the bag and catch hold of the pistol just before he threw the handbag onto the floor and climbed on top of me. He was . . . he was jamming his knee between my legs and . . . my skirt was hitched up and I . . . I didn't think about what I was doing . . .'

Hans waited while Sophie tried to compose herself. She coughed and sniffed, then said in a thicker, colder voice: 'I shot him. Twice. In the chest, I think, or the belly. He looked surprised, then angry. Then he sort of slumped on top of me and I had to push him off. His head banged against the coffee table as he fell. It must have knocked over one of the wine glasses. I remember the sound of it breaking. I stood up and . . . I don't know what came over me then but it was like I was paralysed. I knew he was still alive but I couldn't do anything. I dropped the gun into my handbag and I just stood there, watching him bleed, waiting for him to die. And then you came in.'

Hans nodded and exhaled.

'So now I'm a murderer.'

'No, you're not,' Hans said. '*I* killed him, not you.'

'He would have died anyway. You did it out of mercy.'

'No, that's not true, I—' Abruptly Hans stopped speaking. He could see where this was leading and it was not a place he wanted to go.

'Then why . . . ? Oh.'

He looked up at the ceiling and said nothing. Sophie shivered slightly. It was almost dark outside and the breeze coming through the open window was colder than before. Hans got up to fetch a blanket and covered them both with it. Then he lay next to her on his side so that their faces and bodies mirrored each other.

'Hold me,' Sophie said in a small voice. 'Warm me up.'

He held her tight until she stopped shaking, until his body heat had transferred to her. Her nose and ears and fingertips were still cold, but they always were.

The tension had left her body. She would probably fall asleep soon. He could tell she felt relieved to have told him the truth and he wished yet again that he could do the same.

'One day,' he murmured into her ear, 'nothing will come between us.'

'I think so too.'

'Really?'

'Yes. When we die. We'll be together then, in the same place.'

Hans frowned. 'Are you talking about heaven?'

She pulled back and looked at him with a strange smile. 'Do you really think we're going to heaven, Hans?'

DECEMBER

Max was painting the kitchen when he heard the front door open. He put the paintbrush on the lid of the tin and went to the entrance hall. Sophie was standing there in her coat, hat and scarf, holding up a newspaper. 'Look!'

GERMANY DECLARES WAR ON THE UNITED STATES, the headline read. 'Oh my God,' Max breathed. 'We'll have America on our side. Sophie, we should celebrate! Do we have any champagne?'

'No, but we have cider. Will that do?'

Max went back into the kitchen. The walls were sunshine-yellow, just like the living room of his parents' old apartment in Prinzenstrasse, and in the slanting winter sunlight it looked like the happiest place in the world. He poured the cider into two glasses and watched the bubbles rise. He and Sophie had moved into their new home at the beginning of September. All the apartments at 10 Rue des Princes had been searched by the Gestapo as part of the investigation into Bauer's murder – he'd been seen entering the building a week before his death – and Max had decided it was too risky to continue living there, so the network had offered them this flat on Rue du Cherche-Midi. Max had worried about their finances – how would they survive on only a thousand francs a month? – but Sophie had found a cashbox in Édouard's office and there was enough money in there to see them through the winter.

Sophie followed him into the kitchen and put the shopping basket on the table. 'Look what else I found.' She held up a box of eggs. Then she unwrapped a newspaper package to reveal a handful of mushrooms, the soil still clinging to them.

Max handed her a glass of cider and made a toast. 'To victory.'

'And love,' Sophie added.

'Yes, love too. Especially love.'

They kissed and Max drank half his cider. 'I'm going to make an omelette!' he declared. He hadn't felt this euphoric in as long as he could remember.

He used the entire week's butter and garlic rations to sauté the mushrooms then poured the thick yellow egg mixture over the top. He took gulps of cider as he cooked and began to feel almost intoxicated. When the omelette was ready, Max sliced it in two. He poured himself another glass of cider and was about to serve Sophie when he noticed that her drink was untouched. 'What's the matter? Aren't you celebrating?'

'You have it, Max. I think the bubbles don't agree with me.'

'I'll open a bottle of red.'

'I don't need alcohol. I couldn't be any happier.' Her eyes welled up as she said this.

'Is something wrong?' Max asked.

'No, no . . .'

He sat down next to her at the table. In a softer voice he asked: 'Oh, are you thinking about Jens? Or Édouard?'

'I had another letter from Édouard yesterday, did I tell you?' She sniffed and forced a smile. 'He's still at the detention camp in Compiègne.'

'You haven't told him we're together?'

Sophie shook her head. 'Not yet. Not while he's a prisoner.'

'Did he mention me again?'

'No, nothing like that.'

In his first letter from the camp, Édouard had written: *Have they arrested Max yet? If not, you must report him. It will look better for you if you do. Not only is he a foreign Jew who failed to register when required, but I feel sure he's involved with the resistance.*

'He said they were treating him well,' Sophie went on. 'And he seems to think he'll be released soon.' She looked up at him questioningly.

'It's not impossible. My father was released after a few months. Édouard has a better chance of survival than Jens, put it that way.'

Sophie's face fell and Max wished he could take the words back.

'Poor Jens,' she said. 'It sounds terrible but I'd almost prefer to find out he was dead so we'd know he wasn't suffering anymore.'

'Don't give up hope, Sophie. The Jens in my dreams is still alive, as far as I know. Why shouldn't that be true for our Jens?'

They ate the omelette at the kitchen table but after a minute or so Sophie pushed her plate away and said she wasn't hungry. 'Are you sure you're okay?' he asked.

She sighed and stood up. 'There's something I have to tell you.' Max started to stand too but she gently shoved him back onto the chair. 'It's probably better if you're sitting down for this.'

Max felt an ominous weight in his chest. 'Please don't tell me you're dying.'

She laughed and her eyes filled with tears. 'I'm not dying!' She began pacing nervously around the kitchen. 'Max, I'm pregnant.'

Max was so shocked that all he could say was: 'Oh.'

'I'm sorry. I know this is a terrible time to be bringing a child into the world, and if you feel like it's more than you can handle I'll understand, but—'

'Sophie . . . Sophie . . .' He stood up and put his arms around her, trying to stop the outpouring of words. He rubbed her back and murmured into her neck: 'You're the love of my life. Don't you know that?'

She started to sob. 'Oh, thank God! I thought you might be angry.'

He shook his head. 'I always dreamed of having children with you one day.'

'One day.'

He kissed her cheek. Inside Max's chest, little rats were poking around his guts. How could he go on risking his life if Sophie was carrying his child? How would they earn enough to survive if he didn't? What if she died in childbirth, like the woman in *A Farewell to Arms*? 'You don't think we should consider . . .'

'No.' She placed a hand protectively over her belly. 'This is our child, Max. We made him.'

'*Him?*' Max put his hand on hers and their fingers intertwined. 'You think he's a boy?'

Sophie shrugged. She smiled through her tears. 'I don't know. Maybe? If he is . . . I thought we could call him Jens.'

Max held her tight. She swayed a little in his arms.

'Are you all right?'

'I'm just tired. It's all the emotion.'

'You should take a nap.'

Sophie didn't protest, so Max picked her up and carried her to the bedroom. He closed the shutters, lit a candle and told her he would make her a tisane. But by the time he returned she was already asleep. She looked utterly peaceful in the candlelight. Max gazed up at the ceiling, imagining the vast blue sky above, the black void beyond, and begged fate not to destroy this little pocket of happiness they'd created.

He blew out the candle and closed his eyes and saw again that photograph of the future: himself with Sophie, a baby in her arms, a little boy (or maybe a girl) standing between them . . . Well, Uncle Jens would probably never take that picture but perhaps the rest of it could still come true. Perhaps it was in the process of developing even now, a white rectangle slowly forming lines and shadows in the clear liquid of time, under the warm red light of love.

Hans

He lay in bed beside Sophie at her apartment on Rue des Princes. They had moved into the spare bedroom because the conjugal bedroom held too many memories. It was Christmas Eve and they'd just made love. Earlier he'd taken her to the opera – the first time she'd been in years – and he'd spent most of the performance watching the expression of wonder on her face. Her boylike haircut had got a few stares from other spectators but Hans had glared at them and Sophie hadn't seemed to notice at all. He looked at her now, with her pretty ears and her radiant skin, and felt completely in love.

'Thank you for a perfect evening,' she said, turning to face him.

'I'm the one who should be thanking you.'

'Why?'

'Because you love me. Even though you hate what I am . . . What I do.'

Hans too was starting to hate what he was, what he did. 84 Avenue Foch had been a hellish place to work recently and there was a very real chance it would soon get worse. Dannecker had come back from a visit to Poland this morning, looking like a ghost, and he had told Hans that he needed to speak to him tomorrow, in private. The prospect of that meeting filled Hans with a nameless dread. As he was thinking this, Sophie jumped out of bed and walked, naked, towards the door.

'Where are you going?'

'Idea for my book. Need to write it down. Back in a minute.'

Hans lay back, feeling content. They'd needed tonight, he thought, that moment of connection. Ever since Édouard's arrest there'd been a glassy look in Sophie's eyes that made Hans feel as if she was always elsewhere, distanced from him even in their most intimate moments. Any time he asked what she was thinking about, she always gave the same answer: 'About my novel.' Sophie had begun writing it in the summer but recently she seemed to have grown more obsessed. Sometimes he would wake in the middle of the night and discover that she wasn't in bed with him. He would invariably find her at the kitchen table scribbling in a black leather notebook. Several times Hans had asked her what the title was, what the story was about, but she was secretive. 'You can read it when it's finished, Hans. Not before.'

A few minutes later she came back into the bedroom and slid under the covers to nestle against him. 'I had a dream last night,' he told her. 'We were living together, and you were pregnant with our child. It was a beautiful dream.'

Sophie said nothing.

'Wouldn't you like it if that happened in real life?'

She pulled her head back and frowned. 'Are you serious?'

'Why not?'

'We're in the middle of a war. On opposite sides. I'm married to someone else. How many reasons do you need?'

Hans swallowed his disappointment, but he wasn't ready to give up on the idea. 'You could get a divorce. It would be easy since your husband's a Jew. Then you could marry me and we wouldn't be on opposite sides anymore. And when the war's over—'

'Hans, please stop. We had a wonderful evening. Don't spoil it.'

'But—'

'Shhh.' Sophie breathed out in that telltale way she did when she was close to falling asleep, then shifted the weight of her body over his: lips to collarbone, breasts against ribs, her right thigh draped over his. Within seconds she was asleep. Hans lay there staring at the ceiling and his mind started to race. Why didn't she want his baby? He wondered if she knew somehow that he hadn't told her the truth about himself, if his lies, his secrets, formed an invisible barrier between them. He thought about waking her now and confessing. But perhaps it wasn't only *his* lies and secrets . . . Sophie had secrets of her own. Why wouldn't she tell him about her novel? Hans felt a sudden urge to read it. She might be angry for a while but at least he would know her better, understand her. It would bring them closer.

He carefully extricated himself from Sophie's embrace, got out of bed and went to the kitchen. He turned on all the lights and began to search. Sophie kept her notebook hidden but it had to be here somewhere. Hans opened each drawer in turn, methodically emptying it before returning all the objects to their places. He found the book after about ten minutes, hidden inside a heavy-lidded cast-iron casserole dish that neither of them ever used. He picked it up and took it to the dining-room table. His mouth was dry as he leafed through the pages, puzzling out Sophie's hurried scrawl. Most of the sentences were so cryptic that they meant nothing to him. They looked almost like equations – clusters of capital letters, numbers, signs – or like something written in cipher. But now and then he would find a line in plainer language.

One does not become enlightened by imagining figures of light, but by making the darkness conscious.

A quote from Jung – Hans recognised it from his dreams.

Every time I talk to D, I feel guilty, as though what I'm doing is a kind of betrayal. And yet . . . wouldn't anything else be an even greater betrayal?

D? Who was D? Was this a line from her novel?

Darkness in Paris . . . Life is but a dream . . . The limits of empathy . . .

Ideas for the book's title? He turned the page.

It's terrible, but I think I'd almost prefer to find out that he's dead so I wouldn't have to imagine him suffering anymore . . .

Reading these words, Hans had a sense of déjà-vu. He stared through the archway at the piano and tried to grasp the slippery memory, but nothing came.

He reached the most recent page:

He thanked me tonight for loving him even though I hate what he is. Then he said he wanted to have a child with me. Oh, why did I have to fall in love? Love tortures you, it tears you apart. Love blinds you. It forces you to do things against all reason and morality. It changes you inside, it strangles your conscience . . . but not to the point of death, that's the worst thing. Your conscience is still alive, only weakened, crippled.

My God, Hans thought when he read this, she makes love sound like the Gestapo.

Max

With a flourish Max removed the blanket from the enormous object in the living room. 'Surprise!' he shouted. 'I know it's a bit scratched but it works fine. I even had it tuned.'

Sophie stood in silence, staring at the piano.

'Don't you like it?'

'*Like* it?' She turned to him, mouth wobbling. 'Max, I can't believe it. But how did it get here? How can we afford it?'

'It wasn't expensive. Some friends brought it here yesterday evening while we were out at the bistro.' Max kept his answer vague because the truth was he'd heard about it through the network: the wife of a missing agent was selling her belongings in order to survive and the piano was going cheap. 'So, can we play a duet?'

Sophie spent Christmas morning practising the piano and the afternoon working on a short story – she'd been inspired to start writing again when Max told her about the other Sophie's novel – and in the evening she read him what she'd written and they played together. Max felt certain he'd never been happier in his life. They played Brahms's 'Wiegenlied' for their unborn baby, then the rowboat song that Sophie had sung to him and Jens on the lake that long-ago afternoon. They played and sang and laughed until the neighbours in the flat below banged on the ceiling with a broomstick and yelled at them to shut up.

Hans

'Sophie, we have to talk.' They were standing on the balcony over-looking Rue des Princes, just as they had eighteen months ago when Hans first visited this apartment. Édouard Kahn had opened the door to him that evening. Hans shuddered at the memory. Above him the night was a vast black void.

'All right.' Sophie eyed him warily. 'But let's go inside. It's cold.'

They lay side by side on the bed and gazed up at the ceiling.

'Tell me,' Sophie said in a small voice. She sounded as frightened as he felt. He wondered if she thought he was about to leave her. Or arrest her.

'I learned some things at work today that . . .' His voice trailed off. He felt sick. But he had to get through this: he could no longer keep any secrets from her, not after what he had heard in that meeting. 'My boss returned from a fact-finding trip to Poland. He visited one of the new camps there and he told me . . .' Hans hesitated as he remembered the haunted look on Dannecker's face.

'What did he say?' Sophie asked.

Hans shook his head. This was not how he wanted to confess. 'I'll come back to that. First I need to tell you the truth about me. I'm not the man you think I am, Sophie.'

'What do you mean?'

There was a long silence as he gathered his thoughts. 'You remember the day you touched my scars for the first time? When you made me touch yours and told me about the car crash?'

'Of course.'

Time to step into the abyss. 'I lied to you, Sophie. I wasn't in a car crash, I—' Suddenly he remembered the song the other Sophie had played in his dream the previous night. 'Did you ever play a Bösendorfer Imperial?'

'A what?'

'It's a piano with eight octaves.'

'Yes!' she said, sounding amazed. 'Once. Well, I think I did. But how could you—'

'It was in my father's shop. We had the only Bösendorfer in Vienna.'

Sophie gave a small gasp. 'Hans, that's so strange. I always thought I'd dreamed it. I have a really vivid memory of playing that piano and seeing a boy I liked, and then the next time I was on Prinzenstrasse I tried to find the place and it was . . . Wait. *You* were the boy?'

Hans nodded. 'And the man you and your mother were talking to was Franz Spiegelman, my father. Someone set our house on fire that night. That's how I got my scars. Both my parents were burned to death.'

Sophie, shocked, started to speak but Hans talked over her, trying to keep his voice calm and neutral. The truth, the whole truth, nothing but the truth. He told her his father was Jewish. And he told her about his dreams. About Max Spiegelman and the other Sophie. He told her about their parallel lives, their enmity, their strange closeness.

Sophie reacted just like Max's Sophie had. She asked him why he thought it had started, what he thought it all meant.

'I don't know exactly,' he said slowly. 'But I think you're part of it. And the song you played that afternoon. The one about the rowing boat.'

She laughed and then said: 'Oh! *Life is but a dream* . . .'

'My mother was playing that song when I fell asleep at the top of the stairs.'

'It's like a moment in a fairy tale,' Sophie said enthusiastically, 'splitting your life in two. So now you're in the dark forest . . .'

Hans frowned. 'The dark forest?'

'That's usually what happens in fairy tales: the hero voyages to a faraway land or a dark forest, where he has to perform a brave deed. Slaying a dragon, tricking a giant. Something that changes him. And then he has to find his way back home.'

Hans's mind was racing but he forced himself to concentrate. He had so much more to confess. He told her about being adopted by Frau and Herr Schatten. About Karl, and meeting Bauer. How he'd felt when he first met *her*. Why he'd joined the Hitler-Jugend. How he'd felt when she rejected him.

They both wept, at different times. Sometimes Sophie held his hand. Occasionally she gasped or laughed or said 'Ah' as if the missing piece of a puzzle had been fitted into place. There were some long, awful moments when he wasn't sure what she was thinking. But now the big secret was out, it felt smaller than it had when it was stuck inside him.

'And now I have to do something brave,' Hans said. 'And then find my way back home.' He already had an idea for the brave deed. For a long time it had seemed impossible but now he could envisage the possibility of switching sides. With America fighting alongside Britain and Russia, there was a chance that the Reich could actually lose this war, that – if Hans were to join Sophie in the resistance network – not only would their love be pure, but they might even survive. But how could he find his way back home? How could he close the circle, become once again the person he had been before the night of the fire? The song, the girl, and death. He had Sophie, and that pattern of notes and chords. Someone would have to die. A dream would have to end. He saw it all clearly, for the first time. The whole thing had been a divine test. God had made him dream of Max to show him the life he could have – if he made the right choices. Now Hans had to risk his life to save his soul. If he did, then Max would die . . . and Hans would be fully human. He and Sophie would know true love at last. He felt bad about Max for a moment, but then he understood: Max wasn't real. His life was but a dream. So Max wouldn't really die; Hans would just stop dreaming about him. They would become one.

'But what were you saying earlier?' Sophie asked. 'About the camp in Poland?'

'Oh, yes.' In his excitement it had slipped his mind. The horror returned to him now, but Hans felt a new purpose as he told her what Dannecker had said about the camp. Because he wasn't only telling Sophie, he was telling the resistance. He was taking the first step. 'It's called Auschwitz, and it's a giant factory for . . . destroying people.' He took a breath. 'There's no easy way to tell you this, Sophie. Édouard was sent there. He was gassed and his body was incinerated. Along with thousands of others.'

He lay there in the darkness and listened to her choke on her tears.

Much later, when she had vomited up the contents of her stomach and sobbed herself to a kind of precarious calmness, she asked him several questions and he answered them as best he could.

Hans heard fireworks exploding outside. He had forgotten it was New Year's Eve.

'One last confession,' he said. 'I looked at your notebook last week. I was curious about your novel and I thought, if I read it, I might understand you better. I'm sorry I betrayed your trust, Sophie.'

She didn't say anything.

'That's all,' Hans added, to break the silence. 'I've told you everything now.' He reached out for her hand. It lay limp and cold in his.

She turned to face him, though in the darkness he could see nothing but the whites of her eyes, the occasional flash of teeth. In a thick voice she said: 'Thank you. For telling me the truth.'

Hans held her tight. He felt exhausted and exhilarated. Drained of all the acid that had corroded him for years. Lightened by the loss of those heavy chains of guilt. He wished Sophie didn't sound so sad, but it was understandable after everything she'd learned. 'Everything will be all right,' he promised as she fell asleep in his arms. He knew it was true. Tomorrow he would tell her of his intention to leave the SS and join Liberty, and they would start to make plans together. She would want to marry him then, and have his baby. Smiling blissfully, Hans closed his eyes and for once sleep took him swiftly.

Sophie was still asleep when he woke the next morning. He kissed her warm forehead and breathed in the smell of her hair, half-hoping she would wake. But she didn't stir. Obviously she needed the rest. 'I love you,' Hans whispered. He slipped out of the apartment and went to Rue Orphée to change into uniform. He had a vague plan to steal some papers and hand them over to the resistance. That way, Sophie's comrades would know he wasn't a spy.

In the office he pretended to work as normal while calculating how and when he would take the papers. He was still considering this when Geier came over to his desk. 'Dannecker wants to see you, Schatten.'

'All right, I'm just going to finish up this—'

'You must report to his office *immediately*, Schatten.' Hans looked up and saw that Geier was standing next to an armed guard. Hans's skin prickled with apprehension as he followed Geier through the corridor.

Dannecker was sitting behind his desk, face sombre, arms crossed. 'I received this letter just now. It was hand-delivered to the guards outside.' He took a single folded page from his jacket pocket and pushed it across the desk. Hans unfolded the page. Expensive writing paper: thick, cream-coloured, bordered by tiny golden fleurs-de-lis. The letter consisted of three short, typed paragraphs in French. Hans started to read and his head jerked back at the second sentence: *I wish to inform you that Mme Sophie Kahn of 10 Rue des Princes is a résistante.* A few lines further down he saw his own name. *Mme Kahn has been involved in a romantic relationship for several months with SS-Hauptscharführer Hans Schatten.* Heart pounding, Hans skimmed the last few lines: *compromising information . . . felt it my duty . . .* The letter was signed *A Concerned Citizen.*

Hans glared at Geier. 'Was this you?'

Geier snorted contemptuously.

'It's a serious allegation, Schatten,' said Dannecker, 'and it must be investigated. In normal circumstances this woman would already have been arrested, but given your relationship I thought it best that you bring her in yourself.'

Hans stared. 'But she's innocent.'

'We will decide that. After we've interrogated her.'

'You want me to arrest Sophie?'

'No, Schatten. The Gestapo could do that. I want you to bring her in without arousing her suspicion. She trusts you. Reassure her.

If she's innocent she won't mind answering a few questions, will she?'

On the pavement outside 84 Avenue Foch, Hans walked stiffly away. His thoughts were seething. He would help Sophie escape Paris, go into hiding. Perhaps the resistance network could procure travel permits and fake ID papers for the two of them. They could catch a train to the demarcation line, cross into the Zone Libre . . . Hans heard footsteps and he spun around. Just some civilian. Jittery, he kept walking. As he reached the turning to Rue des Princes, he looked about more carefully. Was he being followed? He patted his Luger, upped his pace.

At number 10 Hans rang the doorbell for apartment 3a. No answer. He checked the street behind him, took out his key and entered. He went upstairs. The door to 3a was open. His mind flashed back to the discovery of Bauer's body, and his heart began to speed. Please don't let her be dead, he prayed. He went to the spare bedroom. The bed was stripped. The wardrobe doors gaped open, the hangers dangled bare. He ran to the kitchen: no food in the cupboards, a plate and a glass drying in the sink. He ran through the dining room and into the living room: books missing from the shelves. He swivelled and stared at the piano: a note on the music stand. He walked closer. A single page with a single word handwritten in blue ink: *Désolée*.

Sorry? She was *sorry*? She'd vanished from his life and all she could say was sorry?

In his confusion, it took Hans a few seconds to notice something else. The paper on which the word was written was thick and cream-coloured, bordered by tiny golden fleurs-de-lis.

1942

APRIL

Hans

It was almost midnight and Hans was sitting at the bar of La Porte Noire with Dannecker and Geier. They were the only customers. The barman had already stacked chairs on top of tables and kept looking pointedly at his watch. Hans was dead tired. He didn't even know why he'd come with them, except that he dreaded returning to his silent apartment. Four months had passed but the ache of separation hadn't faded.

Geier bought another round of beers and shoved one in front of Hans. Dannecker was muttering darkly about Berlin: 'Those bastards expect miracles . . .' Since the turn of the year something had changed at the Judenreferat. There was no longer any room for doubts, delays, exemptions. Moderation was verboten, fear contagious.

'I keep hearing rumours that Sturmbannführer Schatten's going to take over soon,' said Geier, squinting maliciously at Hans. 'Is it true he's your brother, Schatten?'

'Half-brother,' Hans said, gazing gloomily into his glass.

'So I take it from the look on your face that you two aren't exactly close?'

Hans said nothing and Geier laughed.

'He's looked like that ever since his mistress disappeared,' Dannecker grunted.

'Don't worry, Schatten,' said Geier. 'I'm sure they'll catch the bitch soon.'

The black dragonfly fluttered down from the ceiling and landed heavily on Hans's shoulders. Images of Sophie flashed through his mind. He saw her again on that last morning, asleep in the apartment on Rue des Princes. He remembered kissing her fore-head, smelling her hair. For an instant the memory was so precise that he could almost conjure her here beside him, warm and real in this dingy little bar. But then he saw the note on the piano again and his heart hurt so badly he wanted to cry. All over Paris there were posters with Sophie's face on them: in the photograph she was smiling nervously, the white lace collar of her wedding dress just visible at the bottom of the frame, above the word WANTED printed in five-inch-high letters and details of the reward offered for information leading to her arrest. Sometimes Hans wished he could hate her, want her dead, the way everybody imagined he did; it would be easier that way. But how could he when every night he felt love flow through him like blood?

'Anyway, I wouldn't believe everything you hear,' Dannecker said to Geier. 'I think Eichmann would have told me if he was about to give my job to someone else.'

Half-drunk, Hans tuned out their conversation and sank into his own thoughts. *Désolée*, the note on the piano had said: a word that usually meant sorry but could also mean desolate, sorrowful, dev-astated. Was that how Sophie had felt? But then he remembered that typed letter . . . Why take the risk of denouncing herself? Why not just vanish? Was it a form of self-punishment or a way of ensuring that Hans wouldn't search for her? Had she wanted to get Hans into trouble at work? His colleagues still gave him side-ways glances and made sardonic remarks, but Hans had answered all the Gestapo's questions and they'd found no evidence that he'd been aware of Sophie's affiliations. The conclusion to their report had read: *Hauptscharführer Schatten was naive and irresponsible, but there is no evidence to suggest he is guilty of treason.* If only Hans had told Sophie his plans before she'd fallen asleep that night, everything would be so different now. If only . . .

He closed his eyes and heard Sophie breathing steadily in bed beside him. Max was asleep but his hand lay protectively on her swollen belly, and if Hans concentrated he could feel her warm taut skin under his fingertips. Was he still being tested? For a year he'd believed that God had granted him his reward, but perhaps that was just a ruse to make him feel the loss more keenly when it came. What did God *want* from him? Hans remembered how he'd saved Max's parents on the night of the fire by losing his own parents and an idea sparked into life: perhaps this was his role? To risk everything to save Max and the other Sophie. True, they were happier than he was, but they were also in greater danger. Hans had heard rumours that a new mass round-up of Jews was being planned for Paris, a round-up on an infinitely vaster scale than those that had come before. Could he help Max and Sophie escape? If he did, perhaps God would give him back the love of his life.

The word 'Liberty' tore Hans from his thoughts. He looked up. Geier and Dannecker were discussing a new prisoner who'd agreed to give them names and addresses in return for his freedom.

'The plan is to decapitate the network in a single night,' said Dannecker.

Geier leered at Hans. 'Hear that, Schatten? Your girlfriend's about to get it in the neck!'

Hans said nothing. He knew Max was dreaming all of this, that he would wake in the morning with the fear that he and his comrades were under threat. Could that fear help save them? Perhaps. It wouldn't save his own Sophie, though. Only he could do that.

'When is the raid planned for?' Hans asked Dannecker.

Dannecker eyed him suspiciously. 'That's classified, Schatten.'

The barman yawned.

Geier and Dannecker downed the remains of their drinks while Hans left his on the bar along with a pile of coins. The three of them walked out together. A taxi was parked on the opposite kerb. 'Want to share a cab, Schatten?' Dannecker asked. Hans nodded;

he and Dannecker lived on the same street so they often got a ride home together. 'Whereabouts do you live, Geier?'

'Rue de Lille,' said Geier. 'Down by the Seine.'

'Ah, it's dangerous there, isn't it? A few of our men have disappeared near the river lately,' Dannecker said, opening the door of the taxi. 'Get in – we can drop you off.'

'Nonsense!' Geier sneered. 'I always walk home and I always feel safe. We're the masters here, don't forget. Let those French dogs be afraid . . .'

Max

Knock knock.

Max sat up in bed and peered through the darkness. In a sleepy voice Sophie asked him what was wrong. 'Someone at the door,' he whispered.

She sat up next to him. 'You think it's them?'

His heart sped as he remembered his dream: the SS was planning a raid on the Liberty network.

'I don't know. What time is it?'

Sophie turned on the bedside lamp. 'Three o'clock. What should we do?'

'Don't answer it. Keep quiet.'

Knock knock.

His dream . . . Hans wanted to help save them. Ever since the night of the confession, and the morning of the other Sophie's disappearance, Max had felt a growing kinship with Hans. He remembered how desperate they'd both been, back in Vienna, to separate, to flee each other's company. Since Hans had followed him to Paris, though, Max had felt that their fates were somehow bound together. He'd grown used to the sound of that voice inside his head again, to his long and vivid dreams, to the idea that he was two people, that without Hans's presence he wasn't quite himself.

Stop thinking, hissed the voice. *Listen.*

Knock knock knock.

More impatient now. But furtive.

'I don't think it's the Gestapo,' Max whispered.

'Gendarmes?'

'Maybe.'

'Why don't you answer it, then? Your papers are in order. They have no reason to think you're—'

'Unless someone denounced me.'

'But who? Only the network knows we're here. Oh, and the concierge, but isn't she one of us?'

'Who knows,' said Max, who wasn't sure he trusted his new comrades any more than he trusted the fat, beady-eyed concierge. Nowadays the Liberty network was controlled by London; it was regimented, bureaucratic; you couldn't make a move without going through the proper channels . . . Max missed Jens. He missed the warm camaraderie of his early days as a resistance fighter.

Knock knock knock knock.

'Turn off the lamp,' Max said.

He took a small torch and his Modèle 1935 pistol from the bed-side drawer, got out of bed, put on his dressing gown and padded barefoot to the front door. He opened it on the chain and aimed the pistol through the gap while he held the torch in his other hand and shone the light into the corridor. Two faces squinting in the dazzle. Max recognised one. 'Franz, it's me – Danton. Let us in!'

Max opened the door and the two men came in. He dropped the gun into the pocket of his dressing gown and led them to the small living room. Max sat in an armchair. The two men sat on the sofa and stared solemnly at him. Danton's eyes were bloodshot. The other man was thinner and younger; he wore glasses and carried a knapsack. A student, Max guessed. 'It's three in the morning. What do you want?'

'We have a mission for you.'

Max said no before they'd even finished outlining their plan. It was insane – a suicide mission. They wanted him to dress in SS uniform and enter 84 Avenue Foch, to search the detention cells and kill one of the prisoners: a résistant whom they suspected of betraying his comrades.

'You speak German, Franz. You're the only one who can do this.'

'I don't care. Sophie's pregnant. I'm not going to get myself killed and leave our child without a father.'

'We all take risks. It's part of the job.'

'I'm not doing it.'

'I always said we couldn't trust him,' the man in glasses said. 'He's a Kraut. Probably a double agent.'

Max snorted. 'I'm a Jew, for God's sake.'

'Then do your duty.'

'I already gave you my answer. I think it's time you gentlemen left.'

'Franz, you don't understand,' said Danton. 'We're not asking you to do this, we're ordering you.'

'And I'm refusing.'

'Then you leave us no choice.'

Both men aimed guns at Max.

'What? You're going to kill me in my own home?'

'Put the knife down, madame,' Danton said softly, glancing over Max's shoulder.

Max spun around. Sophie was standing in the doorway, gripping a carving knife. 'If you shoot him, I'll kill at least one of you,' she promised.

'There's no need for violence, madame. We're all on the same side.'

The man in glasses took aim at Sophie. 'He told you to drop the knife.'

'Lower your gun,' Max told him. 'Sophie, put the knife down. I'll do what they ask.'

'Good,' said Danton.

Sophie came over to the armchair and hugged Max.

'On two conditions,' Max added.

The man in glasses scoffed but Danton nodded. 'Go on.'

'One: this is my final mission for the network. After this, I retire.' A pause. 'All right.'

'Two: you provide Sophie and me with travel permits to the Zone Libre by the end of the month.'

'What?' said the man in glasses. 'You're retiring and you want special privileges? Who the hell do you think you are?'

'You said it yourself,' Sophie reminded him. 'This is a dangerous mission and you have no one else who can do it.'

'Madame has a point,' said Danton. Then, to Max: 'I'll do my best.'

'Give me your word.'

Danton's eyes grew steely. 'I just did, Franz.'

Max sighed. 'All right. So when's this mission supposed to happen?'

'Tonight,' said the man in glasses, opening his knapsack.

Hans

Ring ring.

Hans sat up in bed and peered through the darkness. He turned on the bedside lamp and looked at his watch. Three o'clock. He'd only fallen asleep a couple of hours ago. Who the hell was calling him at this time of night?

Ring ring ring.

'Shut up!' he yelled at the telephone. It was probably the office again. Hans tried to remember if he'd left any paperwork unfinished on his desk.

Ring ring ring ring.

But what if it wasn't work? What if it was Sophie? A faint bloom of hope. The thought of being with her again was like an opium shot to his heart.

Ring ring.

He picked up the receiver. 'Hello?'

'Schatten? This is Dannecker.'

'Oh.'

'I'm back at the office. You need to get here immediately.'

'Why?'

'I can't tell you over the phone. Just come. And hurry.'

The line went dead.

Hans dressed in uniform and walked numbly down Avenue Foch. He saluted the guards and entered number 84. Climbed the broad stone staircase to the third floor. Entered the office of the Judenreferat, mouth open to ask Geier if he knew what was going on. But Geier wasn't there; the office was deserted.

Frowning, he walked to Dannecker's office and knocked on the door.

'Enter!' barked a strangely familiar voice. A deep, virile voice, very different from Dannecker's usual weary grunt. Nervously Hans opened the door. The first thing he saw was a huge pair of black jackboots dangling in front of Dannecker's desk. Hans stared at them for a second before his gaze rose slowly up the sturdy seated thighs, the massive torso, the muscular neck . . .

Two small blue eyes considered him coldly.

'Hello, little brother.'

. . . identity is HAUPTSCHARFÜHRER DIETER GEIER, a
member of the Paris Judenreferat (Section A, third floor). You
must proceed tonight before his absence is . . .

Max kept reading the typewritten note until he'd memorised it, then burned the sheet of paper in the bathroom sink. He looked at himself in the mirror and felt sick. Danton and his sidekick had left half an hour ago but Max still couldn't quite believe this was happening. His hair was neatly cut and side-parted, his back straight, shoulders straining against the SS uniform he wore. Dieter Geier was at least two inches shorter and ten pounds lighter than Max; more worryingly, the Hauptscharführer looked nothing like him. Even when Max contracted all the muscles around his upper lip, nose and eyes, he couldn't twist his face into the ratlike malevolence of that man he'd seen so many times in his dreams.

Yet what choice did he have? He could try to escape Paris with Sophie but if the network caught them they were dead, and if the Nazis caught them they were worse than dead. Max felt cornered, angry, scared. He caught sight of his reflection again: yes, that was closer to the expression that usually deformed Geier's face . . . He put on the death's-head cap and Geier's dark-framed glasses and looked in the mirror. Perhaps there was a chance – a tiny one – that this operation might succeed.

Max checked his watch: almost four. His window of opportunity was already narrowing. He had two and a half hours at most. By daybreak Geier's corpse, dumped in the Seine by resistance fighters, would surely be discovered. Besides, their escape plan required the cover of darkness.

He went to the bedroom to say goodbye to Sophie.

'Max, are you sure about this?'

'Yes,' he lied. 'The building's practically empty at night and I'll outrank all the guards. I'll be fine, don't worry.'

He didn't tell her about the flickers of dream he'd been having while she cut his hair. In fact he hadn't told Sophie anything about his dreams recently because he wasn't sure they *were* dreams anymore. It was more as if his life and Hans's were once again merging, blurring, intertwining, just as they'd done in Vienna four years ago.

'Take off those glasses. You don't look like you.'

'That's the general idea,' Max said. But he took them off anyway.

Sophie came into focus again, her limpid eyes and her Madonna glow. He leaned down to kiss the dome of her belly, then her mouth. She held him tight.

Hans

SS-Sturmbannführer Karl Schatten lit a cigar. He was sitting on Dannecker's desk and every time he moved, the wood creaked in complaint. Hans, in a chair below, inhaled the second-hand smoke.

'So here we are, little brother. Together again.' Karl was eyeing him intently, a strange smile on his face. He looked leaner than he had the last time Hans saw him. The doughy white face that had haunted Hans's childhood was now tanned and chiselled, and when Karl rolled up his sleeves Hans saw the veins bulge in his forearms. 'Do you remember that night in Bauer's tent on your first summer camp?' Karl asked conversationally.

'Yes.'

'Yes, *Sturmbannführer*!' Karl barked, slamming the desk.

Hans sat up, petrified. 'Yes, Sturmbannführer!'

Karl chuckled then, as if the correction had just been his little joke. He took another drag on his cigar. 'Remember what he said about us that night?' Karl's tone was warm, almost nostalgic, but there was something about his smile that chilled Hans. 'He said one day I'd be taking orders from you. Do you remember that?'

'Yes, Sturmbannführer.'

'And now look at us.'

'Yes, Sturmbannführer.'

'And look at old Bauer. Killed by a woman. By your girlfriend, in fact!'

Hans frowned.

'Oh, you disagree?'

'I don't know, Sturmbannführer.'

Karl stared shrewdly into Hans's eyes as though reading his thoughts. 'I think you do, little brother.'

In the tense silence that followed, Hans stared vacantly at the reflections gleaming from Karl's polished jackboots.

'Do you miss Bauer?' Karl asked, sounding almost sympathetic.

Hans shrugged. 'He was my friend.'

'Oh, you think so? Here's something I bet you never knew about Heinrich Bauer . . . He killed your parents.'

Hans frowned. 'How—'

'How could I know that? How do you think, little brother? That big piano burned beautifully . . .'

Hans remembered standing outside the shopfront of SPIEGEL-MAN MUSIKINSTRUMENTE that warm March afternoon and turning to see three boys in matching beige shirts running towards him. Now, in his mind, two of them had faces. Hans put his hand over his face as he breathed in the sickly-sweet smoke from Karl's cigar. Through his fingers he saw his mother and father screaming in the flames.

I should take my gun out now and shoot him in the face, thought Hans. Karl kept smiling coldly as if daring him to do it and Hans found it hard to escape the idea that all his thoughts were somehow audible. He didn't reach for his gun. He just swallowed and looked at the floor. He felt the same powerlessness he'd always felt in Karl's presence, like a kitten going limp when picked up by the scruff.

'Nothing to say?' Karl asked. 'All right, let's get down to business. Obersturmführer Dannecker is on his way east as we speak and Hauptscharführer Geier is absent without leave. So for now it's just the two of us. And guess what the first item on the agenda is?'

'I don't know, Sturmbannführer.'

Karl leaned forward, blew smoke into Hans's face and announced: 'We're going to hunt down Sophie Kahn, little brother. And when we catch her, you're going to help me interro—'

The sound of a gunshot, from somewhere below. Both men froze.

Karl took out his pistol and barked: 'Follow me!'

Automatically, Hans obeyed. They ran downstairs. On the second landing they heard another gunshot, louder but still distant. Karl checked his watch and said: 'Four forty-four!' As they reached the lobby, Karl shouted: 'You get the lift, I'll take the stairs.' Hans pressed the button for the lift and watched as Karl headed towards the double doors. Before he got there, they burst open and a man in SS uniform ran across the lobby.

'Hey!' Karl called out.

The man turned. He was wearing dark-framed glasses just like Geier's, but Hans had never seen him before.

'Were those gunshots?'

The man stood as if frozen.

Karl stepped towards him. 'Hauptscharführer! I'm talking to you!'

Max

'Heil Hitler!' Max shouted, raising his right arm to the two guards outside 84 Avenue Foch. He thought he saw one of them observing him with narrowed eyes as he climbed the front steps, but perhaps this was just his imagination. Or the distorting effect of the lenses in Geier's glasses. At least he knew where he was going, having visited this building so many times in his dreams.

Max took the lift down to the basement then strode through the dim corridor to the detention cells. The two cell guards saluted him. 'Hauptscharführer? Can I help you?' The guard who'd spoken was young, fresh-faced; more farmboy than soldier.

'I've just arrived from Berlin. I'm here to inspect your cells.'

'Can't this wait until morning?' asked the second guard. 'We're—'

'No, I'm flying back tonight. Eichmann wants details of all the prisoners you're holding. I don't have much time so if you'd give me the tour?'

'Of course, Hauptscharführer!' the first guard said. 'Please follow me.' Eichmann's name had done the trick. Clearly everyone in the building was terrified of him.

'All these cells are empty?' Max asked as they passed several open doors.

'That's right, Hauptscharführer. We had a clear-out last week. Some of these terrorists won't talk, no matter what you do to them.'

'How many are left?'

'Just two, Hauptscharführer, although we're expecting a wave of arrests very soon. One of these two gentlemen is very talkative, if you know what I mean.'

'And the other?'

'Oh, we can't get a word out of him. He's been here for months.'

'Why keep him alive, then?'

The guard leaned close and spoke in a confidential tone: 'Our informer's fingered him as the leader of the whole network.'

Max frowned. Danton? But no, this prisoner had been here for months. 'Let me see him.'

'Of course, Hauptscharführer.'

The guard turned the light on and Max put his eye to the spy-hole. The man asleep in the bunk was Jens. His head had been shaved and his face savagely beaten. As the brightness penetrated Jens's eyelids, he groaned, covering his face with one arm.

'Turn the light off,' Max said. Could he rescue Jens? It seemed impossible. But he couldn't just leave him here, to suffer yet more torture. He thought about going into the cell and putting him out of his misery, but . . . could he really kill his best friend? Later, he told himself. Focus on the mission and deal with this later. 'Let's visit your informer.'

When they reached the informer's cell, Max turned to the guard. 'I want to see him alone.'

'Of course, Hauptscharführer. I'll wait outside.'

'Actually, I'd like a glass of water. My mouth is dry after that plane journey.'

The guard hesitated. 'Visitors aren't supposed to—'

'What's your name, Unterscharführer?'

'Frick.' The guard swallowed. 'Werner Frick, Hauptscharführer.'

'Please get me some water, Frick. I'll remember to commend you for your discretion when I write my report.'

'Yes, Hauptscharführer, thank you.'

Frick turned the light on and unlocked the cell door. Max opened it and went inside. He recognised the man blinking in the corner. When Frick's footsteps had receded, Max closed the door behind him. The prisoner was sitting up in bed. Gérard Blanc was thinner than he'd been the last time Max saw him, standing behind the bar of the Café Bleu. He ran a hand through his sparse, greasy hair. 'Is it done?' he asked in German.

'It's a shame,' Max replied in French. 'Your saucisson was magnificent.'

The bar owner squinted at him. 'Do I know you?'

Max took off his glasses. He raised his right arm and shot him in the head. The traitor's brains splattered across the cell wall and his body slumped sideways onto the bed.

This second murder did not affect Max the way the first had. His heart was speeding as he walked quickly along the corridor to the lift, the Luger still gripped in his right hand, but only because he was frantically trying to calculate whether he had time to rescue Jens before he escaped. Before he could come to a conclusion, he heard Frick running up behind him. Max turned to see the young guard staring wide-eyed with terror, water splashing from the glass he was carrying. 'I heard a gunshot! What happened?'

'Your prisoner attacked me.'

'He attacked you? But is he—'

'He's dead,' Max said testily, grabbing the glass with his left hand. He drank what was left of the water then tossed the glass on the floor. It shattered against the concrete. 'Clean up the mess, Frick. I'll be reporting this incident to Eichmann.' He kept walking, fast and determined, while the guard stammered an apology.

The other guard appeared, his weapon raised. 'What happened?'

'Help Frick,' Max said. 'The prisoner attacked him. I'm going to get the doctor.'

'Stay where you are, Hauptscharführer! You know the protocol. I—'

Max shot the guard and hammered up the concrete emergency stairs. No time to think about Jens now. He pushed open the double doors and saw Karl Schatten standing in the lobby, aiming a pistol at him. Karl called out: 'Hey! Were those gunshots? Hauptscharführer! I'm talking to you!'

'Yes . . . One of the prisoners attacked a guard.' Max's voice was shaking. 'It's under control now.'

'So where are you going, Hauptscharführer?' Karl sounded suspicious.

Max edged away. He thought he could see Karl frowning now, as if trying to grasp a furtive memory. 'I . . . must inform the doctor.'

'Wait!' Karl ordered. 'What's your name?'

'Geier, Sturmbannführer. But this is urgent. The guard needs medical attention.'

A bell dinged. The lift doors hissed open and Karl turned to look. Max bolted.

'Halt!'

Max kept running. One of the door guards turned in surprise. As Max sprinted past him and into the cold darkness outside he heard a loud crack and felt something hit him hard in his lower back, then a sort of hot itch deep inside his body. He heard confused shouting behind and ran down the steps to Avenue Foch but the world was tilting now and he couldn't see properly. His legs were weak, he was stumbling. Was he going blind? I've been shot, Max thought stupidly. He could feel the warm ooze sticking to the back of his shirt and somewhere between his stomach and his lungs the burning sensation was spreading. The roar of an engine up ahead. More gunshots behind. Someone yelled 'Franz!' and Max ran towards the sound. He threw away Geier's glasses and his vision came into focus. Danton was on the motorcycle behind a chestnut tree, as planned. Max straddled the bike and clung to Danton's torso and the world sped away under him as sirens wailed.

Hans

Ring ring.

Hans sat up in bed and peered through the darkness. He turned on the bedside lamp and looked at his watch. Three o'clock. He froze. What the hell was going on? He'd been in the lobby of

84 Avenue Foch with Karl when he closed his eyes. Hadn't he? Or had that been a dream?

Ring ring ring.

But he never dreamed about himself, only – always – about Max. Then he remembered. Max had killed a prisoner and a guard. He'd seen Jens Arnstein in his cell. He'd been shot. Was he . . .

Hans closed his eyes.

Darkness. Silence. Nothingness.

Three o'clock. And it had been 4.44 when he heard the second gunshot – he remembered Karl saying that, remembered memorising the fact for the report he would have to write.

Ring ring ring ring.

Hans picked up the receiver. It was Dannecker. Telling him to report to work immediately. With a weird sense of déjà-vu, Hans got dressed and walked to the office. He knocked on Dannecker's door, saw Karl sitting on his desk, and listened as Karl called him 'little brother', as he repeated the same phrases he'd used before. Even though he knew it was coming, Hans still startled at the first gunshot.

When they reached the lobby Hans pressed the button for the lift even before Karl could give him his orders. He watched as Karl headed towards the double doors and, as in his memory, they burst open and a stranger in SS uniform ran across the lobby. 'Hauptscharführer! I'm talking to you!'

This was where Hans's memory ended. Now he had only the memory of his dream to guide him.

As in the dream, the man turned and ran. Karl shot him in the back. The man kept going, stumbling and bleeding, and Karl fired another shot. This time he didn't miss. The man collapsed to the floor. Karl ran to the body and kicked away the gun. To Hans's relief the man was a total stranger, his face white and streaming with sweat. The man's mouth opened slightly and his eyes rolled back in his head. Karl pressed a finger to the man's neck and said: 'He's dead. Go to the basement and check on the guards and prisoners. I'm going to raise the alarm.' Hans nodded and ran to the emergency stairs. When the doors had swung shut behind him he stood still and closed his eyes. *Max?* he whispered silently. Blackness. Silence. Was this how it felt to be alone in the world? All those years he had wanted an end to his dreams, but now it had happened he felt only horror and grief. If Max was dead, Hans would never see the other Sophie again.

Hans opened his eyes and hurtled down the steps. In the corridor that led to the cells he saw Frick performing mouth-to-mouth on his fellow guard. Hans ran past the two of them, past the cell where Gérard Blanc's corpse lay sprawled in a pool of blood, to the cell at the end. He turned on the light, looked through the spyhole and saw Jens Arnstein fearfully eyeing the door. Suddenly Hans knew what he had to do.

He ran back to where Frick was now weeping over his comrade's corpse. Frick looked up as Hans approached and said: 'He's dead, Hauptscharführer. And it's all my fault.' Hans smashed his Luger against Frick's temple. The guard's eyelid twitched and he slumped to the ground unconscious.

Hans started undressing the dead guard. He prayed to God not to let anyone come down to the basement now: he couldn't think of a plausible explanation for what he was doing. His fingers shook as he unbuttoned the guard's shirt. 'Schneller, schneller,' he urged himself. The last few buttons popped and went flying and he dragged the blood-soaked shirt off the corpse's back. Hans pulled off the guard's trousers, then removed the bunch of keys from the waistband and ran to the cell, carrying the clothes.

He unlocked the door. Inside the cell Jens Arnstein stood in his prison uniform. His body was scarily thin, his face a misshapen latticework of bruises and scars. 'Schatten?' He snorted with disbelief. 'So you're my executioner? Poetic justice, I suppose.'

'I'm not here to kill you, I'm here to set you free.' Hans tossed Frick's gun across the floor. 'You'll need this. But first put the uniform on. It's your only chance of getting out of here alive.'

Jens stared at him, bewildered. He picked up the gun and checked the magazine. 'Is this a trick, Schatten?'

Hans tried to control his breathing but the words came out too fast anyway. 'It's not a trick. We don't have much time. The SS is planning to decapitate the Liberty network. I don't know when, but soon. Find Sophie and the others and tell them to hide.'

Jens took off his prison clothes and began dressing in SS uniform.

'Gérard Blanc is dead, but I think he'd already talked. You need to move your agents somewhere else as soon as you can.'

'I don't understand. How do you—'

'It doesn't matter how I know!' Hans barked. 'If you want to get out of here, just shut up and do what I tell you.'

When Jens was dressed, Hans led him out of the cell, along the corridor, past the guards' bodies and up the emergency stairs. Hans half-opened the door and peeked through the gap. In the lobby, guards were posted at every exit and several men were crouched around the dead résistant's body. No sign of Karl.

'I'll do the talking,' Hans whispered. 'Just limp along next to me. You've been shot, all right?'

Jens nodded.

They set off through the lobby, Jens's left arm draped heavily around Hans's neck. One of the men glanced up as they passed but he didn't say anything.

When Hans reached the door guards at the main exit, he saluted and spoke in a low voice. 'This is Unterscharführer Frick. He was wounded by the terrorist. I need to take him to a secure location.'

The guard looked dubiously at Jens, then back at Hans. 'You have permission from Sturmbannführer Schatten for this?'

'Yes. I'm his brother.'

The guard hesitated.

'Call him if you must, but be quick. This man needs urgent attention and he's an important witness. I wouldn't want to be in your shoes if you let him bleed to death.'

The guard conferred with his colleague for a second then turned back to Hans and nodded. 'You can go.'

The two of them limped down the steps and towards the road. When they'd disappeared behind the line of chestnut trees, Hans turned back to check the building's entrance. No guards in pursuit. He was almost spooked by how easy their escape had been. 'You're on your own now,' he told Jens. 'Go.'

'Wait. Why are you doing this, Schatten?'

'For Sophie,' said Hans, looking into the other man's eyes and for the first time seeing his best friend in another life. 'Jens, if you find her . . . tell her I love her.'

Jens nodded. He ran across the road, jackboots slapping against the concrete, and vanished into darkness.

Hans walked home. He let himself in to his apartment and thought of Max, shot in the back. If Max was dead, then what did Hans have left?

Alone in bed, he closed his eyes.

Blackness.

He couldn't even conjure the memory of Sophie beside him. What if he forgot how she looked, smelled, felt? It had happened with his parents all those years ago. Gazing up at the starless ceiling, imagining the black void beyond, Hans prayed: 'Dear Lord, let Max live. And please bring Sophie back to me. I'll do anything You ask.'

He kept praying until he was too exhausted to speak. His eyelids slowly closed.

Max

His eyes snapped open. The bearded face close to his. The all-seeing eyes staring deep into his soul.

'God?'

The bearded mouth laughed, then turned to the side and called: 'He's conscious.'

Max coughed. His insides hurt. 'I was shot.' Remembering, he looked down and saw his midriff thickly bandaged. He was lying on a mattress, his back and neck propped up on pillows. The man with the beard, he realised, was Danton, not God. But who had he spoken to? Max noticed a figure standing in a doorway. The next thing he knew, Sophie was beside him.

'Max.'

She held his hand and he breathed in her scent and deep inside Max felt a sigh of relief.

'Can I have some . . .' – his mouth was a desert, each word coated in sand – '. . . some water?'

Sophie held a cup to his lips and he sucked the cool liquid. He felt as if he were falling.

'Tired,' he murmured.

She kissed him on the forehead. 'It's the morphine. Don't worry, just go back to sleep. I'll be here when you wake up.'

His eyelids slowly closed.

Hans   Max

They were two souls shifting and sliding in the same timeless space or spaceless time. They were Siamese twins, limbs and thoughts intertwined as they sank through the dark waters between sleep and waking. But this time there was no horror, no repulsion. Only relief.

I thought you were dead, Max.

                                        Ich auch.

I'm so glad you're not.

                                        Really?
                    I thought that was what you wanted.
                                    To be free of me.
                            So you could be fully human.

Yes, but I was wrong.
We're on the same side.

                                    You're right, Hans.
                            We have to help each other,
                            although I don't know how.

There's something I need to tell you.
Something strange that happened
when you were unconscious.

                                Something you saw
                            when you closed your eyes?

No. I saw nothing.
Not until you woke up.
But the moment it happened,
when you blacked out—

                                You went back in time.

Yes! How did you know?

                            It happened to me that first night.
                                At the top of the stairs
                            in our parents' apartment.
                            I dreamed about the fire,
                        and you lost consciousness,
                    and I woke up in exactly the same place
                            at exactly the same time
                            as you had woken up before.
                I remember looking at the grandfather clock

and seeing the time – eleven minutes past one –
then knowing what my parents
were about to do, about to say.
It was like a miracle, a second chance.
Then perhaps that's how.

How what?

How we help each other.

JUNE

Hans

It was dark by the time Hans left the office. His vision swam with exhaustion. Outside, the air was mild and misty and he walked with eyes half-closed past blue-black buildings, receiving glimmers of dream – Sophie's swollen belly, her blissful smile, the smell of her hair – like a radio signal disturbed by interference. Max and his lover were at home, calmly preparing for bed, in a different, over-lapping Paris. Hans savoured these rare moments away from the stale air and typewriter clatter of 84 Avenue Foch. His life was pur-gatorial now, with only glimpses of heaven. But at least he wasn't in hell.

Hans had felt sure that something would happen to him after he freed Jens Arnstein. In all probability, he'd thought, it would be something bad, ordered by Karl: demotion, interrogation, torture, death. But there was also the possibility that something wonder-ful would occur instead, and whenever he was alone Hans would daydream about Jens telling Sophie how he'd escaped, about her seeking him out, sending him a message . . . Instead his life had continued along the same unswerving tracks, week after week, through a grey tunnel of lists and memoranda. Frick, the guard he'd knocked out, had no memory of the event, and Karl had not said a word to Hans about Jens's escape. His act of bravery, it seemed, had made no difference.

Tonight, as usual, Hans did not go straight home. He turned left onto Rue des Princes and stood opposite number 10, looking up at the third-floor balcony. He could see lights and silhouettes in most of the other windows but Sophie's apartment was dark, the red shutters locked. He closed his eyes again and felt her bare skin against his in the darkness. She couldn't lie on top of him the way she always used to because her belly got in the way, so they spooned instead. Hans stroked her hip. He kissed the back of her neck and said: 'I love you, Sophie.'

I love you too, Max.

Hans exhaled and caressed the empty air.

Footsteps. He opened his eyes and saw a man in a trenchcoat and beret walking towards him along the pavement. He tried closing his eyes again but the moment had gone. The man brushed past him and abruptly the footsteps stopped. Hans turned: the man stood facing him, his features invisible in the darkness.

'Monsieur . . . If you want to see her, go inside. The door is open.'

Hans gaped. 'I'm sorry?'

But already the Frenchman was walking away.

Hans caught his breath. Was it possible? He looked up at that third-floor balcony, the closed red shutters. How long had she been hiding there, unknown to him, while he stood on the street below and dreamed about her?

The door is open.

He rushed across the street to the red door. It hung slightly ajar, blocked by a folded newspaper on the floor. Hans stepped inside. He walked slowly upstairs and a thousand moments coalesced in his mind. The first time he'd climbed these steps, feeling hopeful and guilty as he went to his appointment with Édouard Kahn. The last time he'd been here, when he found the apartment stripped bare. That first evening after he'd sent her the piano, when he'd run upstairs buoyed by the knowledge that Sophie loved him. And the morning of New Year's Day, after confessing the truth, when he'd walked down these stairs filled with the conviction that he was at the start of a new life . . . Well, perhaps he had been. Perhaps he was.

He reached the third-floor landing. The door to the apartment was off the latch. He pushed it open. Silence. No lights. She must be asleep. He eased the door shut and walked to the end of the corridor. The flat was so quiet he could hear his own breathing. He looked at the door to the spare bedroom, the room he'd shared with Sophie. It was slightly ajar. His pulse was racing now, his legs were weak. He entered.

The room was in darkness but after a few seconds his eyes adjusted enough to make out a shape under the covers. 'Sophie . . .' She lay very still. Hans tiptoed around the bed to her side and leaned close. He breathed in the smell of her scent. Through the blue-grey dimness he could make out the profile of her face, as lovely as ever. Eyelids closed, hair cut in a bob. His heart sang. 'Sophie,' he whispered, almost laughing with relief. His lower lip brushed the lobe of her pretty left ear. It was cold, as always. *Cold ears, warm heart.* She didn't stir. In a louder voice Hans breathed: 'Sophie, wake up. It's me.' She'd always been a heavy sleeper, but this was ridiculous. 'Sophie!' he laughed. Had she turned into Sleeping Beauty? He bent down to kiss her on the lips, like a prince in a fairy tale, then instantly jerked his head back. 'Sophie?' He reached for the bedside lamp, hand shaking, and knocked it to the floor. 'Shit!' he hissed, bending down to pick it up and put it back on the bedside table. He fumbled for the switch, muttering: 'Please please please please please . . .'

All this noise and she still hadn't woken.

At last the light came on and he saw her.

Her lips were blue. There were thick, finger-shaped bruises around her neck.

'No,' Hans groaned. 'No, no, no. You can't be.'

He lifted up the covers and got in bed with her, wrapping his arms around her shoulders, trying to warm her up. She always wanted him to warm her up. Her body was moving now, quivering slightly, but it was only the vibrations of his own torso as sobs racked him. His tears wet her mottled cheeks. 'No, no, no . . .'

No, no, no, whispered a voice inside him, like a backing vocal.

He looked at Sophie's face again in the lamplight – that regal profile, beautiful in spite of the discoloration – and pain set fire to his body. It began in his chest and radiated through his veins, nerves, bones. It hurt so much that he screamed. Not a scream of anger but of helplessness. When he ran out of breath, Hans closed his eyes and quietly sobbed onto her cold breast. He cried himself into a shallow sleep.

Max

'No, no, no . . .' Max woke in the dark and reached out blindly. His fingertips touched hair, an earlobe. The skin was cold. 'Sophie. Sophie, wake up!'

She turned over, her eyes still closed. 'What's wrong?' She spoke like a ventriloquist, barely moving her lips.

Max sighed with relief. 'You're alive.' He held her closer, inhaling the smell of her hair, kissing her pillow-creased cheek. The other, warmer ear. 'Thank God you're alive.'

Sophie woke up a little. 'Max, what is it?'

You died, he almost said. But he couldn't tell her that. 'Nothing, sorry, go back to sleep.'

She stroked his shoulder, her hand soon slowing as she drifted back into her own dreams.

It was the middle of the night and Max was exhausted, but he was terrified of falling asleep again. Hans kept waking up, remembering, sobbing, and Max couldn't bear the thought of returning there, to that bed with the cold corpse inside it. His body ached – the gunshot wound wasn't fully healed yet – but the pain he felt was nothing compared to Hans's. He was a lucky man, the doctor had told him: the bullet had missed all his vital organs. An inch higher or lower, an inch either side, and he would almost certainly have been killed.

Max had always been the lucky one. He felt guilty about that, but grateful too. Hans had saved the lives of Max's parents when he lost his own; over the years, he had carried more than his fair share of pain and sorrow. And now his suffering was worse than ever. Max wanted to say something to console him, to tell him how sorry he was, but each time he closed his eyes he felt only the silent howl of grief and he knew that his words were poor, small, empty things. So he sat up and watched Sophie breathe until dawn. He focused on each precious breath, each swell of her chest, each flickering pulse in her neck. He held her hand, stroked her belly, and after a while he sensed Hans deeply asleep inside him, soothed by the sweetness of this dream.

Hans

He woke in darkness. He didn't know where he was. For a moment he had no memory of the previous night and then it all came back to him. The black dragonfly dropped from the ceiling and landed on his chest, heavier than ever. He'd fallen asleep hugging Sophie's corpse and he'd dreamed he was watching her sleep, but he was alone in the bed now. No trace of her presence remained. Not even her scent. Hans lay there for what felt like a long time, pinned down by the weight of his grief.

He noticed his uniform neatly folded on a chair beside the bed. Who had done that? The same person who'd killed Sophie? The same person who'd stolen her body while he slept? Hans had nothing else to wear so he put the uniform on and walked to the window.

He looked at his watch: seven in the morning. So many hours to get through . . . He leaned his forehead against the cool glass and closed his eyes and for a moment he was back in that beautiful dream. He stroked Sophie's long hair, lulled by the rhythm and the touch, then his eyes snapped open. Someone else was here. Inside the apartment. He could hear sounds, smell coffee.

In the kitchen Hans found Karl sitting at the table, reading a newspaper, one boot slung nonchalantly on a chair. 'Good morning, little brother.' Karl held up his cup, filled with black liquid. Sophie's cup. 'Want some? It's the real stuff, not that ersatz crap you've been drinking.'

Hans stared at him and Karl looked calmly back. Hans slipped his hand inside his jacket and touched the loaded Luger in its holster. 'You . . . you killed her.' The words like stones, getting stuck in his throat.

'Jawohl.' Karl put the cup down and smiled pleasantly. 'But if you think about it logically, it was your fault.' He said this in a cheerful voice, as if delivering a piece of good news. He got to his feet and walked to the hob. He picked up a metal percolator and poured coffee into another cup, then held the cup towards Hans.

Hans didn't move. 'What are you talking about?'

'Don't you see? You're the one who led us to her. When you freed Jens Arnstein.'

'No . . .' Hans closed his eyes and felt Sophie's head resting on his shoulder. She and Max were on the balcony of their apartment in Rue du Cherche-Midi, looking out at the pale morning sky.

Karl spoke again and the dream dissolved. 'The door guard called me as soon as you left. I guessed who the other man must have been and I sent two agents to follow Arnstein. He led them straight to the flat where your mistress was hiding. Boom! Two birds with one stone.' He paused as if waiting for applause. Seeing that Hans was not going to take the cup from him, Karl placed it on the table and carried the percolator back to his own seat. He poured himself more coffee and sat down. 'We had to shoot Arnstein, of course. But we got the Kahn bitch alive.'

Eyes closed again, Hans kissed Sophie's forehead, warm from the sun. He slid his index finger through the trigger guard.

'I know I said you could help interrogate her, little brother, but in the end I didn't think you had the stomach for it.'

Hans placed a hand on her belly. He took the gun from the holster.

Karl glanced at it but carried on talking in the same unconcerned tone. 'It took a long time to make her talk. A *long* time.'

Hans staggered under the weight of loss and rage. Vengeance was possible, he told himself. It was easy: a second of pressure. But still the Luger hung uselessly by his side.

'She told me everything.' Karl took a sip of coffee and paused as if savouring a fond memory. 'Some of it didn't make much sense, if I'm honest. She said you'd told her that you dreamed of being a Jew every night and you thought maybe your dreams were becoming real . . . ?' He scoffed. 'But, you know, pain can do strange things to the mind.'

Hans opened his eyes. He aimed the Luger at Karl's head and hissed: 'Get out of here.'

Karl raised his eyebrows sceptically, as though he didn't believe in the gun's existence. 'All right, little brother.' He finished his coffee then stood up, steady as a rock in front of Hans's trembling arm. 'You can take today off but I'll expect you back at headquarters tomorrow.' Suddenly his eyes were hard and cold. 'I have a few questions for you.'

Karl walked away. He didn't look back. Hans continued to aim the Luger at him until he'd left the kitchen. When he heard the front door click shut, Hans smashed the gun barrel down on the cup of coffee Karl had poured for him. China shattered. Hot liquid splashed. Hans screamed. Why was he such a fucking coward? He dropped the useless Luger, picked up the hot percolator and flung it against the wall: a black splatter stain, trickles of coffee running down the white-painted walls. He heaved the wooden table onto its side: Sophie's cup fell and broke. He opened the cupboards and began dropping stacks of plates onto the floor, kicking away the shards that accumulated around his feet. He opened the top drawer and threw fistfuls of cutlery across the room. From the middle drawer he grabbed pots and pans and tossed them blindly over his head, bellowing over the sound of crashing metal. He threw lids, smashed bowls, plunged his hands into piles of broken crockery. When he pulled them out again they were smeared with blood. Hans pressed them to his face and hair as he stood groaning and surveyed the carnage. With one last surge of anger he yanked open the lowest drawer and picked up the lid of the cast-iron casserole dish where Sophie used to keep her notebook. He hurled it with all his strength at the ceiling lamp and the light went out with a blue flicker and sizzle. Glass rained softly down. Hans collapsed to the floor. He was an empty husk. In the corner of his eye he caught sight of an envelope inside the cast-iron dish. He picked it up and stared at it. *Hans*, it said. In blue ink, in Sophie's handwriting. He ripped open the envelope, unfolded the letter, and his red fingerprints stained the thick, cream-coloured writing paper.

New Year's Day, 1942

Oh Hans, I wish I didn't have to write you this letter. I don't even know where to start . . . With last night, I suppose. First of all, that was such a brave thing you did: you made yourself completely vulnerable to me. I want you to know that I realise your confession was an act of love, and that, until the very end, I never once

– 341 –

thought about leaving you. But then you told me that you'd read
my notebook.

You may not have understood what you were reading, you may
even already have guessed I was part of a resistance group, but my
network chief always told me I must contact him urgently if my
cover was ever endangered. So I called him last night after you'd
fallen asleep. He told me to leave the apartment. He wanted me
to kill you first – a razor across the throat while you slept – but of
course I couldn't. He says that when you discover the truth about
me, you will tell your superiors everything. Perhaps he's right, but I
can't bring myself to believe that. I believe you love me like no one
else ever has or ever will.

Perhaps this letter is a mistake too, but I couldn't bear the
thought of just abandoning you with no explanation, no last
words. I hope you'll think to look in the place where you found
my journal, and that your colleagues won't search the apartment.
Such slender hopes . . . But they are all we have at the moment.

I want you to know I always loved you, Hans, that I was never
simply using you. I joined the network more than two years ago,
after the execution of those protesters in November '40. At the time
I thought I would never see you again, so it was purely an act of
conscience. But I missed you so much, and then you had the piano
delivered, and I knew I was inextricably in love with you, that
our fates were bound. At first I didn't tell anyone in the network
about you, but the truth came out eventually. I was ordered to get
information from you. I remember being shocked by how easy it
was. I asked and you answered. It made my chief suspicious, in
fact: he thought you might be using me to spread misinformation,
or – he never said this, but I'm intuiting – that I was a double
agent. But then I shot Bauer. He didn't doubt me after that.

This is so hard. I don't want to live without you, Hans. I can't
help believing we were meant to be together. But in the end I have

to choose between my heart and the fate of the world. And I choose the world. However much it hurts, I can't ever regret that.

I'm running out of time, and it's difficult to remember everything I want to tell you. I'm haunted by all the if-onlys. If only you'd saved your parents from that fire. If only you were Max Spiegelman, not Hans Schatten. If only I was the Sophie in your dreams. If only we were on the same side . . . In the next world, we will be. Or perhaps the two of us will live on in Max and Sophie. Perhaps that's who we were all along.

The sky outside is lightening and you'll be awake soon. I have to stop writing now, Hans. I will kiss you goodbye and fall asleep beside you. For the last time.

I'm going to miss you so much. I already do.

love,
Sophie

Hans stared at the words on the page, then at the chaos that surrounded him. All his fury had gone now and he felt only sadness. Sophie was dead and he was alone in a world that held no meaning. In the next world they would be together again. Hans tried to imagine the afterlife. Would they be reunited in hell, amid torment and flames, or in Sheol, which he'd always pictured as a dark and silent cavern? Or perhaps he and Sophie would find each other in that nameless place between sleep and waking where he sometimes spoke with Max, surrounded by warm black water, their intertwined souls shifting and sliding, free of all cares and worries.

He closed his eyes and saw the sky above the rooftops again, felt Sophie's warm body close by. But it wasn't really him, and it wasn't really her. In this world Hans would never see or touch her again. He caught sight of his abandoned Luger floating on a sea of smashed plates and leaned over to pick it up. He could have used this gun to kill Karl, her murderer. But he hadn't. He'd been too weak. Was he strong enough to kill himself? He stared through the black hole of the barrel, then placed it to his temple. Cold metal on skin. He released the safety. His finger curled around the trigger. He closed his eyes and inhaled.

No, said the voice inside. *Don't do this, Hans. We need you.*

Hans exhaled. He clicked the safety back on, dropped the gun on the kitchen floor. Max placed his hand on Sophie's belly and Hans felt the baby kick. He jumped, a thrill of fear in his throat. Something had slid under his fingers, something tiny and alive and vulnerable. Hans opened his eyes, picked up the bloodstained letter and walked to the bed he used to share with Sophie. There he lay down, his arms around her absence, and fell asleep so he could dream of her alive again.

Max

As evening fell above the darkening city, Max and Sophie stood on the balcony holding each other tight. Max had told her what had happened, and they had spent most of the day here, talking and grieving and watching clouds roll slowly across the pale-blue sky. Inside him, Hans was dreaming all of this. They'd kept him alive, but for how long? Max could feel Hans's hurt and despair infecting him even now. 'What kind of world are we bringing our child into, Sophie?'

'A *beautiful* world.' She pulled away from him, her eyes full of passion. 'Look!' He followed her gaze. Swallows were swooping and squealing joyously across the vast violet canvas of the sky. A warm breeze fluttered their hair. 'All this was here before we were, Max,' she said quietly. 'The sky and the sun and the birds and their songs. And all of it will be here after we're gone. Bombers and battleships and guns will all melt, bullets will dissolve in the air, tyrants will rot in the ground, and empires will sink under waves. But *this* will endure. Life will endure.'

'I hope you're right,' said Max, watching the birds in the bright sky and then looking down at the city below, its elegant boulevards stained with the shadows of dusk, where swastika flags hung from thick stone walls, where murderers sat comfortably behind windows eating meals, where unmarked black cars patrolled the streets and under those streets the young and the brave were tortured and killed in cold basement cells, their screams unheard. 'I just don't believe that good will ever vanquish evil.'

'No, of course it won't,' said Sophie, and he looked at her, surprised. 'And evil will never vanquish good.'

He nodded slowly, seeing the truth of this for the first time. The endless struggle, the eternal balance.

'We just have to live, Max. As well as we can. For as long as we can. Keep fighting, keep finding happiness and love. And try not to forget how lucky we are.'

Max sighed, thinking of Hans. 'I can never forget that.'

'Listen, I know you scoffed when I told you this before, but . . . what if Hans really is your guardian angel? What if these things are happening to him so they don't happen to you? Maybe that's his purpose.'

'Maybe.'

'If I speak to Hans now, will he remember what I said when he wakes up tomorrow?'

'Yes.'

Sophie put her lips close to Max's ear, her arms around his shoulders, and murmured: 'Please don't abandon us, Hans. I know it's hard without her, but stay alive. For our sake. I think you're here to save us.'

Hans

He woke with Sophie's words in his head, with the memory of her arms around him, her face close to his. But in the real world Hans was alone, except for the black dragonfly. He went to the bathroom and washed his face in front of the mirror. A gaunt, ghostly figure stared back at him as he tried to work out his next step. He could go to Danton's apartment and ask to join the network. But what if he was being watched? He had already led them to Sophie by freeing Jens. After that, Danton probably wouldn't trust him anyway. And the only way he could help Max and Sophie was to return to 84 Avenue Foch and try to find out more information about the Liberty raid. It would mean seeing Karl again – Hans felt sick to his stomach at the thought – but what choice did he have?

He dressed in his SS uniform and went outside. A grey wet day, the pavements glistening, water dripping from the trees on Avenue Foch. Hans walked until he was outside number 84. The dragonfly was so heavy on his shoulders that he could hardly climb the steps to the front door. Wearily he saluted the door guards and crossed the threshold. Behind the reception desk, one of the officers eyed Hans as he spoke into a telephone receiver. Hans heard the sound of jackboots hammering down marble stairs. He turned around and began making his excuses to the door guards: 'I forgot my briefcase, I—'

But both guards were pointing submachine guns at his chest. 'Hands above your head, Hauptscharführer.'

Hans was taken to the basement and locked in an empty interrogation cell: a small, white-walled room lit by fluorescent tubes, with no furniture except for a concrete bench set two feet off the floor in the centre of one wall. The air smelled of bleach. Hans sat on the bench and held his face in his hands.

The scratch and clunk of a key inside a lock. The door opened and Karl walked in. He stood in front of Hans and beamed down triumphantly. 'Sorry about the temporary accommodation, little brother, but we're going to arrest all Sophie Kahn's comrades next week and I didn't want you sneaking off to warn them.'

Hans looked up through his fingers at that hated face. 'Why don't you just kill me and be done with it?'

'Kill you? Why would I do that?' Karl looked genuinely surprised. 'If you die, there's one less Jew in the world. But if I can train you, mould you into a weapon, you could kill hundreds of them. Thousands.'

Hans shook his head, disgusted. 'I'm not going to help you.'

'We'll see,' said Karl with a little smile. 'I've got nine days to turn you from a pathetic traitor into someone worthy of this uniform. Two hundred and sixteen hours, little brother. And each hour is going to feel like a lifetime.'

Hans said nothing. He stared at the concrete floor, making calculations in his head and waiting for Karl to leave. As soon as he heard the door slam shut, he closed his eyes.

Today is the twenty-eighth of June, he told Max. *In nine days it'll be the seventh of July. You have to get Sophie out of Paris before then.*

Max

A spring breeze rustled the leaves of the birch tree above. Max glanced up at the golden-green dazzle, then down again at the page that shivered slightly in his hands. He was sitting at one end of a bench in Parc Monceau, the man in glasses at the other end, as if they were two strangers. Max was verifying the layout of the offices and cells at 84 Avenue Foch, a page for each floor, marking the placement of the guards with a red pencil. 'What will you do with this information?' he asked before turning to the final page: a plan of the building's basement.

'You don't need to know that, Franz,' said the man in glasses, legs crossed in a casual pose, pretending to read a newspaper. 'Just make sure it's all correct.'

'But you've warned the others? About the seventh?'

'Yes, as I already I told you,' the man replied in a bored voice.

'And they all have somewhere to go?'

'We've located a new hiding place.'

'What about the travel permits that Danton promised me?'

'You'll have them soon.'

Bientôt: the man had been telling him this for weeks now. Danton had been arrested in May and the man in glasses was now Max's only contact in the network. He hadn't revealed his codename but Max instinctively thought of him as Robespierre.

'Give me a specific date or I'm not going to help you.'

'Keep your voice down, Franz, and don't look at me when you speak,' Robespierre muttered as a woman pushed a pram along the path in front of them. When she had moved out of sight, he added: 'I can't give you an exact date. It's a difficult situation.'

'But it has to be before the seventh.'

No answer. Max glanced up from the page to Robespierre's eyes, which were gazing blindly at the newspaper from behind his glasses. At last he nodded.

JULY

Max

He sat in the conciergerie of his apartment building and waited.
It was a small room furnished only with a desk and two chairs.
The air was humid, his shirt sticky with sweat. The concierge sat
behind her desk and leafed through some papers. Max glanced at
his watch: quarter past three. Where was Robespierre? The concierge had told him this morning that the network chief would
meet him here at three.

For the past week Max and Sophie had been cooped up in the
apartment, distractedly trying to read books or play music while
they waited for their travel permits. He'd even taught Sophie chess
but the game seemed to mirror reality too closely – angles of escape
being cut off, the final move looming – and in the end she decided
she would rather watch clouds instead.

Max checked his watch again: twenty past three. He stroked the
pistol inside his pocket. If Robespierre didn't hand over the permits today, Max would aim the gun at his face and . . . and what?
He leaned back in his chair and ran through various scenarios in his
head. None of them ended well. He wondered if he would have to
kill the concierge too.

At last there was a knock at the door. The concierge struggled
to her feet and went to answer it. 'I'll leave you two in peace,' she
said in the doorway, before disappearing. Max wrapped his fingers
around the pistol butt and waited for Robespierre to enter.

But he didn't.

The man who came in was even taller and thinner and did not
wear glasses. Max gasped. Jens gave a lopsided grin. 'Not who you

were expecting?' Speechless, Max leapt to his feet and hugged him tight. Jens whined like a dreaming dog. 'Shit, I think you may have rebroken a few ribs there, Max.'

'Sorry. I just . . . I didn't think I'd ever see you again!'

'Yeah, I had my doubts about that too.'

The months of incarceration and torture had changed Jens, that was obvious. His gaze was steadier, his voice hoarser, the lines around his mouth and eyes a different shape. For a moment Max felt awed by his friend's new gravitas. Then he remembered: 'Oh, I have news. Sophie's pregnant!'

'That's wonderful. So I'm going to be an uncle.' Jens's voice was warm but unsurprised.

'You already knew.'

'I'd heard, yes.'

'Come upstairs now. Sophie will die when she sees you!'

Jens gave a mournful smile. 'That's exactly why I can't go upstairs. She already knows too much. The last thing the two of you need is any further connection to me.' Max opened his mouth to protest but Jens put his hand on Max's shoulder and said in a low voice: 'Please don't argue, Max. There's no time.'

'All right. But at least tell me how you escaped.'

'I was rescued. Voltaire ran the operation, but it was the information you gave him that made it possible. The map of the cells. I owe you my life, Max.'

'Who's Voltaire?'

'The man you were expecting to meet today.'

'Robespierre?' Max said incredulously. 'The tall guy in glasses?'

'Is that what you called him?' Jens looked amused. 'Yeah, he could be a dick. But he was good at his job.'

'*Was?*'

'He died saving me. I'm not sure that was much of a bargain, from the network's point of view.'

So the man Max had spent weeks cursing had saved his best friend's life . . . Max's thoughts were a tangle of remorse and confusion. 'When was this?'

'Three days ago. Sorry I couldn't come earlier. I had to lie low, as you can imagine.'

'Of course, but—'

'You need the travel permits.'

'Yes.'

'I have them here.'

'Oh, thank God.'

Jens took the documents from his pocket and placed them on the desk. Max eagerly examined them. 'Try not to get into any deep conversations with the police. I'm not sure these identities would stand up to much scrutiny.' Max nodded and Jens handed him more papers. 'This is a map of the spot where you'll cross the demarcation line and these are the names and numbers of some comrades on the other side: memorise them, then burn this paper. Here are your train tickets. And some cash. I wish we could give you more.'

'Thank you, Jens. Thank you so much.'

'You should go now. There's a train leaving at five from the Gare de Lyon.'

Jens sounded businesslike, perhaps even impatient, and Max couldn't help feeling hurt. He'd just got his friend back and already they were about to be separated. 'Jens, please come and see Sophie. This might be the last chance we ever get.'

Jens shook his head but less brusquely than before. 'Oh, enough with the puppy-dog eyes,' he said, looking away. When Max still didn't move, Jens sighed. 'All right. I can't stay long, though.'

Max ran upstairs with the documents and burst into the apartment, calling out excitedly: 'Sophie, look who's here! And he got us the permits. We can leave Paris today.'

He found her on the sofa. She was wearing a dressing gown and looked pale and worn out. When Jens entered the room, her face was briefly transformed by joy. She stood up and the three of them hugged, together for the first time in eight years.

'Sophie, what's the matter?' Jens asked as soon as he caught sight of her face.

'My waters broke,' Sophie said. 'The contractions have started.'

Hans

He was asleep on the concrete bench. His limbs twitched and his eyeballs darted back and forth beneath the thin lids. In his dream he was holding Max and Sophie's tiny newborn baby on his shoulder. Even after the bell started ringing and electric light flooded his vision, even after the image of that sweet little girl was obliterated, he could still feel the warmth of her soft round cheek against his, the almost weightless bundle of flesh and bones in his arms.

Mechanically Hans swung his legs around and groped with his hands until he was sitting up. Squinting against the dazzle, he could see the young guard still shaking the bell as he yelled: 'On your feet! What is your name?'

On the floor beside the guard, as always, was a metal tray containing a hunk of bread, a tin mug of water, and a whip.

Hans resisted the temptation to close his eyes. 'SS-Hauptscharführer Hans Oskar Schatten,' he muttered, pushing himself up from the bench. The ringing stopped.

'Louder!' said the guard.

'SS-Hauptscharführer Hans Oskar Schatten!' Hans shouted.

He was so hungry and thirsty and sleep-deprived he could hardly stand. If it weren't for his dreams, he knew, he would have cracked long ago. But Max and Sophie's baby, little Suzi, had kept him moored to himself, fed him with a secret source of hope when all else had been stripped away.

The guard put the bell on the tray and picked up the whip. Hans flinched at the sight of the leather cracker dangling from the end of the long cord. The wounds on his chest and arms and back were only just starting to heal. For the past three days he had given no wrong answers.

'Who is our guiding spirit and protector?' the guard demanded.

'The Führer, Adolf Hitler!'

'To whom do we owe our allegiance?'

'The Führer, Adolf Hitler!'

The words were like a deeply carved groove through which Hans rolled unthinkingly.

'Who is our greatest enemy?'

He half-closed his eyes and glimpsed the sleeping baby in his arms. 'The Jews.'

The whip twitched. 'Louder!'

'The Jews are our greatest enemy!'

'What must be done with them?'

They must be saved, Hans thought.

The guard raised his right arm and Hans's knees buckled momentarily. He forced himself to stand straight.

'What must be done with them?' the guard shouted.

'They must be destroyed!'

'Louder!'

'THEY MUST BE DESTROYED!'

At last the guard told Hans he could drink. Hans knelt down and crawled over to the tray. He raised the mug to his lips. His hand was shaking so badly that some of the water spilled down his chin and he frantically tried to push it back into his parched mouth. Even while he drank, he was hungrily eyeing the piece of stale bread. As he carefully set the mug down, still half-full, and reached for the bread, the guard unexpectedly stood in his way, the whip still dangling menacingly from his hand. Hans looked up, dumbfounded by this change in routine.

'What is today's date?' the guard asked.

'I . . . I don't know.'

'What is today's date?'

Hans understood. He would not be allowed to eat until he had guessed correctly. He had no idea how much time had elapsed since he'd been locked in this cell. At random, he said: 'The third of July?'

'Wrong.'

'The fifth of July?'

'Wrong.'

'The sixth of July?'

'Wrong. You know why?'

Hans looked blankly at the guard.

'It's past midnight,' the guard said.

'The seventh of July?'

Without a word the guard picked up the bell and turned on his heel. He left the cell, locking the door behind him.

Hans ate and drank with a pleasure and relief so great that they turned to shame when he caught sight of his reflection in the metal tray. How could he care so much about staying alive when Sophie had been murdered? He ought to be stronger than thirst, than hunger. It sickened him that his body had such power over him. When he'd finished the bread and water, he crawled slowly over to the bench, lay down and closed his eyes.

And then he remembered what day it was.

It was just after midnight: half-moon rising over rooftops, the first hint of chill in the air. Max and Sophie were leaving their apartment on Rue du Cherche-Midi. Max carried their belongings in a knapsack and their sleeping daughter wrapped in a blanket on his shoulder while Sophie peered at the hand-drawn map. They didn't speak at all. While they walked through darkness, they listened out for the echo of other footsteps, the hum of distant car engines. It was long after curfew and anyone they met on the street at night would almost certainly be an enemy.

Tonight was the seventh of July. They didn't know whether the raid would take place tonight or tomorrow night but they'd decided it would be too dangerous to stay at home. Max had gone to the Gare de Lyon earlier in the day and tried to buy train tickets to the Zone Libre but he couldn't get one for Suzi because she didn't have a travel permit. In fact they couldn't even rent a hotel room without a third ID card. Jens had told them he could manufacture new identity papers for their baby but they would not be ready until the next day. So Max and Sophie were left with no choice: they had to go underground.

They reached the iron fence that surrounded the Jardin du Luxembourg and followed it along Rue Auguste-Comte. As he walked behind Sophie, Max kept checking that his daughter was still breathing. How perfect she was, so small and frail, and how wrong that she should be in such danger in only her second day of life. Poor little Suzi . . . He'd wanted to call her Sophie, in tribute to Hans's lost love, but his Sophie had said that would be too confusing, so in the end they'd settled on Suzana, a contraction of their mothers' names. Suzi for short.

They came to a house, and a figure emerged from the shadows. Max tensed but Sophie kept walking. The man spoke in a murmur and Sophie recited the words Jens had made her memorise. The man turned and disappeared into a doorway. Max and Sophie followed. When the door was shut behind them, the man turned on a lantern and they caught a glimpse of his face in the yellow light. He was a boy, not a man: he couldn't have been older than sixteen or seventeen.

The boy led them down a steep staircase into a basement and Max concentrated on not losing his footing. At the far end of the basement, hidden behind planks leaning against the concrete wall, was a small door. Max had to duck his head to get through it, and the corridor in which he found himself on the other side was narrow and not much higher. 'Close the door,' the boy said in a neutral tone, and as soon as Max did they were encased in a cool, humid blackness that the halo of light from the lantern seemed only to deepen. Max breathed in the damp smell of rot and felt the first stirrings of panic.

'Where are we going?' he asked in a whisper.

'The catacombs,' said the boy. 'Safest place in the city.'

Hans

He was mumbling and twitching on the concrete bench for several minutes before Karl rang the bell next to his ear. He gasped and sat up, covering his eyes with his forearm. In his dream everything had been so dark and silent.

'On your feet!' Karl barked. 'Name!'

'SS-Hauptscharführer Hans Oskar Schatten.'

Hans's ears were still ringing and he could barely hear his own voice.

'Louder!'

'SS-Hauptscharführer Hans Oskar Schatten!'

'Who is our guiding spirit and protector?'

'The Führer, Adolf Hitler!'

'To whom do we owe our allegiance?'

'The Führer, Adolf Hitler!'

'Who is our greatest enemy?'

'The Jews!'

'What must be done with them?'

'They must be destroyed!'

'Louder!'

'THEY MUST BE DESTROYED!'

'Good,' said Karl with a smile. 'And what is today's date?'

'The seventh of July.'

'Yes. The night of the Liberty raid. Are you ready, little brother?'

Hans looked into Karl's eyes and felt an inkling of dread. 'Ready for what?'

Max

The boy took Max's knapsack and carried it down an iron ladder that led through a sort of dry well. Sophie, carrying the lantern, went next. When she was about six feet into the narrow hole, she looked up at Max and said: 'It's all right. Come on.'

Sophie knew all about his claustrophobia. She understood that the prospect of hiding in the Paris catacombs – that vast network of tunnels sixty feet underground where the bones of six million corpses lay neatly stacked – was Max's worst nightmare come to life. Suzi, now strapped to his chest, whined quietly. Her eyes were still tightly shut. Was she was having bad dreams or did she sense her father's fear? Max pressed his lips to her forehead, stroked her silky hair, and said 'Shhh.' Then he turned around and began to climb down the ladder.

At the bottom the boy took the lantern from Sophie and silently walked ahead of them through the narrow corridor. Sophie held
Max's hand and asked: 'How is she?' She spoke in a low voice but
it was amplified by the strange acoustics of the tunnel and the boy
turned around with his finger to his lips.

'Still sleeping,' Max whispered. 'Still breathing.'

Sophie squeezed his hand.

Max filled his lungs with the stale, putrid air and tried not to
think about the massive weight of earth pressing down on them
from above.

They followed the boy for what felt like hours, their feet trudg-
ing through foul water, until at last they reached a small opening
where the ground was higher – and dry. Someone had lit a fire. The
boy held up his lantern, illuminating the squarish shape of this
underground room. There were half a dozen other couples there,
with small children. Piles of blankets and pillows. Some food and
flasks of water. The sound of coughing and wailing, whispers and
lullabies. The palpable tension of fear. The boy carried the lantern
to an unoccupied corner and dropped the knapsack onto the rock
floor. 'You're the last ones,' he told them. 'I'll be back in the morning.'

'Thank you,' said Sophie.

The boy nodded and walked away, the lantern's glow shrink-
ing then vanishing and leaving them in the dim flicker of firelight.
None of the others spoke to them. They were busy with their own
little ones, and besides, they were all aware of the network's rules:
the fewer comrades you knew, the fewer would be endangered if
you were caught. Now Max had stopped walking, Suzi started to
fuss again. Sophie loosened the straps tied around his back and
lowered the child into her arms. She sat next to Max and the two
of them watched their daughter breastfeed in the smoky orange
glow, arguing in low voices over which of them should sleep first.

In the end Sophie won the argument and Max lay on the blanket, a pillow under his head, Suzi curled up inside his arm. He felt guilty that Sophie, who had given birth only yesterday, should be the one to keep guard, but it was true that he hadn't slept much recently: his dreams were unendurable and he'd been constantly on edge at the thought of the looming raid. Would he even have trusted himself to stay awake?

The baby was silent but wide-eyed, so Sophie sang her a lullaby in a hushed voice. 'Row, row, row your boat, gently down the stream . . .' Max's breathing slowed and in place of the mass of earth suspended above his head he found himself in a boat floating on a glassy lake, water lapping against the hull, on a perfect summer afternoon long ago.

When Suzi had fallen asleep, Sophie leaned across and kissed Max on the lips. 'Süsse Träume.'

'What time is it?' he asked drowsily.

She looked at her watch in the faint glow of firelight. 'Ten past one.'

'Wake me if you hear anything. And wake me after an hour no matter what.'

'I will. Now get some sleep.'

Hans

In the cold cell, Hans's fingers were numb as he tried to button up his jacket. He was so tired he could feel himself swaying as he stood. His eyes closed for a second and he heard the notes of the lullaby echoing slowly inside his head. The song, the girl, and—

Karl slapped him hard in the face. Hans reeled but stayed on his feet. His cheek stung, his ear hummed. 'Time to wake up, little brother. You remember what the Führer said about the Nazi of the future? "He must be tough as leather and hard as Krupp steel." You're too soft.' Karl grabbed the back of Hans's hair and pulled his face close. His breath smelled of meat. 'I'm going to change that,' he whispered. 'I'm going to melt you down and forge you into something new. Tonight we will hunt down your weakness . . . and kill it.'

Sophie

Max groaned in his sleep. Suzi lay beside him, cradled in a nest of blankets. Sophie stroked Max's back and shushed him. The last thing she needed was him waking up their daughter. Other than the echoing drip-drip-drip of water in the tunnels, there was almost no sound at all. The fire was dying and in the spreading darkness she couldn't tell if any of the others were awake. But there was no way the Nazis could find them down here, Sophie told herself. The catacombs were a labyrinth: she and Max probably wouldn't even be able to find their way back to the surface without the boy's help. What was happening up there now? She imagined the SS raiding their apartment on Rue du Cherche-Midi, Karl Schatten smashing her piano in a rage when he realised his prey had escaped. She tried to picture where the boy might be hiding, then felt a jolt of panic at the thought of what would happen if he were killed or arrested during the night. Would they ever make it out of the catacombs? Sophie went over to the embers of the fire and looked at her watch. Two twenty. She had let Max sleep longer than he'd wanted, but he looked so peaceful now that she was reluctant to wake him. He'd been sleeping badly ever since he was shot. Besides, she felt wide awake. She sat down beside him, her back against the hard rock wall, and thought about the book she was going to write.

Hans

He sat in the back of a limousine, flanked by SS guards with sub-machine guns. Through the windows he saw the monuments of Paris flash past. The Arc de Triomphe, the obelisk in the Place de la Concorde, the Seine glittering in moonlight. The streets were empty and they made quick progress. The thrum of the engine lulled Hans to sleep and he dreamed of silent blackness, dripping water.

The car stopped and Hans woke with a start. The guards pulled him out and he found to his surprise that they were not parked by any of the safe houses on the Liberty list. They were near the Jardin du Luxembourg. They entered a brightly lit building. A for-mer school, by the looks of it. Not the same place where Max and Sophie had gone, he noted with relief. The clock on the wall in the entrance hall told Hans it was half past two in the morning. Karl led them down a series of steps into an underground bunker, where soldiers saluted them. Their 'Sieg Heil's echoed in the cav-ernous dark. The air smelled of paraffin. One of the soldiers took a wooden stave from a rack on the wall and dipped its end into a large bucket. Another soldier held a lighter close. The flaming torch lit up the space around them. They were in what looked like a disused Metro station. The walls were painted with swastikas and train tracks swept past the platform where they stood. Karl and the two guards were each given a torch. Karl's face shimmered demon-ically. 'Follow me,' he said, before jumping off the platform and striding along the train tracks, torch aloft.

Fearful now, Hans asked: 'Where are we going?'

'The catacombs, little brother,' Karl called over his shoulder. 'You're not afraid of ghosts, are you?'

One of the guards prodded Hans in the ribs with the barrel of his submachine gun. Hans jumped onto the tracks. Stumbling over sleepers, he caught up with Karl. 'Why are we going to the catacombs?' he asked. His voice sounded shaky. It was hard to get enough air in his lungs.

'The resistance found out about our raid,' Karl explained. 'But we discovered their new hiding place.'

Hans closed his eyes and silently hissed: *Wake up.*

Sophie

Max's body twitched and he made those little grunting, humming noises he always made when he was having a nightmare, as if he had a mouthful of bees. He was desperately trying to break the surface of his dream, to come up for air and yell, but Sophie was worried he might wake Suzi or the others. One of the men had rebuilt the fire an hour ago but they all seemed fast asleep now. So she lay down next to Max and curled her body around his, resting her chin on his shoulder and whispering: 'Shhh, it's all right, Max, everything's fine, we're safe, go back to sleep'. At last he calmed down and the twitching ceased. After that there was no sound but the dripping of water, the crackle of the fire, her loved ones' breathing.

Hans

They fell into a steady rhythm and Hans listened to the crunch of their boots in the ballast, the quiet roar of the torch flames, his own ragged breathing. After a while they turned into a narrower corridor and left the train tracks behind. Here the air was closer and damp cobwebs clung to Hans's face. The crunch of ballast was replaced by the slosh and squelch of muddy water. A vile smell filled Hans's nostrils and stung the back of his throat. The guards walked in single file behind him and the light from their torches illuminated walls crammed with human bones. So many dead bodies . . . Where had their souls gone? Hans thought of Sheol. Was *this* what the afterlife would be like?

They came to a place where the tunnel divided. Three identical-looking arteries branched out in different directions. Karl stopped and stared into each, frowning. Hope flared in Hans: perhaps they were lost? Karl ordered one of the guards to step closer and hold his torch, then took a sheet of paper from his jacket pocket. He unfolded what appeared to be a map and examined it. In the wavering light Hans caught a glimpse of some words painted on a wall in one of the tunnels: YOU ARE ENTERING THE EMPIRE OF THE DEAD. Hans shivered. Now he was no longer moving forward he could feel fatigue unfurling through his body, like blood in water. His legs wobbled, his eyelids drooped. Perhaps it was just the effects of sleep deprivation, but there seemed something unreal about tonight. The watery silence, the undertow of dread, the maze of tunnels, the interminable quest. It was like a dream – a normal person's dream. The kind that quickly vanishes upon waking. Maybe I'm dying, Hans thought. Maybe my body is stretched out even now on that concrete bench in the brightly lit cell but my soul is retreating inward, spiralling down to the underworld in search of Sophie. Is she here somewhere? He looked around but saw only Karl and the guards and beyond them darkness. Surrendering to exhaustion, he closed his eyes and found himself staring into a vast black sea. Sleep or death? Either way, it looked peaceful and inviting. Was this where he would find her again? Hans yearned to dive into its depths, to let his soul swim with hers in night eternal. He staggered and his hand caught hold of a wall to stop himself falling.

'Wake up, little brother,' said Karl, laughing. 'We're almost there.'

Karl folded the map and led them into the tunnel with the writing on the wall.

The empire of the dead.

Sophie

She was deep in thoughts of her novel when little Suzi started to fidget and moan. In the flickering firelight Sophie looked at her watch: almost four in the morning. Only a few more hours and the boy would return to lead them back to the surface. She picked up the child's small warm body and felt it wriggle in her arms. Suzi's mouth opened wide – here came the howl – but Sophie inserted a nipple between her daughter's lips before any sound could emerge and after that all she could hear was the sucking of breastmilk. She exhaled with relief. Beside her, Max was breathing regularly, finally at peace.

Hans

Had time slowed down? Hans felt as if he'd been walking through this tunnel for hours. He'd grown numb to the endless parade of stacked bones, the sightless skulls staring out at them as they passed. Slosh and squelch, drip and roar. The music of the catacombs mesmerised him and he fell into a sort of trance. You're dying, he reminded himself; this is all an illusion. Karl and the guards are not real, they will fade and vanish as you walk these tunnels and eventually you will find her and the two of you will be together again. This is God's final test. Just keep going.

But how would he find her? There were six million souls under Paris alone, and if he really was in Sheol then that figure must be multiplied six million times. How could he locate Sophie among such a crowd? With love, he thought. Rebuild her. Pile memory upon memory, desire upon desire, until she is standing there before you. So Hans remembered Sophie playing the piano in the apartment on Rue des Princes, and in the window of the shop on

Prinzenstrasse years ago, the tendons in her neck fluttering beneath the skin. He remembered their first kiss in Frau Schatten's living room, their sad farewell on the train station platform in Vienna. The duet they'd played at the Konzerthaus and the duets they played in Paris. The stars on her ceiling. His fingertips tracing that scar on the back of her head. Her fingertips touching his scar, the tingle of electricity under his skin.

Sophie

She held her breath and listened. She thought she'd heard something far off in one of the tunnels. Were those lights in the distance or just the after-image of the fire in her eyes? Suzi's body stiffened and Sophie looked down at her daughter's face. Her little mouth was screwing up. Was she about to scream? Please don't scream, Sophie thought. She stood, gently patting her daughter's back while she bounced up and down on the balls of her feet. 'It's all right, my sweet,' Sophie whispered. 'Don't cry, everything will be fine.'

Hans

Squelch and slosh, drip-drip-drip. Water, water everywhere and not a drop to drink. Hans imagined licking the moisture from the walls. He stared at Karl's thick fingers holding the torch a few feet ahead and remembered Sophie's swanlike neck, so pale and slender, covered in gross bruises. The coldness of her earlobe. The blueness of her lips. *Hold me, warm me up.*

At last Karl stopped. He lowered the torch. He was peering into the darkness ahead. Hans followed his gaze. Was that firelight? Karl turned to the others and whispered: 'This is it.' He slid his torch handle into the eye socket of a skull and motioned the guards to extinguish their torches in the puddles at their feet. A hiss and the scent of smoke. In the feeble light of the one remaining torch, Karl put his finger to his lips then took off his boots. The guards followed suit. Hans understood: they were going to sneak up on their victims. Karl took a flask of water from his knapsack and drank from it. A waterfall pouring down his throat. He wiped his mouth then looked at Hans. He held the flask up, eyebrows raised questioningly.

Hans nodded.

Karl pointed at his boots.

Obediently, Hans took them off. He held out his hand for the flask.

'Who is our guiding spirit and protector?' Karl asked in a whisper.

'The Führer, Adolf Hitler,' Hans whispered back.

'To whom do we owe our allegiance?'

'The Führer, Adolf Hitler.'

'Who is our greatest enemy?'

'Please can I just have—'

Karl grabbed him by the throat and squeezed. He let go and repeated: 'Who is our greatest enemy?'

Hans swallowed painfully. 'The Jews are our greatest enemy.'

'What must be done with them?'

'They must be destroyed.'

Finally Karl passed him the flask and Hans drank every drop. He closed his eyes with relief and saw the vast black sea again. But his Sophie wasn't here; he understood that now. He wasn't dying – this was real. Max and Sophie were not at the end of this tunnel, of course, but someone was. Liberty agents, frightened fugitives, sleeping children. And, in their world, Max and Sophie were being hunted down by another Karl Schatten, as hateful and relentless as this one.

Silently Hans screamed: *Wake up!*

But Max slept on and the only sound Hans could hear in that world was Sophie murmuring, 'Please don't scream, everything's all right.'

Hans gave the flask back to Karl, who dropped it in his knapsack, then held something else out to Hans. In the shadowy half-light it took Hans a few seconds to see what Karl had in his hand. A pistol.

'Take it,' Karl ordered softly. 'This is where you start to redeem yourself, little brother. Kill them and all will be forgiven. You'll have as much food and drink as you want. You'll be free.'

Hans took the gun from Karl's hand. It was his old Luger. The same pistol he'd had since the age of eighteen, and which he had never once used.

Sophie

What was that? Sophie stopped bouncing for a second. A shushing, splashing sound. Distant, but amplified by the tunnel's acoustics. Footsteps through water? She felt Suzi's body tense in her arms and began to bounce again. But Sophie was alert now. She edged towards the fire and kicked ashes over the embers. Darkness shrouded their hiding place. She looked through the tunnel again. Those really were lights, weren't they? It could be the boy coming back early. But hadn't he arrived from the opposite direction when he brought them here? Sophie's heart was speeding. Her calves were cramping. She wanted to wake Max, to warn the others, but if she stopped bouncing up and down she feared Suzi would begin to howl. And that would give their position away.

In a hushed voice, she started to sing her daughter's favourite lullaby.

Hans

They crept closer to the fire and someone there must have heard them because the glow abruptly vanished. In the distant, intermittent light from the last torch flame, far behind them, Hans could see the other three turned towards him as if frozen: the guards holding their submachine guns, Karl with his pistol dangling casually from one hand. Had time stopped? No, the light still flickered, illuminating Karl's eyes, a guard's mouth, a swastika armband, a tensed trigger finger. The three of them were watching Hans, waiting for him to move past them through the tunnel towards the prey huddled in darkness. But Hans didn't move. He was remembering something Sophie had once told him about fairy tales: 'The hero voyages to a faraway land or a dark forest, where he has to perform a brave deed. Something that changes him. And then he has to find his way back home . . .'

But how could he find his way home? How could he find his way back to Sophie? Close his eyes and tap his heels together three times and think to himself: *There's no place like home?*

He closed his eyes. And that's when he heard it. The sound of her voice.

'Row

      row

          row

              your boat . . .'

That song. The same tune Sophie had been playing when he first saw her. The same one his mother had played as he fell asleep at the top of the stairs that night. He could hear it again now, slowed down and breathy. A long silence between each word. The jaunty melody transformed into a lullaby. A magical incantation. A way back from the dark forest.

Time to close the circle. The song, the girl . . . and death.

Karl was opening his mouth now, words were about to explode into the air, words that would puncture this unnatural silence, burst the bubble of this expanding moment, and send two Nazis with submachine guns into the darkness to kill. Hans had to stop them. That was his purpose, the meaning of his life. He was a guardian angel. He had to save them, he had to die, and then he really would be in Sheol and the Nazis would fade and vanish and he would be together with Sophie again. *Rebuild her*, he urged himself. *Pile memory upon memory, longing upon longing, until she is standing there before you.* Hans remembered all the letters Sophie had written to him, the faith to keep writing even when she received no reply. He remembered the words in her last letter. *Perhaps the two of us will live on in Max and Sophie . . .* He felt a sudden touch-memory of Suzi's soft round cheek pressed against his. Her silken hair, her weightless body. He remembered swallows swooping across a violet sky. *I think you're here to save us.* Sophie stood before him; she held his hand and smiled. How wrong he had been to curse God for all the obstacles He had thrown in their path. Hans had been so lucky ever to have known Sophie, to have loved her, to have felt her love. The bitterness inside him evaporated and was scattered to the winds. Still Karl didn't speak and now something odd was happening: as her voice sang softly in Hans's head, slowly, stutteringly, like birds hatching from eggs, words emerged from between his lips, which curved into a strange smile as he opened his eyes to the torchlit darkness and sang in faltering English:

'Gently

      down

            the

                  stream . . .'

Karl snorted contemptuously. He took a step towards Hans, his face close and dimly illuminated. 'You're as crazy as your bitch was at the end, little brother.'

But Hans sang over him, raising his voice and smiling that disturbing, scarred smile of his.

'Merrily
    merrily
        merrily
            merrily . . .'

As he sang, Hans calmly raised the pistol, invisible in the darkness, until it was level with Karl Schatten's temple. And shot him dead.

In the long, stunned second that followed, as Karl's massive body fell backwards through dancing fingers of torchlight, a black-edged red hole burned in the skin beside his eye, all his certainty and superiority and hate spurting in a black gush from the larger hole on the other side of his skull, as the women and children at the end of the tunnel cried out and began to run, as resistance agents fired shots into the darkness and submachine guns crackled in response, as the two SS guards turned back to gape at their commander's fallen body and trained their guns on his killer, Hans raised the pistol's barrel to his own temple and closed his eyes.

He had killed his weakness. He'd performed the brave deed. He had changed. Now he had to find his way home.

The song, the girl, and death.

Max

He was rising towards the surface as Hans sank down through black water. For a moment they were together, souls intertwined, face to face.

Hans, don't!

It's the only way.

But—

You need time, Max.
And I need to find my way home.

    Thank you, Max tried to say. *For everything.* But Hans had gone, plunging into darkness as Max rose towards the light.

Hans

Sophie was with him now, down here in the dark. Hans felt her skin warm against his, felt her love surrounding him, felt himself easing into it, swimming through its bottomless ocean. Love like black water, like dreamless sleep. I don't ever want to wake up, he thought.

    In the tunnel, time had stopped. The guards were paralysed. Even the torchlight no longer flickered. Eyes squeezed shut, Hans whispered: 'Das Leben ist nur ein Traum.'

    He caressed the trigger and a thousand swallows soared into the sky.

    It was five past five in the morning.

Max

He woke with a start. He was lying on a blanket in an underground cavern and when he opened his eyes he saw firelight reflected on the low ceiling. His heart was racing and he assumed it was because of his claustrophobia. But it wasn't.

    Rubbing his eyes, Max wondered what had woken him. A noise, he thought vaguely, something loud and violent. An explosion? A gunshot? A sound in his dream? His eyes were still half-closed and a familiar tune was circling his head. As he sat up, he followed the thread of the descending melody towards its end –

> *Merrily*
> > *merrily*
> > > *merrily*
> > > > *merrily . . .*

– and the memory of his dream coalesced around those words.

Karl Schatten.

Nazis with submachine guns.

Sneaking through the tunnel towards them.

Max felt a surge of fear and hope. His eyes opened wide and he saw Suzi asleep beside him in the nest of blankets, Sophie sitting by the fire.

'Sophie,' he whispered. 'What time is it?'

She turned, amused. 'Same as it was the last time you asked.'

'What time?' Max insisted.

Sophie looked at her watch. 'Eleven minutes past one.'

For an instant Max was at the top of the stairs in the Prinzen-strasse apartment, a thirteen-year-old boy waking disoriented after a nightmare. Then he remembered that last conversation with Hans, the pistol barrel cold against his temple. And he understood. His guardian angel had saved him again.

'Sophie, we have to leave now!' Max said. 'They know we're here.'

Max

Green fields roared past the window. Only another ten minutes until they reached the demarcation line. It was hot in compartment 50, even with the window open. Max had been sitting in the same position for hours and both his hands were going numb. Sophie's head was lolling heavily on his right shoulder while Suzi lay across his lap, her tiny skull nestled in the crook of his left elbow. He watched fields of wheat and corn flash by one after another in the morning sunlight and marvelled at how normal everything looked. He contorted his wrist under Suzi's body to check his watch: eleven fifty-one. The second hand took an eternity to tick its way around the full circle.

Eleven fifty-two. The night was a smashed mirror. He saw it reflected in fragments: waking the other agents in the catacombs and telling them they had to leave, getting lost again and again in that labyrinth of tunnels, frightened parents shushing crying children, before finally finding the ladder, the door, the building, and going outside to breathe the cool, fresh air of night-time. The look of surprise on the boy's face when he saw them there, then the waiting while he spoke on the telephone before guiding them all to a new hiding place. Hours of dark silence and broken sleep until, haloed by the light of dawn outside, a tall figure entered the room . . . and then the relief at hearing Jens's voice, the elation as he gave them Suzi's freshly forged papers. The hurried explanations, the tearful goodbyes, followed by the long wait in the Gare de Lyon, watching the exits and talking about Hans until they could finally board their train . . .

'Papers!' a voice barked from somewhere down the corridor. The train was starting to slow. Max looked at his watch – eleven fifty-seven – and caught his breath. They were approaching Vierzon.

Max remembered the night train he'd taken from Vienna to Paris four years ago, the terror he'd felt at the idea that the SS guard examining his identification might, impossibly, be Hans. Now he would have given anything to see that scarred face again, but he knew it wasn't going to happen. Hans was dead and he, Max, was alone.

He closed his eyes. If he'd done that yesterday he would have seen the world through Hans's eyes, inhabited Hans's body, but now he saw only the reddish insides of his own eyelids, heard only the wind whistling through the open window, felt only the sticky warmth of Sophie's skin against his. A whole world had vanished. The black dragonfly fluttered down and landed on him and for the first time Max sensed its true weight.

He felt different now, he realised: not merely relieved and grateful and guilty and grief-stricken, but as if his soul had grown deeper, darker, vaster, like the vision of Paris he'd glimpsed down in the catacombs. That black vastness scared him, but it was part of him. And it always had been; Max understood that now. This was how it felt to be whole, to be fully human. The light indivisible from the shadow.

'Papers!' A fist hammering on a door close by. Max watched his daughter's face, expecting her features to contract into a howl, but Suzi continued sleeping peacefully. He twisted his arm and looked at his watch.

Eleven fifty-nine.

Outside, fields gave way to the backs of houses, parked cars, brick walls, a steel roof. Inside the station in Vierzon, the train juddered to a halt. The pressure on Max's shoulder lifted. He turned to see Sophie gazing groggily through the window.

'We're here?' she whispered.

He nodded, too nervous to speak.

Bang! Bang! Bang! The door of their compartment shook, then opened. A pair of black jackboots stomped heavily across the linoleum floor and a man in SS uniform barked: 'Papers!' Still cradling Suzi's sleeping body, Max reached into his jacket pocket and took out the fake ID cards, the travel permits, the train tickets. Without looking up, he held them out to a leather-gloved hand. The hand took them. Max glanced at Sophie's face: she was staring down adoringly at Suzi, stroking her daughter's peachlike cheek with the back of a little finger, as if the guard was not even there.

Max held his breath and looked up at the guard. He was staring at Suzi.

'Cute baby,' the guard said at last, in strongly accented French. 'Congratulations.'

'Merci,' sighed Max and Sophie as he gave them back their papers.

Five minutes later they crossed into the Zone Libre.

Somewhere in Dordogne, Max fell asleep.

And he dreamed.

In the dream he was swimming underwater, sliding through a warm black sea. And she was there with him, their limbs and souls intertwined.

As he woke, these images dissolved, leaving only the serenity he'd felt, the unfathomable relief of being held in her arms again, the two of them together. Opening his eyes, Max tried to catch hold of the dream but already it was evaporating from his memory, like breath from glass.

He looked out of the window: trees and green fields, sunlight and shadows. The train was slowing down. Beside him, Sophie was breastfeeding their daughter.

'Where are we?'

'Almost in Toulouse. We made it, Max.'

Max smiled, exhaled. Then closed his eyes again. He saw blood pulsing through the veins of his eyelids, heard birds singing through the open window, felt Sophie's cool hand squeezing his.

He was seeing the world through different eyes. He was seeing it through Hans's eyes. He leaned his head into the hollow of Sophie's neck and breathed in the scent of her hair. They were alive, they were safe, they were free, and they were together.

Sophie

17 Rue du Cherche-Midi, Paris
Tuesday, 8 May 1945

Dear Hans,

This is the fifth letter I've written to you since you saved our lives almost three years ago, and I think it will be the last. I'm alone, as I always am when I write to you. Max has taken Suzi to the Arc de Triomphe to celebrate the Allied victory. They wanted me to go with them, but this felt like the perfect time to tell you our news . . . and to say goodbye.

The last time I wrote, we were still living at my mother's farm in the Hautes-Pyrénées. It's beautiful there, but in the end it became uncomfortable sharing a house with Mama. She's not anybody's idea of a doting grandmother. We moved back to Paris just after the Liberation. We did think about moving into the apartment on Rue des Princes. We visited the street a few times and looked up at the balcony and the red shutters, as I know both you and Max used to do. But in the end it felt too haunted by dark memories, so we moved back to this flat on Rue du Cherche-Midi. It's where Suzi was born, and it feels like home to us.

The whole world is haunted by dark memories now. All the Nazis' death camps have been liberated over the past year and we discovered that your father and Édouard were both killed at Auschwitz. We will always feel an undertow of guilt about Édouard, but your father is the one we miss and mourn the most. Max likes to believe that he was optimistic until the end, that he was never worried or sad or afraid.

Max often thinks about you, I know he does, even if he rarely speaks about it. Some things are too deeply embedded in us to

- 377 -

be easily articulated. You are part of him now, Hans. He's been different since your death. More prone to dark thoughts and melancholy, perhaps, but also kinder, gentler, more patient and understanding, more appreciative of what he has. He believes in forgiveness and redemption in a way few people do these days. He's horrified by all those poor women having their heads shaved (or worse) for having fallen in love with German soldiers. And I know he dreams about you sometimes, even if he says he no longer remembers his dreams, because I can see it in his eyes when he first wakes. The dreams he has now are not like they used to be. He told me once that they're like a normal person's dreams: fragmented, nonsensical, times and places all mixed up. I asked him if he misses the dreams he had before, and he said yes and no: that your absence is simultaneously like a lightened burden and a phantom limb.

And what about me? Am I different? Your Sophie was so brave and fierce and principled, I used to envy her sometimes. But I started writing again when Max told me she was writing a novel. And after she died, I knew I had to write the book she was never able to finish. Is she part of me now? I think she is. I hope she is.

But Max and Suzi will be home soon, so I should give you a quick update on what everybody is doing in our world:

Max is studying to be a psychoanalyst. He makes money teaching the violin to some neighbourhood children. And he's a wonderful father to little Suzi, just as you would have been.

Jens is working for the Provisional Government and will stand as a representative for the SFIO socialist party at next year's elections. He's kind of a big shot now but he still comes to eat dinner with us most weekends. Suzi, who adores him, calls him her Noisy Uncle.

Your mother is still living in Vienna, still married to Herr Oberhuber. She and Max are in regular contact again now and she's hoping to come and visit us in Paris soon, probably without her husband.

My father is planning to visit too, or so he says. He recently remarried and has two young children with his new wife, so he's rather busy at the moment. He did write me a nice letter begging my forgiveness for his 'regrettable choices', though, and Max persuaded me not to hold a grudge. Suzi deserves to know her grandparents, however flawed they may be.

I recently heard that Frau Schatten, whom you knew so much better than I did, overdosed on sleeping pills in February 1944 after Karl was killed on the Eastern Front. I suppose the loss of both her sons was too much to take. Herr Schatten still repairs watches and lives alone in the house on Trauergasse.

And I am sorry to report that your teenage girlfriend Paula was killed, along with her children, in the bombing of Hamburg last year. I don't know what happened to her, or to any of these people, in your world. All I know is that in your world I was murdered by Karl Schatten, while here, thanks to you, I am still alive.

What else should I tell you? I suppose the last big question is why . . . Why did your life split in two that night? I've asked myself that so many times but I'm not sure I really have an answer. Max has developed a persuasive psychological explanation – that you were his Jungian shadow, that the dreams were part of his journey to individuation – and he told me that before the end you had come to believe you were on a divine mission. Do you think God sent you to Max to be his guardian angel? Or did he send you to me – the other me? What I find hardest to grasp is my own role in all of this. Was it destiny that led me to the music shop on Prinzenstrasse that afternoon? Was it fate that directed my fingers as I played that simple nursery rhyme on the Bösendorfer? Is life just a dream? Sometimes I feel as if I'm on the verge of understanding it all, as if at any moment these disparate puzzle pieces will suddenly fit together and I'll comprehend the precise workings of cause and effect, the exact blend of magic and religion and random chance that connected the trajectories of the stars to those split-second decisions in a handful of lives and brought the four of us together, like single notes miraculously transformed into a melody: you, me, Max, and your Sophie. But then the spinning-top of my mind starts to slow and it all comes crashing down and I am left staring at the impenetrable core of mystery at its heart. And the only certainty I feel is an immense wonder and gratitude that I was part of it all.

I can hear Max and Suzi's voices in the stairwell. Any minute now they'll open the door and this apartment will once again be filled with the vibrancy of the present. Life will start again. And I will let go of you.

I don't know where you are now, Hans, but I hope and believe that you're with her and that nothing can come between you anymore. No lies, no secrets, no war. Only love.

Goodbye, Hans.

Always,
Sophie

ACKNOWLEDGEMENTS

Thank you to the early readers of this novel in its many drafts: to Robert Dinsdale, who helped me realise that I had to set it in the real world; to my former agent Victoria Hobbs, for her kindness and patience over many years; to Clémentine Beauvais, for her incredibly generous six-page analysis; to my brother Matthew Taylor, who read at least two different versions; and to Emma Knight, for her advice and encouragement.

Thank you to my agent Adam Eaglin and the team at the Cheney Agency who read the book at various stages, especially Claire Gillespie, who – in a brainstorming session with Adam – came up with a title we all finally loved. Thank you to my editor Louisa Joyner for believing in the book, and to Jordaine Kehinde, Krys Kujawinska, Lizzie Bishop, Josephine Salverda, Josh Smith, Tara McEvoy, Phoebe Williams, and the rest of the team at Faber who worked so hard to bring it into the world. Thank you to my copy-editor Silvia Crompton for her thoroughness and thoughtfulness, and for teaching me how to crawl correctly.

And, above all, thank you to Kathy, for whom this story is a love letter that took me twelve years to write.